THE CHOSEN:
PAST 2 PRESENT

By: J.E. Runnion

ARTIST: JOHN W. R. RUNNION

COARTIST AND EDITOR: MARY M.
RUNNION

ASSISTANT ON ARTWORK:
FAITH R. RUNNION

ISBN: 978-0-578-13064-4

CUSTOMER REVIEWS:

These are customer reviews from our first book THE CHOSEN in the Chosen Trilogy Series. They were taken from reviews on Amazon

The story was at first hard for me to understand, the writer used a different dialogue than I'm used to reading and I usually don't read any books containing any type of religious aspect. Once I reached page 64 I became enthralled with the storyline and the characters are compelling and likeable. This book was a great mix of romance, action/adventure, mystery and fantasy. I would definitely recommend this book to my friends and family.--Janelle

The author does a great job of incorporating a multitude of urban legends, mythology, and mainstream religion in one package with intricate details and conclusions that though they are fictional they are also believable. I especially like the occasional twist to the story that keeps you interested in "what happens next".

It was also refreshing to read a story with roots in the bible but a connection to the present without feeling that the author is trying to connect dots that don't fit. There is a good flow to the book with regard to feeling informed as to what is transpiring in the story. Can't wait for the next book to come out on kindle format.--Andrew

I had heard about this book because the first time author, J.E. Runnion, was doing a book signing at a local bookstore later that week. First thing I did was go to the Kindle store at Amazon in hopes to purchase it immediately if I liked the description. It did not hurt that the price was right at 3.99. The book description was short and to the point. It describes the overall book as God sends the archangel Michael down to earth so that God may create a "shifter" to help rid the world of demons. JD, the main character, is granted the ability to change into a large owl, a wolf/wolfman, and a 30ft Siberian tiger to do battle with Satan's demons. The book is much deeper than the description reads. It is a Christian based fiction, with paranormal characters, good physically battles evil, purity and the heart ache of a long ago lost love. There are also a few other hidden prizes that unfold as the book goes on. I found the book is easy and fast to read. It is not a kid's book, but it is clean enough for a tween to read. As I read the book, I found there was no need to go back and forth because I felt I missed something in the timeline.

My only complaint, I WAS FINISHED TOO FAST! If I was not able to sit down and read, I listened to it using the "text to speech" feature on Kindle. I stayed excited throughout the entire book. The ending completed the current journey, and yet left you wanting for more. I do not like when serial books end on a cliffhanger, which makes you have to buy the next book whether you want to or not just to find out what happened. The author stated the second book is written and will be out soon, and Mr. Runnion is now well into the third book. Doing a face-to-face review of the book with the author and his wife was fabulous. It was easy to bring the characters to life, and review each one of their personality and roles in the book. I have already told several people about this book, and I will be in like to get the next one. Demons Beware!— C.Tilson

The Chosen: Past 2 Present

Glossary

Measurements

Cubit: About eighteen inches.

Stadia: About 607 feet.

Chosen Characters

Deliverers: Average men appointed by God and given powers to fight evil in the guise of animal forms. Deliverers are very powerful, yet are limited by their own character and traits, due mostly by pride.

Shifters: Generic term referring to the original chosen men of God and those chosen by them to assist in the fight against Lucifer and his minions.

Demonic Characters

Mastemas: Aggressive and at times playful shadowlike entities. Mastemas are lower-order demons.

Samaels: Highly intelligent and technologically savvy beings. They are not very aggressive, preferring to use low-order demons to carry out certain missions. Samaels are medium-level demoniacs.

Bael's dragons: Four out of the two hundred original fallen angels that were deceived by Lucifer; they can no longer take on angelic form but are in the guise of dragons or reptilian humanoids. They are second in authority under Lucifer.

Lilith: Mother and queen of all demoniacs; her beauty is as intense as her hatred for mankind.

The three immortals: The spawn of Lilith and Stul the dragon. They are the original vampires that feed off the life force of mankind and shifters alike. They are obedient to no one, though they relent to their father's authority from time to time.

Giants: Spawn of the fallen ones and the daughters of men. Their size and shape vary along with their strengths and weaknesses; they rule over and enslave mankind.

DEDICATION

I dedicate this book to my parents, Robert and Caroline (Dad and Mom); thank you for your many sacrifices to ensure I received a private-school education. Motivation, discipline, and positive will must be forged by fire and proved and sharpened in the hands of God, and to this end a child requires parents who are not fearful in stoking such fires. Though it was certainly a rough road dealing with my early beginnings, you softened and hammered metal in the furnace of life to produce a quality sword for the Lord that is me. I have arrived, thanks to you and your love for me, your son.

Chapter 1

Basking in the warmth of the spiritual light that illuminated and energized Paradise, J.D. and Mary lay holding each other near a meandering crystal-clear stream. A soft wind cascaded across her body, fluttering through her long blonde hair and catching her sweet scent to tease J.D.'s nostrils.

"I can't get enough of you, woman."

An impish grin on her face, she replied by saying, "I can't get enough of you either, you animal, you." Embracing, the couple kissed and stroked each other as only lovers can until they heard someone clearing his throat.

"If you don't mind, I'd like to speak with you both, please?"

A little embarrassed to see Larz standing with arms crossed and seemingly annoyed with the two of them, J.D. quickly stood and said, "Larz, old friend, how… how are things with you? We're good—that is, we are just fine. How… how are you?"

"Yes, well, aside from the awkward position I find myself in, everything is fine. Here, take this and eat, the both of you."

J.D. looked at Mary, and then at what appeared to be a nectarine in Larz's hand, and then back at Larz.

Talking with upward inflection in his voice, the young man queried, "Larz, why are you offering us fruit? Fruit in Paradise? My friend, I believe an incident like this happened once before, and it ended poorly as I recall."

Frowning, Larz said, "Right, and no, your humor is not lost on me. Ha ha. The fruit, when ingested, will produce an outer skin of clothing much like mine. When transforming from animal to human, you will no longer be naked, and I will no longer have the sensation of—how is it humans say?—ah yes, 'tossing my cookies,' as it were."

Grinning, J.D. replied, "I could see how our naked forms would affect you in such a way. If the situations were reversed, I'd feel the same."

Stepping forward, Mary grabbed the fruit from Larz and, seeing it was good for food, took a bite and then gave it to J.D. and told him, "It's not bad at all. Like a nectarine, but better."

Once he had eaten the fruit, the couple looked at each other.

"J.D., do you feel anything?"

"No. Larz, I don't think—"

Suddenly, a sensation of pins and needles struck the shifters as a dark bluish liquid oozed from their pores, creating tiny honeycombs over their entire bodies, including their faces. Then a silver film formed over their eyes, making them almond-shaped and large, much like Larz's eyes. Thin silver lines raced up and down their arms, legs, and torsos like living veins of light.

They looked at each other. JD exclaimed, "Mary! You look incredible! I mean, that suit really does justice to you, and then some!"

Giving a shy glance down and away, she said, "J.D., you're making me blush, silly ole bear."

Interrupting, Larz stated, "Yes, nice... Now, if I may have your attention. J.D., the suits will last forty days and nights. After that, you must feed again. Once you are comfortable moving around in them, you'll learn to control the amount of skin to cover."

Cocking his head to one side, J.D. asked, "You mean if I didn't want my face covered, I could just think to uncover it?" As he spoke, the blue suit receded from his face. "Whoa, it's like a reflex. This is great! Mary, try it; just think it off your face."

As she concentrated, the suit receded from her head, retiring at the nape of her neck.

"Okay, this is cool, really cool!" said Mary.

Larz continued. "Now, when you change from one form to another, you won't be nude, and with your faces covered, no one will know who you are—humans, I mean."

Puzzled, J.D. asked his former instructor, "Dear friend, is this fruit that makes outer clothing something new, or has it been around all this time?"

"It has always existed, J.D., from the beginning. Why do you ask?"

"I've been naked when transforming this entire time, and you're only supplying me with it now—why?"

Without skipping a beat, Larz explained. "I really didn't think you were going to work out as a chosen one of God, so why waste resources?"

A bit annoyed, J.D. shot back, "Why waste resources? Why waste resources!"

Cutting in, Larz asked, "Are you feeling well? You keep repeating yourself like a person with a brain disorder or a tumor."

Growling through his teeth, J.D. replied, "It's not a tumor but aggravation." Larz nodded in understanding. "Ah, well, in time this too shall pass."

Still annoyed, J.D. replied, "I guess it will at that. Well, we are covered now, so that's one challenge solved. Now let's get down to business, my friend. Patel—where and how do I find him, and will he even help us with the demons?"

Searching for words to explain how the chosen should handle their quest for Patel, Larz said, "J.D., I think it would be best if you tracked Patel on your own while Mary stayed behind. Just for now."

"Mary stay behind—why? We're a team, Larz. I need her with me."

Larz sighed and tried to explain, "J.D., Patel is very old. His ways are old ways, and Mary would be a hindrance rather than a help in this situation."

Waving off his former trainer's comments, J.D. said, "Well, my friend, times change and so do people if they wish to survive. Besides, he should be elated that things have changed for the better. Patel could take a wife if he wanted now, as I have."

Pleading with the couple, Larz said, "Please take a seat, my son, Mary. I will explain to you certain sensitivities regarding our dear Patel. In the time of men, before God's wrath against the fallen ones and their offspring, Patel fell in love with a beautiful woman named SedicEve. She loved him as well, and soon after, they became one flesh, transforming her into a shifter like him. Everything seemed to go well for the couple as they fought and banished many rebellious angelics and their spawn to the abyss, and then it happened…"

Mary, intrigued, asked, "What happened, Larz? It sounds as though they were successful and loved each other."

Continuing, he said, "Yes, they were a very powerful couple, but soon her eyes fell upon another shifter. Vul was his name; his heart was impure and greedy, seeking venerations for himself rather than God. SedicEve noticed how man revered changelings as well, turning to them rather than God for the way that they should live out their lives. This behavior infuriated and frustrated Patel, who pleaded with mankind to turn to God—with very little success"—he paused momentarily—"mostly since there were other shifters who fell prey to power and pride, fueling the deception of men, which affected his beloved as well. She wanted adoration and worship from what she began to perceive as lower life forms and despised Patel for not wanting to share in it. Time and again, he begged her to turn from such wicked ways, but it was useless. She left Patel and became queen to this Vul, and they made a people for themselves, building a city—an entire empire built with the assistance of giants, among others. Broken, Patel and a few other chosen ones left, desiring to serve the Lord rather than man. Because of the shifters' loyalty and obedience to God, He made them immortal. Those who turned away from the Most High remained mortal and, after becoming abusive toward them, died by the hands of their human subjects during a revolt. The changelings' bodies were cut into small pieces and burned, and the remains were placed in a large sarcophagus with an eighty-ton lid placed over it. Though man killed them, the people still feared a resurrection of the changelings, seeking revenge against those who took their lives. Every reference to the shifters was struck from written history of that kingdom; however, some priests of Ra maintained hidden records of the secret wisdoms of watchers and shifters in a room under the right paw of the Sphinx. Patel holds women in contempt, thinking all fall prey to the desires of fame, fortune, and power as Eve and his love, SedicEve, did long ago."

Speaking up, Mary replied, "Not every woman falls as they did in the past, Larz, just as every man doesn't fall in the same way."

"I am aware of this, young one, but some entities think as they do and will not see logic because of this bias. I'm sorry; that's the way it is."

Chiming in, J.D. said, "I will show our old friend how times have changed." He pointed toward Mary. "And we will change his mind together."

Seeing that the couple was set on completing the mission together, Larz relented. Nodding, he turned and walked off toward a crystal-clear waterfall, stopping only to answer J.D.'s last question of where Patel could be found.

"In the forests of the northwest, Patel resides in many hidden caverns strewn throughout the region. Look for large boulders that seem out of place from the surrounding landscape. Move them aside, and you will find one of Patel's lairs. Godspeed to you both." Larz turned and slowly walked away, disappearing behind a large waterfall.

Chapter 2

Focusing hard on a thought, J.D. didn't acknowledge Mary's question to him even when she walked up and placed a hand on his shoulder.

"J.D., what is it? What's wrong?"

Suddenly, he came alive. "I know where he is! Come on. Come on and I'll show you!" Grabbing Mary's hand, J.D. called for a portal to a ridgeline where he'd seen a large boulder that a creature had disappeared near some time ago.

When they popped out next to the boulder, J.D. pointed. "He's behind this boulder, Mary. I saw him disappear in this brush next to the boulder." Running his fingers where the immense stone and earth wall met, he could feel space between them and a cool breeze escaping from a crevice on the outside. "There's a room behind this boulder, but I can't seem to budge it."

Mary spoke up. "What if you change?"

Pausing from his efforts to move the stone, J. D. smiled, looked deep into her eyes, and said, "Beautiful and smart. God, I love you!" He moved in to give her a kiss.

Mary pressed a hand against his chest and said, "Okay, no time for this now, my love—later. Right now, the stone—okay?"

Collecting himself, J.D. nodded and shifted into a werewolf. He took hold of the boulder and effortlessly moved it to one side. Peering into silent, thick darkness of the cave, Mary shifted as well, thinking it was better to be safe than sorry since neither of them knew what to expect.

After they entered the cave, J.D. replaced the stone and the duo headed down a long, dark tunnel. They could see perfectly in the dark, and their sense of smell told them an animal of some kind was here—somewhere. After walking down the long, snaking, musty tunnel for what seemed like an eternity, the couple came to a large chamber littered with stalagmites and stalactites. Glowing quartz crystals of various sizes and colors lined the floor, making a wide path for the two to follow.

They entered another tunnel and continued moving toward a brightly lit area off in the distance. A much bigger room met them which held a large crystal table and several chairs. Running their hands over the furnishings, they were amazed how smooth the glowing table and chairs felt. The crystal gave off a warm sensation that made them feel something akin to euphoria. Sitting at the table and talking among themselves, they were unaware of a figure looking on from a nearby room.

"What are you doing here, Deliverer? Why have you entered my home unannounced?" Startled, the couple looked all around but could not find the source of the voice.

J.D. spoke up. "We are here to find Patel the Great. Who and where are you?" He received only silence mingled with his echoed entreaty. "Are you Patel? We are chosen servants of the Lord as well and want to ask your assistance!" Again, not a sound was heard in response to J.D.'s question. "We just want—"

Cutting in, Patel replied as he walked nonchalantly past the table where J.D. and Mary sat. "Stop yelling; I'm right here." Feeling a little embarrassed, J.D. fell silent as he watched Patel walk around and take a seat at the head of the table between them. As the shifter stared at Mary, J.D. took time to size him up.

Patel was almost ten feet tall. Dark, matted hair covered his broad, powerful body with the exception of his face, his palms, and the bottoms of his feet. His intense orange-red eyes were sunk deep into a thick skull with a pronounced brow and flat nose; his teeth were large and humanlike except for long, sharp canines that hid behind thick lips. When Patel placed his hands on top of the table, J.D. could make out thick finger and thumb digits covered with fur, but the fingernails appeared to be normal. J.D. thought, *Normal fingernails—what in the world is normal for a bigfoot?* Peering under the table, he could make out five digits on each of Patel's feet—feet that measured at least eighteen to twenty inches long by twelve to sixteen inches in width.

Glancing at Mary as if to ask, "What kind of sneaker do you think he wears?" J.D. could make out a concerned look on her face; that's when he noticed Patel's glare directed toward her. "Patel, this is my wife, Mary, and I am J.D."

The bigfoot's attention did not change; nor did he acknowledge J.D.'s introduction.

"Excuse me, Patel, but I said my name."

Gruffly he responded, "I heard you the first time J.D."

"Ah—good, then maybe you can stop looking at my wife and speak to me."

Letting out a low grunt, Patel turned away from Mary and said, "My apologies, deliverer. It's been a very long time since I've talked with my kind, let alone seen anyone or anything other than wild animals. I certainly didn't expect a female shifter. I believe you referred to her as your wife. Wife—really?"

"Yes, we are one. A lot has changed, Patel—"

Interrupting, Patel said, "…and some things will never change, young one, like a woman's deceptive character and mankind's overall desire to do away with God in favor of worshipping bushes, crawling creatures, and even other men. Taking a wife was foolish." Standing and walking away from the table, Patel continued. "In time you'll see for yourself how foolish it is; my condolences in advance."

J.D.'s blood began to boil white-hot as Patel's words lingered in the young man's ears.

Seeing that her husband was ready to blow, Mary stepped in. "Patel, I'm sorry for you—for the pain your lost love put you through—but not all women are as she was, and it isn't fair to lump us together like that."

Turning with eyes ablaze Patel shot back, "You know nothing, woman; nor am I inclined to educate you or your man in the ways of this life, or mine for that matter. Now get out of here, the both of you, and do not bother me again!"

"How dare you speak to my wife that way!" Teeth bared, J.D. morphed into a tiger, prompting Patel to change into a sixty-foot silverback gorilla.

"You wish to challenge me boy!" Patel beat his chest. Patel continued,

"Then bring it!"

J.D. lunged toward his opponent, clasping hold with claws and teeth to the ape's body. Releasing an earth-shattering yelp, Patel stumbled backward from J.D.'s attack, but he soon recovered and ripped the tiger from his body, flinging him across the cavern to slam against a wall, where he fell to the floor dazed. As Patel began to charge, a sleek black panther moved between him and J.D.

Bellowing a roar in both their directions, Mary continued, "Stop this right now; both of you! Have you lost your minds? Why is it whenever a disagreement between two men happens, the only solution is to fight like little boys! Nice to see that hasn't changed over time." Turning to J.D., she said, "And you should know better. We are a guest in his home, and attacking him like that was uncalled for. Now put away the testosterone and apologize."

Protesting, he said, "What—he started it! I came here to ask for help with the dragons and he—"

Scolding him, she said, "John Doe Ryan, you change back right now and apologize for attacking Patel!"

Looking like a whipped puppy dog, J.D. morphed into his human form and, glancing down toward the ground, said under his breath, "Sorry."

Raising her head, Mary replied, "What was that? I don't think Patel could hear you, because I sure didn't, and I'm closer!"

Louder, J.D. replied, "I'm sorry!"

Facing Patel, Mary said, "And what do we say when someone apologizes?" The great ape looked at Mary, then J.D., and back again; after a few moments of silence, he began to laugh as he morphed back into a Sasquatch. Still charged up, J.D. yelled back, "What's so funny!" Suddenly, Mary began to laugh as well as she watched Patel, who was now lying on his side, shaking with laughter.

Confused at the sight of his wife and the fellow shifter's strange behavior, J.D. walked off, mumbling as he went. He tried to ignore the two but found it quite difficult and joined in the laughter. After they had gathered their wits, Patel calmly gestured for the couple to join him at the table. "I had forgotten a women's persuasiveness; something so delicate— fragile, really—and yet it wields a power over man and even a few angelics too great to measure. Please, take a seat and I will explain and answer any questions you may have about our origins and mankind's."

Chapter 3

As the couple took their seats, Patel retrieved a large crystalline orb from an adjoining room and placed it in the middle of the table. He sat, and as he began to speak, images formed within the orb. "Seventy thousand times seventy thousand times past, the Lord God Almighty created the universe and everything in it; turning to the sons of God, He bade them to go forth and see all He had created. Traversing all that was and discerning rules that governed it, the sons of God came upon a non-binary star system that held a unique water-filled blue planet. A massive continent dominated a quarter of the deep blue orb that sat under a clear atmosphere rich in oxygen and nitrogen gases. No life was found in the water, on land, or in the sky, prompting several of the sons to say, 'Let us make, with the Father's approval, life upon the rock that we may watch as it goes to and fro.'"

With that, Patel began relating the long tale being displayed to him in the orb.

***

Twelve sons agreed and sought the Father's approval; it was granted, with provisos that they were strictly required to follow, the most important of which was that there is only one God of all creation and only He was to be worshiped as such.

In agreement, they first set out to build a great city where they would meet to plan operations. An area was chosen on the continent, centered and close to the West Coast. The sons built their city, having concentric circles of broken land and fresh water—seven bands that cradled the inner buildings, which stretched into the sky. Meeting together in council chambers located at the apex of a solid crystal central tower complex, the sons of God appointed an overall leader of their project to ensure conformity.

A tall, fair-haired being stood before the members and said, "First, thank you for entrusting me with coordinating our newest project. I'm confident that we will be successful in our endeavors as we work together to bring forth something unique. Please, everyone, be seated and we will get started. I would like to take roll and assign groups with particular tasks if I may, and a record shall be kept of each meeting embedded within these crystals for anyone to access if agreed."

Receiving a silent nod to proceed from everyone, the being continued. "As you already know, but for the record, my name is Ecegre, overseer of project earth—yes, earth will do for a name, and everyone at this table will assist in completing it. To my left: Tazec, Nayam, and Canni will be in charge of various types of foliage to cover both wet and dry areas; Rosen, Glanend, and Gnuloms, your charge will include various animals. Now, as a group, work together to produce and place eclectic life forms upon the earth's surface that it may exist and manipulate the three dimensions of air, water, and solid ground.

"To my right: Airmuse, Diani, and Gypet; I leave knowledge to you, while Hanic and Aafric shall deal in the arts to include precious gems and fine ores. Together we can make a great civilization unto the Lord dedicated to His Glory. I put forth that we should come together at least once a day to update the council on everyone's efforts—what say you all?"

Finding the eleven members in agreement, Ecegre released them to their tasks, hopeful that all would go well. Setting about their work, the three sons responsible for foliage understood that they were in charge of preparing food energies for whatever 'high-end' life forms were created, and the fact that plants were living organisms was not lost on them. Therefore, they made some plants good for food; and others, though not precisely edible, would clear the atmosphere of chemicals toxic to animal life.

It took many days of years for the new world to flourish in foliage alone, but when it was complete, Rosen, Glanend, and Gnuloms brought forth varying life from single-celled to complex organisms. Their first attempt at producing complex animals led to large, warm-blooded reptilian creatures that lived off of plant life. Many more days passed, and when the sons came together for a meeting, Ecegre broached a particular subject. "Gentlemen, we have life flourishing upon this planet, living off of plant life, and producing too well. If calculations are correct, animal life will take over plant life, and soon there will be no land for the air breathers to exist upon; therefore, I suggest we come up with life spans to control and balance our creations."

Glanend stood and, taking hold of his toga at chest level, protested. "Why must our animals be affected—their life spans cut short? Just make more dry land for the beasts to roam."

Sympathetic to his brother's entreaty, but standing firm, Ecegre replied, "My dear brother, as you know too well, we are governed by specific rules set forth by our Father and we need to ensure His wishes are followed. Perhaps we can make a slight compromise; we will inject life spans; however, we will use nothing under a day, and we shall install predatory creatures to assist in keeping populations in check."

Rosen stood up from the table and, with great anger, protested Ecegre's proposal. "How dare you make such a request! Why should our creations prey upon one another! The very thought is outrageous, and I will not support any ideas that cause harm to my work!"

After hearing Rosen, Tazec calmly chimed in. "My plants are eaten every day by your creatures, and I have yet to say anything against it, dear Rosen; the predatory idea seems acceptable to me."

Rosen continued his rant. "It was long known before the beginning that your plants would be used for food—nutrients for my creations—so don't give such a glib response and expect me to stand by and swallow it!"

Feeling he was being ignored, Ecegre watched as the entire table exploded with tempers flaring. Only Airmuse, Diani, and Gypet along with him stood silent, watching as the others flung barbs back and forth.

When Ecegre could take no more, he slammed a powerful fist upon the table, sending out a shockwave that knocked his brothers backward and made the ground around the crystal tower quake. Silence fell over the room, and after a few moments had passed,

Ecegre said, "Arguing solves nothing. It is imperative that we work together. It is logical to install a balance with all things for proper function, or over time our project will fail. Some plant life is consumed for food, and so shall it be among the animals as well. I suggest we implement predation immediately and watch to see what happens as time passes; if it does not seem to work in maintaining a natural balance, we can always change it." Looking around the table at his fellow watchers, Ecegre asked, "What say you all?"

Receiving a positive majority, Ecegre affirmed the decision, and predation was instilled in a select group of animals; a taste for flesh locked away in their DNA.

Everything proceeded as they commissioned, and yet there was a feeling of emptiness; something was missing from the earth—an intelligent being so different from anything else found in nature. Ecegre called a special meeting of the sons and put forth his proposal. "My brothers, I have taken time away from you to ponder an idea which haunts my very being." Looking intently at everyone and after drawing in a breath he said, "After conferring with Father and omitting very few details from Him, let us make an intelligent being in our image. One just a little lower than us which we can teach the way of the Father; otherwise all life will stagnate, reaching its potential and halting altogether."

Airmuse said, "Ecegre, what you ask is too much for any of us to do—not without the Father's expressed permission. I mean, are we twelve here experienced enough to do such a thing? I have doubts, my brother."

Gypet said, "What of wisdom, Ecegre? None of us possess the ability to impart wisdom, and without it how could any being we create properly wield knowledge? Therefore, I am in agreement with Airmuse; we must not do this thing you ask."

After looking around the room, searching for support of his idea and finding no one, Ecegre continued with great firmness in his voice. "What is this I am witness to? Where is the boldness, the desire to explore and go beyond the normal bonds of what is—to reach out for what might be? Animals, plants, elements—these are the things you find acceptable and content to dabble in? Anywhere in the vastness of the universe these things can be done. But listen to me, my brothers; we can develop a unique creation found nowhere else. A being that we can call our kind, and watch as it goes to and fro within the world—the world of men. They will be just a little under us in abilities but possess the drive and ambition to explore, wanting to understand and ask the ultimate questions in the universe: who and why am I? Think of it, my brothers. Gypet, we the Majestic Twelve can and must do this to show the Father what is possible in His own creation. If wisdom is the only challenge that worries you, then I say put your mind at ease. For just as their intellect grows, so will wisdom along with it because evil will not be imparted to man. No, my brothers, we shall keep mankind free of the knowledge of evil, which will allow wisdom to flourish. Only good can come from this endeavor, and we will control every aspect of it. What say you now?" Everyone but Gypet stood and applauded their mentor.

Once the brothers fell silent, Gypet stood and said, "Since you all are in agreement to do this thing, I will not protest, provided we each create our own version of man and, though we teach him the way to go, we allow for diversification within their separate civilizations—one God with many evolving cultural societies based in what is good and righteous."

Ecegre was more than happy to concede to such a request since it meant the immediate production of his pet project—man.

Chapter 4

As the sun slowly rose in the east, the watchers picked their sections of land and created their versions of man. Setting them among the animals, they taught their new creations about nature and all its workings. The fruits of trees, bushes, and plants, the fruit thereof were given them to eat as food, and they were instructed to go into the land, be fruitful, and multiply.

Man made dwelling places in caves and dug-out underground chambers. They also learned about pigments made from plants and how to make tools from stones and bits of wood that littered the landscape. Many days of years passed, and mankind flourished. They moved out of caves and into wood-and-brick cities and sometimes into the sides of cliffs. Eventually, one race of men met with another and was fascinated to find others of their kind in the land. They lived and shared ideas with one another in peace, for they did not know evil and war was not a part of their psyche. Harmony reigned supreme, and the whole earth prospered for many more years.

One day the angelics of God were summoned to stand before the Lord of Hosts; knowing the twelve must obey and leave their creation behind, Airmuse proposed a solution. "Let us call upon the lower-ranking angelics and have them protect our world until we return from the Father."

Gypet, uncomfortable with such an idea, spoke up. "Brothers, leaving man in the hands of lower-order angelics burdens me greatly; our creation of him was carried out without Father's explicit approval, and that is troubling enough, but man is vulnerable on his own, open to many ideas and concepts which he cannot fully understand in this, his infancy. Some of Father's Angels are quite volatile and unpredictable, as all here know too well. If placing him in the hands of His messengers' appeals to you, then I ask that Lucifer, His highest angel, be named mankind's protector until our return."

Debate among the watchers as to what should be done with their project while they were away grew in intensity until finally Ecegre spoke. "Enough, my brothers, please calm yourselves and listen. We are left with very few choices and an infinite number of challenges with regard to our project. Therefore, I have determined that Gypet's proposal to assign temporary guardianship to Lucifer is the best solution. He is the bright morning star, God's most favored angelic among the lower order. With mankind in his hands, what then could go wrong?"

Once the choice was unanimously accepted among them, Lucifer was summoned; he answered their call. They felt that if there was ever a perfect being outside of the Lord, it was him. As the Lord's favored, he was placed above all other angelics, including the watchers, not so much as a ruler, but as a summoner of all God's creation, for his voice was beautiful, holding all who heard it in awe. His raiment was unsurpassed, and nothing in heaven could compare itself to it.

Yes, indeed, he had earned the title "bright morning star." Yet, as with even the most wondrous gem, minute flaws abounded in him. His imperfection was vanity mingled with a prideful heart. Lucifer believed himself to be above all creation rather than a part of it; that he possessed the same authority as the Father simply because of his station among the realms. He felt rules did not apply to him, and he wielded a free hand wherever the mood and situation suited him. It annoyed him that after summoning the watchers to present themselves before the Lord, he was summoned by them. Yet he was curious, since he had never been summoned by anyone other than the Lord before. Lucifer's curiosity was peaked, and it gave him a false sense of importance that he, rather than God, had been called upon.

Manifesting before the twelve inside their council chambers, Lucifer intensified his radiance, catching the crystals that made up the room. Light streamed unopposed through the crystals, where it was effortlessly bent into brilliant multiple colors that filled the sky as far as the eye could perceive. Once he felt everyone's attention was on him, Lucifer drew back his radiance and addressed the watchers. "I heard and responded to your entreaty—a unique request, to be sure."

Rising, Ecegre said, "My brothers, if it pleases you, I would speak with Lucifer alone so that our meeting with the Most High is kept, and I shall follow shortly thereafter." Nodding, the eleven left to keep their appointment with the Lord, leaving Ecegre behind to speak with Lucifer.

"Lucifer, dear brother, let me be the first to welcome you to earth; a project which we, the Majestic Twelve, are now working on for the Lord."

A bit confused, Lucifer asked, "Project earth— Majestic Twelve? Why have I not heard of any of this, nor seen plans put forth by the Father?"

Ecegre explained. "What we do here is unique in His universe; so unique, in fact, that we have kept it quiet from everyone—save the Father, of course. Permit me to show you around, and afterward, we may discuss the reason we have called upon our dear brother for assistance."

Lucifer slightly nodded his approval, and the two angelics left the crystal tower. Ecegre explained to Lucifer all the plants—those that bore fruit for eating while other plants simply renewed an atmosphere of oxygen suitable for biological and organic life forms. Next, Ecegre drew Lucifer's attention to animal life, which grew, scurried, and ran around them oblivious to their presence, since fear was not a part of any animal's instincts at that time. Moments passed, and then Lucifer, growing impatient, asked, "Ecegre, forgive me, but none of this is even remotely unique; literally millions upon millions of planets possess the same life forms upon them. As far as I'm concerned, dear brother, your 'earth' is mediocre at best. Unique? I don't think so."

Nodding in agreement, Ecegre explained, "This is not everything which inhabits our planet." He took Lucifer to an area just past a thick wooded forest, and on the other side of a large meadow, Lucifer finally beheld multiple images of an organic life form much like himself but not. "Behold—man!"

At first the angel was dumbstruck at the appearance of man. "How—how is this possible? What have you done?"

Ecegre replied, "Something new—a unique life form found nowhere else in the universe." A look of shock fell upon Lucifer's face that startled Ecegre at first, and then he continued to explain. "Brother, these creatures are unlike us and yet are very much us, in a sense. They are organic, made up of matter, whereas we are not—oh, we may take on an organic form whenever we like, but they cannot transfigure. They are a little less than us, possessing only that knowledge the Majestic Twelve see fit to impart. We have watched mankind develop over many days of years. We wanted to keep each group separate from the other; however, we found that man is curious, possessing an innate desire to explore and learn, which is exactly what we were hoping."

Interrupting, Lucifer asked, "Each separate group—are you saying there are more of these creatures roaming earth?"

Excited, Ecegre continued. "Yes, twelve in total—one group for each member of the Majestic Twelve, which is what we call ourselves. As I was saying, when one different cultural group met another, they embraced and accepted each other; we did not teach them about evil, and since it was not taught, mankind does not engage in it. Look for yourself; they know not of war, greed, or envy, and so man does not murder, steal, or do any type of harm toward one another. I will show you all the groups of man, and you will know why we called upon God's most favored angel to watch over them."

Ecegre took Lucifer around the continent and showed him every culture of mankind that thrived upon the earth at that time. Once the tour was over, the two angels arrived back at crystal tower to talk over Ecegre's proposal. "Well, my friend, man is why we need to ask if you will watch over this planet in our absence. Something this unique and unpredictable cannot be left to its' own; otherwise, we would not ask this of you."

Walking around the room as if to reflect upon Ecegre's words, Lucifer turned to him and said, "I'm at a loss as to why such an endeavor would take place and find your explanation lacking. However, I am at my brother's disposal and will reluctantly watch over the men created here."

With a sense of relief in his voice, Ecegre thanked Lucifer for accepting the request, but he saw a troubled look suddenly wash across the angel's face.

"Brother, I cannot help but notice something troubles you. What is it?"

Lucifer answered, "I was pondering. The separate groups of men shown to me possessed subtle figural changes unlike the others; some had darker tones and curled, coarse hair, while another group had straight hair and lighter tones, and yet their symmetry is as we are. Why?"

"Ah, yes, we wanted a way in which to identify what group belonged to its Watcher, and so we gave them distinctive qualities. Of course, it wasn't until after doing so we realized that eventually they may encounter the other groups and intermingle, rendering invalid our way of 'tagging' them. Although the land mass on which they live and thrive is great, it was their sheer will to explore that we did not count on which drew them to others of their kind."

Sounding a bit bored, and with a lazy swipe of his hand through the air, Lucifer replied, "Yes, of course, of course. Free will, exploration"—he turned his back to Ecegre and continued in a muffled voice— "and a lack of wisdom."

"What was that? I couldn't hear you too well with—"

Abruptly answering, Lucifer replied, "And lack of nothing, my dear brother. Now then, I think it best if you do not keep Father waiting for your presence before Him any longer. Rest assured I will keep man for you as if they were my own."

Nodding, Ecegre replied, "Thank you, Lucifer; I will not forget this and will, in fact, call upon Father to confer a commendation for your selflessness in this matter."

"Nonsense, dear brother, I would rather we kept this just between the thirteen of us; otherwise, how could it be considered selfless. Others of our kind might look at it as a grab for attention—so please, allow my humility to remain intact as well as my pride and keep all this a secret for now."

Shocked in amazement at how humble a being Lucifer was, Ecegre replied, "Never have I witnessed such humility among Father's creations; is it any wonder why you are his favored among us!"

Waving off his comment, Lucifer replied, "Thank you again, kind sir, but I must insist that you leave immediately. He waits."

After one final nod, Ecegre left earth to present himself before the Lord of Hosts, leaving Lucifer to guard a unique being found living on a small rock that orbited a single yellow star.

Chapter 5

Sitting alone in council chambers at the apex of the crystal tower, Lucifer plotted his next move. His hand was set against mankind, as he thought they were a great abomination, an experiment that should not be, and he intended to destroy them before they could increase in knowledge and branch out from the earth to other parts of the universe. Man's demise, he decided, needed to happen in such a way as to keep blame from himself. He would prefer that it be placed squarely on the shoulders of mankind's creators, the Majestic Twelve. As he gazed upon large crystal screens that showed all twelve tribes of man going about their daily activities, he pondered different fates.

Freeze them to death. No, no. Nature is perfect. Volcanoes, droughts, or anything involving nature will work as an excuse for man's demise. But if the system is perfect, then no such occurrence shall happen. A rogue asteroid from deep space—yeah. It smashed into the planet, causing all kinds of destruction and killing everything. How could I have not known of its existence, though? Let alone allowing it to impact the earth, which I could easily have kept from happening. Frustration and anger welled up within him as he watched each set of crystal monitors that projected images of the loathsome human creatures busying themselves with food gathering and dwelling construction. Then it hit him.

Man destroys the area he occupies, and anywhere he spreads out into dies. Nature is disrupted; all regular cycles are harmed. Man kills, so why not have man kill man—that's perfect! I'll pit man against themselves and let them annihilate each other. Bah ha ha ha—it's perfect! Perfect!"

Pacing back and forth, Lucifer suddenly discovered a huge flaw in his perfect plan. *Man doesn't possess the knowledge to kill or to make weapons, nor do they have a reason to kill in the first place. They must be taught to kill, but I cannot involve myself directly. No, I can't risk being blamed. I'll need help to pull this off: those angelics loyal to me… a small group of my choosing—and I know just who to call upon.*

Soon after Lucifer sent out a call, four angels appeared in the council chambers where he would plot the demise of mankind. The beings were strikingly handsome, possessing a glow all their own. They took seats around a table, and one of the angels spoke up. "Dear Lucifer, to what do we owe this frantic summons that simply could not wait for the four of us to finish the work we were engaged in ourselves?"

Walking around the table with a great seriousness firmly affixed to his face, Lucifer explained. "The 'what,' gentlemen, is more important than you could possibly imagine." Pointing to monitors littering a side wall, he continued. "Behold, a new creation—an abomination!"

The four beings watched as different types of mankind went about daily routines. A thick silence settled itself within the chamber, uncomfortable and unnatural, until finally an angel spoke up. "What are we seeing here, Lucifer? They appear to be like us, but they are not of the angelic realm. Look how they scratch the dirt and collect seeds of plants. What is this that you have created, and by whose authority?"

"No, I did not create these … things. Rather it was twelve watchers calling themselves the Majestic Twelve. Allegedly, Father gave authority to do this, but I highly doubt it since they wish to keep man's existence a secret even from Father. That's why I called you, Torel, Tubel, Deenal, and of course you, my dear Larz. I want to do away with these beings, and I need your assistance in doing so."

Larz spoke up. "Lucifer, we are not needed for this. Simply wipe them out with a cataclysm. After all, they are not immortal, I'm sure."

Focusing intently on Larz, Lucifer responded, "My friend, I know nothing of their abilities, let alone whether they are immortal or not. The other challenge is the fact that they may indeed be a legitimate project. I just can't accept it—I mean, why? I ask all of you, does this make sense? For what purpose?"

Tubel broke in. "What would you have us do with regard to these ... creatures?"

Pacing back and forth as he spoke, Lucifer said, "I've thought long and hard about the best way to disrupt and perhaps destroy mankind. They do not know evil, which works in our favor. I want you to teach them every aspect of evil, especially the taking of life. If they are not immortal, they'll die by their own hands, keeping us free from their blood. Deception is the word of the day my friends; draw them away from good, and lead them like lambs to slaughter. Above all, we must conduct ourselves in such a way that they do not know what or who we are. As angels of the Lord, we must remain above reproach."

Larz spoke up. "To do what you are asking, Lucifer, we must have hands-on contact; how then are we to explain ourselves?"

Looking away from the group, Lucifer answered, "You are to say to them that you are gods." One great gasp resonated within the crystal room.

"You speak of blasphemy! It is blasphemy, Lucifer! How could you even think of asking us to involve ourselves in such an ill-conceived plot—you, of all beings? God's most favored angel—how could you?"

"My friends, please hear me out; I'm not asking you to commit heresy, because these beings, albeit, have our appearance for the most part, but they are not us! They are creatures made up of dirt and dust from a floating rock in space. They are no different from the two- and four-legged animals that thrive around them. Man is not our equal, and so we would not be violating Father's command by saying we are gods."

Chiming in, Larz rebutted, "Your argument is very thin, Lucifer—very thin, for everything comes from God and is God's."

Frustrated with Larz's attitude toward his idea, Lucifer shot back, saying "Then what, Larz? What will work for you or any of you here to do this thing? I need your help, my friends, or these animals—these humans—will continue to proliferate and use up and destroy resources around them, eventually moving out into the rest of the universe to continue creating and spreading their chaotic ways. Can't you understand that? Man is an affront to God, not a blessing."

Moments passed in silence until finally Larz replied, "Beings from the stars above? Perhaps..."

"What was that?" asked Lucifer. "Did you say something, Larz?"

"Yes. We can say that we are beings from other star systems on a mission. At least it will keep us from saying we are gods, which frankly I cannot—and will not—agree to do. We are beings on a mission to observe and help in advancing their societies in exchange for raw materials, which we need and this planet possesses, to... I don't know... save our own planets from destruction, I guess."

Lucifer's face lit up, making everyone else in the room more at ease. "Yes. That's brilliant, my dear friend—absolutely brilliant! Why didn't I think of ... Is everyone here more open to Larz's idea, and if so, will you help me?" All four beings stood up and, with one voice, agreed to take on the mission put before them.

"Destruction of man must be complete before the Majestic Twelve return; otherwise, we may have to deal with their wrath, and our actions might touch off a war between angelics—something I would like to avoid at all costs for now." All were in agreement that a war would not serve the heavenly realm, and so the four angels immediately went to work on mankind to bring about its destruction.

In the beginning, Larz and the three other angels chose four cultures to teach the ways of evil. Keeping to their story of planetary travelers from distant star systems, they taught astrology, giving different stories as to their origins in space and how to track the stars and their cycles. Next, they put the humans to work excavating metal ores, precious stones, and quartz crystals, which would be used in the many building projects soon to take place. Larz taught each group how to plan and create various dwelling structures as well as temples for worship and underground storage areas. Torel passed on the art of forging tools and various types of weaponry made from bone, wood, stone, and metal. He also showed man how to track and hunt animals as well as what parts of the animal other than the meat were good for such things as clothing, sinews for bow strings, and animal fat which made up a part of paints, adhesives, and medicines.

These concepts were strange to man at first, since until this point they did not eat animal flesh but lived off the land, consuming only vegetation. Once they tasted flesh, it delighted them greatly—with the exception of a few humans that would not partake in flesh-eating frenzies; instead they kept themselves apart from groups eating animals. Tubel took it upon himself to teach man war and reasons for it. Though many fell under his spell, there was one with a desire to oppose his teachings. Because of his defiance against Tubel, this warrior would go on to become one of the Most High's first chosen.

"Why should we war against one another? The reasons you give do not make sense!" A large, muscular, slightly dark-skinned man stood defiantly waiting for this star man to answer his question.

Tubel remained seated and patiently reiterated the reasons for man to make war. "Patel, my friend, war is the only way to ensure the strong receive the choicest of foods and resources. The strong—such as you—breed with the best women found on the face of this planet. We need strong men to leave in place when we return to our own star systems to rule in our stead— someone such as you, for instance—to be king over mankind."

Sternly, Patel replied to Tubel with great confidence, making all who witnessed his speech look on in awe. "We do not require kings to rule over us; each goes his own way knowing that his neighbor comes before himself. We share in labor as with the harvest, and it's in this sharing that our strength in community flows to every person and their families. The men are free to choose a woman or women as they are able to love and care for them, knowing it is not quantity but quality which drives us—not just in selecting a mate, but in all things. We have no need for ideas which teach that the taking of human life is good or that ruling over those who remain is acceptable. I could not lay hands upon my brother and then ask his family to follow me. No, I will not!"

Great anger arose within Tubel, but he kept his tongue sheathed since the group of men now standing around them roared with excitement and elation for what was said by Patel on their behalf. Glaring at Patel through the crowd, Tubel nodded and disappeared before them. Appearing in council chambers, Tubel released his pent-up anger by throwing chairs across the room. He slammed his palms together and then extended his fingers, sending forth a thick stream of bright blue plasma that blew a hole through an opposite wall.

Lucifer appeared at the other end of the plasma blast, absorbing its energy. "Redecorating, I see, Tubel." He looked through the hole made by his underling, Lucifer continued, "Are you looking to increase airflow or let more light into our chambers?"

Annoyed, Tubel said, "I find these … things … most insufferable. How many days and years have we squandered on these creatures? Still they have yet to take up arms against each other. Lucifer, you stated to us that mankind had not obtained wisdom, and yet there are a few—not many, but a few men—that speak as though they have wisdom from the Lord of Hosts. How is this possible?"

Slowly walking in the direction of Tubel, Lucifer replied, "I do not know, my dear Tubel; perhaps our prey perceives more than we give credit for. But as far as having true wisdom—wisdom which only comes from the Father—I don't think so. I know they can't possibly possess what hasn't been instilled within them. Do not get so tied up in these creatures; remember that we are greater than they will ever hope to be."

Placing a hand on Tubel's shoulder, Lucifer continued. "Stay the course and keep an open mind as how to deal with our quarry."

Nodding, Tubel acknowledged what Lucifer was saying but was still troubled. "We cannot just destroy them outright—I'm only asking for a few to kill in front of the others. Let the fear of us enter their hearts and then see how they bend to our will."

"No, Tubel. To be honest with you, we began this journey to annihilate these creatures, and now I'm not sure how much of what we have done can be kept from Father—if any. We cannot turn aside from what we are doing, but perhaps the punishment for our deeds will be lessened if life isn't directly taken by us."

Fear washed over Tubel, threatening to crush him where he stood. "The Lord knows of what we have done—is that what you are saying? He would not approve of our actions?"

Once again, Lucifer spoke softly and cunningly to his fellow angel. "Sometimes the Father does not see clearly, allowing the question 'What if …?' to always work to a positive end. We must assist from time to time to show the folly of such thinking by taking action ourselves—action that proves we are right. Tubel, we are His advisers, not anything else in creation—and definitely not man. We are doing what is right."

After hearing Lucifer's words, Tubel felt more at ease. "You make a great argument, my brother; it appears the Lord provided you with a silver tongue for His goodness. Very well, I will continue to work against the humans without taking life. But what of these meddling ones that simply refuse to listen?"

Glancing toward the newly formed hole in the wall created by Tubel's fury earlier, Lucifer said, "Exile—separation from the rest of the herd. We'll stick them in a hole where no one will hear them speak. Be patient and identify the troublemakers, but do not act against them; instead, we will wait and round them up all at once. I want to keep mankind pliable in their thoughts. When they ask where their friends have gone, we will say other planets were in need of strong leaders and so we transported them to where they were needed most."

Smiling now, Tubel replied, "I am in awe. It will work—your story will work in our favor. Very well, I'm off to train our herds on how they are to go and identify those creatures which go astray."

"Good, my friend, but one more thing before you go. Keep to yourself what was spoken about the Father and His potential knowledge of our actions. We don't want to upset our brothers needlessly, especially your twin, Torel. His constant questioning of things is most unnerving at times. Progress and speed are key to our eventual success, and we cannot afford any more delays, right?"

"Yes, of course. My brother is most insufferable at times. It will be kept between us, then. I'm off to complete our mission." Disappearing from sight, Tubel left Lucifer and returned to the humans, not realizing Lucifer's real motivation. In case the Father *was* aware of their actions, he would use the others as a scapegoat should he need to deny knowledge of what was happening in a little part of the Lord's creation.

Chapter 6

A few years had passed since Lucifer and Tubel spoke when, sitting among the elders in a small village settlement near the ocean and only a few miles from crystal city, Patel listened to the inhabitants argue over their teachers. "Adamu, you are the oldest sitting here, and your words will stand as wisdom among our many clans; what say you of these teachers from other worlds? Should we fear them? Or can we finally state their benevolence in wanting to ensure our progress maintains itself, rather than buy into an idea that they mean us harm? What say you, sir?"

Glancing around and after making eye contact with everyone present, Adamu began, "It is true, my brothers; I was one of the first created and placed upon this great part of the Lord's creation to be. At that time, we had different teachers who guided us in the way we were to go and we did what was asked. But now we have had in our midst a being not unlike those which taught us then, with one exception—and that is the knowledge they wish to impart. It is quite strange, and so different from that of the former fathers, just as dear Patel, who sits among us, has pointed out many times. I will not try to persuade this council one way or another.

"These beings are here and among us, which tells me they are supposed to be here and that what is taught is imperative to our growing society whether I or anyone else possesses the knowledge to understand the 'why' of it."

Patel stood and protested. "So we are to follow blindly what is taught to us, no matter how harmful it may be—is that what I am hearing from our oldest elder?"

Calmly, Adamu said, "Your passion, more than your great physical strength, is found to be noteworthy, my dear Patel; but it is much like an unbridled ass— wild and stubborn at times. We do not follow blindly what we learn or are taught but use the information to better ourselves."

"How can taking the life of animals and brethren be considered a benefit to our society, Adamu?" Patel asked.

Adamu continued. "The taking of animal lives for sustenance was at first odd, since we did not require such actions in the past. Our people grow stronger from this, not weaker. Second, no one has taken the life of his brother; yes, it is taught, but we do not act upon it, and no human life has yet been lost at the hand of another. The instruction is given for a 'just in case' and nothing more. Please, Patel, we are all friends within the council. Sit and we will ponder these ideas together."

Holding contempt for what he perceived as harmful thinking, Patel answered. "For all the years I have walked upon this ground, let it be known that my diet has only consisted of fruits and plants found in abundance for all of us to consume. Do I appear to suffer from a nutritional deficiency which can only be cured by consuming the flesh of animals? Please tell me exactly what situation we could possibly face that justifies the taking of human life or any other life? If it is the will of the council to accept these ideas as proper teachings, then I am not a member of it; nor will I condone behaviors which I know will eventually destroy rather than positively propel and help progress our civilization into the future!"

Patel stormed out and headed for the crest of a hill that overlooked the entire settlement. "How crazy must everything become before they will open their eyes and see as I do?" he said.

"The loss of life," said a voice from behind him. Patel turned and saw that Ackal, a council member from the Ecegre clan, had joined him on the hill. "Patel, I'm in full agreement with you. It doesn't make any sense to learn how to kill each other. I'm afraid my clan agrees with yours, though, and they will not be swayed." Ackal sat next to Patel. "We need to do something about all this, my friend, but what I don't know."

Looking intently at Ackal, Patel replied, "We—who is we?"

"Well, you, me, and the others of course."

"There are others of your clan which are against this new teaching?"

"Not just my clan; I have visited the other ten, to include yours this very day, looking for people who believe as we do."

Curious and hopeful at the same time, Patel asked, "Would they be willing to leave their clans to start one of our own—separate from the others?"

"This I do not know, but to what end, Patel? Do you want to tear people from their clans forever?"

Shaking his head Patel explained, "Not at all. I want to eventually reunite them with their own people as leaders—leaders who are willing to teach proper doctrine. We've failed to make changes from the inside, so I want us to try from the outside as these new beings have done. Something else has nagged me for some time now. Why have people from other star systems been allowed to come here and influence the people of this world? We were taught of our uniqueness in the universe, and yet here are others which we were not told about that look like us but are not us; they are able to do things no other person is able."

Ackal nodded. "Yes, they are quite powerful, as you say, so what's to keep them from disposing of us? We are no match for them, Patel."

"I don't care, Ackal. What they are doing threatens the very existence of everyone down there— my people, as well as all the clans. If losing my life protects our people from harm, then I am ready. I would happily lay it down in their defense."

"I am with you, Patel, and if you were to explain this to those of other tribes in the same way as you have explained it to me, then I think they will follow you as well. We'll take back our people from the star men, with the Holy Father's assistance!"

"Yes, I'll go with you to speak, and once we have taken our people back, I must seek out our Father and speak, asking why all this has taken place under His watchful eye."

Cautioning, Ackal said, "Patel, do not overextend yourself; keep humble. No man may see God and live—this was taught to us by the watchers!"

"What you say is true. I will still seek Him out; remaining humble, I will ask my questions, and hopefully He will answer. Let's gather provisions for our journey and select an area for building a new settlement dedicated to our God."

***

Days and years came and went, and with each passing day, man grew closer to the brink of war between clans. Patel no longer visited the separate settlements, since his entreaty to turn from what he considered evil doctrine fell on deaf ears. Instead, he decided to work on building an army to fight against the star men. He figured that if they were done away with, then their doctrine would eventually fall away to be forgotten. The number of men that followed him grew from six plus Patel to seventy times seven times. Each of the original seven men commanded seventy soldiers of their own. Hand-to-hand and armed combat training went round the clock. Patel personally instructed every soldier in stealth tactics, using large reptiles that roamed the jungles as targets.

Early one morning Patel awakened to an annoyed follower named Vul. "Patel, our numbers keep growing. We are our own clan, mixed from all the others. Now is the time to place a ruler as head of the clan, and yet you persist in putting it off. Why?"

"I'm not putting it off, Vul. I've cancelled it altogether. Each man is free to do as he sees fit; no man is subjected to any one man."

"Then how do you propose to keep these men in line without a true leader to lead them?"

"Each man will follow his heart, and the One true God will lead them—us. Who are we—who is anyone, for that matter—to know the proper way to govern a group of men or people?"

Puffing out his chest, Vul replied, "I believe leadership is born within, which makes me very capable of leading these men."

Smiling slightly, Patel answered, "My dear Vul, a good leader is first and foremost a great servant. You must serve these men if you wish to lead, and that's something I have not seen from you at all."

Angrily Vul replied, "I am to serve them? Nonsense! They are to serve me—or go into exile!"

Leaning into Vul's face, speaking in a low tone, Patel said, "And that is why you will never be a true leader of anyone, Vul. Pride and vanity rule your character and cloud good judgment. These men are free, and free is how they will stay. This is the last time I will speak to you of this, Vul; do not bring it up again." Patel walked away, leaving Vul to stew in his thoughts. He knew he would have to keep an eye on him and his ambitions of leading a supreme dictatorship.

Chapter 7

Torel, much like his brother Tubel, was growing impatient with the progress made in destroying mankind. After much debate with himself, he decided to bring in three other angels known for their rebellious natures. Bael was the worst of them; however, each was notorious in his own right. Stul and Ridep followed Bael across the universe, displacing stars and planets to keep them from promoting potential life. The trio despised everything in existence, including themselves. They were locked in their stations, knowing they could never excel and would remain where they were. It was their desire to destroy rather than assist in God's creation.

Torel was very aware of this, and the fact that no one save the Lord could control them interested the being greatly. He also knew how volatile such an alliance with the trio would be. After all, how does one control a renegade, let alone three? Despite this, Torel brought his idea before Lucifer, who agreed that the angelics' assistance could prove useful. Dismissing Torel, Lucifer would make contact with the three alone and attempt to convince them to assist in the destruction of mankind. After putting out a call across space, Lucifer waited for a response. He didn't have to wait long.

The three angels appeared before Lucifer and glared on with great disdain for their summoner. Grunting Bael said, in a booming voice, "What would you have with us, favored of the Most High?"

Lucifer took a seat at the conference table located in the crystal tower where he had met with the watchers previously and began. "Straight to the point, Bael, as always—I admire that about you. Please, take a seat—all of you. I have a proposition that I'm more than sure you will enjoy with great relish."

After a long pause, Bael turned and nodded to the other angels to take a seat. Sitting himself, he stared through Lucifer with a look of contempt upon his face. "You … have a proposition for us? What business do we have with one another, most favored, and why now?"

Lucifer said, "Watchers of the Lord have created, on their own, a creature who possesses our likeness in every way but not our power. It is an abomination and must be destroyed from all creation, and I need your help to ensure a swift completion of this particular mission."

"If these creatures are as you say, then why not do away with them yourself? Why use us? And what is in it for us?"

Lucifer stood and walked over to wall monitors and brought up images of man for the angelics to view. "What do you most desire, my dear Bael? Name it, and it is yours—provided it is within my purview to give, mind you."

Glaring at Lucifer, Bael bellowed, "You know what we want! Your station for all three of us and nothing le—" A vision on the monitors caught Bael's eye, turning his attention away from Lucifer and toward the image. "What is that—that beautiful creature?"

Looking as though he were going to be ill, Lucifer said, "That thing is not beautiful; it is man's opposite—called a woman—who requires annihilation, not our adoration!"

Bael was mesmerized; never had he seen such a wonder in the universe. Long, shimmering hair covered her head, framing a triangular face that possessed almond-shaped eyes that sparkled green in the light of the sun; full breasts gave way to an hourglass-shaped body covered by silky, soft skin. A powerful feeling surged through Bael's entire body, electrifying and exciting him for the first time—and he liked it.

Seeing his reaction, Lucifer decided to use women to his advantage. "Of course I cannot give you a station, Bael; that is out of my hands. However, I can give you that woman and as many others as you would like to keep for your own—as pets, I guess. What say you to that? Is it a deal?"

Taking his eyes off the screen for only a moment, Bael answered, "It's a deal, favored one—as many as we want, and you stay out of our way?"

Smiling, Lucifer said, "My dear Bael, I wouldn't have it any other way. Please, go forth and check out the men of this planet for they reside on the face of it. Take what you want of their female stock, but kill the rest. Oh, and try not to implicate yourselves as the killers; otherwise, the watchers may take you before the Lord for punishment. Other than that, welcome to earth; as the watchers state, it is a unique rock in space that harbors the only living nonangelics—for now."

Bael and the other angels with him settled in amongst mankind and took for themselves wives and entering them, they begat hybrid children who were most powerful. As time went on, Bael dismissed the idea of killing man in favor of his offspring and decided instead to teach man, particularly his wives, alchemy and those things that are referred to as magical or mystical.

He groomed his children to be leaders of men; their knowledge of constructing various buildings and temples surpassed what had already been taught to man by the watchers. In fact, as massive blocks of stones were quarried by regular men, Bael's children, with knowledge of mass nullification, moved them with levitation, placing each stone where it should go. They even taught the secrets of heating and pouring of stone into perfectly sculpted bricks and monuments that would last for eons. All was well in the land for the angelics, but one man would not look upon the things taught as gifts to mankind. He saw Bael as a worse curse than Tubel and his crew; Patel was his name.

Patel created a separate settlement where those who wished to could leave their tribes and join with him. Though he did not perceive himself as a leader, everyone in the settlement looked to him for direction. Within the council hut Patel held a group meeting in which he discussed at length the plague of the star men and what needed to happen in order to rid the world of their influences. "Men of the one true God, too long have we waited for the curse of these aliens to our world to be lifted from us. I tried to speak with Him for guidance and received no answer. So the time has come for us to act and strike. All who sit here are trained in fighting, and every man in the village is also ready to fight. If it seems good to everyone, I would like to set a date for when we attack the other settlements and retrieve our brethren from the bondage which was instituted by the star men and their offspring."

Glancing around the room, Patel acknowledged every nod given by those present. It was then that Vul walked into the room and, with an air of arrogance, said, "I see we did not wait for everyone to arrive before starting this gathering."

"The meeting started on time, Vul; you are late."

"According to whom, Patel—you? Have you taken it upon yourself to be leader of these people? I cannot recall a vote cast to echo the same sentiment—so by whose time am I running late?"

Attempting to be civil, Patel responded, "No one has been made leader over anyone, Vul. It was known by everyone present that once the sun had cast a long shadow upon the water bowl the meeting would begin."

"I see," said Vul. "Everyone here was made aware of this information—everyone. And why am I just now hearing of this meeting time? Are you saying that I was made aware of this? Because if you are—"

"Vul! Brother, we can speak about this later in private. For now, I apologize for not ensuring everyone was made aware of the meeting time." Though Vul fell silent, he brewed hot inside. His ambition never swerved from his goal of becoming lord over a group of people. Since everyone held Patel in great esteem and always went to him for answers, Vul considered him an obstacle that needed to be removed in order to accomplish his goal.

As the council discussed plans, Ackal spoke up. "Patel, I have seen a great many things regarding the children of our foes. They are not like us. What I mean is that they possess great strength, speed, and agility. I doubt we can even do any type of damage to them. Some of these creatures are large—as much as ten or twelve cubits in height. Do you really believe we can take down such creatures with our weapons and dispatch them all before they do us harm?"

After thinking for a moment, Patel answered. "What I do know, Ackal, is this: The star children hold our people against their will. They have enslaved our families, including my father and grandfather. I will fight against them with my bare hands, if necessary, to gain the freedom of my family and our people. Is that a fair answer, my brother?"

"Yes, I imagine it will have to do for now, but I'm still apprehensive. We have never taken a life except those of the animals for sustenance. Regardless of their origins, some of our blood flows through their veins. Do we have the right to try and kill these creatures—to do them harm?"

Calmly, Patel said, "Our people suffer under their rule, enslaved by those beings to do their will. The land has been marred because of greed—greed for a metal they call gold. They search the depths of the earth for it on the backs of our people, and for what— scraps of food and a guarantee not to be harmed? I tell you, any man made a slave by another suffers—deep inside he suffers, and I will not rest until all our clans are freed from their oppression!"

As Patel's words resonated within the chambers, everyone present stood and clapped their hands as one, and once the applause began to die down, one man kept slowly clapping—Vul. "You make quite the speech, Patel; why don't you answer the question that was posed to you earlier? Can these beings be defeated with what arms we possess? All present understand that you would fight the enemy of man to the bitter end; your courage is not in question here.

Rather, are you prepared to sacrifice the lives of men under your command because of your feelings towards the hybrids? We live here in peace; not one of the star men has even ventured into our borders, but you wish to invade theirs to do them harm. Is the desire of your heart based on what is right or as an act of vengeance?"

Patel rose from his seat and looked around the room at every man present. Casting his gaze downward, he left the chamber in silence. Vul was a troublemaker for sure, but Patel started to wonder if perhaps he was right. *Is it vengeance that guides my thoughts or the freedom of my brothers? And how can I know for sure?*

Late in the evening, Patel called for another gathering, and he personally escorted Vul to the council chambers. Once all were settled, Patel said, "I had much to think about because of Vul's words earlier, and I realized he may be right. I'm not a leader of men, and you all know I've tried my best to keep one person from making decisions for everyone—all should have a voice in the way they are to go. I certainly do not wish to send anyone into harm's way because I told him to do it, and so I withdraw my plans to attack our enemy."

Silence within the chamber gave way to low, rolling gasps of surprise. "Just as Vul pointed out, we have lived here unopposed for a very long time. Instead, I wish to create a superior council of six who will represent and speak on behalf of all within our society. I would like to propose this to ensure that no one man's desires rule over anyone else's. I spoke of war without taking into consideration your thoughts, and for that I am sorry. I believe you all possess great minds and that you work to see to the desires and needs of the people are met, instead of your own agendas. If this sounds agreeable to you, I would like to begin selections for the six members of the council."

After an hour or so of speaking amongst themselves, the group came to a decision. Amos was the oldest member of the group—as old as Patel's grandfather—and he spoke for the people. "Patel, we will agree to this arrangement and allow the council of six to make decisions based on the desires of the people, with one proviso. A good leader is first and foremost a great servant. Good character is more precious than water and much harder to come by. Charisma masks both evil and good alike, and so it is through a person's deeds and inner being that one can discern good character from bad. You do yourself a disservice, my son, by running down decisions that you have made, but it is because of your love for the people that you do so. This is a long-winded way to say that, provided you sit on and head the council, we will accept its creation. Additionally, you must choose the other five. I'm old, but don't let my age fool you any; I'm stubborn. And on these points there are no negotiations—take it or leave it. There, I'm done."

On cue, Vul stood and began his ranting. "This is outrageous! Who is he to say what members can make up the council? I protest and find the group's idea ludicrous!"

Patel turned to face Vul. "I thought you would have some misgivings, Vul. That is why my first act as council leader is to make you a member of the council."

Once his brain accepted the statement made by Patel naming him a member of the council, Vul replied, "I knew this group had made the right choice from the very beginning. I was just playing out the cons to even the pros. Very good then. I accept the position."

"I thought you would. And for the others, please come forward when you hear your name: Ackal, Nob, Norhi, and Rave." Once all of the named members were standing before the group, Patel stated loudly, "People of Xmi, I present your ruling council of six."

Chapter 8

It came to pass that the watchers, minus Ecegre, returned to the crystal tower, but not before looking in on their prized possession—man. Shock turned to anger as they realized the drastic changes that had taken place, such as giants ruling and oppressing the people.

Gypet was the first to speak. "What is this? What has Lucifer allowed to happen?" Upset, Airmuse answered, "I don't know, but Lucifer has a lot of explaining to do—and now!" When they arrived at the council chambers, the eleven found Lucifer calmly waiting for their arrival.

Standing near the monitors, he addressed the group. "My dear brothers, welcome. Welcome back to—"

"What in all of creation have you done to our people?" said Gypet.

Lucifer remained calm. "Brother Gypet, please, I assure you—all of you—that I did nothing to your creatures. However"—Lucifer moved to a chair at the table—"I'll admit that overseeing all settlements was a bit tasking, so I took the liberty of recruiting other angelics to assist me. After all, there are twelve of you, and so—"

Still outraged, Gypet interrupted, "You were the only angelic we ordered to be the overseer, and so it should have been you alone, Lucifer!"

Arrogance mixed with a great annoyance spilled out from Lucifer's being as he responded. "Ordered—you *ordered* me, Gypet? I take orders from only one source, and none of you are Him. Yes, I took it upon myself to bring in helpers because no one else was around to ask what should be done. If you wish to release your anger on someone, then it should be against those who committed the acts which led to your ire, not me. As I was saying, four angelics came to assist me, and then another four after that, and they also brought one hundred and ninety-two others. The latter are the responsible parties, for they looked upon the females of your creatures and entered them, leading to hybrids—powerful, out-of-control hybrids. Since the last angelics' arrival, I have had zero contact with any of them. I never could find where they were going or what they were up to, I'm afraid."

Still visibly upset, Gypet fought to keep his anger in check as he questioned Lucifer. "Dear Lucifer, I apologize for saying 'ordered.'" We entrusted man to you alone, and now man is—well, a mess. Their blood cries out to us, which means death has come to our creation, and you show us hybrids ruling over them.

How should we feel or think when the person placed over man is calm and doing nothing to fix a grave error that happened under his watch?"

A focused glare met Gypet's as Lucifer said, "The error was man's creation in the first place, my dear brother. Secondly, how or why you care is not a concern of mine. I've stayed near this abomination entirely too long and will take my leave of all of you. If an intelligent watcher exists among your group, take my advice: destroy it—all of it—and never speak of the existence of man to anyone, ever!"

Lucifer turned away from the group and disappeared in a blinding flash of light and thunder. Most of the eleven sat silent, not believing what they had just heard from the keeper they thought would care for mankind. Gypet stood up, and after a few minutes had passed, he spoke. "My dear brothers, I am truly sorry for all that has happened. How blind I was to think Lucifer would have made a good watcher—so foolish."

Airmuse, with a consoling voice, said, "It wasn't just you, Gypet; we all settled for him because of time constraints. Anyway, the real issue is what to do about our creations. How do we fix it without destroying everything and starting over?"

Hanic interjected, "Destruction is out of the question. Let us go out and annihilate the hybrid scum! Then we stay with and reeducate the settlements that use force, teaching that killing is wrong."

"I like your enthusiasm, Hanic, and if it were possible to wipe violence from man's mind, I would say okay. But mankind is designed to experience and learn, and once an idea is introduced, it stays firmly seated within their psyche. Additionally, the mutants which we are now faced with are angelic hybrids, and we may be unable to dispatch them from the realm of organic life. As spiritual beings, they may have the ability to manipulate organics as we do, so nothing man-made will kill them."

After hours of silence, Airmuse spoke. "We empower man."

"What was that, Airmuse?" Gypet asked. "What did you say?"

"We empower man with the abilities needed to fight against and defeat the hybrids." The more Airmuse spoke, the bigger his smile became.

Shaking his head, Gypet spoke of his misgivings. "Brother, the purpose of this exercise was to create a being unlike anything in all creation—an entity that learned as he grew over time, not a new type of angelic to add to our ranks. It's not possible, my dear friend."

Airmuse argued, "Not all humans would be affected, just enough to do away with hybrids among each settlement. We can take back their powers once every hybrid is … no longer living. As for the angelic part, our champions will have the ability to send the creatures' spirits to the abyss, where they will be held until the Lord of Hosts passes judgment upon them."

Wanting to weigh in on the conversation, Aafric stated, "Power corrupts, as we have seen with those of our own ranks. I fear for what might come to pass if man is given such power. What would keep one or all of those given power from dominating and forcing their will on the people?"

Airmuse replied, "It's difficult to really know a being's heart and what it holds, save for the Lord, but we cannot stand by and do nothing. People are dying, and whether we like it or not, man knows life can be terminated and that he possesses the ability to do it."

Gypet was still unconvinced, thinking man should be left as man and not manipulated as the other angelics had done, because the council then would be no different from those who caused this chaos in the first place.

Airmuse could read the frustration on Gypet's face and tried to alleviate it by offering a way to choose their champions. "Let us go forth and find men that the settlements look to for guidance, and we will empower them. This will work, Gypet—it really is the only way for us to go. Time is ticking, and the people are suffering. Let's do what's right—now."

Looking around the table, Gypet studied each face of his fellow brothers. Once he was done, he stood. "Very well, my brothers; we will do this, and if it is good and agreeable with all of you, Airmuse and I will go forth and search for candidates." Everyone nodded in agreement, prompting Gypet to say, "So be it. We will deliver mankind from the grip of those who do evil with our chosen!"

Chapter 9

Sitting on top of a hillside overlooking the settlement, Patel pondered his people's successes in raiding and smuggling groups of men and women from other villages controlled by the star men's offspring. As the sun rose and slowly began its descent to bring on the night, anxiety and excitement took control of his thoughts. Tonight's target was his old settlement, where both his grandfather and his father had stayed behind to rally and keep their people together.

The giant Utt had taken charge of their people soon after Patel's leaving. It had been many years since Patel had received word from either of them. He planned on going in first to scout out the area before sending in a large party that would direct and light the way for his clan to escape. All other missions had gone off without a hitch; and yet he was nervous and didn't know why.

Looking up, he could make out some of the stars, a few at first. Then, as the last of the sun's rays disappeared, an explosion of stars lit the clear, crisp sky, prompting a question that had nagged his mind since he could remember. *Why does God not answer me? Did I do something wrong? Maybe the Creator doesn't see me as being worthy of an answer.*

Regardless, he wasn't going to quit asking; he was determined to receive a reply. Many in his new settlement thought it silly that he kept trying to speak with God, but it would not deter Patel. When he did attempt to speak to Him, he did it in private, hoping that what the Lord saw in private would be answered in public. Not for validation, to be sure, but so that everyone could benefit—not just one, or a few, but everyone.

Patel heard a voice coming from camp and knew it was time to go. Still on his knees, he asked the Creator for a smooth mission and that he might be reunited with his family and bring them back to a safe place. The one voice multiplied into many, urging him to hurry. Patel got up from his place of prayer and solitude on the hill and ran to the waiting group and into the arms of a new destiny.

Coming to the outskirts of the village, Patel looked around and found things quite strange. The night fires were not lit; everything was dark and quiet—too quiet. As he approached a family sized brick-adobe dwelling, he slowly entered with a sword in one hand and a shield firmly grasped in the other. He quietly glanced around to see who dwelled there and if he knew them or not. To his surprise, the dwelling sat empty, as though no one had ever lived in it. There wasn't so much as a jar of water or a sleeping mat on the floor. Patel stepped back out and strained to hear any sound to indicate that someone lived in the village, but none came to him.

Walking down an exposed path a couple hundred yards from the old dwellings, he saw a small glow in the distance. He headed straight for it but kept his wits in case it was a trap. Soon the soft glow gave way to a roaring fire right in the middle of what looked to be brand-new dwellings made of stone. Patel guessed the dwellings weighed over a hundred tons. The homes were built around a huge fire pit that measured eighty cubits across and about twelve cubits deep, with an active fire giving off extreme heat and light. So impressed was he by the size of the fire that he paid no attention to a giant man leaving one of the dwellings to enter another.

Long iron rotisseries ran from one side of the fire pit across to the other side. He could barely make out what was attached to them. It appeared to be animals of some sort roasting over a huge fire. He moved closer to the buildings at the bottom of a steep embankment, Patel was, extremely careful not to be seen by anyone. It seemed he didn't need to try too hard, since it looked as desolate as the old village he had just left. He reached a stone wall that he followed around to the front of one of the buildings. A wooden door that led to a large room was ajar enough that he could take a glimpse inside without disturbing it, and that's when he saw her for the first time. A beautiful woman with long silky brown hair, barely covered by a thin sheet lay on the ground with chains secured to her ankles and attached to a stone wall. She lay sobbing in the dark, and it touched his heart.

After peering left and then right, he quickly opened the door and ran into the room with his sword and shield poised for battle. When he could see that she was the only person in the room, Patel ran up to her. Surprised to see him through her tears, she screamed. Throwing his sword to one side, Patel covered her mouth with his hand, and tried to communicate that he was there to help her. She could see by the look in his eyes that he spoke the truth, and she began to calm herself. After assessing the chains and the wall, Patel decided to use his sword to break a link. He placed the blade into one of the links and twisted the sword with all his might, snapping the link in two and freeing her from the wall. In gratitude, the woman threw her arms around Patel and kissed him on the face over and over again. After pulling her off, he placed a finger over his lips and gestured that she follow him out of the room. She nodded, and she stayed very close to him as they left. Once outside, he pointed in the direction she was to travel, where his men would be waiting for newly freed people, and he watched as she went up the trail. Once she was out of sight, Patel turned to reenter the village, but a blow to his shoulder sent him reeling.

He looked up from the ground and could make out the looming figure of a very large man. "You are not one of my slaves! Who are you, and what are you doing in my district?" The voice boomed so strongly that Patel could feel its power. Patel was speechless as he watched the huge man reach down and pick him up with one hand. "Well, answer me! Who are you?"

Patel pulled his sword from its sheath and struck at the giant's neck, catching him by surprise. The huge man released Patel and fell backward. He clenched his neck and began to laugh. "You cannot harm me with weapons made by men, little one. Ha ha ha!"

Standing and taking up a defensive pose, Patel answered, "I am Patel, giant, and these are my people. I'm here to free them from you!"

Again the giant laughed. "What—all by yourself, little one? You are like a locust to me, for I am Utt, leader of this territory, king of your people, and god to everything under my power!"

Firing back, Patel replied, "You, oh Utt, are nothing more than an undeserved burden to me and my people. I will free them from your tyrannical grip this very night. How they are freed is up to you"—he raised his sword over his head—"the easy way or the hard way! Choose, Utt!"

A look of arrogance came over the giant's face and then retreated as he pulled out his sword from its scabbard. The sword's blade was as long as Patel was tall, its width equal to the width of his torso. "Very well, insect. I choose the hard way." Utt raised the massive blade over his head and slammed it downward, intending to slice the warrior in two from head to foot. Patel moved quickly to the left, allowing Utt's sword to drive itself into the ground. Using the partially buried blade as a ramp, Patel ran up its length and struck the giant's temple with his own sword, which had little effect. Bounding up and flipping over Utt, he narrowly escaped the giant's grasp. As he landed behind the monster-sized man, he attempted to plunge his sword through Utt's back, shattering the blade into small, jagged pieces that fell harmlessly to the ground.

Utt turned quickly, landing a back fist to the side of Patel's body, launching him twelve feet into the air and slamming him into a stone wall, where he fell to the ground in a heap.

As Utt walked over to where Patel lay slumped over, just before he reached out to crush his foe, a loud, commanding voice came from behind the giant. "Release!" Streams of arrows rained down on Utt like a swarm of bees attacking someone disturbing a hive. None of the projectiles penetrated; however, it was just the distraction Patel needed to get to his feet and retreat from the giant. Another volley of arrows was fired at Utt, with two lodging in the bottom of his left eye socket, causing him to reel backward cursing as he scratched at the protruding arrow shafts at his eye. Patel bounded up the trail and met the raiding party, and they all made their way back to the settlement.

When Patel arrived at the village infirmary, Norhi, physician and medicine man to the group, examined him and found a few cracked ribs and blunt force trauma to one shoulder; but other than that, he was fine. After removing the last of the chain from their rescued female, Norhi could see her skin had been rubbed raw and was bleeding in the shape of a shackle around her ankle. He smeared honey on the whole wound and then wrapped her ankle with clean bandages. After giving her a drink of gall for pain, she fell fast asleep with a look of comfort and peace upon her face. Patel was mesmerized by her beauty and wanted to talk with her but could see she was exhausted and needed rest.

"Patel," said Norhi, "I've wrapped your torso to keep the rib bones from moving about so they may heal properly; it may take weeks, though, and you'll need to rest yourself. Here, drink some gall; it'll help with pain." Patel didn't respond or look away from the dreaming beauty that slumbered before him. "Patel!"

As if snapping out of a trance, he turned and acknowledged Norhi's entreaty. "I'm sorry, Norhi, what was that? Ribs broken and take time to heal? Gotcha. And thanks, you're a good physician."

"Yes, well… anyway, what is it with you? I can't tell if your brain sustained an injury or not. You can't seem take your eyes off this female; just staring and staring—"

Cutting him off, Patel said, "I'm fine—really. It was just a difficult battle with that giant is all."

Norhi nodded. "Okay, Utt is one of the largest men I've ever seen in my life, and watching you take him on all by yourself was something to see. I mean, from our vantage point you appeared as a doll in his hand, being tossed this way and that. Ha ha ha! If I hadn't seen it with my own eyes, I wouldn't have bet anyone could walk away from a fight with that thing and live."

Appearing annoyed as he winced from the pain in his ribs, Patel said, "Yes—yes, thanks, Norhi; I was there and don't care to relive the experience. If you don't mind, I'll sleep here and wait for our guest to awaken, okay?"

A bit puzzled, Norhi agreed to Patel staying near the newly freed female. "Please drink the gall; it'll help with pain."

"Thanks again, but no, I want to be in my right mind when she wakes."

"Look, Patel, you may not be in too much pain right now, but when the pain comes, you'll know it big-time. Take the gall; it'll help. Trust me."

Patel waved Norhi away, determined not to take any gall. The physician left it close to him in case he changed his mind later. Once Patel was alone with the woman, he resumed watching her as she slept, trying to understand why she so moved his heart, she was incredibly beautiful in slumber. She had a soft caramel skin color, long brown hair that fanned out around her waist. *She's been through much at the hands of Utt; I vow to protect her from everything evil and cruel.* Eyes heavy, he fell asleep dreaming that he and the woman were walking along a clear blue ocean holding hands, smiling and laughing with one another as they went.

The sun's rays pierced a small hole in the roof of the infirmary, striking Patel in a closed eye, rousing him from sleep. He quickly sat up, and a sharp pain in his side brought back memories of the previous night's brawl with the giant. Tenderly holding his ribs, Patel slowly rose to his feet and looked for the rescued female, but he found the infirmary empty. Walking outside, he saw Norhi grinding leaves and other items to make medications. Norhi glanced up from his work, moved to where Patel stood smiling, and inquired as to how he was doing.

"A little sore, especially when I breathe, but I'm functioning. Where's the girl?"

Shaking his head, Norhi asked, "You didn't take any of the gall did you? Patel, you must take it for the pain. It's only going to get worse before it gets better."

Cutting him off, Patel asked again, "Norhi, where is the girl from last night?"

Norhi knew arguing wasn't going to do any good, "Oh, well she woke up just before dawn and insisted on knowing where you lived to make a meal— to thank you for saving her. I'm sure she's still there. You know, if I didn't know you any better, I'd say you were taken with her, but that's not possible, I know.

None of the females in our own village have ever turned your head … Patel?"

Turning from his work on the table, Norhi watched as Patel walked off toward his dwelling place. "Could he be taken with this woman? Nah, crazy talk. Okay, back to work we go."

Slowly opening the door to his dwelling place, Patel peered in to see the woman busying herself with food preparations it smelled of spices, onion, and a delicious meat. Looking about his own home seemed strange, but he couldn't quite put his finger on why. Moving from a firepit on the front left wall to the table, the woman dressed in a green toga, was startled to see Patel standing there staring in her direction with a look of bewilderment on his face.

"Oh—I didn't hear anyone come in. I must look a mess. I was making a nice meal for you to say thank you for saving me last night. Oh, but you're hurt— more than I from the looks of it." Patel just stood and stared at her, which made the woman feel a bit self-conscious. "Forgive my appearance; I must look a mess."

"You said it."

A tinge of hurt feelings could distinctly be heard and felt in her response. "What? Well I'm sorry if I am not to your liking; perhaps—"

"You are very much to my liking; what I meant was that you said earlier that you must look a mess. I think you're the most beautiful of all creations found under the sky, and why you are here in my home is puzzling to me."

A shy yet coy look fell upon her face. "I'm here because you saved me from a terrible situation and I wish to spend the rest of my life thanking you."

"There's no need for that, woman; I was fortunate to stumble upon you chained to a—"

She interrupted, "Nyeve."

"What's that?" Patel asked.

"My name is Nyeve, daughter of Kilil," the woman replied,

"Right, you are right; we haven't been properly introduced. I am Patel, son of Shir. Our village where you were held captive is where I and my family are from, and I was going to rescue more of my people to include family members, but that giant had other plans." Terror and pity swam across Nyeve's face, and it was obvious to Patel that something was bothering her. "Is everything all right? You seem frightened of something."

Moving away from the table, Nyeve continued to speak as she prepared and put mutton stew before him. "The village that you speak of is of your people, not mine. I was a gift to Utt from his brother, Demar the Detestable One. I was to couple with Utt to produce more star people."

"Not exactly the way I think a man would treat his woman—chaining her to a wall and all."

"It is if the woman is not willing to couple and continues to escape from the man. I have never known a man, and sometimes the women given to those giants do not survive the closed-door ritual."

Confused, Patel pressed further for information, hoping to find something that would give him the edge to infiltrate and free his family from Utt's grip. "Closed-door ritual? I don't understand."

Taking a seat next to Patel, Nyeve explained. "Women enter the coupling chamber deep within the ground so that no one can hear what is happening. A survivor told me that."

"Hold it, I'm getting confused with "survival" and "survive"; what do these words mean?"

"I thought everyone knew. It means you do not go with death—you know, suffer the dying time." Seeing the confused look upon his face, Nyeve tried harder to properly explain the concept to him. "Do you eat the flesh of animals?"

"Yes, of course," Patel answered, still not understanding.

"Good, then you know when an animal is killed, it goes with death."

"Nyeve, the animal goes nowhere. We eat it, so where would it go? Besides, people do not kill each other; this is forbidden."

Frustrated, she attempted one more time to help Patel understand. "You say you are the son of Shir, right? Shir went with death along with his whole family—except for you. Utt gave them over to death."

Shock, confusion, and anger welled up, electrifying every part of Patel's being. He couldn't understand why Nyeve would say such things—false, impossible things. Even when battling Utt he hadn't been trying to take the giant's life; only hurt him enough to get away to free his people. "To kill is forbidden!" Tears of agony and rage began to well up in his eyes. He got up from the table and turned his back to Nyeve so she wouldn't see the emotional cocktail that was on the verge of spilling out.

Feeling her soft hand lightly touch his back as her arms moved to embrace him, Patel was able to fight back the emotional pain so he could ask more questions. "Do you know where death took them and how Utt gave my family to death?"

"Patel, I've hurt you with the telling; perhaps it's best if we rest for now."

"I cannot and will not rest until I know everything regarding my family and where I might find them now that death has taken them."

Reluctantly, Nyeve took Patel by the hand and led him to his bed, where she motioned for him to lie down. After he complied, she sat close and began to tell Patel all he wanted to know about his family. "Before the days of the giants, there came to us star men who taught many things, such as how the stars move, why the sky is blue, and how things work on earth, which is the name of this ground we live on. Then star people coupled with women, and some of their children are the giants, such as Utt. Others are quite like us, though they possess different powers we do not possess. Their numbers grew quickly since their time within our wombs is less than half the time a man's child requires.

"Those star children that are giants ruled over man, while the others showed us how to dig for metals and construct intricate buildings, and some taught secret things, such as mass nullification—taking something that weighs more than the dimension it's found in and making it equal that dimension. It sounds hard but is not really; it helps to levitate materials, which I can show you later. Anyway, your father and grandfather rebelled against Utt because of his cruelty toward the people. They were so brave, Patel, never giving ground on their stance. One day, Utt sent out guards to arrest the whole family, and somehow your father knew it would happen. He had the women of your family smuggled out of the village, but all the men stayed behind to give them a chance to escape. Utt was furious and threw them in a room where he tortured each of them to find out where the women went, but no one talked. The giant called for his brother to assist him with making what they call a citadel; that's where you found me. When it was complete, Utt brought everyone out of the old village and placed them in this citadel. He celebrated by taking the men from your family and roasting their bodies over the pit. That's when death took your fathers—to where I do not know."

A great pain stabbed at Patel's chest worse than cracked ribs could ever produce. "Where are the bodies? After they were burned, where did the bodies go?"

"My dear, sweet Patel, I don't think you need to know that."

Patel sat up and grabbed Nyeve by the arms. "Tell me!" He shook her, desperate to know where to find them.

Wincing in pain, Nyeve yelled out, "They were consumed!"

Patel released his grip. Nyeve stood up, walked across the room, and began to weep in a corner. Patel, momentarily in shock from hearing of his father's demise, soon became aware of Nyeve's sobbing. He rushed to the woman and spun her around, taking her in his arms. He apologized over and over again, kissing her head while stroking her long, beautiful hair. Nyeve started to melt into his arms.

Nyeve snuggled closer and confided, "How wonderful it feels to be in your arms; so safe, secure, and comfortable, as though I've known you from the dawn of time rather than just one day." She pulled away enough to look up into his eyes. Her eyes shone her excitement and the fire coming from core of her being; electric jolts exhilarated every part of her as evidenced through Patel's mutual touches and feelings. Nyeve moved closer as if wanting to fan the flames of passion growing within, she rose up on her toes and kissed him softly upon the lips. As he kissed back, Nyeve snuggled closer to his muscular frame pressed against her body, and it felt good to her—very good. Patel enjoyed watching her breathe in as she rested her head against his chest, as if she loved to feel and hear the rhythmic dance of his heartbeat. She looked so ready to give herself and all her feminine beauty with him.

Suddenly, Patel stopped and pulled back from Nyeve. "I can't do this—not now. I'm sorry, but a remnant of my family is still out there somewhere, and finding them must come first. Once I find them, though, I want you to be mine if you want me."

"Oh Patel, I do want to be with you. I'm afraid you may not want me to stay when you get to know me better—thinking I'm strange and so leave me."

"Nyeve, I would never leave you. You'd have to leave me—I promise to love you forever if you'll let me."

Through tears of joy, she replied, "I'll never leave you—not ever. And yes, I'll be your woman. I can wait to give myself to you until your family is safely returned. We'll go through this together, okay? Stay with me, my love, and I promise it'll never be boring!"

Smiling at each other, they embraced one last time and sat at the table to figure out how to find death and the women of Patel's family. "Nyeve, what does death look like? Did you see in what direction they were led off by him?"

"No, no one saw death; only that the men of your family's bodies were missing their heads. Either

Utt or death took off their heads to remove them from the body—I guess. I mean, no one has ever been taken from their body before, so I don't know. The women did escape in their bodies, though, to the east of Ibog, to a place never known."

Frustrated and unable to make sense of the information given him, Patel decided he would need to confront Utt and make the giant tell him where death had taken his father. He kept his thoughts to himself so Nyeve didn't worry and the council could not stop him.

Night fell over the settlement, and a council meeting was arranged to discuss the previous night's successes and failures. In an accusatory voice, Vul questioned, "Patel, why did you circumvent the village and raid, on your own, a stone construct never before seen?"

Humble, yet firm, Patel replied, "It wasn't my intention to go into the citadel. That's what the new village is called—a citadel. My old village was abandoned in favor of this citadel by Utt the giant. I did not raid the stone dwelling but happened upon a woman chained to a wall and wasn't about to leave her there like some animal, Vul. This is, after all, the reason we are doing this, isn't it?"

"Well," said Vul, "I think we all agreed to certain procedures—procedures that must be followed to ensure not just one person's safety but the safety of the entire group. Or has that now changed? Wouldn't you say that due to actions taken by you personally, you put others in jeopardy?"

"No, I would not—I alone was in harm's way."

"To be sure, everyone here on the council would agree, including myself. However, I contend that placing yourself as you did—in harm's way—with your being a leading member of this council; losing you could, indeed contribute to the harm of this body and ultimately the people who rely on you and this body to rule over them."

Becoming annoyed with Vul's banter and knowing his heart, Patel said, "I'm sure if ever I were captured by our enemies, you would have no problem filling my position. In fact, I'm sure Vul the Great would enjoy that very much. This is why I will ensure to keep myself free to serve the people of Xmi. Oh, and one more thing, Vul; we do not rule the people, and as long as I am the leading member of our council, we never will." Leaving Vul fuming in his seat, Patel left the chamber and returned home to Nyeve.

Lying in silence upon his bed, Patel contemplated how to leave the settlement with no one knowing and what he'd do when face-to-face with Utt. Nyeve, from the table watched her man, *I wonder what could hold his focus for so long.* She was used to men of her village "doing" rather than being steeped in thoughts and ideas. Of course, the giants really never allowed time for personal reflection but worked them to exhaustion. By doing so ensured the men they controlled couldn't find time to think of freedom—or anything else, for that matter. "Patel, what troubles you so? I'm afraid for you my sweet."

After a moment of silence, he answered. "What can you tell me of Utt? What are his weaknesses and routines? Where does he reside within the citadel? Does he ever leave the settlement?"

Nyeve tilted her head, thinking. "Why do you need to know such things, my love? Are you thinking of taking on Utt by yourself?"

Letting out a long sigh of frustration, Patel sat up and looked Nyeve in the eye. "Nyeve, I must do this, and I wish to place only myself in danger; not my people, the settlement, or you—you whom I love deeply."

She argued,"Patel, Utt is not a person to deal with lightly; he's lethal. He kills people without caring. Death follows him and takes our kind away—forever. I know because … because he took from me my parents and a man I was to be betrothed to. Please, abandon your thoughts of revenge and stay with me; I don't wish to lose you as well."

"You mean more to me than anyone could know. As long as Utt is out there, we live in constant danger; can't you see that? Once I return, we can start a life free of fear. I know I can defeat him and death. My father and forefathers need me, just as I would expect them to come to my aid if needed."

Staring into his eyes, Nyeve could tell that with or without information from her, he was determined to confront Utt and nothing would stop it from happening. "No weapon forged by man will cause harm to him. Weapons are more of an irritant than anything. Rarely does he leave the citadel unless a possession he dearly wants back which was lost to him is fairly close and retrievable. I know of no way to kill him, as he has done to our kind. Removing the head of our people does the job; maybe it would work on him, but I cannot be sure. Patel, I doubt he's just going to give it to you without a battle.

"During the day, he watches over the citadel from a spire located north of the fire pit. This way he is able to keep an eye out for anyone approaching or attempting to leave the citadel. His senses of smell, sight, and hearing are very good—better than those of any man or animal walking the earth. When the light of day is gone from the sky, he enters a great hall located to the east of the fire pit. There are two large rooms inside; the first is where he keeps women, and he always beds at least one but as many as six before bathing and heading into the second room alone to sleep. While he slumbers is when Utt is most vulnerable, and yet when some of the men attempted to subdue him while he was sleeping, they failed and were roasted in the pit as the light came up. It hasn't been for a lack of trying, Patel, but Utt can't be defeated. Don't you see that? I don't wish to lose you to him as well, my new love."

As tears welled up in her eyes, Patel tried to comfort Nyeve as best he could, but determination ruled his heart. He was full of a determination to take out Utt, an enemy of mankind. After a deep kiss and loving embrace, Patel gave three light taps to Nyeve's behind, signaling it was time for him to go.

Patel could tell Nyeve was struggling with letting him go. She finally released him so she could take a few steps backward. Pushing her garment off her shoulders, she exposed a flawless beauty that was woman before her man. "If you must do this, Patel, I will not stop you; but don't leave without first giving me a child—your child. Take me, for I am yours."

Mesmerized by the incredible sight before him, Patel took a step toward her and then stopped. "I swear by the Heavenly Father my heart will never belong to any other woman but you, and upon my return, dear Nyeve, we shall become a couple forever. Now, however, I must leave with all my strength intact if Utt is to be confronted successfully." After praising the Lord for giving him a woman of perfection, Patel gave a quick kiss to Nyeve and set out to seek and confront Utt the giant.

Chapter 10

Night fell quickly across the face of the earth, allowing starlight to illuminate a cool, crisp sky. Reaching the outskirts of the old settlement abandoned by Utt, Patel was suddenly hit by and bathed in a great white light that forced him to his knees. Once his eyes adjusted to the brilliance, he made out images of two fair-haired beings floating in the air before him. Wanting to speak, he couldn't find words but struggled to push out a question. "Who… who are you?"

Smiling, one of the beings answered, "Do not be afraid, Patel; we mean you no harm. Where are you going?"

"I go to confront Utt the giant, an enemy of man—my people, I mean."

"Where are your weapons, Patel of man?"

"I possess no weapon that can harm Utt, for no weapon of man will do harm to him."

"Why do you wish to confront Utt; why do you consider him an enemy?"

"He has enslaved my people, chased away the women of my family, and given my forefathers to death and roasted and eaten their bodies. I cried out to the One Father but received no answer, so now I go against Utt to destroy him and release my people from bondage."

The beings answered, "Patel, the outcries of your ancestors' blood has come to us. We have heard the entreaty of you and your people. You may consider it answered. Behold, in the Name of the Lord of Hosts, we send you as His chosen to confront, fight, and destroy the evil in this world. We shall set upon you power from the Spirit so that you shall possess the abilities needed to defeat evil."

Humbly he asked the visitors, "Please sirs, if I may be so bold, could not the One Father and His army easily defeat the giants of this—as you call it—world?"

"Evil shall be defeated by the Lord's army of mankind, for you shall lead it most favored; for man must defeat this enemy with the assistance of the Most High."

Patel, dumbfounded, said, "I beg your indulgence, sirs, but who am I that the Most High God would wish for me to lead His army of men? It's not my wish to be over my brothers but rather to serve them."

"It is because of such a quality, a desire to serve rather than be served that makes you a leader of men and chosen of the Most High." Moving toward Patel, one of the beings placed a hand on his head, saying,

"Man of the One true God, behold; His power shall overshadow you. Spirits of the beasts of the field and air times three are given that will conceal who you are, O man, so that no one gives false veneration and so your identity is kept secret from the enemy. At times, during certain battles, the body frame of man is of necessity; at these times you may fight as half-man, half-animal so as to conceal your identity; additionally, a gold band will form, encircling the upper left part of your arm. Attached to the gold band is a solid-silver hilt of a sword which only you can remove, and once removed, a flaming blade shall appear. This flaming blade is the finger of God to use in dispatching your foes. Removing their heads will destroy their bodies and send their spirits into the abyss, where they shall stay and rise no more without permission of the Lord, God."

"Sirs, what do I call you, and if I need assistance, how may I call upon you?"

"We are the watchers, guardians from the sky. Simply speak requesting our help, and if we are able to intercede, so be it; however, if we are not allowed, so be it. Trust in the Lord, use the power given for the good of mankind, and keep the Lord close to your heart. If it was not in your character to be God's champion, then we would not be here speaking with you. Now go; confront and dispatch Utt the giant using the skills given. As you deploy your powers, you'll see how reflexive and second nature they become, dear Patel. Keep the faith. Stand strong—in the Name of the Lord!"

Suddenly, the light and beings were gone and Patel stood alone, trying to comprehend what he had just experienced. Looking around, he noticed the sun was beginning to rise. *Did I fall asleep? Was it all a dream? Why is the sun rising? When I set out, it was setting. And how do I know the light in the sky is called sun?* His mind seemed more open, and he understood many things that were not known to him before now. A flood of new knowledge sprouted within his head, and a feeling of dread followed, for he now understood the concept of death. He realized that his forefathers were forever lost to him in the flesh but one day he would reunite with them in spirit. Then Patel considered his own mortality. He could be lost to this world as easily as his fathers. Though the idea was grim, his spirit was set on completing the mission he had started out to fulfill: destroy Utt, free people from the giant's tyranny, and return safely to Nyeve.

Overlooking the citadel from atop a cliff where the old village stood, Patel contemplated the folly that was Utt's fortress. *Only a fool would place a defensive stronghold in a low-level area surrounded by high places.*

Patel climbed down from his vantage point and entered the citadel, looking for signs of life. People moved about, bringing wood to keep the central fire burning, and gathering food and water, seemingly oblivious to Patel walking among them.

Just then, a large boom that vibrated the ground below turned his attention away from the people and toward the giant that stood before him. "Little one, you returned to me, and with no weapons this time. Is your intention to give up and become one of my slaves along with the rest of these creatures?"

Confidently, Patel replied, "O, mighty Utt, I have noticed that you have no soldiers to protect you and this settlement. Do you not fear death at the hands of such like me?"

Laughing, Utt replied, "I fear nothing on this rock, little one. Nothing of man can harm me; I alone am king. Who would dare to take a stance against me and live?"

Patel smiled. "Then you do not fear the Lord of Hosts or His chosen, for if His hand is against you, then how can you stand?"

A grunt of arrogance and pride led Utt's reply. "The Lord of Hosts has forsaken this place and its people, and no chosen exists. Therefore, I say to you, bow to me and pledge your obedience to my rule or die like the rest!"

Looking all around, Patel could see that no one was watching the two square off. The people hid in their homes, knowing full well that Utt's wrath, once unleashed, took time to subside; to be in his path meant death. Concentrating, Patel chose to morph into a half-man, half-ape standing over twelve cubits in height, equal to Utt. As the giant stood shocked at what he saw, Patel said, "Here is my answer, Utt: you are condemned to die for your mistreatment of man—"

"Impossible. There's no such thing. It is not I who will die, but you!" Utt lunged for Patel, took hold of an arm, and threw the beast over the fire pit, where he smacked into a wall of the spire.

Picking himself up, Patel looked intently at the giant and said, "My turn." Taking a running leap, Patel launched himself into the air with such speed that Utt could not move out of the way in time. As Patel's shoulder impacted Utt's chest, the two fell backward, slamming and crashing through a stone wall and rolling across the floor until coming to rest against an interior wall. From a corner in the room, Patel saw three people huddling in terror with eyes wide, wondering what was happening. He didn't want to endanger any of the people in the citadel, so he picked Utt up off the ground and hurled the giant through the opening in the wall. Once outside, Patel leaped and landed straddling the giant, where he began to land powerful blows to Utt's face. One of Utt's thighs hit Patel from behind on his buttocks with enough force to send him reeling over the giant's head.

As Utt stood up, he ran stumbling and grabbing for a weapon that lay waiting. Seeing Utt go for his lance blade, Patel remembered what the guardian had said about a hilt on his left arm. He grabbed the hilt and removed it from the gold band, and a blade of fire formed out of it. As the two squared off once more, Patel noticed for the first time a look of dread on Utt's face. Attempting to reason with his opponent, Utt grumbled, "Chosen of God, I do not deserve to die. These creatures, humans, were forsaken, left by themselves without a protector. How else could we have taken control of them so easily?"

No sympathy was found in Patel's reply. "This day you shall die, for the Lord has delivered you into my hands. Prepare yourself!"

As blade smashed into blade, large sparks shot off in every direction, and when Patel had positioned himself in a way that gave a clear trajectory to Utt, he took it. Patel's fiery blade passed without resistance through the giant's neck, removing Utt's head from his body. The giant's body remained standing for a few moments and then slumped to the ground, where it lay motionless before Patel. Silence fell over the citadel as the chosen looked over his kill with relief and great satisfaction. Calling out to everyone in the fort, Patel told them not to be afraid. "Come forward, all who live here, and see that you are now free—a slave no more!"

It took some time, but eventually all that could do so assembled before him and the lifeless body of Utt. Speaking to a few of the residents, Patel wanted to ensure every person found within the citadel was free.

"Master, there are many of our people chained in rooms underground. What is your bidding, master?"

Upset at being called "master," he said, "First, I am Patel, not your master. No man or half-man shall ever be master of you again. You are free, and so shall those chained be made free as well. Show me this underground and take me to all who are bound, and I will release them."

The young man bowed and took Patel into underground rooms. With the use of his sword, Patel freed the people there, who were very grateful to the giant, hairy creature. Once everyone was accounted for and all were assembled, a crowd pushed Utt's body into the fire to watch it burn. One man, the oldest among them, took Utt's head and presented it to Patel, thanking him for freedom. Accepting the head, Patel ordered the crowd to take anything useful from the citadel and prepare to follow him to a new settlement where all would be welcomed as family returning from a long journey.

Chapter 11

On the outskirts of town glancing up from his work table from time to time and panning the coastline, Norhi thought he saw a large group of people walking on the beach in the distance toward the village. A fragmented marine layer of thick fog had rolled in, obstructing the beach in various areas and making him think he was seeing things. It wasn't until an alarm sounded that he realized a flood of settlers were truly headed his way. Leaving his work, Norhi ran to meet the group with great enthusiasm.

Walking and talking, the people told him of a great beast that had defeated Utt with a sword of fire and released them from bondage. The creature had showed the people the way to go and told them to ask for Norhi when they reached the village. Perplexed, Norhi tried to make sense of it. "I do not know of whom you speak unless it is Patel, but he is hardly a beast possessing a sword of fire. Let's not worry about it for now. I shall have a meal prepared for everyone, and then we can sit and try to figure out what exactly happened, if this is good to all of you."

The members of the group nodded. The older men went with Norhi, while the women met and followed the women of the village and assisted in preparing meals for those freed from Utt's evil hand. Nyeve was very happy to see all the people she knew coming into the village by the thousands, but where was Patel? His strange absence from the group worried her deeply, and she thought about returning to the citadel to look for him. Nyeve headed back to Patel's home, and as she began to pack provisions to take for the journey to the old settlement, she felt hands softly grasping her shoulders.

Startled, she spun around to find Patel's smiling face. "My love, where have you been? I was so worried and scared that they captured or killed you!"

"I'm fine, my sweet; and except for a little tiredness, everything is good. I have something for you on the table—sort of a gift, but more for your relief than anything else." Curious, Nyeve walked over to the table and found an old brown sack sitting in the middle of it. As she opened the mouth of the sack and pulled it down by the sides, Utt's head emerged, its eyes closed, appearing to be at peace. At first she was shocked and moved away from it, but as she gained her composure, she moved closer to gaze upon an enemy that had brought pain and terror to all she knew. Wondering how such a giant could be defeated, Nyeve looked to Patel with questioning eyes.

"It's strange to me as well—or was at first— but, Nyeve, I had help from above." Patel glanced back at Utt's head. "He would have killed me easily without it. His strength and power—I didn't have time to think about it during the confrontation, but I've had plenty of time now. He actually shook the ground as he moved toward me, and the pressure from his blows should have turned me to dust."

Looking back at Nyeve, Patel became more animated. "The Lord bestowed upon me His spirit, which surged through me like the lightning in the sky. It was so intoxicating, Nyeve; so freeing that I knew deep inside Utt would fall before me, and he did."

Confusion filled Nyeve; she didn't understand what Patel was trying to explain. She believed every word because she loved him but just couldn't understand the new concepts. "Lord? Who is the Lord? And lightning? What is this lightning? I'm trying to understand it, my love. I have not heard these things before."

It was then that Patel understood. He had been given new information, a mind opened to a lot of new knowledge. Patel took Nyeve by the hand and led her to his bed, and as he sat, he propped himself against a corner wall, allowing Nyeve to comfortably lie in his lap. Using great patience, he took the time to explain everything to her. He taught his second heart new vocabulary and concepts of life, death, and how all things worked in nature. The brightness in her face as her eyes lit up whenever she grasped a new concept encouraged Patel to continue his instruction. After some hours had passed, a knock at the door broke them from their concentration.

Heading to the door, Patel met Norhi, who was happy to see his friend's safe return.

"Patel, why didn't you lead the people into the village? I thought the worst when you never showed. We are having a banquet to welcome our new arrivals and honor the man who freed them. Come, come we are waiting for you to—"

"Norhi, my friend," Patel said, cutting in, "I'm sorry for not coming to you earlier, but I did nothing—that is, it wasn't me, necessarily, but the Lord who released them and killed Utt."

"Such modesty—and it's getting old. Come now, so we can begin. The freed men have a story to tell about a beastly man saving them all from Utt, and I keep trying to tell them you're no beast, so let's go!"

Not wanting to disappoint his friend or make anyone wait on him to eat a good meal, Patel fell silent, grabbed Nyeve by the hand, and made his way to the banquet. They had cleared several large trees and cut them in half flipping them to use as a long tables to feed the newly arrived people and would later use for building furniture and home furnishings. There was plenty of seafood, fish, and vegetables. Entering the middle of an overcrowded part of the beach, Nyeve released Patel's hand as Norhi led him to a large rock outcropping. Once the two men reached its apex, Norhi waved his hands over his head and instructed the people to take a seat.

As noise from the crowd died down and prepared food was dished out in group portions, Norhi began speaking. "My dear friends, freedom is no small thing to be taken lightly, and from the very beginning, when man was made slaves to star people, one of our own made it his personal mission to do whatever it took to free us from their tyranny. None of this—the food we eat, the water we drink, the free air we breathe—would be possible without this man's personal sacrifice. We now all live outside the evil will of others because he decided life under slavery is no life, and so without any further ado, I give you Patel, my friend and your deliverer—Patel!"

Stepping forward, Patel was both surprised and annoyed at the words Norhi spoke. He wanted to rebuke the statements made, but the crowd was on their feet, clapping and chanting his name. Waiting for the people to end their applause, he asked everyone to take a seat, after which he began to speak. "Thank you for … I did nothing to free you"—he glanced down at Nyeve—"any of you. The Lord of Hosts worked through me to free you from the giants and star people. Give thanks for what is received to Him and know that I am satisfied to work for His honor and glory. Please understand that I am nothing without the Lord; we are nothing without Him. Thank you."

Silence fell like a thick blanket upon the crowd. Only waves hitting the shore and the crackling of the night fires could be heard. Turning to walk down the rocks, Patel glanced over at Norhi and said, "It wasn't me."

Watching Patel as he walked away, Norhi stood slack-jawed for a few moments and then turned to the crowd and said, "Okay everyone, please enjoy the meal, and afterward we'll show all their temporary living areas. Thank you."

Nyeve quickly walked over to her man, and after she caressed his face, they kissed. She grasped his hand, and the two moved off to his dwelling, leaving the crowd behind. The newly liberated elders presented themselves before Norhi and stated they had never seen Patel before and insisted that a large hairy beast had defeated Utt, not the man walking with his woman toward the village. Norhi was perplexed at both his friend's behavior and the elder's insistent story of a creature never before seen.

"Well, I did say we would talk of this beast, didn't I? Shall we sit, eat, and ponder then?" Nodding, the elders moved to an eating place and spoke of their encounter with a great creature. "We did see and speak with this ... animal—I guess that is the best word to describe it. He stood as tall as Utt and wore a coat of blackish-brown fur. Massive muscle and sinew of stone moved freely under its hair. The face could pass for human except these four teeth were longer and came to a point, the nose was a little flat, and his eyes glowed yellow-orange with power. His hands were large, but the feet—huge, strong—next to mine, they were very big. The beast was gentle with us, though, and said he was our protector sent by the Lord. We did not know what 'Lord' meant, but he explained 'Lord' is the One, and this we knew from old times, when the guardians used to speak with us, but no longer do. We must have done something wrong to incur wrath in the form of giants and other children of star people, yet no one knows what it was. Praise the One Lord for sending a champion now to save us."

Norhi replied, "You spin a great tale, um… what is your name, sir?"

"Of course, I am foolish to not have introduced myself. I am Scribe, son of Dar."

"Scribe, son of Dar, welcome. You said the beast—let's call him Bigfoot for now—he told you to seek me out?"

"Oh yes, he was very firm about it. 'Go to no one but Norhi and say nothing to anyone except Norhi until I return,' he said."

Norhi shook his head in confusion, "Return—return where?"

Scribe replied, "I'm not certain, but it was pressed upon us that he meant here—the village of Xmi."

Scratching his head, Norhi tried hard to figure out why Bigfoot would say 'return.' "Well Scribe, if Bigfoot comes here, we will welcome and honor him. Until then, if you have had enough to eat, I'll show you where everyone will stay in the village."

Excited, Scribe remembered something else Bigfoot had said to him. "The beast spoke of underground living areas already prepared for us just east of the village. He showed the opening before sending our people to you; may we go there now to see it?" Confused and curious, Norhi nodded, stood, and headed with six elders to the underground village said to exist in the east by Bigfoot.

Entering his dwelling, Patel decided to remove Utt's head, which relieved Nyeve. He placed it outside on a large stone. The couple washed their bodies and changed clothing before lying back on Patel's bed to resume their teaching session about knowledge given to Patel by the guardians. "The giants and other star men are really offspring of rogue angelics; their children do more harm than good to us. So we must fight to rid ourselves of their teachings."

As her curiosity began to wane, a more intimate part of her being awoke inside. Nyeve wanted to inquire but wasn't sure how to approach Patel about it. Sitting up on one arm, she looked deep into his eyes and finally asked, "Patel, do you find me beautiful?" Taken off guard, he answered, "What an odd question. Of course you're beautiful; why ask such a question?"

Coyly she said, "I'm sorry, it's just… well, you haven't tried anything with me." Raising an eyebrow, he said, "Tried anything? Like what?"

Being very coy now, she said, "Patel, you know—something physical."

Suddenly it came to him, slamming hard like a brick to his head. "Nyeve, I love and respect you; I want us to be together forever and would do nothing to destroy that. It's not that you're unattractive; believe me—not at all." Seeing understanding yet disappointment on her face, Patel continued. "Look, you're beautiful, and if I could, I'd make love to you right now, but so much is—"

Suddenly, Nyeve's eyes brightened as she hurled herself upon him. As they kissed passionately, they knew this would be the first of many nights they would know each other intimately; and to them it was good—very good.

Chapter 12

Entering the underground complex, Norhi couldn't believe what he was seeing. Passageways extended endlessly throughout it, with large, clear crystals embedded into ceilings and walls that lit up as people approached them. Spacious rooms branched off of each corridor, with intake and ventilation shafts supplying fresh air hundreds of feet below the surface. Fire pits for cooking and warming the caverns were concentrated away from living and sleeping quarters to ensure against out-of-control fires. They had proper ventilation to remove smoke from the living areas and worked like modern-day stoves or fireplaces. Clean water cascaded from the ceiling of a massive room and pooled in a large stone cistern the size of a small lake. Solid and liquid waste even had a place for disposal, as water overflow from the cistern washed over a three-mile-deep crack within the cavern floor.

Norhi was absolutely awed. He never knew such a facility had ever existed. Thinking back, he recalled seeing strange lights dancing around the area, but he had never heard any sound that might indicate earth being excavated or removed. "It's unbelievable! And you know about this place because a bigfoot creature that our people have never heard of or seen in the area brought you to it?"

"Yes," said the elder. "He directed us to you and gave instructions we must fulfill at first light." Norhi tilted his head in questioning the elder. "And what would that be? Just so we're on the same level of understanding."

"We must begin to bring in foods and resources, of course, before the battle."

Puzzled, Norhi continued to ask questions of the elder. "Resources before a battle? A battle with whom? Our people are not at war with anyone, and Patel—Patel conducts raids on settlements to release those enslaved by star people. But there haven't been any battles ensuing from the raids."

Leaning in to Norhi, the elder said in a low whisper, "It's coming; and you will participate in the battle to come. Be strong, my son, for you are chosen."

"Chosen for what?"

Smiling, the elder patted Norhi on the shoulder, turned, and headed toward the surface, leaving Norhi dumbstruck, not knowing what to make of the old man's statement.

At daybreak, the village and shoreline came alive with people loading litters to carry food stores while others carried them into the caverns below. Men cast nets into the ocean, immediately filling their snares to the brim with fish, crabs, and other crustaceans. Hundreds of sacks containing wheat, barley, dry beans, nuts, and corn littered the upper shore along with smoked and cured meats. Stalks upon stalks of green sugar cane and wood piles were stacked next to the dwellings on the outskirts of the village. Startled awake by a commotion outside his home; Norhi stood up, stretched, yawned, and headed for the outside. Seeing all the resources scattered along the shore, and smelling meats cooking over fires, he was mesmerized once again.

Norhi found the elder supervising people, and he approached excitedly and asked, "What is all this? Where did it come from? Did you bring it with you and just hide it in the jungle?"

The elder known as Scribe shook his head. "No, my son, it all arrived last night, given to us by the guardians."

"Guardians?" Norhi asked. "Who are the guardians? Why have I not heard of these generous people?"

Smiling Scribe continued, "Oh, the guardians are not people; they watch over us from above. We are creations of the One Lord of Hosts, and this bounty is to keep us until after the wars have ended and before the beginning."

Frightened by the words of Scribe, and not understanding any of what he had just heard, Norhi slowly withdrew and, after a few steps, turned and ran for Patel's home. "I don't understand any of this—war, guardians, the One Lord of Hosts? Patel will know. He has to know, or I think my mind will explode from all this craziness!"

When Norhi reached Patel's house, he burst in ranting a slew of unintelligible words, startling Nyeve from a sound sleep upon Patel's chest.

Patel, half asleep, sat up. Nyeve scolded Norhi, saying, "Norhi, what's wrong with you? Don't you know how to call from without before coming into someone's dwelling place?"

Attempting to calm himself, Norhi answered, "I'm sorry, Nyeve. The elder, Scribe… a war… wheat and fish. Why am I speaking to you? Patel—Patel, I need to speak with you now! Please!" Patel fully awoke with a smile on his face; he looked at Nyeve and sighed. "How beautiful you are; I could stay here with you forever."

Giggling, Nyeve redirected him. "Patel, I love you also, but someone is here to speak with you— Norhi." Shaking cobwebs from his mind, Patel looked over to see Norhi standing with anxiety set squarely upon his shoulders.

Tilting his head to the side, he asked, "Norhi, what is it? What's wrong? Are we at war? What's all the noise outside from?"

"That's what I need to speak with you about. Please come with me now so I may show you!" Norhi motioned Patel towards the door. After kissing Nyeve, Patel left the hut with Norhi and headed straight for the shore.

Norhi tried to explain what he knew and was shocked at Patel's response. "Everything is moving along nicely. Good—good. I'm not sure when the battle will begin, but at least we will have our people safe and out of the way."

Norhi, shaking his head in alarm, asked, "Patel, what is going on? You act as though you knew this was going to happen. I can't believe all of this seems normal to you! What is going on?"

Calming his friend, Patel assured Norhi everything was fine and not to worry.
"Do me a favor and collect Ackal, Nob, Vul, and Rave. Meet me atop the hill over there to the west, and I will explain everything. All is well my friend—I promise."

Once again Norhi felt as though he was in the dark, and it was beginning to annoy him, but he did as

Patel asked and rounded up the council members, taking them to a hill west of the village. Waiting for Patel atop the hill, the council talked amongst themselves, debating what was happening in the village and how it all came to be. Vul was the most animated of the group. "Could all this have been brought by those villagers? I don't think so. What if it's tainted to make us sick, or perhaps it could affect fertility in our women? The enemies have power, you know, and the giants may very well have brought in that food to do us in as a society. I mean, have any of you been intimate with a woman, because I haven't. What if it robs us of our desire to be with women? Huh? What about that? And these caves appeared out of nowhere—really? How long have we been in this area and are just now finding out about their existence? It's an attempt to get us underground and bury us there forever. Is that what we're supposed to do? Are we going to fall into their trap? Because that's not for me; we need to be fearful of—"

Suddenly, a voice from behind Vul broke his rant. "Fearful of what, my friend? I say, do not be afraid." Turning toward the voice, all five members were awestruck to see a large, hairy creature with big feet smiling at them. "I can see in your faces that you are still afraid. Shall I take on more recognizable features? Very well." Slowly morphing back into a human form, Patel stated, "Greetings my friends," extending his right arm toward them. With an open hand that held a red, yellow, and blue flame, he said, "May the Lord be with you—His chosen."

The flame leaped forward, separating into five flickering tongues of fire that came to rest upon them. The flame slowly sank into their heads, awakening each of them. Immediately, the five men spoke, praising the Lord and stating future events. Then the men fell silent, levitated, and shone with the brightness of the sun for only a moment. As they touched the ground once again, the light faded and all were looking at Patel.

"My friends, we have a purpose on earth: to protect people from evil, which is so pervasive at this time, and to send angelic children called nephilim, the giants, and ariyons, those who teach forbidden mysteries to the people and are soldiers of the nephilim armies, to the abyss. We possess power to do so, but it comes with a price. We cannot live among the people or allow them to know who we are, to ensure against misled veneration. Glory to God, not us, and I fear ariyon influence has turned some people to idolatry already—yes, and even cannibalism.

"Once we leave the hill and enter the village, pick from the elders your replacements, then have them choose five from the new arrivals to be members of the council for a total of twelve men. They shall act as stewards of the forty thousand men, women, and children which make up both groups. We shall then guard the settlements until all are underground. Once they are, we leave to hunt our enemies and destroy them from the face of the earth. Take time now, however, to become accustomed to morphing and knowing which animals you'll shift into. Each of you has different animal spirits to call upon and different gifts. No weapon of man will harm you, but death is possible. Decapitation releases us from our bodies and we cannot return once this happens—but it's not an easy task to take our heads—we are strong—very strong."

While he continued to speak, his five friends practiced morphing into various animals, finding that they each possessed three animal spirits and that the third spirit was a juggernaut, larger and more powerful than the others. Patel's power spirit, the silverback gorilla, stood sixty feet tall. Nob's baboon was just as tall. Vul morphed into a sixty-foot-long lion, while Norhi changed into a sixty-foot-long rhino; which left Rave, who morphed into a timber wolf that was just as long. Their animal growls and roars shook the ground and chased off wildlife around them.

Settling his brothers down, Patel instructed everyone to change back to humans and cautioned them not to change in front of people. "You see why it is important for us not to morph in front of people; they may very well try to worship us, and that is strictly forbidden. We have other powers as well and can discuss them later. Let's get back to the village and begin preparations for the upcoming battle."

As they walked down the hill, the six men focused on the tasks given them. They were bound and determined to ensure the survival of mankind and the destruction of evil. One in particular, however, had his own agenda but would keep it secret until a more prosperous situation presented itself. Unknown to himself and the others, his future actions would spell demise for most of the chosen and those around them.

Chapter 13

Staggering as he fought his way through a dense jungle floor, a man determined to reach the great citadel lurched forward step by step. Four days of traveling on foot without food, water, or rest had taken its toll on his body. He fell to the ground and stopped fighting momentarily to catch a breath. As he turned onto his back, yellow beams of sunlight penetrated through the thick, green, lush upper canopy, striking and bathing him in warmth. His thoughts turned to the last time a cold, wet drink had touched his lips or a nice piece of fruit had livened his tongue. *Where will I get the strength to go on?* He thought.

Perhaps he should give up and fall asleep, but dread and fear filled the man, compelling him to move forward. When dizziness and a weakened body restrained him, almost breaking his spirit, he saw a pair of arms that seemed to him to come from the sky; they picked the man up from the ground. A feeling of floating through the air enraptured him as something cool and wet washed over his lips. A disembodied voice directed him to take little sips and rest. Complying with the voice, he took in water, bringing some comfort to his body. Glancing around, he could see sides of a wagon he was in, and he could hear the voice telling him to rest and asking his name.

"En—Endo… my name is Endo." His strength depleted, Endo fell into a deep sleep, placing his life in the hands of a stranger—not that he was in a position to protest anyway.

The sound of metal scraping against stone slowly brought Endo out of his slumber. The room he occupied was dark and cool, and it smelled of rotting flesh. Sitting up, he tried to peer through the darkness with very little luck. He got to his feet and supported himself against a stone wall. As he started to move toward another side of the room, he noticed his movement was restrained by chains on his ankles. It was the first time fear crept up his spine. Sitting again, he tried to remove the shackles, but it was no use. Yelling, "Hey, is anyone here? Hey, can someone hear me?" He tried to get someone's attention, but his entreaty was met with deep silence.

Many hours passed before he heard footsteps coming toward him—soft at first, and then growing louder. A key clicked into the lock on a massive door. Hearing the tumblers clicking within a lock brought both dread and excitement to him. Light pierced the darkness, shining a dim yellow hue upon him. A gritty voice summoned Endo to stand up, and as he did, a dark human form blotted out the light. He saw the figure of a large man with numerous teeth missing and only one eye. The man's scent was repulsive and filled the room and Endo's nostrils.

"You! Walk to me so I can unlock your shackles, and don't get any funny ideas of running or I'll roast your legs for my dinner this night." The gravelly voice was very confident, rendering Endo implicitly compliant with his jailer. "Walk to lord Demar's throne. Stay next to me! Remember what I said about your legs; I'm famished!"

Trying not to look directly at the big man, Endo nodded his head and kept eyes forward. The whole reason for his coming to the citadel was to meet with Demar, so he wasn't in any hurry to run away—not yet anyway. What seemed like endless corridors and stairwells finally gave way to a huge, open room. Walls, ceilings, and even the floor were covered in fine gold with glowing precious gems all around. At the far end of the room, a staircase led to a throne of gold and silver with embedded gemstones decorating the frame. Sitting upon the throne was Demar. He was twelve cubits in height, and although he was sitting, he still looked imposing and intimidating. A shiny silver helmet covered his head; two horns made of solid diamonds rose out of the front of it in an S curve. In between the horns, a type of blue-red plasma of energy floated, continually moving and reforming between the two horns in the air in front of the giant's forehead.

Endo was awed by the sight before him, but he was soon snapped back into reality by his jailer's grisly voice. "On your knees, dog; and bow your head before Demar the Great, ruler of all that is conquered!" A push from his jailer aided Endo in finding the floor with his knees, and a smart slap to the back of his head helped bow his head immediately.

After what seemed like an eternity to Endo, Demar spoke. "Why is it that I know you, dog? Are you one of my slaves attempting to escape?"

Endo shook his head quickly. "No, my lord, I am Endo, of your brother Utt's citadel. I've escaped to bring news of your brother, oh mighty Demar."

Demar's voice slowly rose in volume. "So you are an escaped slave! A slave of my brother, and yet you search me out? Do you not know the penalty for escaping our jurisdictions, man of mud? You shall be taken from my presence and prepared for roasting with the other foul men of your ilk!"

Attempting to remain calm while shaking in fear, Endo spoke. "My lord, may it never be that I would leave the service of my master Utt. But he is no more, and so I have escaped to come and give myself into your service—respectfully."

Intrigued at the fool's comments, and put off at the idea that his brother had been taken to the gods, Demar bade Endo to speak after waving for the jailer to leave the room. "Are you telling me, little man, my brother was taken by the gods? And that you saw this? I warn you, lying to me will bring a slow and torturous existence for you! You'll beg me for death. Speak now!"

After drawing in and releasing a long breath, Endo continued. "My lord Demar, I did not see gods; at least I do not believe it was a god. But a great creature took your brother's head from his shoulders, and the people threw the body into the pit of sacrifice, which is where I believe it still is—to this day."

Sitting up now and squaring his jaw, Demar said, "Did I not warn you of lying to me, dog! No weapon of man can harm us! We are immortal! Demigods, rulers of this world by virtue of our blood! Insects like yourself hold no power over us and therefore cannot kill us!"

Confused by the giant's words and their meanings, Endo continued to explain what had taken place at Utt's citadel. "Great Demar—a man's weapon was not used. A beast of enormous size took Utt's head off with a great flaming sword—something I've never seen in the forests, woods, or jungles, my lord."

Sitting back on his throne, Demar tried to make sense of the information. As he pondered the possibility of his brother's death, he focused a glaring stare toward Endo. *My brother killed by a beast never before heard of or seen, wielding a sword not of this world. It couldn't be a creation of man, to be sure—or this man standing before me is making it all up in an attempt to save his own skin. There is only one way to validate this information, and that is to go to Utt's citadel and look for myself! But not alone; the creature may be in the area, and what if more wait in hiding to take off my head.* Demar reached for and blew a solid gold horn situated to the right of the throne, and within minutes his ariyon generals prostrated themselves before their ruler.

"I will take one thousand times ten groups of soldiers with me to my brother Utt's citadel! Prepare the troops; we leave at daybreak!"

The Ariyon soldiers looked at one another other and then back at Demar, one of the generals asked, "Sir, do you mean to lay siege against your brother Utt or to send him into exile?"

Demar's anger burned from the question put forth by the ariyon. Power from between the horns on his helmet glowed bright and shot forward like a charged plasma ray of energy, consuming the ariyon general, leaving nothing but ashes where he once stood. "Does anyone else here question the love I hold for my brother Utt?"

His question was met by silence until another general rose up from his place and asked, "No one questions the love you hold toward your brother, my lord. We must have information to know what weaponry and other supplies are required, Oh great one."

His anger subsided and Demar nodded, speaking and directing his generals, "You will outfit each soldier with standard weapons. No siege armaments are required. Bring enough supplies for thirty days"—he glanced over at Endo—"thirty dawns to dusk. We will take Endo along with us; if what he tells me is true, I'll reward him with freedom and a position on my staff—a minute position, but one nonetheless. If what he says is a lie, my brother and I will celebrate my visit with a roast in his honor, beginning with Endo as an appetizer. For now, take him with you. When I dismiss you, ensure he is thoroughly washed and put some clothes on him that are not revolting in my presence. I leave him in your charge and will meet you at the gates come first light."

Bowing to Demar, all were dismissed to prepare for the trip, which would take at least four days to complete. He puzzled over what kind of creature could kill his brother, and his thoughts turned to his gods. *They will know what I am dealing with and how to defeat it, but what if Endo is telling a story? I'd look foolish in front of my gods. No, I will wait to contact them until after seeing my brother alive or dead. They said we were immortal; that nothing of man could harm us—nothing! Yet Endo speaks of a creature—a creature never seen or heard of before. Could Endo make up such an incredible story? A mortal man, possessing little knowledge and a slave of my brother Utt? Time will tell; time will tell.*

Chapter 14

Entering the village, Patel and the other men worked through crowds to pick out elders to replace them. They brought the first six replacements to council chambers, and Patel spoke with and welcomed each member to be of service to the village by joining the council. "Greetings to all of you who have been chosen to take our place within the villages. Six more are needed, but we leave you in charge to choose them. Your names shall be on the lips of the people, and they will rely on your wisdom to lead them. As I call out your names, please stand that we may know who you are: Kram, Tamwhet, Jsame, Ojhn, Teper, and Sula. Again, greetings. We will teach you everything required for proper leadership of the people. Your responsibility is great in that you are to serve rather than be served. You are not to rule by your will, but to serve them with your heart and in following of the One, the Lord Most High. Keep this as your center and everything else will fall into place; you'll see. In six days—six dawns to dusk—we will teach you, and then we must leave here to serve as protectors of man. In times of trouble when we are not seen and you require assistance, use this ring to summon us and we will respond."

Patel's open hand held a ring of solid gold with a bright silver face that bore a figure of a candleholder with seven candlesticks. Placing the ring on a table, Patel directed the men to place their right hands palm down on the table; as they did, the ring vibrated, moved, and came to rest on the index finger of Teper. "Teper of Sol, the Great Spirit has chosen you to be the ring-bearer, and it cannot be removed. Use its power wisely and know the Lord is with you always. Work and edify each other in all things, and lead the people with hearts free of selfishness and full of mercy." Leaving the council chambers, Patel and the five other shifters looked around and saw that all of the supplies had been moved into the underground complex.

Looking intently at Patel's dwelling, Norhi asked, "Patel, old friend, have you talked with Nyeve yet—about leaving, I mean?"

Eyes downcast, Patel replied, "No... no I haven't... not yet."

Frowning, Norhi asked, "When will you, if not now?"

Patel growled a reply. "The moment I see her! The very moment I do."

Vul watched Nyeve emerge from the cave entrance and slowly walk across the shore to where they stood. "Ah, you're looking in the wrong direction, gents. There she is, Patel—no time like the present, right?" Seeing her walking across the beach, Patel glared back at Vul as he made his way to Nyeve. Vul put his hands up in surrender and shrugged his shoulders. "Hey, I was just trying to help you, Patel. I didn't think you could see her from your vantage point. Break it to her easy; no need to be a jerk about it."

Vul ceased talking as Norhi pulled him away. "What's the matter with you? Leaving her won't be easy, and you're acting like a moron about it. Now let's go talk with the elders while we wait for Patel to return, all right?" Pulling his arm away, Vul was not accustomed to being handled or lectured. Vul gathered his thoughts, *Everything he did had to look as though it was by his will and not someone else's. Never someone else because eventually Vul would rule! Rule, rather than serve, and that's was the way it would be to all.*

Smiling, Nyeve ran to Patel and threw her arms around his neck, kissing the man she loved passionately. Pushing her away, Patel looked deeply into her beautiful jade-green eyes, which made her feel something was wrong. "What is it, my sweet one? Why are you troubled? Did I do something wrong to anger you in some way?"

Smiling back, Patel replied, "You, upset me? Nonsense, my love; in fact, just the opposite. Let's go home so we can talk in private, okay?" Her beautiful eyes smiling back, she nodded, and the two of them walked hand in hand to Patel's house to talk about what was on his mind. Sitting at the table, Patel tried to find the words that would best state what was going to happen in a positive way, but the words were lost to him.

Seeing the conflict and struggle painted across his face, Nyeve spoke first. "Sweetheart, is everything all right? Are you hungry? Now that all the supplies and most of the people have gone underground, we're almost completely alone, and we still have plenty of provisions on hand, so I could make a very tasty supper for us if you would like."

"No thank you, Nyeve. I'm not hungry. In fact, I haven't required food or water ever since… Hm. Okay, I'll tell you what it is. See, I—"

Cutting in, Nyeve matter-of-factly said, "You know, I don't have an appetite either. Isn't that strange? Since we were together, the need for food and water hasn't come to me, now that I am thinking about it."

Patel gathered his courage and blurted out what he had to tell her. "Nyeve, I must leave you—for good! We can no longer be together, and I'm so very sorry."

Slack-jawed and with tears welling up in her eyes, she couldn't believe what Patel was saying to her. "Why? Why do you want to… Don't I please you; I can do better. Just let me know what I'm doing wrong, but please don't leave me! We are one in the same aren't we? Oh please, Patel, please help me to understand why you feel this way?"

Patel turned away and hung his head. His voice shook as he tried to explain. "It has nothing to do with you. Yes, you are what happiness means to me in this world. Now I must devote everything I am to the Lord—in His service. So I am unable to stay among the people because of what I am—what I have become."

Frustration and anger filled Nyeve's being, cluttering her mind as the thought of losing Patel overpowered her emotions. Suddenly she began to change. Thick fur grew out of her skin as her muscle, bone, and sinew grew in size and strength. Top and bottom canines sprouted large and sharp in her mouth, and her eyes glowed with a soft yellow-orange hue. All was taking place while Patel had his back to her. When she saw the hair on her hands and torso, she let out a scream that sounded like an animal's howl more than it did human. Patel turned and was shocked to see that Nyeve had morphed into a bigfoot.

Patel let out a sigh of relief and ran to her. "Praise the Lord, Nyeve; you're beautiful!"

"I'm… look at me! I'm… I'm… what am I? I don't know!" she shrieked, looking down at her hands and body.

Laughing with excitement, Patel tried to console his love with little effect. "You'll be all right, Nyeve. This is a sign—we can stay together; don't you see?"

Nyeve, becoming angry and hysterical, worked her response out carefully. "What are you talking about? Look at me! So now you are saying I can stay with you because I look more like your pet than your woman? What? Look at me! Why am I like this?"

Taking her to the bed, Patel told Nyeve to sit and watch him closely. Watching through tears, Nyeve beheld Patel changing into a bigfoot; his head broke through the ceiling of their dwelling place. Going to his knees, he spoke to Nyeve. "See, we both change into creatures now, and it's okay. We can stay together. I don't know exactly why you changed, but it tells me you were accepted by the Lord and we can be together!"

Tears were still streaming down her cheeks. She shook her head while looking at him in shock. "Oh, Patel, I don't understand any of this! Why are we beasts? Look at me! My feet—they're huge! This is not a good look for me—not at all. And what is this gold band on my left arm, Patel? We really need to talk about this before going any further."

Patel explained how he and the other five members of his team had become shifters in service of the Lord.

Nyeve still couldn't fathom the fact that she was able to shift. "No, Patel, I understand why you and the other men can do this, but why me?"

Suddenly, a brisk wind moved through and around the room they were in, and simultaneously a still voice was heard by both to say, "And the two shall become one flesh." As quickly as the wind had begun, it diminished, leaving the couple to ponder the words that came from within it.

Then it hit Patel. "We coupled, and in doing so, we became one flesh. We are one in the same, Nyeve; that's why we both change. It also means we are to stay together forever. Is that good with you?"

Smiling with great relief, she said, "Oh, Patel, of course it's all right. I've wanted to hear you say it for so long, and I will fight by your side against all evil that comes our way; I promise." The two beasts embraced and exchanged kisses, reveling in the love that was theirs to cherish. Nothing could stop them from holding each other—that is, until Norhi barged in. At least that happened before the couple had gone too far.

"Hey Patel, we have a situation out—um… I'm going to wait outside for—is that Nyeve?"

Laughing, Patel said, "Norhi, we'll be right out, if you don't mind. We were just talking over a few things. We'll be right there, okay?"

Standing mesmerized, Norhi couldn't pull away as he was trying to figure out how she had changed.

"Norhi, please, a little privacy; we'll be right out!" Stumbling backward through the door, he said, "Right! Right—sorry—I'll just wait outside for you two. Any more strange things happen, and I swear I'm outta here. People morphing left and right, possibly others as well, who knows what."

Patel and Nyeve looked at each other and started laughing a nervous yet excited laughter as they thought of what might be and what would become of the future. "So you're okay with this, right?" said Patel.

Nyeve smiled and touched his cheek. "Patel, as long as we are together, I can endure anything—including enormously large feet."

They laughed as they shifted back into their human forms, and Patel said, "You know your feet are proportional to the size of the beast, so, I mean, they're not as huge as you might think."

Tired of all the attention being paid to her feet, Nyeve turned with Patel on her arm. "Okay, enough about feet. Let's just catch up with the other guys and find out what's going on with Norhi."

"I'm glad to see you taking everything in stride, sweetheart—I think we'll do fine together." Walking out of the dwelling, they found Norhi waiting and Utt's head missing from the stone it had been sitting upon.

"What's up, Norhi? Where did the head go?"

Norhi replied pointing, "Well, that's what we wanted to talk about; the other four are up on the hill with it."

"Ah, okay, so I take it we are supposed to go up to the hill?"

"That was the idea, but I don't know about you-know-who coming with us."

Cocking his head to one side, Patel asked, "You mean, Nyeve coming with us?"

Nyeve, speaking up for herself, said, "I'm right here and can hear you both—and I'm going."

Looking at each other, Patel and Norhi said simultaneously, "She's going."

When he reached the summit of the hill, Patel found the four sitting in silence with the head of Utt a few feet away from them. Vul was the first person to break the silence. "Ah, Patel, you were going to lose the woman, remember? Why is she still around?"

Before Nyeve could fulfill her desire to tell him off, Patel said, "Nyeve is one of us and will be welcomed as such—any problems with that?"

"Yeah, I got a problem with it—because she is not one of us, and you know why." Annoyed, Nyeve morphed into a bigfoot, grabbed Vul by the throat, and lifted him off the ground. Unimpressed, Vul growled. "Patel, call off your bitch before I hurt her!"

Patel replied, "Her name is Nyeve not bitch. It's comments like that which exasperate the situation, Vul, rather than resolving it."

"I mean it, Patel."

Chuckling, Patel nodded in agreement. "Nyeve, you proved your point, sweetheart. Please release him."

Nyeve released her grip so Vul dropped to the ground, and she then shifted back into human form and sat next to Patel. "I let him go because you asked me to, my sweet."

"Thank you. Now then, why are we on this hill with Utt's head?" Patel asked.

Norhi explained. "Patel, I noticed that Utt's head has yet to, well, decompose, which I found fascinating, and so naturally I took it for observation."

"Naturally," Patel replied.

"Yes, well, it seems the head may reattach itself to his body if placed in close proximity to it." Standing back and looking puzzled, Patel asked, "And you know this how?"

Norhi moved quickly toward a nearby log pile. "I placed the head inside this frame of logs to keep it from moving. Now watch what happens when I take one of the logs away." When Norhi moved one of the logs, the head immediately started to move on its own. Norhi continued, "See—anywhere you place the head, it always moves in the direction of the citadel. I think it's looking for the body—and that's not even the creepy part."

Patel looked at his friend with raised eyebrows. "Norhi, I'm watching a head move on its own! I don't think it could get any creepier, my friend."

Waving a hand, Norhi said, "Listen carefully and you can hear it speak." Bewildered, everyone fell silent to listen to the head. It was low and quite garbled, but a distinct word could be heard as the head moved along the ground.

"Revenge… revenge… revenge."

Shocked, the group looked around at each other wondering how it was all possible. Patel was the first to speak. "What should we do with it, then? I'm at a loss."

Norhi's idea made sense to them all. "We must burn it to ashes, which means that any hybrids we come in contact with must be beheaded and burned; otherwise, it's quite possible for them to reanimate."

Vul commented, "The undead—is that possible?"

Norhi corrected, "Yes, it is possible because the opposite of undead is living, which we all are at this time. These, then, would be ever living—unless properly disposed of, and even then I can't be sure. I do know this: Utt has not grown a new body; nor has his body grown a new head—so he rests for now. We must burn the head and body separately and bury the ashes either in the ocean or in the ground to be sure. I'm sorry, but that's the best I can come up with since all this is new to me—to us."

After thinking about Norhi's advice, Patel came to a decision. "Very well, let's burn his remains. I'll travel to the citadel and take care of Utt's body, while the rest of you dispose of the head—agreed?"

Vul stepped forward and said, "Burn it with what, Patel? Norhi, we don't even know if it will burn—except for me, that is. I tried to rid the settlement of that … thing once before, and no amount of fire even singed a hair."

Intrigued as to why Vul had wanted the head burned prior to now, Patel asked, "Why did you try to burn it earlier?"

Vul pointed at Patel. "Why should you have a lasting reminder of your battle and defeat of an enemy when none of us had ours? It may lead to the people worshipping you as their champion, and that wouldn't be right—or would it?"

Patel knew Vul was merely jealous of him and the way their people respected Patel, but he didn't want to give an opening for Vul to say it was all right for men to venerate those persons they chose rather than God. "No, Vul, it was wise of you to think such a way. I can tell you, though, the blaze of fire given me to defeat Utt severed and burned the flesh at the same time. Perhaps if we place our swords together, we can devour the head with thick flame."

The seven of them agreed. They morphed into their animal spirits and drawing an hilt from the band on their left arms produced a flaming blade. When they crossed the swords, a great blue light of enormous flame leaped upward, and within the flame a figure formed. It was Airmuse. "Greetings, my children; why have you summoned me?"

Only one person knew who it was, for he had seen him with another being some time ago. Patel addressed him. "Greetings to you, Airmuse, the guardian of the sky. Please forgive us; we didn't know what we were doing would summon you."

Airmuse replied, "I sense you wish to do away with the body of Utt, and you are right to do so. He is not just flesh, but angelic as well. Before disposing of his body or any other nephilim or ariyon encountered, you must first banish the spirit within to the abyss; only then will these hybrids be unable to regenerate and return to your world. Powerful are your enemies, my son, both within and without. Guard yourself and know the power of God is with you. Dispatch all enemies of men in this way, Patel. Rid the world of the pestilence that infests it and mankind will have a chance to flourish in peace." Then Airmuse turned, glaring into the eyes of Vul, knowing the evil desire that resided in his heart. "Be very mindful of the black hearts of men, for what they perceive as success and victory is only an illusion." He disappeared as quickly as a candle's flame being extinguished.

Patel set out to show the other six how to banish the spirits of their enemies. Picking Utt's head up from the ground, Patel looked into his eyes and said, "To the abyss with you, in the name of the Lord!" A great cry went out from Utt's head as a mist of smoky, green plasma-like energy ascended from the severed head and disappeared into a great whirlwind. Shocked at the sight of it, the six became fearful—none more so than Vul.

"What if we are sucked up into that thing?" Vul asked. "This I cannot do; you all will have to, because I will not!"

Patiently Patel replied, "Calm yourself, Vul; we all are empowered to fulfill the Lord's will, and so we shall—all of us."

"Very well, Patel. I'm no coward by any means, but know this: if anything strange happens to me, I will find a way to come back and avenge myself on you!"

Smiling, Patel replied, "Vul, I can hardly wait."

Chapter 15

As the sun rose in the east, Demar exited his citadel in full armor, holding a thick shield made of silver, gold, and platinum that stood eight cubits high and four cubits wide. In his other hand was a spear, made of the same metals as the shield, standing almost eighteen cubits from end to tip. Fastened around his waist was a belt made of thick leather, engraved and decorated with ornaments of various reptilian creatures twisted around, holding, and supporting a large sword made of a material unknown to man and created by angelic knowledge of warfare. The metallic scales that made up his body armor were each the size of a normal man's head and covered the giant's entire body, exposing only fingers and toed sandals. The armor gleamed brightly, reflecting the sun's rays like a watchtower, a beacon in the darkest of nights. So bright was it, in fact, that he had to lead his army always taking up the front, lest the soldiers be blinded by the light.

Each soldier was equipped with the same kind of armament, but at a smaller size since ariyons only grew to four or five cubits. They were fair-haired and fair-skinned, possessing strength, cunning, and knowledge of warfare. The ariyon loyalty fell to the nephilim and their angelic fathers of Bael. Nothing on the planet, whether man or beast, could withstand them.

Lined up in separate columns of ten soldiers long and ten soldiers wide, ten thousand soldiers made ready to set out for Utt's citadel. Demar summoned his personal weavers to bring forth his aerial carpet. He and his generals would ride above the army to scout out the pathways ahead and scare off any large reptilian beasts that roamed the jungles and woods between the two citadels. As a rite of passage, all nephilim giants had to track down and kill one of the large carnivorous reptiles that prowled the land. Demar wore an outer neck chain of the sharp teeth, half a cubit in size, of the beast that he had killed bare-handed many years ago.

Great respect was given the giant because of this particular act, but mainly people feared him because of his prideful heart and heavy-handedness shown toward people and some of his own kin. Utt was the only person Demar treasured dearly, mainly because of the way his brother felt about humans. To him they were insects to be crushed and best used for food. Even though their mothers were of human origin, it did not matter; the union of their fathers to daughters of men was nothing more than a lustful misjudgment.

Demar took a seat upon the carpet front and center, and his generals sat in back. He bellowed a command, and the carpet rose slowly into the air and rode the winds aloft. One of his generals blew a ram's horn, which received a united response, and the army began marching forward. Soaring just under the clouds, Demar could see all ten thousand of his soldiers as they marched. Behind the army, human slaves pulled supply carts and other weaponry, such as bows, thousands of quivers of arrows, and battle axes for their ariyon masters. Most of the food and water was to support the many slaves, since ariyon and nephilim warriors required very little food and could be active for many days without anything to eat or drink.

Demar considered his own army as an anchor and hindrance since he wanted to go forward quickly to check on his brother. He didn't want to wait for the soldiers to catch up, but an uneasy feeling kept him in check—for now anyway. What could defeat his brother? That is, if Endo was telling the truth. Looking back, Demar tried to read the face of his new human, General Endo. Why would he lie to Demar? He seemed so relaxed knowing his life hung in the balance. No, the giant could tell Endo was genuine, and that's what struck fear deep within Demar's heart. That fear was driving Demar to get to his brother regardless of the risk that he might encounter.

Turning to his generals, Demar spoke. "I have decided to go forward without the army; they will catch up to us in time, but my brother may need me now!" There were no protests from his staff, because they knew the giant would merely drop them from the sky if they voiced their disagreement. Demar gave another command, and the carpet zoomed through the sky, making its way to the citadel of Utt.

***

Large columns of smoke rose from the center of Utt's citadel as the chosen seven set his body and head ablaze within the fire pit where the giant had roasted so many humans, including Patel's family years earlier. All of the shifters, save Patel, felt avenged as they watched the giant's body consumed by blue-white and orange-red flames of fire.

Deep within Patel's mind, a voice kept saying over and over again, "The way to avenge oneself against his enemy is to forgive." He moved away from the pit; he no longer wanted to watch or take delight in his enemy's demise; what he did had to be done, and nothing more. "…for the future of our people."

Looking over her shoulder, she placed a hand on his arm and coaxed the warrior to turn and take her in his arms. He complied, as he didn't want to upset the love of his heart. She was all he had left in the world, and he didn't want to lose Nyeve, not ever. "What's the matter, my love?" Nyeve asked. "Why so sad?"

Patel sighed. "I'm not sure, Ny. I don't know for sure. I mean, I should be happy—right? The person that took my family from me has been done in himself, but Utt's death brings no relief to my grief. It might even be adding to it—I don't know. How are you, my pet?"

Nyeve, concerned, said, "Worried—worried about you. I want to make you feel as I do in your arms: safe, secure, and comfortable. I know nothing can harm me as long as I am within your strong embrace, and it seems as though I'm unable to give that to you."

Patel raised her face to his with a finger under her chin, locked eyes with her, and said, "I am complete with you in my life! If it were possible, I'd permanently meld into your body, making us one together forever. In time this down feeling will pass and all will be well again."

Acting coy and running a finger around his chest, Nyeve replied, "I think I know a way to get you happy and relaxed, but we need privacy. Let's go back to your place and—"

Norhi ran up to the couple and interrupted. "Sorry, guys, but we have company coming in from the west and in the sky!" About seven stadia out from the citadel, a large rectangular platform with a huge, brightly lit giant riding upon it was heading in their direction.

Patel yelled out, "Get under cover quickly, and do not come out until you see me come out first!" Running into stone buildings near the west wall of the citadel, the seven took cover, hoping they hadn't been seen by their adversary.

Demar brought his carpet in for a landing within the walls of the citadel and was the first to disembark. He ran to the fire pit, leaving his shield and spear behind. Looking into the pit, Demar could make out an ashy outline of his brother. Endo met the giant near the pit to see the body that would vindicate him. Gazing hard at the ashen pile, Demar's grief engulfed him completely, driving the giant to his knees. Nothing could snap him out of the trance which had overtaken his very being. Not even Endo pulling at his arm to warn the giant of the enemy battling his generals.

***

Vul saw an opportunity to strike at Demar's men and took it without waiting for Patel's signal. He morphed into a man-lion, leaped out, and grabbed hold of a soldier, sinking teeth and claws deep into him. Following Vul, Rave jumped out of a darkened doorway as a wolf-man, slashing and tearing into a soldier as well. Seeing two of his fellow generals ambushed from doorways, a third soldier launched a spear through the air at an entryway close to him, striking an apelike creature in the shoulder, sending the beast reeling backward into a room.

Glancing over, Patel found Nyeve lying on the floor with a spear stuck in her. He was enraged more at Vul, for not waiting on him before attacking soldiers, than the enemy. He walked out of the room and morphed into a forty-cubit-tall gorilla. A spear flew by his head, and when he looked in the direction it had come from, Patel locked eyes with a general. He charged the soldier, picked him up, and launched him toward the giant, impaling the general on one of Demar's helmet horns. As blood dripped down the helmet, sprinkling his nose, Demar came out of his trance and was enraged himself. He turned and ran at the large gorilla, jumped into the air, and landed a blow to Patel's face. Tumbling backward from it, Patel was startled at the strength this giant possessed.

Running to fetch his spear and shield, Demar knocked Vul through the air with one forearm sweep. Vul impacted a stone wall with such force his body blasted it to pieces. Taking hold of his spear and shield, the giant turned to face Patel. At the same time, Rave and Nob made a run at Demar only to hear Patel yell and order them to stop. "Leave him to me! Check on our wounded; I'll dispatch this giant myself!"

At hearing the beast speak, Demar said, "You think too much of yourself, creature. I've yet to be bested by anything or anyone, and no manimal will have my head as a trophy!"

Morphing into a bigfoot, Patel took the hilt from his armband, producing a flaming blade of fire.

A determined look fell across Demar's face as he witnessed the mutated thing before him. "Strange beast, are you responsible for the death of my brother?"

Patel nodded to the giant. "Yes."

"What are you, beast?"

His jaw firmly fixed, Patel replied, "Your demise."

With a gut-wrenching laugh, Demar said, "Like my brother, creature?"

Again nodding, Patel answered, "My name is Patel, giant; and exactly like your brother!"

Demar, tense with rage, took two steps and hurled his spear toward Patel while simultaneously removing a sword from his belt. The spear nearly struck Patel on his left, cutting tuffs of his hair as it went but never making contact with his skin. Demar's blade sliced through the air, missing Patel and smacking hard upon the ground below. Recovering, Patel launched a blade attack of his own, striking the giant's helmet and easily removing one of the attached horns. Backpedaling, Demar was amazed at how quickly his opponent moved. Patel stepped forward and lunged with his sword, striking Demar's shield. Recovering quickly, he then swung his blade from one side to the other, knocking the giant's shield from him.

Demar immediately countered with three blows of his own but could not find his mark. Frustrated, the giant swung the blade over his head, forcing the sword downward with great might, once more slamming it into the ground. In doing so, he gave Patel a clear shot at his head, which he took. The flaming blade cut clear through Demar's neck, just as it had his brother's. The giant's body fell in one direction while his head rolled in another. Standing over his kill, Patel took in huge breaths of air, attempting to calm his inner being.

Glancing around the arena, Patel was able to see that all enemies had been dispatched except for one—Endo. The little general sat shaking in the corner of a stone wall that surrounded the citadel. Wiping blood from his muzzle, Vul glared intently at the little man and moved in to kill him; but before he could strike, a large fist slammed squarely into the side of Vul's face. His vision blurred and slightly loopy, he looked up to see where the blow had come from. He could barely make out the figure of Patel looming above.

"Patel… wha…? Who do you think you are, hitting me like that?"

Patel pushed his chest forward, still ready for battle. "Vul, I should rip your head off for putting the team in danger with your antics, and if Ny is badly hurt, I intend to follow through with my threat!"

Vul countered, "Hey, I saw an opening and took it, pal. We were about to be discovered anyway, and the only reason you're ticked off is because I acted on my own, not waiting for his majesty's permission! You should be thanking me, you maniac!"

Patel wanted badly to knock Vul's head off, but Nyeve required his attention more. Patel walked to the room where she had been struck and checked on her. Norhi had removed the spearhead from her shoulder and had bandaged her arm and bound it in place. He gave her a drink of gall for pain, and Nyeve slept peacefully.

Norhi said, "Looks as though we can be harmed, injured, and thus killed if not careful, Patel. How many more of those giants with flying things are there, and what kind of army will we face when they arrive?"

Not taking his eyes off Nyeve, Patel said, "I don't know, my friend, but I will find out. Watch her; I'll be right back."

Patel stepped out of the room and made his way over to Endo. He pushed Vul out of the way and spoke to the last general alive. "My name is Patel. No harm will come to you. I only want information, and once you give it to me, you'll be released back to your people."

Protesting, Vul cut in. "He's not going anywhere. No mercy to the enemy, Pa—"

Before Vul could finish, Patel turned and punched the lion-man so hard he became aerial before smacking into a stone wall and falling to the ground in a crumpled heap. Turning back to Endo, Patel continued. "Do you believe me when I say you may go free after I receive the information I need?" Trembling, Endo could barely respond by nodding his head. All the color had drained from his face, and Patel was afraid the little man would die from fright.

"This is no general. Look into my eyes. Be calm, and tell me your name."

Suddenly, the general's body stopped shaking and color returned to his face as he stared deep into Patel's eyes.

Hearing the ape man ask him his name again, and the general said, "My name is Endo, the servant of Utt."

Patel nodded, glad the glare had worked. Patel further inquired; "That's good, Endo. Why do you wear a general's frock and armor?"

"I was made a general by Demar, brother of Utt, ruler of all he surveys. He commands the nephilim and ariyon warriors throughout the land."

"How many warriors are on their way here?"

Endo was a little slow to reply. "Ten...ten..."

"Ten's not so bad," said Rave as he walked up to Patel and Endo.

Endo continued. "Ten times a thousand march to Utt's citadel as we speak."

Overhearing from the building, Norhi ran out and said, "Are you serious? Ten times a thousand warriors! Is that even possible?"

Using his hand to gesture for Norhi to keep quiet, Patel asked, "Endo, are you sure of the number of warriors heading this way?"

His answer was matter-of-fact. "Yes."

Unable to keep silent, Norhi asked, "Now what, Patel? We cannot hold off, let alone attack, so many soldiers and expect to survive!"

Knowing the situation was as Norhi stated, Patel thought quickly and developed a plan. Weak as it was, he had to try something. Gazing deeper into Endo's eyes, Patel said, "Endo, you were told by Demar to return to the army on the flying--carpet to take command and turn them back home because everything is fine. Do you understand? Demar states all is well."

Answering, Endo said, "If all is well, then I am a liar and will be put to death to be roasted and eaten since I was the one that delivered the news of Utt's death by a great beast."

Smiling, Rave said, "It sounded good to me, Patel. Nice try anyway."

Endo chimed in, "There is a way to show I am under the protection of Demar," said Endo. "A pardon. I need the neck chain that he wears; if I return with it, they will believe all that is said by me."

Relieved to hear his plan would work, Patel ran over to Demar's body, took the neck chain of teeth from his body, and raced back to Endo. Placing the chain in Endo's hands, Patel said, "Remember, all is well. The army must return home, and after forty sunsets, you and you alone are to return for Demar, understand?"

Nodding Endo agreed, "Yes, I understand."

A sigh of relief escaped Patel. "Good, climb aboard the flying carpet and leave; remember only what I have told you." Endo stood, walked to the carpet, sat on it, and commanded it into the air. As he watched the flying machine take to the sky, Patel said, "There, that's the best I could do. Hopefully it works." Ackal, Nob, Norhi and Rave stood before Patel with puzzled looks on their faces.

"I know; it's called gazing. You all can do it, but only to humans."

"Yeah, thanks," said Norhi. "That's part of it, but why did you tell him to return in forty days? When he returns, Utt and Demar will be just as dead."

Patel stroked his chin, deep in thought. "It gives us time to build our own army—an army of shifters—so the odds will be as even as possible."

"And just how do we make an army of shifters?" asked Norhi. "Not only that, but how do we train them in time for little man's return?"

He replied, "We'll discuss it later. Right now I need Rave and Nob to strip Demar's body of armor and weapons. Set the body and head on fire, and then bring the armor and weapons back to the settlement. Norhi, carry Ny to my dwelling, and I will carry our 'friend' home."

Laughing and shaking his head, Norhi went to scoop up Nyeve. Patel threw Vul over his shoulder and started to walk back to camp. Partway there, the lion-man stirred and groaned. Patel slammed an elbow to the side of his head, putting him back to sleep until morning's first light.

***

When Endo met Demar's army, he easily turned the soldiers back. Taking lead, he flew toward Demar's citadel compelled to take charge of everything while the giant was away. Upon landing in the dusty and deserted courtyard, he immediately headed for the throne room and, with the chain of teeth wrapped three times around his neck, sat upon Demar's seat of power, looking like a small child in his father's chair.

Mutt, keeper of the fortress and head jailer, was told of Endo and his flying carpet's return. This surprised him greatly. When he entered the throne room, his jaw dropped at seeing the little man seated upon his master's throne. "Scum of the earth! How dare you sit on the throne of power? Removing your entrails will bring me much joy—dog!"

Great confidence flowed from Endo's response to the ogre. "You are the dog! Mutt, what right do you have to address me in such a way? Do you not see with those grotesque eyes that I wear the chain of power?"

Sharpening his sight, Mutt peered closely at Endo and swiftly acknowledged Endo's authority by falling prostrate on the ground. "My lord, forgive me, but what does a human have to do with the rule of nephilim kingdoms?"

"What concern is it of yours who Demar elects as his minister, O Mutt?"

Nervously, Mutt said, "None, O lord of the lands. Forgive my ignorance. Shall I prepare a human for roasting to honor your highness?"

Repulsed at the idea of eating man flesh, Endo said, "I want no celebrations until the return of Demar to his rightful place upon this throne. Bring me fresh fruits and animal flesh instead. I will also partake in the drink of angelics—what's it called again—fermented grapes, I believe?"

Nodding feverishly, Mutt replied, "Yes, my lord, I know of what you speak; wine from grapes—Demar's favorite of all drinks, including the blood of humans."

Feeling queasy, Endo replied, "Yes, that will do—the wine; no blood, thank you."

As Mutt crawled out from Endo's presence, the human felt good about his position and proud that Demar held such admiration for him. High-ranking soldiers of the ariyons demanded an audience with Endo, not fully understanding or accepting the human's authority. The man sitting upon Demar's throne, however, did not fear, and gave them entry.

Panter, with two other subgenerals, walked into the room to confront Endo. "Human, what makes you think demigods would serve an insect such as you?"

Endo Cautioned,"Really, soldier choose your next words carefully." He motioned for his guards to move forward with spears at the ready to cut the angelic down where he stood, and the subgeneral sheathed his anger as Endo continued to address him. "Look with your eyes, hybrid, and see that I not only wear the chain of power but hold control over your fellow angelics—who with one word would reduce you to slabs of unrecognizable meat."

Nodding in acknowledgement, he said, "My name is Panter, Lord Endo, and I humbly ask for forgiveness for my earlier outburst, which was unprovoked."

Endo accepted his apology and provided seats for the soldiers, a table, and wine for drinking. Once the soldiers were seated and comfortable, Endo explained. "Demar is enjoying time with his brother Utt at his citadel and did not want to return for now."

Panter still questioned Endo. "My lord, why did the generals stay behind? If no battle was to take place, then they would have returned—with you, my lord."

Thinking for a moment, Endo could not retrieve a reason other than Demar wanting to spend time with his brother. Then an idea that made sense entered his mind. "Demar, along with his senior staff, is making plans, with Utt's assistance, to take an expedition to other human settlements to bring them under their control as well—yeah, that sounds right."

After some time had passed, Panter replied, "What you say indeed reflects Demar's actions when dealing with prior conquests, but wasn't the purpose of this last expedition to take down Utt's enemies? Some kind of beast, or beasts, harboring intelligence? That was the information given to us before starting out from here."

"Yes, well, it was also reported that Utt had been killed by a beast, and of course that proved false. Demar thought a campaign as large as this last one required more planning rather than acting out of haste. Would you not agree with Demar the Great?"

Again, what Endo said made sense to Panter, and he didn't want to say anything against Demar or his decision making. "Yes, my lord, I agree completely! It is good judgment by our esteemed leader."

Pleased with himself, he said, "Good. In forty days I am to return to Utt's citadel, though where the extent of power begins and ends under my reign stands until Demar says otherwise. I promote you three to full general in charge of Demar's army and protectors of his realm. It is sensible to me to promote angelics so others of your kind feel more at ease taking orders, since, as pointed out earlier, I'm human."

The three soldiers stood and bowed before Endo, and they swore allegiance to his reign while Demar was away. Feeling everything was under control, Endo dismissed his generals and headed to Demar's bedchamber for a relaxing rest.

Chapter 16

His hand slowly caressing Nyeve's thigh, Patel sat and watched over her as she slept. The spear tip was angelic and had pierced her deeply, cutting not only into her flesh but her soul as well. Feeling helpless, he tried to ease her suffering by wiping the sweat from her brow while tenderly speaking words of love and encouragement to her ear. Soon Patel spoke inwardly to the One Lord of Hosts, asking for her life to be spared. A blue-white light shone brightly within the room, and Patel could perceive the image of Gypet.

"Your prayer has reached us in reference to this woman; she will die."

Pleading, Patel asked, "Why, my lord? Please spare her life, and I will be forever in your service, in the service of the One.

Explaining, Gypet continued, "This woman, if left to live, would corrupt man as queen to a pseudo-god—a corrupting influence, a benefit to no one and a great harm to you."

Patel shook his head. "No! I know this woman; we are one in the same! Nyeve fights evil at my side, loving the people as I do. She could do no harm to me or any other person. Please, help me by healing her!"

Moments ticked slowly past in silence, and then Gypet spoke. "Remove the bandages from her wound and place your hand on it. Say the words 'El Ekter,' and she will recover as you wish. But know this, Patel: great shall be your loss—a pain rivaling death and separation. Your days shall be filled with despair, leading to a life spent in self-exile with no relief given until that day!"

Suddenly, the light and being were gone, leaving Nyeve and Patel within the room. Ignoring all Gypet had said other than how to heal his woman, he lifted away the bandages, exposing her wound. Dark green, yellow, and red murky fluids oozed from a large black slit just inside her left shoulder. Placing his hand across the slit, he said the words "El Ekter." A bright yellow glow surrounded Patel's hand and penetrated Nyeve's wound.

As her back arched, relaxed, and arched again, he could see through his hand the wound begin to close. Once it had completely sealed, Patel's hand ceased to glow and the power holding it in place released. In a soft, low voice, he tried to coax Nyeve awake. Slowly, her eyes opened, and as they focused on his face, she smiled. "Where am I?" She looked around. "Why are we back here? I remember getting ready to fight in the citadel—and that's it."

Smiling and touching her, Patel said, "Everything's fine, my sweet. You were injured, but you are better now. How do you feel?"

Nyeve sat up. After looking herself over, she said, "I feel great—like awaking from a long nap."

Laughing in relief, he said, "Thank the One true God; He's given you back to me!"

Still puzzled, Nyeve asked, "The battle with the giant—did it happen? Did we win?"

Patel explained all that had happened after her injury, and as he was about to finish, Norhi knocked and entered the room. "Nyeve, you're awake—and healed. Outstanding! My roots-bark paste really did the trick then, huh?" Keeping quiet about Nyeve's true recovery, Patel nodded as the couple smiled at each other. "Well good! Good! Uh, on another subject, Vul is awake and really ticked off with you, Patel. He's saying things like, 'I'll stuff his big feet up his own'… up… 'behind'; and when he's done that, he'll shove your head up his… well… to fight for air. You get the idea; he's mad."

Frowning, Patel rose. "I'm sure he is, and I'll deal with him now. No sense in putting it off. Ny, stay here and rest; are you hungry or thirsty? I'll bring you back something if you want."

"No thanks, love; I'm good, really."

Norhi asked, "When did you want to start training others as shifters for the upcoming battle?"

Taking in a deep breath, Patel answered, "Right, the army. Well, after I deal with Vul, I guess; the sooner the better."

Patel knew confronting Vul would be a difficult endeavor because he had humiliated him in front of other shifters, not to mention the enemy. Taking his time to reach the hut where Vul was imprisoned, Patel pondered over proper words to use that would appease a loose cannon such as Vul. An idea suddenly presented itself. Upon entering the hut, Patel looked around the cell specifically made for a shifter. Vul sat within a cube of pure crystalline quartz eight cubits high and just as long and wide.

Looking up at Patel with a great blazing glare, Vul bared his teeth from behind a snarling, evil grin. "You have some nerve to come in here as though nothing is wrong while I sit in a cage like an animal, you bas—"

Patel cut him short. "I don't have time for this, Vul. You're here because of an uncontrollable impulse to be a man of importance, which put lives in danger. Luckily for you, Nyeve is well and I need as many fighters as possible for what's about to come against us."

Chuckling, the shifter shook his head in disbelief. "And so you come in here thinking I'd help after this! Are you insane? The moment I'm released from this box of" —he smashed a side of the cell with his fist—"whatever the blazes this thing is made of, I'm going to rearrange your face!"

Sitting on a bench close to the cage and rubbing a side wall, Patel replied, "Amazing isn't it? Quartz crystalline of such purity, translucency that it can absorb and hold energy; it can even focus such energies for use in countless applications—something the watchers taught me. Second only to death, it is our only weakness. Now, you can spend an eternity in this cell or train and lead fellow shifters to victory against a powerful enemy."

A silent glare followed by an unbelieving laugh escaped from the trapped man. "Only if I train and lead them under you is what you are saying? Patel, I'm no fool—go fight them yourself, and stop messing with me. I don't want to play!" Turning away from Patel, Vul waited to hear him walk out, but he was surprised at what he heard next.

"They would be under your authority, not mine."

"What?" Vul asked with a hint of suspicion.

"You heard me right, Vul. As general of the Vulinese, you alone will lead them into battle." His interest piqued, Vul turned, walked over to where Patel sat, and, after squatting down, said, "I'm listening—for the proviso. I know you, Patel; there's always a proviso."

"Only that our attacks are synchronized. I don't want to put people or shifters in unnecessary danger—deal?"

"I and I alone will rule over the shifters?"

Correcting, Patel replied, "No—over your army of shifters you may have full command, not any others." Frustrated, Vul replied, "See! I never know what the abyss you're talking about—how many armies of shifters are there anyway?"

Calmly Patel answered, "Seven total—a thousand changelings per chosen one. You, me, Norhi, and so forth and so on. Each of us will recruit, create, and control our own army."

"In that case, I agree to your terms. Know this, Patel: the moment I feel betrayed by your words, I'll pull your spine from its moorings and keep it as a trophy. Just so you understand."

Patel nodded. "And just so you understand, if I think you are being deceptive or attempting to undermine our true and only mission on earth and needlessly placing personnel in danger; I'll throw you right back into this cell and dump it deep within the ocean, where you can wait for the end of days in solitude—deal?"

An impish grin and bow to Patel was his answer, but Patel waited for something more verbal. "Done. Now please open the door and release me from this thing!"

Stepping back from the cell, Patel raised his hand toward it and said, "Tak eck nel." At that, a side of the cell melted away, allowing Vul to jump clear of his prison. Seeing Patel's hand extended to him, Vul looked at it and wondered what he wanted from him. Reaching down, Patel took hold of Vul's right hand and shook it with his own. "It means we are united in purpose, friends and allies, opposed to being foes."

"You're just full of all kinds of information, aren't you?" Vul took his hand back. "We're allies; don't push it."

Grinning, Patel said, "That will have to do for now; let's get the others together and begin building our army."

Vul and Patel left the hut, rounded up the other shifters, and headed for Patel's dwelling, which would serve as a headquarters until enough men were recruited as shifters. As the seven sat around a table,

Patel explained how selection and turning the shifters needed to take place.

"We each will pick, from the men of Xmi, our soldiers to train as we see fit—a thousand per each of us. Once trained, we will occupy Utt's citadel and wait for the angelic hybrids to come to us."

Protest of the plan came quick from Vul. "Why are we waiting to strike them within the citadel, when it was you who said the army of nephilim is ten times a thousand? We will only be seven times as much, and I believe it will lead to a massacre of our people because they will be trapped inside a stone structure."

Norhi added, "I hate to admit this Patel but he is correct. It could lead to an unnecessary slaughter of our people if we wait it out."

Patel looked around the table, stopping at Vul's grinning face. "Very well, I'm open to suggestions. Vul, what is your idea on confronting the enemy?"

Vul took a breath and began explaining. "I take four thousand out of the seven thousand men. We station ourselves between the citadels since we know the route they will take, and we lie in wait to ambush. Additionally, I can cut off supply lines and attack from behind the columns, pushing the enemy toward what they perceive as a friendly ally—Utt's citadel. Then we encircle and slaughter every last hybrid. We confiscate weapons, shields, and supplies, then target the rest of the settlements and release more of our kind to worship us in gratitude for their newfound freedom!"

Silence fell over the members, some of them holding looks of shock on their faces, until Patel finally broke it by saying, "Vul, your plan is a good one, and I think I speak for everyone here when I say you possess the intelligence of a professional tactician. As I've said many times over, we are not looking for people to venerate or worship us. We do this for the veneration of the Lord, and it is to Him—and Him alone—the gratitude of their freedom belongs."

Feeling all eyes rested upon him in judgment, Vul quickly retracted his statement. "Please forgive me. I was caught up in the moment and certainly didn't mean that we should be worshipped. The plan, however, stands as a good plan—you said it yourself, Patel."

"Yes I did, and it is a good plan." Patel motioned to the group. "Do we have any volunteers that won't mind placing themselves and their armies under the temporary control of Vul? Please signify by raising your hand."

Ackal and Nob quickly lifted their hands in agreement, which met with Patel's nonverbal approval. Just then a lifted hand plunged an arrow of anxiety deep within his heart. "Nyeve, I think it best that you stay within the citadel, where it's safer."

Cutting in, Vul stated, "She is a shifter as we all are, and I think if Nyeve wishes to fight along with us, she should accept the risk that comes with such a decision like the rest."

Shooting back Patel replied, "Ny has done her part, Vul! Her body was violated by an enemy spear— not yours. There's nothing she needs to prove to anyone at this table, so she will—"

Standing, Nyeve said in a firm and determined tone, "Excuse me, but I have a voice and I will speak for myself. I don't have anything to prove—that's correct. I'm not looking for special privileges because Patel is my man and I his woman. We fight together— face the same risks together—and I'll accept nothing less from anyone. My hand is raised in decision, and I will be respected, as I respect the decisions of others here. Vul, I will be honored to fight with you, Nob, and Ackal outside the walls of the citadel against the enemy. Now, I'm no warrior; I possess less knowledge of how war and tactics are completed, and so I hold no delusions of who I am. I'm Nyeve, and I believe that I could learn from a proper instructor in things of war. Patel, you've taught me true love. You are a gentle man that makes me feel safe, secure, and comfortable.

I'm yours because of it. So now I require a barbarian—an animal of a man—to teach me the ways of aggression, battle, killing, and death. Therefore, Vul, I subject my army to your leadership, and I'll be yours to command in conflict."

Patel couldn't believe what he was hearing from his woman. Submitting herself to anyone seemed out of her realm, let alone to Vul out of all the shifters. Protesting would only make matters worse, but he had confidence and knowledge that she loved him. Besides, Nyeve had made it clear in front of the others what her wishes were. Patel didn't want to show weakness or mistrust in front of them by forbidding her requests. When the meeting was adjourned, the chosen went their separate ways to begin recruitment procedures, envisioning an army that could level the playing field for man against demigods.

Chapter 17

Deep within the universe, four angelics set about their work of tracking each galaxy to ensure pathways traveled were in synch, as the Lord commanded. As one of the angels moved a single galaxy back on a proper path, two voices caught his attention. Low at first, the voices grew, and as three other angels rendezvoused with the one, they too heard the cries.

"Bael, I've heard these voices before."

He replied, "Yes, they are of my sons—cries of my sons from the abyss!"

Stul said, "Impossible. How did they wind up in the abyss?"

In a rage-filled voice, Bael replied, "I don't know, but the entities responsible will pay for it! C'mon, follow me!" After heading through the spiral-shaped galaxy and through one of its solar systems, the four angels were intercepted close to a small, rust-colored planet by Lucifer. "Greetings, dear friends."

Bael spoke hurriedly as he continued forward. "Lucifer, I have no time for you right now. My children reside within the abyss and—"

Interrupting Lucifer continued, "I'm well aware of your sons' demise, Bael and I advise you to turn around and go back to your tasks. Leave it alone."

Bael, shocked by Lucifer's announcement, said, "You know! How do you know? Why are you here talking with me instead of releasing my sons?"

Lucifer lowered his voice. "Perhaps we could talk in a place a little more—well, out of earshot of other angels. I have a very nice place in the core of Mars where we can sit, share some energy, and talk about how better to release the kiddies; whatcha say?"

Suspicion mixed with interest led Bael to accept Lucifer's offer. The five headed for a large scarred area located on the surface of the red planet. They dove into it; close to its bottom, a huge metallic door loomed before them. Lucifer took a smaller entryway into the base's interior and led the angelics into a chamber filled with metallic chairs and a large conference table. Lining the walls encompassing the room were orbs of energy both pure and very rare in the entire universe. Lucifer levitated five of the orbs from a shelf and placed each sphere on the table corresponding to seats where they were to position themselves. He then took a chair and gestured to the other angelics to follow his lead. As they sat and drew out energy from the orbs, Bael and his followers waited for their host to speak, and when he did, "Now then, about your boys; I'm afraid they are lost to you for now. As unfortunate as that may sound it is the truth."

"Lucifer," said Bael looking mad enough for his his blood to boil white-hot, "You hold influence over the Lord; after all, you are favored among all the angels in heaven. And you sit here waving my son's futures off as though they were dust for the wind to play with. They are my—"

Cutting in Lucifer replied, "They are dust! Well, partially dust, that is. I did not take it upon myself to mate with the daughters of men. No, you brought that on yourselves, and so the rules of celestial laws apply, making it impossible for me to rescue them—at this time."

Calming his inner being Bael asked, "If you think I will let this go, my friend; you are very mistaken. Who's responsible for their demise? What angelic possesses the intestinal fortitude to take away the flesh life of my progeny, and where may I find him?"

Attempting to hold in a grin of satisfaction at knowing his plan was working well, Lucifer said, "Utt and Demar did not fall by the hands of an angelic. Well, not directly." He leaned forward in his seat. "It was by the hand of man, my dear Bael—by the hand of man. It was fairly quick, too, as I recall. Don't you find that odd—because I sure do."

Bael leaned forward. "You were there and watched as a man killed my sons? Ha ha ha ha ha! Oh, Lucifer, you had me going, and using unique energy to cloud my mind so you could spin your tale of exceptional humans. Very good; very good indeed. But a hu—"

Cutting in once again Lucifer said, "I'm sorry, Bael; perhaps you are a bit clouded by the quality of this energy, but I did not say that what toppled your sons was human. I said that angelics were indirectly responsible by giving to man certain skills and knowledge which led to the demise of the giants, along with top generals on their staff, which led to the release of settlements of men—freedom. Now that I think about it, I may not have been as precise in telling you everything, which I guess would mean the energy is very good and affecting me quite well. Yes, I watched as actions unfolded. It's called observing your enemy to find weaknesses, Bael, and did I learn a lot."

Lunging and taking hold of Lucifer's throat, Bael shouted, "What's to keep me from crushing God's favorite music maker's vocals into nothingness? Tell me!"

Lucifer raised a hand, and a great bolt of energy went forth, levitating Bael and pinning him to a wall. Watching wide-eyed, the other angelics stood up, ready to rush Lucifer, but found themselves stuck to the floor by an invisible force generated by their host. Walking slowly toward Bael, Lucifer kept his eyes locked on his guest, who was struggling to free himself from the wall. "I am above you. I am all-powerful. I am, so do not presume to hold anything against me or the things I do. Whether they meet with your approval matters not to me, Bael. I can be a friend of abundance or an enemy most merciless—your choice. This is the last time that I'll allow an outburst from a subordinate in one of my realms! Are we clear—angelic?"

Bael gave up on trying to free himself from the wall, and after looking over at the other angels. He nodded to Lucifer showing he felt compelled to relent to Lucifer, and the host turned his back to Bael and released him from the wall. After falling to the floor, Bael collected his faculties, approached the table, and took a seat next to Lucifer. He asked, "Lucifer, if in fact what happened was perpetrated by angels and men, how, then, was it done, and what must I do to exact revenge—my lord?"

Unable to suppress a grin any longer, Lucifer answered. "Very good, my friend—I'll tell you everything." Lucifer explained how the watchers had appointed chosen ones among man and empowered them with angelic abilities and knowledge.

Bael listened closely and Lucifer noticed him began working a plan in his mind to attack with vengeance against the enemies of his sons. All these plans were shattered, and he noticed Bael's dissapointment however, when Lucifer continued to speak. "Angelics are forbidden by celestial law to harm or harass things of creation without first receiving consent from the Lord. Unfortunately, man is a pet project of His, which forbids you from taking revenge, my friend."

Looking desperate, Bael asked, "There must be a way, Lucifer, or you would not be here! What is it? We are at your disposal; just give me justice!"

In a sober tone and with a firm look upon his face, Lucifer replied, "Justice is the furthest thing from that which you desire, Bael. You and your posse decided to desecrate your stations by lying with animals found on an insignificant rock, staining creation! But if you are truly willing to take this path of self-destruction to avenge your sons and keep others from falling into the hands of men, then listen. Shifters use deception by reconfiguring their outward appearances—taking on the guises of animals to carry out their plans. I can give the four of you that power as well—for a price. No haggling, and whatever the outcome, I will not be implicated in any of this by you."

Bael, leaning forward, asked, "What's the price for your assistance?"

"It's very simple: your undying loyalty and, when the time is right, assistance in an endeavor of my own to be named later. What say you one; what say you all?"

After the group of angels talked among themselves, Bael turned to Lucifer and said, "We are yours to command. Although control on how we do things will rest with us, we will honor your leadership."

Sealing the deal, Lucifer placed a mark on each angel's chest—a symbol of the dragon, which would stand as Lucifer's mark forevermore. "You all shall be disguised as dragons, fiery reptilian beasts with the power to destroy flesh. Though you may be opposed by an enemy, it's doubtful any opponent could overpower you. However—"

Bael becoming annoyed cut in, "Why in Hades is there always an 'however' with you? "It always comes up after we agree to one of your ridiculous plans!"

Ignoring the outburst, Lucifer continued. "A strong enemy—if there is such a thing—can and will banish my dear friends to the abyss for a time."

Ridep spoke up. "How long a time are we talking about?"

Lucifer answered, "Really time is relative, isn't it? A second can seem like an eternity, while an eternity may feel like mere seconds—so try not to dwell on it. Now, I believe you have a rendezvous with the third rock from this star, and good luck to all of you. Remember, do not under any circumstances reveal your true identity to anyone; it could start a war between the angelics. I'm not ready for that just yet, understand?"

A look of disdain was all Lucifer received in the form of a response before Bael and his team flew from Mars and headed for earth.

Chapter 18

Dawn on the thirty-ninth day from when the killed Demar brought with it warm golden rays that penetrated rooftops, stirring awake seven thousand shifters of the chosen. The original seven met for a morning conference to go over final plans before setting out to complete their first mission. Distressed with some observations he had made of the soldiers, Patel said, "Is it only me, or do the shifters we recruited seem... well, less—I mean in strength and agility?"

Answering Norhi said, "I've noticed it too. What they lack in total strength they make up for in intelligence and the ability to change, at will, into any animal desired—not just three, as we are confined to. I think they'll do fine, Patel."

Vul chimed in. "They are all trained well in hand-to-hand combat and weaponry. I'd stack our bowmen and swordsmen against any enemy, easily."

Norhi nodded. "And since I was able to synthesize and create the metals that make up our swords, arrowheads, and blades, they should take down the ariyon soldier with ease. I can't be too sure about the giants, though; their armor may prove difficult."

Nob injected, "Unlike us, these soldiers of ours require food and water sources as well. They are able to travel and fight for around thirty days or so without them, but after that they must eat and drink."

"It appears our copies are… limited," said Patel, "but they will have to do. Nob, come up with a logistical plan to maintain food and water stores while traveling. Vul, I expect you will set out for your positions when the sun is at its apex. What can we do to support?"

Vul said, "Communication is key to the entire operation; the five hundred trained for this will be our eyes in the sky relaying information to the citadel and soldiers in the field. If we run into a situation not anticipated, I'll need reserves on hand and stationed at the citadel to bring immediate assistance to cover our retreat as we prepare to regroup and counter their attack. We wiped out most of Demar's generals at the last ambush, so I'm not expecting too much trouble."

Nodding in agreement and understanding, Patel replied, "Vul, you make one amazing general, and we are blessed to have you on our side."

In his stylized sarcasm, Vul replied, "Save the honey for women, will ya; just make sure we have reserves ready to go if needed."

Smiling, Patel replied, "We'll be ready, general; don't worry. If there's nothing else, let's get the last of the preparations together; we leave at sun high."

As the chosen set about their tasks, Nyeve approached Patel with a look of inquiry on her face. "Patel, can I talk with you for a moment?"

Smiling, he said, "Sure, my love. I can see by your look that something's on your mind; what is it?"

"Why am I the only woman shifter? I'm not trying to complain or anything, but I'm the only one out of seven thousand. It's just weird, ya know?"

Patel shrugged. "I'm not sure, Ny. You picked your shifters from the village along with us; weren't there any women among the people you felt could perform the tasks?"

Not quite comforted by his words, she replied, "That's the weird part; I tried to pick a few women, but something inside compelled me to stick with men— single men."

Nodding his head Patel answered, "As was I— none of the men picked in my group have women of their own either. I imagine it's for the better now that we are discussing it. Think how we'd be—to lose the other part of us."

"I'm sure that's the reason; you're not worried about me going into battle without you, are you?"

Gazing into her eyes, he responded the only way open to him. "Of course I'm fearful, Ny. If it were possible, you would stay behind those stone walls with me, but you pledged to go into the fray under Vul's leadership. I can't override it now. My standing with the people would suffer, and your honor would be stripped from you, and I don't want that for either of us."

"I love you, Patel, and once this battle is behind us"—she placed her hands upon his broad chest Nyeve purred, " I'm going to show my man how much."

Vul walked over to the couple with sheer determination on his face. "If you two are done, it's time to go. Patel, the signals to look for from the eagle's flight overhead are a wide circle for enemy spotted and a small circle for enemy engaged; quick dives mean we need to send the reserves—fast!"

Nodding Patel answered, "I'll look for them, and we'll be ready. Take care of Nyeve for me; I want her back in one piece."

Walking off, Vul said, "She can take care of herself. Focus on the mission at hand, Patel!"

The couple watched as he morphed into a lion-man and walked away. Annoyed with him, but knowing what he said was true, Patel and Nyeve hugged quickly so the could hurry to take up their positions; lives were at stake!

Sitting in Demar's throne room with his newly appointed generals, Endo made ready to return to Utt's citadel. Ten thousand soldiers, fully equipped, waited outside the castle walls for first light to appear over the horizon. Slaves and supplies for the journey were kept off to one side, with men standing guard over them. Armor, once too big for Endo or any other man to wear, was custom made for him, as were the weapons he wielded. A person not knowing that an ariyon's height averaged four or five and a half cubits could easily mistake Endo for one of them. He securely wore Demar's neck chain over the armor to ensure everyone was aware of his authority at all times. Once his meeting with the generals concluded, Endo went to his bedchamber to rest before the expedition. He was still human and required food and sleep to sustain strength and alertness.

As he lay upon a couch within the room, a bright light filled the area, startling and blinding him. Then a voice spoke to him from out of the light. "Endo, who are you that I find you sitting upon the throne of an angelic seed?"

Shielding his eyes from the intensity of the light, Endo responded, "I am the elected leader of the land while Demar is away visiting his brother. Who are

195

you, my lord?" The light diminished, revealing a man-shaped figure standing before him. "I am Lucifer, your god, man of dust! Now listen carefully, for there is not much time. Four great beasts are coming to exact revenge against those who have killed their sons, the giants. If found in Demar's place, you will be killed; your body pinned to the outside walls of this citadel."

Frightened and confused, Endo cried out. "My lord, Demar lives and has placed me in com—"

Interrupting, Lucifer continued, "Your mind has been cloaked from the truth." Lucifer moved forward and placed a hand on Endo's head, removing the veil placed over his mind so he recalled what happened at Utt's castle and Demar's death.

Kneeling before Lucifer, Endo asked, "My lord, what am I to do? I don't want to die. Please help me!"

Grinning down at the man, Lucifer said, "Surely, you will not die! Instead you shall be my vessel to do my will among men. Your form is my signet, and you shall be called Serpent, general of my dark army on earth."

Immediately, Endo's shape took on the appearance of a reptilian manlike creature. He grew and broke the armor covering his body. When the metamorphosis was complete, he easily towered over the ariyons. He now had scaly emerald-green skin, shiny gold eyes, and a muscular frame as thick and solid as stone. Twin retractable fangs, sharp and filled with lethal venom, protruded from his mouth when his jaws were open. He had long, sharp black claws extending from his fingertips, strong enough to slash through metal and stone.

Lucifer commanded, "Rise, Serpent, and leave the neck chain where it fell. You will come with me."

In a low, gravelly voice, Endo said, "But, lord, we are about to march on Utt's citadel, and since both giants are dead, we can go to battle against those responsible and crush your enemies!"

Dismissing him, Lucifer explained, "The Baels will see to that, my dear Serpent. Your task is with me. I require the seed of men to breed my army—a prize stud for the vessel Lilith, to sire sons of rebellion and of great renown which will be under my command as you serve me, Serpent. Oh, and about Lilith—she can be a handful. She is dominating and talkative, and she complains about anything and everything. But you should be all right; just say 'yes, dear'—a lot."

Lucifer placed his hand on Serpent's shoulder, and the two entities disappeared to journey and bring into fulfillment one of many conspiracies perpetrated by Lucifer, the enemy of mankind.

Chapter 19

Endo's generals, seeing that the sun was clearly over the eastern horizon, went to the bedchamber to rouse their leader. Meeting them at the door was Mutt, who stood guard, not allowing entry.

"The master is human and requires rest, my lords; he cannot be disturbed until he rises."

"Mutt," Panter replied, "we are in need of his highness to begin the march to the citadel. We do not dare show up without him in the lead and incur the wrath of Demar and his top generals."

Nervously, he said to them, "I understand, but my orders are strict and must be enforced. Tell you what—take the army, and before you reach the citadel, my master will catch up with you by using the flying carpet."

After thinking it over, and wanting to reach their destination quickly, the generals relented. They moved the army without Endo, hoping that he would do as Mutt said and catch up prior to the time they reached Utt's citadel. About four or five stadia from Demar's fortress, several soldiers and generals noticed great birds flying high overhead, far away in the distance. It wasn't strange to see animals—especially birds taking to the air—as the army went forward, since the rhythmic sounds of metal and feet striking the ground sent many creatures running in panic, but these birds seemed to move with purpose and focus.

One general said to another, "What do you make of it?"

"Not too sure, but we have had many birds of prey overhead when slaughtering men. It makes for an easy meal."

Nodding, the lead general agreed. "Yeah—yeah, maybe you're right. I just don't remember this many before, and in such a linear pattern. This is why I wanted to wait for his highness; before Demar ever sent our troops into battle, he always mounted the carpet and flew over a settlement, letting us know what to expect on the gro—"

Pausing in his statement caught the other officer's attention asking, "What... expect what?"

"This is an odd thing for me to say, but could these birds be some kind of scout, like an early warning system, letting an enemy know we are coming?"

Skepticism flowed from the officer's response. "A warning system comprised of animals? Really—to what enemy? We are rendezvousing with Demar, our leader, at the citadel of his brother—an ally. It's going to take much more than a few large birds in the distance to make me worry about any unseen enemy.

Besides, who would dare come up against us and expect to walk away? We are the reigning entities on this planet. No man could dislodge us, let alone think about rebelling against our stations. Not to mention they are slaves, my friend. So any talk to the contrary is defeatist at best."

Panter felt uncomfortable being thought of as a defeatist and said, "Maybe you're right. No, I mean to say you are right. When do you think we will arrive at the castle?"

The other officer looked around, especially focused on the slaves to the rear. "Slaves always slow us down. Perhaps four days before we see it in the distance.

The overgrowth of the jungle and forests are more of an enemy to us than anything else. Hopefully the six roads we travel upon will stay free of debris and plant overgrowth; otherwise, it could slow us to a crawl in some places."

Under his breath, and more for himself than anyone around him, the other general replied, "A perfect place for an ambush."

Vul arrived at barriers placed along the six roads leading to the citadel and went over plans with Nyeve one more time before deploying the troops to their places of attack. "All the barriers look like they belong to the end of the jungle and beginning of the forest. This is our squeeze point and kill zone, which is two and a half stadia long. Place your soldiers along the whole length of it, but keep a few behind in reserve. I will take my troops to the rear of their column to attack. When I do, it's sure to cause a great commotion within their ranks, which will be a signal to attack the front."

Speaking up Nyeve said, "The slaves will reside in the rear, Vul; what will you do to protect them from harm?"

Vul shrugged her off. "They are of no consequence. Consider them collateral damage. We must focus on the big picture, Ny, and that's the way it is."

Annoyed with his attitude toward fellow men Nyeve shot back, "Only Patel may call me Ny, and you're no Patel. We need to protect all men from the angelics, Vul. We don't pick and choose who is salvageable and who must die; are you God?"

"Look Ny… eve, you were the one to volunteer for this mission. None of the other chosen had a problem with me being in charge of this part of the operation. So don't think you can change what I know is required by trying to make my heart bleed like that of Patel's. I'm no lapdog, woman; the quicker you find that out, the better!"

Nyeve turned crimson with rage, she shot back, "I'm here to ensure the safety of our peoples—every one of them! They depend on us, Vul, to rescue them from a terrible and cruel master. I know because before Patel found and released me, I was one of them. I lived in complete terror, chained to a cold stone wall, waiting for my turn to be taken by Utt. My only crimes were beauty and not knowing a man. For that, Utt would have taken me at first light if not for dear Patel. You're a chosen one as well, Vul, which means a good heart must beat within your chest just as it does in Patel's. We need to save our kind"—Nyeve stood before him and placed a hand gently upon his cheek—"otherwise, who else will do it?"

As Vul looked deep into her eyes, a feeling strange and unusual washed over him, but only for a moment. Grasping both of her arms below the shoulder, he pulled her into him and said, "You are very beautiful, and I can see why Patel is so easily led by the nose. Maybe I'll take you for my own—make you a queen among men!" Suddenly, he pulled her up to his face and forcefully kissed her, mashing their lips together. Then he threw her to the ground and turned his back to her. "Then again, maybe you aren't as wild and beautiful as I thought."

Anger filled every part of her body as she glared at him from the dust-covered ground. Getting to her feet, she walked around to Vul's front and slapped him smartly across the face; he reciprocated. Once again she found herself on the ground, looking up at the man.

Vul bellowed, "This is my operation and if you can't accept that fact, then run back to your lover."

She stood and approached Vul in humility. "You're in charge; I'll listen to you, but please let me go with you, and I will ensure the people's safety while you fight the Ariyons. Please, I beg you."

Relenting, Vul said, "Very well, they are your responsibility—not mine. I will not be slowed down or interfered with, and that's final!"

Nodding in agreement, Nyeve left him momentarily to assign in her place another general who would lead the attack from the front of the Ariyon column while she accompanied Vul to the rear.

After their confrontation, Nyeve experienced an emotion she had not felt before, which led her to the idea that Vul could be changed. She wanted to flatten and make smooth the creases of his character. She wanted to fix the traits she deemed as flaws that kept him from becoming a more mature and thoughtful person, like her Patel. As Nyeve walked rubbing the cheek Vul had struck when he knocked her to the ground, a slight tinge of attraction welled up in her, something she tried to wave off but found impossible to do. She would fix him and that was that.

***

Upon arriving at Demar's citadel, the four dragons shook walls, knocking various items of pottery and armor to the ground. Running out the main hallway to the courtyard, Mutt thought an earth shaking was taking place. As he looked up at the dragons, he could not believe what he was seeing. Frozen in place, he didn't move until a deep, snarling voice bellowed in his direction. "Where is the army of my son Demar? Why have they left the confines of the citadel? Who are you, ugly one?"

He tried to find words, but they escaped him, leaving only a grunt and a passing of flatulence as his answer.

Reeling from the odor, Bael addressed the ogre-like giant again. "Where is the army located, you disgusting glob of flesh?"

Mutt, finding his voice and recovering from his shock, said, "I'm sorry; I've never encountered such beasts as you before. My master, Demar, is with his brother Utt at Utt's citadel. His Lord Endo sleeps in the upper chamber while the army marches to Utt's citadel to escort Lord Demar back here. Did you say you are the father of Demar?"

Bael moved and brought his massive head to Mutt's level and continued speaking. "Perhaps my appearance is too much for you to bear, stinky one. Let me know if this suits you better. Rising up, the four Baels concentrated and morphed into large reptile-like men twelve cubits tall with two large, prominent horns that curled up from their foreheads. "How is this, bag of rotting meat? Can you speak now?"

Mutt, still nervous and scared, replied, "My lord's... Lord Endo was placed in charge by your son Demar. He slumbers while the army marches on to Utt's—"

"Yes, you said that already. Take us to this Endo; we will have words." Bowing as he moved backward, Mutt turned and led the Baels to Endo's bedroom. Mutt knocked on the large wooden door and received no reply.

Pushing him aside, the four Baels broke through the door and entered the room. The area was devoid of any living creature, and the only thing that showed Endo had been in the room was his miniature set of armor and Demar's neck chain lying in a clump on the floor. Examining the armor, Mutt noticed some of the metal scales seemed to have ripped apart, leaving jagged, sharp pieces. Bael picked up a familiar scent on the air. "Lucifer was here and must have taken Endo with him—but why?" Receiving only looks from his fellow dragons, he turned to Mutt, thinking the grisly giant held answers to his questions.

A scarcely toothy grin and shoulder shrugs were the only replies Mutt could give to the visitor who called himself Demar's father.

Turning back to his team, Bael said, "We need to find the army of ariyons and protect them from the enemy. Once we turn them back to this citadel, we will hunt for the killer of my sons and take revenge. Keep the shifter leaders alive and as untouched as is possible. It will be my pleasure to kill them slowly—for eternity, if I have my way." Before leaving the room, Bael turned to Mutt and ordered him to take a bath and scrub the filth from his body and then see to the cleaning of the citadel since Bael would return to rule mankind from within its walls.

Chapter 20

After checking on all the reserve soldiers located in Utt's citadel, Patel noticed a light of bright blue and white hues coming from within a room directly in front of him. Compelled to enter the room, he walked through the threshold, and immediately the door to the room slammed shut behind him. From within the light came a voice he knew very well—the voice of a watcher. "Patel, four supernatural enemies greater than the army of ariyons are on their way to attack your soldiers." A holographic image of four dragons formed in the space between Patel and the light. "The dragons of Bael mean to exact revenge for the death of their sons. Many are in danger. They are looking for you because their sons died at your hands and were cast into the abyss. Go forth in the power of the Lord and confront these dragons. You must tear from their heads the horns of power; this shall make them weak—weak enough for you to send them into the abyss, where they shall reside for ten thousand years." Immediately, the light that had filled the room suddenly disappeared, leaving Patel with questions without answers. After a few moments passed, he collected his senses and ran out of the room.

Motioning to the reserves, he made them take to the sky while he morphed into an eagle. He took lead as they made their way to where the armies were located, carefully watching the sky and land for any signs of the dragons. Thoughts of Nyeve at the hands of Bael made him even more determined to reach the group as quickly as possible.

The shifters kept silent as they watched ariyon soldiers marching on the roads leading to Utt's citadel. They waited patiently for the attack signal to come from Vul as the soldiers moved deeper and deeper through their lines. Vul and Nyeve sat and watched as the final columns of soldiers passed their position. A few hundred cubits behind, male slaves carried and pulled supplies and replacement armaments. They were far enough behind the ariyons for Nyeve to personally ensure no harm would befall them during battle.

Signaling his troops, Vul pushed forward, beginning an assault on their rear lines. Nyeve moved to where the men were and told them to not be afraid and follow her to safety. She led them off the roads to take up a secure area within a nearby cave. She then returned to the battle at hand. Soon the entire area where the ariyon soldiers marched was under attack by shifters. Vul's plan seemed to be succeeding, making the lion-man quite satisfied with himself.

From the west, a terrible roaring screech sounded the arrival of Bael and his dragons. Diving into the lines, each dragon picked up and flew off with a shifter in his claws. They ripped and shredded them to pieces, which fell to the ground like rain. In awe at the sight of the beasts, it took a few moments before Vul signaled the archers to take aim to down the dragons. Volley after volley of arrows found their mark with no affect against them.

One of the dragons caught sight of Nyeve and made his way toward her, reaching out with claws extended. Nyeve had just enough time to catch a glimpse of the beast a few paces from her before a large eagle smashed into the dragon's side, sending it reeling into thick jungle brush. Touching down, Patel morphed from an eagle to a gigantic gorilla. After glancing over to see that Nyeve was safe, he moved into the brush where the dragon had landed. Sounds of a great struggle came from the jungle, but the only signs of the creatures came from flying debris and tremors in the earth shakes.

As another dragon moved in from the air to assist his brother, the one fighting was thrown skyward with great force. The two dragons collided, sending them both tumbling into a deep ravine that ran alongside one of the roads.

Bael's eyes burned with anger as he watched, prompting him to take on the gorilla himself. Launching toward Patel at a dizzying speed, Bael plowed the ape across the jungle floor before grasping him by a leg and soaring skyward. Shaking off the hit he sustained, Patel reached up, took Bael by the throat, and squeezed until the dragon loosened its grip on his leg. Once free, he swung up onto Bael's back and, taking hold of his horns, rode the beast as though it were a horse, forcing it toward the ground. Just before impact, Patel pulled the horns with all his might, tearing them away from their roots. He then leapt free, allowing Bael to slam hard into the surface of the road. The impact caught everyone by surprise, and for a moment all fighting stopped. Bael crawled out of the impact crater, green fluid oozing from where his horns once were, and fell to the ground, too weak to move.

Walking over, Patel took hold of his enemy and said, "The name's Patel, and I killed both sons for the atrocities committed against my people. Now I send you to meet their fate."

Looking into Patel's eyes with a half grin upon his face, Bael replied, "I'll be back."

Confidently Patel said, "Somehow I doubt that very much. But if you do return, I'll be waiting. Now, into the abyss with you!" A vortex formed above the dragon's head and sucked the creature into it, and it then vanished. Turning, Patel changed into an eagle and took to the sky, where he addressed everyone with a thunderous voice. "Fight on if you desire, ariyons, but know this first: I have killed Utt and Demar, and their father is no more. If fighting continues, I will destroy you in the same way. You have the choice to head back to your dwellings now, and I will assure safe passage. Release all men from their bondage and molest them no longer; otherwise, I'll hunt every last one of you down and cast you off this planet forever. I give you forty days to comply. After that, defy me and prepare for war!"

The dragon Azel, though he did not tangle with Patel, was very fearful of him. Diving into the ravine where Stul and Ridep had been thrown, he found his comrades and petitioned them to leave and return to Demar's citadel to recoup. Stul, hearing of Bael's demise, took up the mantle of leadership and agreed on returning to the castle for now. Trying to find a general among them still alive, the ariyon's waited to see what they were to do—fight on or go home. Finally a soldier named Akan took from his side a gold-and-silver horn, the sound of which could be heard as far as Utt's citadel. Listening to its tones, the soldiers cast off their weapons and walked back toward home, disgraced. Of the ten thousand that battled, only five thousand survived.

***

Although the shifters had won a victory, four thousand out of the seven thousand that fought were lost. Watching the soldiers make their way back home, Patel felt a little saddened. He was happy to have won a victory, but compassion for his enemy made it difficult for him to revel in his success. They did not march back but walked in shame, shuffling and tripping as they went forth. A remnant of shifters still alive cheered and shouted Patel's name, saying victory was theirs because of him.

One shifter did not share that view, however, and he simmered in rage and contempt for Patel. Morphing into a large vulture, Vul took to the air and met Patel above the battlefield. "What the blazes do you think you're doing? Allowing the enemy to just leave when we clearly have the advantage, and taking credit for a successful campaign that you did not conceive or even execute?"

Patel didn't want to deal with Vul's ego, yet he knew that if it wasn't addressed now, he would have to face it later. "Vul, I did nothing to prompt any of the adulations coming from our people. Once we return home, I will publicly give personal testimony to you for coming up with the plans and seeing them through. Second, we cannot continue to fight the ariyons without suffering greater losses than those already sustained. Third, and lastly, we have just been shown a new and terrifying enemy; I personally can attest to its raw power—a power which has drained from me enough energy that I cannot transform from this back to human form or the form of any other being. The fact that I am still flying is incredible, but the thermal updrafts are helping. We need to study this new threat and find its weaknesses, along with how many there are. If there had been more of those beasts, how long do you think any of us would have lasted?"

Pacified but still annoyed Vul replied, "What you say makes sense? But you did defeat one of them, as though you possessed foreknowledge of how to do it. Why did you enter the battle anyway? We never made a request for—"

Cutting him short, Patel replied, "Vul, I don't have enough strength for this right now. I need to get back..." His strength depleted, Patel lost consciousness and plummeted to earth.

Diving after him, Vul reached out with talons and secured him before he hit the ground. Flying off toward Utt's citadel with him, Vul had thought of ways in the past to do away with Patel, and when this one presented itself, he felt compelled to save the vulnerable leader of the people, but he couldn't figure out why. Perhaps he wanted Patel to die by his hand and not in some freak accident, or maybe he desired the people to witness his demise at Vul's hands. One thing was certain, Patel had been in mortal danger and Vul had saved him. The thought left a bad taste in his mouth as he flew toward Utt's citadel. "The son of a jackal... he'd better be grateful for this."

***

Norhi met up with Nyeve at the rear of where fighting had taken place and said, "We need to clean up this mess. Confiscate weapons, armor, and supplies. Then we need to bury or burn the bodies. I've already given orders to my men to decapitate all ariyon soldiers and to build a large pile for burning, but I need your troops to bury our dead, and I figure Vul's can collect the weapons and supplies; what do you think?"

Smiling Nyeve agreed, "Sounds like a good plan, but I also have slaves—former slaves—hidden in a cave close to here. They'll require an escort back to the citadel, and I want to ensure safe passage. If you don't mind, I'll take them back home. Did you see where Patel went after his speech? It was very good."

Norhi shrugged. "Ny, there was so much happening, I'm surprised to know where I am. And where did Vul go, for that matter? I'd think he would be furious with Patel for ending the battle and sending our friends here on their way home unharmed."

Her smile grew larger. "It just shows how much compassion he has, that's all. It's why I love him so."

"Who—Vul?" Norhi asked confusedly.

"No, idiot, Patel. Vul does not know the meaning of compassion. I intend on changing that part of his character in time."

Norhi smiled back. "Good luck on that. Just be careful when grabbing a tiger by its tail. Er—lion, rather." The two laughed as generals from Vul's, Nyeve's, and Patel's shifters approached requesting new orders. Norhi told Nyeve he would take care of things if she wanted to leave with the humans, and she did.

Nyeve placed the people in two carts, one hitched to the other. She then morphed into a large grizzly bear and pulled the carts toward the citadel. The road traveled was littered with carnage never before seen on such a scale. One of the slaves asked Nyeve what all of this mutilation and death was for—gold, riches, or power. Her answer was matter-of-fact. "For you—for your freedom!" Sitting back in the cart slack-jawed, the man wept as he pulled his legs up to hide his face.

Seeing the man's response stirred emotions within Nyeve. She knew they were tears of gratitude; no words were needed to express it. The rest of the trip was completed in silence as they passed shifters working to dispose of dead bodies and clear the road of all battle debris.

***

The three dragons who had landed in Demar's citadel wondered over what had just happened. Unfortunately, Azel was the only dragon unharmed by the battle with Patel, and the others could not keep focused.

"What power does this shifter possess that he can affect us in such ways?"

Stul said, "Azel, I'm too weak to think. We were drained by him as well, I'm sure of it, but I don't..."

Both Stul and Ridep suffered from a lack of energy and required time to reenergize their beings. Wondering if they could change back to their angelic forms, all of them found it too difficult to do so. However, they were able to transform into reptilian humanoids. When they did so, Mutt came forward and led them to a place in the castle where they could rest unmolested.

While resting, Azel kept trying to figure out where the shifters might have received such incredible powers—if, indeed, they were men of dust. Resigned to find out, he made it his mission to contact Lucifer after recharging. If Lucifer wasn't available, then perhaps Deenal, Torel, or Tubel had answers. Drifting off, his thoughts turned to the battle with Patel and the shifters and how quickly Bael, their leader, had been defeated.

***

Soldiers met Vul at the citadel and took charge of Patel's limp body. They moved into a large stone room and placed him on a bed of soft straw and feathers. After covering the eagle with a blanket, they left the room and stationed two guards at the door. Vul then turned his attentions to the aftermath of battle, wanting to ensure everything moved along smoothly. He didn't care for the fact that Patel had allowed the enemy to walk home. He didn't trust that they wouldn't rally for a counterattack. Questions boggled his mind. *Where did the dragon beasts come from? And how was it that Patel seemingly knew of their existence and potential for attack? We were fine until dragons showed up— almost at the same time Patel appeared. How—how did he know they would show, and the way in which to dispatch them? He's intelligent, but not that intelligent. These watchers he keeps talking about, I've only seen one. Why show up to him all the time, but not any of us—me? Something doesn't seem quite right with that. I will not be controlled by them or anyone else. I will learn how to control these watchers, you can count on it!*

After checking to see that the roads were being cleared, Vul headed toward a pull cart with people in it that was being pulled by a very large grizzly bear. Grinning, he teased Nyeve by saying, "I see you decided on a new fur coat. Looks expensive; where did you come by it?"

"Ha ha ha, very funny, Vul; it is to laugh. Where did you take off to, anyway?"

Realizing she had no idea about Patel, he decided to keep it to himself. "Someone needed to ensure our soldiers were safe after your lover allowed them to leave unharmed for home."

Nyeve started to lecture him. "You know, you could learn a lot from a man like Patel if—"

"Yeah, yeah, he's great; wonderful personality, fun at parties, blah, blah, blah. If you haven't noticed, I am the one flying beside you right now, watching out for your safety, securing you so that you're comfortable as you go."

Seeing through his sarcasm, Nyeve replied, "Safe, secure, and comfortable—nice use of words that express how Patel really is. You can only wish to be like him."

Vul baited her. "Oh, now, you can't tell me there isn't an attraction, Nyeve. I've felt it many times."

Annoyed she replied, "I'm not sure what you were feeling. Oh wait, I do—yourself! You think so much of yourself, and it's really sad. Yes, I've made it my personal mission to change you from what you are into what you should be, but that's as far as it goes. I belong to Patel, and I always will, and neither you nor anyone else will ever change that, okay!"

Confidence oozed from his voice as he replied, "We'll see who changes their mind. Once you see how strong and appealing I really am, you'll leave the routine and comfort of a weak man like Patel for a world of wild, uninhibited passions and desires. You'll dive deep into the pool in which I swim every day, and, in fact, you'll watch in awe as I perform many different types of dives into the waters with you as my woman."

Trying hard not to show her attraction to him, Nyeve snorted and turned away, saying, "You don't know what you're talking about, Vul; go find something to do. I believe there are bodies waiting to be burned needing your attention."

Relenting, he replied, "Very well, Ny, I'll leave you for now; wouldn't want your passions to overheat in front of the slaves, now would we?"

As he flew off, Nyeve corrected him. "Former slaves—they are free now and not—"

Vul simply laughed noticing she didn't say he was wrong about her passions overheating, as he soared higher into the sky. Partially upset with Vul's goading, she kept her course, taking the freed people to Utt's citadel, which soon would be renamed in honor of Patel and the shifters under him.

Chapter 21

Azel flew quickly through the solar system, arriving on
Mars in the twinkling of an eye. Once there he plunged
quickly to Lucifer's secret base at the bottom of an
unzipped part of the planet's crust. Utilizing a word
only known by Lucifer and the four dragons, he opened
a large bay door, allowing him to enter. He located the
orbs of power and took two of them in tow as he
secured the facility. He then raced back to his fellow
dragons and placed an orb on each side of the spent
dragons. They immediately drew in energy, becoming
stronger and more aware. Azel warned both of them
not to take in too much of the pure energy; otherwise, it
would affect them like alcohol affects man.

Stul, having enough energy, stood up and swore
death upon the creatures that had defeated them in
battle.

Azel tried calming his rage, explaining that they
needed to study this enemy to find weaknesses before
launching another attack.

When Ridep was able to stand, he asked about
Bael, prompting Azel to recount the battle. "Bael was
banished to the abyss by a large and powerful shifter.
He warned of more fighting if man is not released from

our children's bondage, and I believe he means it sincerely."

Ridep responded, "It warned—us? We are angelics! What in hell's deepest pit are these beings with the power to summon portals to the abyss—and not only that, but to banish us to it?"

"We only have the information Lucifer supplied, and by the way, I haven't been able to make contact with him to ask for clarification. However, he was quite adamant about the fact that these beings are endowed with angelic abilities. However, we never needed to change our appearance to access our powers, as they do. Why that is required, I wonder."

Bael possessed the most wisdom out of the four angels, yet Azel and Ridep were no slouches when it came to knowledge. Stul was ruled by his emotions rather than logic, which made him the most dangerous and reckless entity in the group. Bael could control him when others could not; he used Stul when it fit his needs to gain his own heart's desires. Stul sat off in a corner as the other two worked through their ideas on what should be done next.

An idea came to Ridep which made sense, "It's about worship. The watchers are worried that their dust balls will worship other entities other than the Lord. So they disguise and empower these… things… to free mankind from our children so they can worship Him freely. I think I know a way to deal with them now. We'll teach man to worship all sorts of things, from rocks and plants to angelic beings—anything but God."

Puzzled, Azel asked, "So how does that help us exactly? So, man venerates everything but God"—suddenly it hit him—"so the Lord is made aware and He destroys man for us. Brilliant!"

Ridep looked puzzled. "Well, that wasn't what I was thinking, but sure—it works for me."

The dragons went on to develop a plan. They knew they would require angelic images, which they could no longer change into. In order for their plan to work, they needed the assistance of others who shared their goal—the annihilation of mankind. Only a few entities had such desires other than Lucifer, and those were Deenal, Tubel, and Torel. Three angelics they required to bring about the destruction of man from all creation.

***

When she arrived at the citadel, Nyeve unhitched herself from the carts, morphed into Sasquatch form, and directed a few soldiers within the castle to care for the people she brought in.

Just then, Norhi flew in and morphed into human form. "Nyeve, have you seen Patel? I can't find him anywhere."

She shrugged, as she thought Patel had been with Norhi collecting weaponry while watching over the ariyons' retreat. One of the soldiers posted at a door spoke up, telling the duo that Patel was in the room he was guarding. The two shifters looked at one another and then back toward the soldier, and they then moved quickly into the room to find Patel lying on a bed, sleeping. They tried to wake their friend by calling out, but they received no sign of consciousness.

Norhi then examined Patel. "I'm not sure how to help him, Nyeve. His vitals are very low—so much so, I don't think he has enough energy to transform. That's likely why he is still in the form of an eagle."

Worried Nyeve replied, "How is this possible? During battle not more than two sunrises ago, he was in powerful health and vitality. The way he went at those dragons Norhi, he was incredible, not requiring anyone's help to tangle with them. Oh, and the speech afterward—I mean, his voice boomed in our ears; it was magnificent."

"He fought them alone?" Thinking about what might have happened; Norhi paced the room for some time until it hit him. "The dragons have an ability that allows them to extract energy from their opponents. It's the only thing that makes sense to me. Did you see the entire confrontation that took place between Patel and the dragons?"

Nyeve answered, "Yes. Well, no. Some of it, I guess; I don't know."

Puzzled and confused by her answer, Norhi continued. "Okay—better yet, tell me what you do remember of the fight."

Nyeve, staring down at Patel, said, "Everything happened rather quickly. Vul and I had just begun the attack on the ariyons' rear when these large dragons— four, I think—swooped down and started attacking our soldiers with great ferocity. I was fighting two enemy soldiers when one of the dragons came at me. I remember feeling a little tired on its approach, but the feeling went away quickly because Patel came out of nowhere and wrestled it to the ground. The jungle obscured most of the fight, but when a second dragon dived at the two fighting, Patel must have thrown his opponent at it, because they collided in midair and fell into a ravine close to the outer road. That was it; then he had to take on a different dragon, and he sent it into the abyss. Once the dragon disappeared, Patel took to the air and gave an ultimatum, which they accepted, and the battle was done. Vul was so upset with Patel for letting the ariyon survivors leave, he took off. That's all I remember, Norhi. Sorry."

Sympathetic he replied,"No, no, your story helps me to confirm what I thought. These creatures have the ability to draw energy from us. I think we possess the same abilities to draw from them, but what happens to the energy once it is extracted, I just don't know."

Suddenly, Nyeve jumped up and down like a child excited to be getting a treat. "I remember something else. I do! I do! Patel pulled the horns from one of the dragons that he sent into the abyss. The other two lost a horn apiece when they slammed into each other—I remember! I remember!"

Lost, Norhi asked, "Okay, so what. Some horns came up missing. How does that help us?"

Excitedly, she explained. "No, listen; when Patel grabbed the horns, they glowed. In fact, anytime one of the dragons came close to him, the horns would give off a glow. Once my love pulled the horns off, the dragon became weak like a baby. The horns are the answer, Norhi. We pull off the horns which extract energy from us and we're good to go!"

Nodding to show his acceptance of her explanation, Norhi turned to Patel and said, "Removing the horns may make them weak, but we have a fellow shifter here that possesses no horns and lies unresponsive. There must be a way to revive him, but I don't know how—unless it's dependent on time alone. If that's the case, Ny, he'll be vulnerable. We must get him underground."

As they pondered over what to do with Patel, a bright bluish light filled the room, and from within the light a figure emerged. Silently, the entity moved toward Patel and placed what appeared to be a red-hot coal on his beak. A white glow branched out from the coal and encompassed Patel's entire body. Suddenly, he morphed into human form. He turned his head and opened his eyes to see the angel. Smiling, he thanked Airmuse for the assistance and sat up in bed. Airmuse glanced at the three shifters and said, "Your tribulations will be many, my children, and power can be drained from you by angelics, so take care." He waved his hand over the floor, and seven smooth and clear large spheres of pure quartz appeared. "Within the spheres, energy is produced and stored that you may use to energize after an encounter with those who have fallen. Calamity sits upon the horizon which must be faced by you. This is the last I will appear before you until the time of the end. Prepare yourselves, and always trust in the Lord of Hosts." The light and Airmuse disappeared, leaving the three to wonder what he meant by "the time of the end." It could wait, though, because Nyeve was happy to see her man awake and healthy. Excited about Patel's recovery as well, Norhi decided to leave as Nyeve was kissing Patel. He decided to leave the couple alone. Outside the room, Norhi gave instructions to the guards that no one was to enter without his permission.

Nyeve loved Patel because of how much he loved everyone else. Not a day went by that he didn't think of helping a person in need. When she heard from Vul he had allowed the ariyons to drop their weapons and leave the battlefield unmolested, her heart had flown that much higher toward the sky that was his heart. What she failed to say verbally was made known through her loving physical prowess. She wanted Patel to know beyond all doubt that she was his now and forever. He felt the exact same way about her. After hours of lovemaking, the two fell spent onto the bed, drifting off into a deep slumber full of peace and silence.

Four angels entered Demar's citadel. They were summoned by Azel, who stated an emergency existed that required their assistance. In the golden throne room, Azel sat upon the seat of power when they entered. "I did not summon Larz, only you three; why is he here?" Azel had never cared for Larz because he had too much of a good streak running through him. While the others didn't mind breaking celestial law, provided something was in it for them.

Torel said, "We are a team—a team which was here before you and your knuckleheaded brothers decided to take human wives and defile yourselves with animals. Now then, what do you want?"

Azel squirmed slightly in his seat. "Before you pass any kind of judgment against us, you better check yourself first. We didn't teach the humans secret knowledge in alchemy, sciences, and levitation capabilities. Sure, we had our fun with the women of this planet—so what? Very few of them resisted, and we brought forth great races of men—men of renown and great power. What have you created?"

"Azel, I don't think we are here to confess sins committed by any one of us, so why are we here, and what is it with you and your reptilian appearance? It's repulsive to us. Please change to a more angelic look, if you don't mind."

Azel moved quickly from the throne to Torel, Azel reached out, and took him by the throat, lifting the angel off the ground. Bringing him close to his face, Azel said, "Don't you dare say a word about my appearance. Don't… say… a word!" Azel released Torel and moved back toward the throne, speaking as he went. "We are stuck in this form, powerless to change back into angelics, and we don't know why."

Looking around the room, Larz asked, "Who is we, Azel? I see only you in the room."

"There are… were… four of us. Bael, Stul, Ridep, and yours truly—we are Bael's dragons." After Mutt brought out chairs for the visiting angels, Azel explained all that had happened, including Bael's fate of being sentenced to the abyss. Listening to every word on the edge of their seats, the four couldn't believe what they were hearing but knew they were as culpable as, if not more than, Azel's crew for interfering with the progression of mankind.

Once Azel fell silent, Tubel spoke. "Dear brother, we have also fallen under Lucifer's spell in dealing with the men of dust. We fed them information and related secret teachings as well. Things have gotten out of control, and we all need to work to fix this mess before the Lord gets involved. It amazes me that He hasn't involved Himself yet, which makes me think we are being given a chance to deal with all of this ourselves. He's very forgiving and quite patient, but there are limits."

Larz replied, "Man was meant to cease to exist by its own hand. What Lucifer required of all of us was to bring his vision to pass, which we failed in. Gentlemen, we were all tricked into doing evil against a part of God's creation. The best thing to do now is to stop, face the Lord, and ask for His forgiveness. Let's return to our stations as celestial beings of the Father rather than puppets to a rogue angelic."

Amazed at Larz' words and annoyed with the being, Torel said, "Larz, are you preaching to us as to what is evil and good? Who are you to question Lucifer and judge us in the process? You're right, though, in that we started this and will finish it with Lucifer as our leader. If fear has entered your heart because of what's happened so far, then leave, but don't think the rest of us feel the need to shame ourselves by turning against our oaths to Lucifer. In time, he will take charge of heaven and we will be rewarded for our efforts."

"Torel is correct," said Azel, "and this goes for all of you. Turning from Lucifer now will do us no good. We are marked by his hand, and our oaths cannot be revoked. Stand with him, Larz, or fall, but you fall alone."

Answering Larz stated, "Since when did God's angel's exchange wisdom for folly? Our loyalties are to the Father—the Creator, and not the created! I'll not have any more to do with this ill-conceived plan or its architects. I go to turn myself in and pray for mercy. I urge all of you one last time to do the same. Accept judgment now rather than later, my brothers—please." Deep silence stifled and crept into every part of the room they were in, and then each in turn gave his back to Larz as an answer to his plea. Nodding, Larz turned and disappeared, making his way back to heaven and his fate.

Once he was gone, Lucifer's angelics plotted their next moves. First, they needed to turn man against themselves. Something their leader had wanted from the very beginning. Second, they needed to receive positions from Lucifer placing them above other luminaries that they may bask in the glow of God's glory to reap the benefits. The only obstacle seemed to be the shifters acting as mankind's personal protectors on earth. They needed more information on this threat before acting again, since the powerful foe possessed skills and abilities far above those of regular men.

Pondering the threat, Azel said, "Lucifer told us shifters are men with powers given to them by watchers. Even though they are not full luminaries, they possess great power. I can vouch for it firsthand; Bael and the other dragons would tell you they are strong!"

"Yes, very well, they have the ability to send us to the abyss," said Torel. What weaknesses did you observe? How best can we deal with these shifters?"

Azel responded, "I saw nothing which could be taken as weakness. Well, some soldiers seemed more prone to death than others. I mean, we attacked the bulk of their troops as they moved against the ariyons, and they were easy to dispatch; but then a large eagle swooped out of the sky, flew past me, then attacked Bael as a large ape. It was very powerful! Actually, he put down Stul and Ridep before dispatching Bael to the abyss. He had to be in charge, because all fighting ceased once he transformed into an eagle again, flying over the battlefield, giving those ariyon soldiers still living a chance to retreat back to this place unharmed. About that time was when I went into a ravine and took hold of Stul and Ridep to bring them here to rest up. So—any thoughts?"

Tubel was the first to speak. "The shifters are not completely angelic and therefore must reside somewhere on this planet. We need to locate and destroy their nest or lair—or whatever it is they live in— along with all of their kind. Otherwise, we will have to fight on two fronts, dividing us once again from Lucifer's stated goal—the destruction of man."

Torel interjected, "I agree with you, brother. However, we need some way to keep safe from being placed into the abyss by those animals. What can we do to protect ourselves from them?"

None of the angelics spoke until Torel continued. "Exactly! We don't know how, and therefore we can do nothing until we find a way to protect ourselves from the shifters, which means we need Lucifer here. Now! We need him to tell us what our options are with regards to the enemy; otherwise, I'm going to do nothing, my friends. This is not my project; nor is it yours—other than that we all have desires to secure higher stations for ourselves. So whose mission is this? Lucifer's, and he needs to equip us for it or forget it!"

Just when each member was set to agree with Torel, Lucifer appeared before them and answered him with a voice rich in syrupy sarcasm. "Imagine my elation upon hearing my fellow comrades speak so confidently about my plans for man. Truly awe-inspiring—melts the heart."

Surprised at first, Torel answered, "Enough of your quips, Lucifer. We need real assistance if you expect your plans to see the light of day."

Biting back Lucifer responded, "Light has nothing to do with it, my dear Torel, it requires deep darkness and the strength of great luminaries to pull it off. What? Did you expect everything to be easy? We are fighting to destroy a piece of God's creation: not some rebellious system of higher-ordered intelligences, but rather the gnats and bloated flies under the protection of Him. So it's going to take some time and energy to destroy it! I need the strength and power of angelics—powers and principalities—to pull it off, and that's why I came to those present. Do I have strong luminaries or weak men before me? I need to know now if my plans require alterations."

Speaking up for the first time in a very long time, Deenal asked, "Why is it important to you, Lucifer? Why must men be destroyed? As you pointed out, mankind is nothing—insects."

Lucifer fixed upon Deenal a gaze meant to burn a hole through him as he answered, "Because He loves them… more than us. Can you imagine being in His presence and hearing such a thing? I will use every resource available to bring about man's total destruction with or without your help."

Azel wasted no time giving an answer for the group. "Lucifer, you know we are here for you, but we require protection or a weapon—something to use against these shifters."

Thinking for a moment as he paced about the room, Lucifer said, "There is something I can do under celestial law. It's not much, but anything is better than nothing, right?"

Excited, Tubel asked, "What? What is it? A weapon of some kind—tell us!"

"I'm authorized to alter frequencies of both nature and luminaries. However, balance must be kept at all times, which means I cannot alter angelics unless they give consent, and only two of nature's four dimensions may I change, ever."

The others looked around at each other with great confusion, and Tubel replied, "Okay, so what does that mean?"

Lucifer explained, "It means I can produce havens, such as space and water for instance. By changing the frequencies at which you and, say, water and space vibrate, a barrier to the shifters is produced, making it impossible for them to enter space or bodies of water."

Azel was still confused and asked, "Lucifer, we can do these things now, just as we are. Space and water—actually any form of matter—are nothing to us. Why do we need to be changed?"

Lucifer replied, "My dear Azel, you of all angelics should know this. You and the rest of the dragons enjoyed the daughters of men, producing hybrids. Changing your frequencies will ensure your spawn make use of the barriers as well."

Torel stated, "Anything is better than nothing, Lucifer. Make it so and we will start to create an army to replace the one devastated by the shifters."

His brother Tubel shot back, "Easy, brother, before speaking for any of us. We need to think about what's being presented. The barriers are fine with me, but I will not—will *not*—defile myself with an animal for anyone or anything, including new stations!"

"What are you trying to say, Tubel?" said Azel. "I'm defiled? That I am less of an angelic than you because I knew many daughters of man? I'd be very careful talking about something of which you have no knowledge, my friend!" Suddenly the room erupted with many words of damnation exchanged, leading to a physical brawl among the team.

Prior to the fight breaking out, Lucifer had moved to the throne. He now sat upon it watching while shaking his head. After a time, a brilliant light shot forth from the throne area, knocking the group to the ground and blinding them each from the other. As the light subsided, Lucifer spoke. "This is the great wisdom of the luminaries—infighting, cursing, jealousy? Is your confidence in me and the mission such that you must act like the very creatures you are expected to extinguish? The brawling amongst you ends now! Cooperation with one another is paramount; I'll accept nothing else. To ensure this"—He stood with arms raised—"I alter the dimensions of space and water. Barriers of vibration against your enemies they shall be—havens to my elect from now until the end. Tubel, you shall dominate space, while Torel controls the seas and bodies of water upon the earth. Azel shall control land, sea, and air to bring calamity within and without. And so shall it be."

Feeling a bit dejected Deenal spoke up. "Not to incur your wrath, Lucifer, but what is my charge, if any?"

Lucifer nodded. "Yes, Deenal, of course. You shall assist all three with their areas and create for yourself a base of operations from my base on Mars until further notice. Perhaps we can place a satellite above the earth later for you to work from, but right now Mars will have to do. Now, please take your seats and I will explain my plans for the future."

Sitting in front of the throne on chairs of silver and gold, the angelics listened as Lucifer told them of his plans. "Some of you worried about whether defiling yourself with an animal was necessary—it is not. In an area on the surface of the earth and known only by me, a servant is busying himself with creating an army—an army of darkness. Serpent and Lilith, as we speak, are hard at work producing spawns which will worship and serve only me, following my every command."

Torel, under his breath, said, "Demoniacs— heresy."

Having heard him, Lucifer responded, "Yes, dear Torel, demons under my control. And when I have taken my rightful place in heaven, heresy will no longer exist. Far too long have I sat and watched as parts of His creation deserving of destruction are forgiven and reinstated. I will not forgive, and mercy will be an obsolete concept relegated to the past. We will ensure all things are in submission—and remain in submission—to us, or they shall perish to the ground under our feet, where they will remain so that others might see and tremble. Nine days from now, my army will be ready to strike out against those in heaven, and I intend to be sitting upon a throne greater than His by the tenth day. It shall be a great army, my friends, and along with it will be those loyal to me in the heavens. I intend on taking over all of creation, and when I do, you will be my generals, holding stations higher than any other luminary—aside from myself, of course. Questions—I'm sure there are many; please feel free to ask them."

Azel inquired, "Lucifer, your plan is—well, both complicated and foolish. Nine days—I assume that means nine thousand earth years? We need an army now to fight against the shifters. Otherwise, what's the point? Are we to wait until you take over heaven and then deal with man? Why should we put ourselves in harm's way for nothing? Do you really think enough of the heavenly realm will follow you against the Creator?"

Torel said, "I agree; what makes you think overcoming the Lord will be so easy?"

Annoyed but patient Lucifer replied, "Leave that to me, brothers. I have it all under control. Just focus on what your rewards will be when I am in charge. As for mankind, I need you to keep working toward their demise so that the watchers along with other angelics are kept busy. While they deal with you, their focus is off of me. There will be times when I must protest against your actions to keep up appearances. Keep that in mind when I chastise you in front of other luminaries. This will work; be confident and keep your place. I assure you the rewards will be great. And no fighting amongst yourselves. Stay united in the cause, and good luck with the shifters. I must leave now but will return in time."

A bright light winked out from the throne area and Lucifer left the five angels to sit and ponder over what their leader had just told them. Deenal still had more questions than answers, but he knew asking would be pointless. Lucifer will return when Lucifer returns and not before. As they spoke amongst themselves, the idea on how to test the new boundaries made by Lucifer to restrain shifters from entering water or space came up.

All eyes turned to Deenal making the entity very nervous. "Hey, now wait just a minute, everyone! I do not now, nor will I in the future, desire to test our incredibly skilled enemies on how barriers work in the realm of earth. What about Azel or one of the other dragons? They're bigger, faster, and far scarier than little old me."

Answering Azel said, "This is true, but you are the least-ranking in our group, and one should always send the least-ranking person into a potentially dangerous situation."

Deenal shook his head. "Says who?"

Azel shrugged. "Well—I don't know; that's just the way it is. Now go out there and get one to follow you into a pool of water or lake or something and see if he can get at you."

Still shaking his head, Deenal said, "Oh, no—not this angelic, pal. You want one, you go get it!"

Torel stepped forward and said, "Enough, the both of you! I'll go and round up a shifter; after all, the waters are my domain now. Azel, I want you to keep close but out of sight. If the barrier fails to work, you will need to come to my assistance—immediately! Will that suffice for everyone?"

The other angels stated their approval with great enthusiasm and then set out to devise a way to draw out one of their enemies and decide where it should take place. Since Torel was taking most of the risk, he decided on a lake close to Utt's former citadel. A cavernous tunnel a stadia from the surface ran and linked up to a pond just outside of Demar's citadel. The brothers had it excavated and filled to ensure fresh water supplied wells scattered between their dwellings for human slaves that were used to build roads and conduct mining operations for precious metals. Additionally, the lake had two mountains on its west side, giving Azel a place to hide and spring from if Torel needed help. Tubel and Deenal would remain in Demar's citadel along with Stul and Ridep in case their experiment led to shifters mounting an assault against the castle. Torel decided to wait until first light before starting out. Azel agreed. The two rehearsed the plan over and over again, first on paper and then using the pond next to the castle, hoping everything would go well the next day.

Chapter 22

Entering Patel's domicile, located within Utt's citadel, Vul, with a typical swagger that oozed arrogance from every pore, sat before his supposed leader to begin an interrogation wrought in sarcasm over earlier actions. "Well, I see we are doing fine now. And how was our rest, then, hmm?"

Patel was very aware that Vul could care less about his physical state or any other state for that matter, yet he was curious himself about actions taken by Vul at the end of the battle. "Only because of your assistance am I still among the living. Thank you for saving me. May I ask why you did it?"

Vul shook his head. "Please, don't mention it. Ever! I mean that sincerely. The fact is, you are still among us, and I did not come here to listen to gratitude bellowing out from my 'leader.' Speaking of leadership and the reason for my presence here, dear Patel, why did you allow the enemy to retreat from the battlefield unharmed? Why did you interfere with my war plans? How is it that you somehow knew about those flying reptiles coming to the assistance of our enemy? And how did you know how to defeat them, since the other day was our first time encountering such creatures? Can you explain that, dear comrade?"

Cautiously Patel mulled over answers in his head before speaking, knowing full well Vul's volatility and his being prone to physical confrontations rather than verbal debate. After all, it was Vul who had saved him from plunging into the earth and perhaps the open arms of death.

Patel smiled. "Tell you what, Vul, I'll answer every part of your question if you'll tell me why you saved me the other day."

Frowning, Appearing annoyed with the question, Vul stood up and turned his back to Patel. "For whatever reason, I was compelled to do so. It wasn't something I wanted to do, but I did it." He swung around and stared Patel directly in the eyes Vul continued, "Now, answer my questions—leader."

A confident and compassionate smile jump-started his answer. "For whatever reason, Vul, I too was compelled to do so."

Vul sneered. "How convenient and typical— use my own words against me. Nice, nice. I bet you're proud of yourself—always finding a way to use my words to your advantage."

Cutting in, Patel replied, "Vul, I never intended—"

Interrupting and shooting back, Vul said, "Save it, Patel; I've grown weary of your explanations. Why the watchers chose you as leader over me, I will never understand. I am a man of action! Of blood! We need to completely destroy the enemy, not coddle them and show them mercy. Do you think for one moment they would have shown us the same compassion you showed them?"

Calmly Patel answered, "No, they would have annihilated every last one of us. It is for that reason, Vul, that we show mercy and compassion—it's what separates us from them."

Vul snickered. "No, Patel, what separates us from them is knowledge, not mercy. I have scouted out other settlements, watching as these hybrids teach our people how to manipulate blocks of stone the size of mountains to build fortresses and cities. They teach them how to melt rock and pour it into molds to design temples honoring the hybrids and their fathers. You and I have both felt the enemy's blades. How strong and superior their metal is opposed to ours. They use flying carpets, attacking us from the skies with great numbers of soldiers, Patel. You want to talk about mercy when we have none of this for ourselves.

"The next settlement that you want to liberate possesses technologies far greater than anything we've faced. I watched gleaming shields made of metal flying through the sky, leveling walls with rays of fire. The stone forts our people hid in, the people were fearful of the attacks from the hybrids. The hybrids teach the people how to fly these things so they can sit back and relax as people engage one another in battle—and you want to speak of compassion?"

Patel's answer was not what Vul was looking for, but he knew deep down it was what he would receive. "Yes—yes, Vul, because we are not them. What they have done destroys more than taking a life could ever do. These rogue angelics are turning the hearts of men from the Lord, even turning them against themselves. I'm not foolish, though; you may mistake my compassion for weakness. I wish I knew the words which would set your mind at ease, dear brother, but it appears I do not. We need to be above our foe in character, because as you have pointed out, the angelics are training man to battle against man for them. If you had to stand before a fellow brother that is lost to the 'hybrids,' as you call them, what would you do—strike him down or try to reason with him instead? As we evolve in battling the angelics, so they change their tactics as well, to the point that we will soon fight against our own people—our own flesh. Taking the heads of giants and ariyon soldiers is one thing, but to fight our people—I can't imagine."

Growing weary of Patel and his excuses, Vul sighed, "If you wish to keep this mind-set of yours, then so be it. I have a responsibility to the people as well, and that's to keep them safe from the enemy. I'm taking those shifters loyal to me and will set up an empire of my own. I tell you this so you will not be kept in the dark about my intentions. Heed this as well: do not attempt to interfere! If I am wrong in what I'm doing, won't your invisible God stop me like He stopped the hybrids from becoming lords over us and our people? Oh, wait—He didn't, did He?"

Shocked but not surprised with his plans or attitude Patel replied, "Vul, I'm tired of fighting with you over every little thing that doesn't go your way. If taking people under you will make a difference, then Godspeed, and if your actions are not in keeping with His plans, then may it be as you say—the Lord rebuke you. Take only those with the will and desire to follow you. Force no one, or I will come against you with all my power. A divided camp serves nothing, and yet you wish to do this thing. I only hope wisdom comes to you before it's too late."

Vul smiled. "Don't worry about me, pal; I'll be just fine!"

Shooting back, Patel replied, "It's not you I worry for. Remember, Vul, the shifters we created are imperfect in that they have the ability to change into many forms but possess less wisdom to control themselves, meaning that they may very well turn against their leader."

Vul nodded. "The same goes for you, my friend! I'm doubtful I will face conflicts within my ranks before you do. I'm not encumbered by such ideologies as mercy and compassion, as you are, Patel. We'll see whose empire falls first—yours or the Lord's."

Patel shook his head. "Vul, I'm not creating an em—"

Cutting him off as he left the room Vul replied, "Of course, of course; you're too good for that!"

As Vul made his way out of the room, Patel mulled over their conversation in his head. *What is it with that guy anyway? We have enough enemies to deal with; we don't need to make foes within our own ranks. He's correct about one thing—the demigods are training men to go to war against other men. Their technologies are far superior to anything we have, and I'm not sure how to change that to our advantage. I can't call upon the watchers for assistance, so what do I do?*

Norhi stood outside his door but seeing his friend deep in thought, couldn't decide on whether to bother him or not. Glancing over to the door, Patel caught him turning to leave when he yelled out for his comrade to enter the room. "Norhi, my friend, please come in. I was just thinking about you!"

Surprised, Norhi entered the room and, with a manly embrace, took hold of his friend. "You were thinking of me—really?"

Patel chuckled. "Of course, of course, dear friend. Please, take a seat. Norhi, you are one of the most intelligent men I know, and your knowledge is what I need. Tell me, could you construct a working vessel if you saw one?"

Thinking, Norhi said, "A vessel? Sure, anyone could—"

"Really, you're sure? Because I couldn't even if it were in my hands, let alone look at one and copy it."

Norhi gave Patel a quizzical look. "You're pulling my leg, right? I mean, we must have made at least a hundred vessels from the red clay found near the western shore of—

Cutting in Patel replied, "I'm sorry for not being clearer. I'm talking about a flying vessel like the shields of Ecris in the east, or the carpet of the giants— that kind of vessel."

"Oh. Oh—oh no, no; not a chance, Patel. The precision, metallurgy—let alone propulsion systems—I mean… no."

Norhi stood up and paced the room. "If we found one along with a few of their engineers, perhaps—*perhaps*. But don't hold me to anything. Why do you ask?"

Patel explained, "I've kept things from you and the others, but Vul is aware, so I might as well tell you. The angelics are changing up their tactics. Soon we may be facing off against our own kind. They use people to construct everything as it is, and now, using advanced technology, man will go to war against man."

Norhi exhaled a deep breath. "That is hard to take in, but it may work to our advantage. Right now, Nyeve is training shifters on the bow and arrow."

Not understanding how the one had anything to do with the other, he said,

"Okay, but what does that—"

Norhi continued, "Please, Patel, let me finish. We take the time to train our warriors, so they must be training theirs right? If we can find out where they train, we might be able to sneak in, capture a vessel with a few of its crew, and return here to study it and make replicas."

After thinking about it for a moment, Patel said, "Norhi, that sounds like a lot of work, and time that we don't have."

Norhi shrugged. "I'm sorry, Patel, but that's the best I can do. Unless we possessed an intact vessel along with a few engineers, I wouldn't know where to begin."

Patel frowned. "It's not your fault. We'll need to think of some other way, I guess."

"What's wrong with the way we've been doing things? Look how many settlements we've liberated, not to mention underground dwelling places that have been built."

Patel shook his head. "Norhi, we didn't have dragons before now, and believe me when I say fighting them is no easy matter. Plus, Vul is going solo; he's taking those shifters with the same mind-set as his own and building an empire."

Norhi raised his eyebrows. "I didn't know that."

"He told me just before you arrived. Vul is many things detestable, but as a tactician he is unsurpassed. Don't ever tell him I said that, though; it'll only inflate an already out-of-control ego."

Norhi smiled. "Well, it explains why he has taken Ustin under his wing, training the lad in tactics and leadership. I believe he means to make Ustin his second in command. Before coming in here, I heard him talking to the young man about that very subject. Of course you know how Vul enjoys making himself look important among the new shifters, so I really didn't give it much thought, but now…"

This news troubled Patel even further. "I can't stop him, Norhi. Even though I know deep down any small split amongst us will most certainly cause a great rift. Two camps of shifters, which do you follow? Which one is right? No—I think the young men will go with the camp most appealing, dependent on how they are feeling at the time." He paused for a moment. "Do you think I am doing right by God and the people, Norhi? Or are my actions based more on what I want, rather than what is good for others?"

Slapping Patel on the back with a smile on his face, Norhi said, "Patel—that is the most ridiculous question I've ever heard you ask! Believe me; in the past, you had some real whoppers, but you were chosen because of your character to be one of God's champions! Not anyone else—you. Then you picked us for whatever your reasons, and although I questioned Vul being chosen at the time, I understand now. A man may possess a lot of negative qualities on the surface— and I do mean a lot! When it comes to Vul, you looked past it all to see a good quality buried way below the surface of the man. For whatever reason, we needed him, and you knew that from the beginning. Don't ever doubt yourself, Patel. A leader must appear in control at all times, and even if he may not have the slightest idea what to do or where to go, his troops are to think he does."

Patel shook his head in protest. "Norhi, I believe a good leader is a great servant—so what service am I providing by lying to the people? Because if I proclaim to know the answers and don't, eventually the people will see this and distrust me."

Norhi walked across the room in silence, turned, and said, "What are you doing right now? Questioning—trying to find answers to recent problems in counsel and out of the earshot of people and shifters alike, right? There is no deception, but as far as the people know, their protector is taking care of them. You are always concerned about their welfare rather than your own. You are a great servant of the people, Patel, and that's the plain truth of it. Stop questioning and keep serving as you've done from the very start."

A smile of gratitude and a nod was all Patel needed to give his friend in response.

"And hey, I'll always be around to give a slap upside your head when needed."

Norhi had Patel laughing. "Gee, thanks."

Norhi smiled and nodded. "No need to thank me; after all, it's what friends are for."

At that moment, a trumpet sounded, alerting the citadel of an enemy's presence. Running from the room, Patel and Norhi went to find out what one of their foes could possibly be doing so close to them.

Vul and Ustin were the first to respond outside the citadel walls, where they saw a being hovering over the lake on its' farthest side. Vul hollered up to the shifter that spotted the entity, commending him on his alertness. Turning his attention back to the being, he looked the area over thinking to himself that the whole situation seemed odd. Keeping his gaze fixed on the entity Vul asked Ustin what he thought.

With his head tilted, Ustin said, "I think it's only one being—maybe a spy or lookout, sir."

Vul said, "If he were a spy, my dear boy, he'd be a very poor one. Detected so far from his objective? As far as a lookout, it's quite doubtful, since there is no smoke from troop fires in the distance. No, it's certainly strange indeed." Looking to see where the sun was positioned in the sky, Vul devised a plan to capture the entity. "Ustin, listen carefully; I believe there is only one being over there for whatever reason, and I intend on finding out why. I need you to slowly sneak up toward where he is on land, using brush and trees to partially conceal yourself from him. Every now and again as you approach, let the entity see you. I'm going inside and leaving through the other gate to the exterior. I'll then take to the sky and use the sun to blind him from my approach and take him by surprise from the sky, understand?"

Nodding, Ustin morphed into a jackal and stealthily made his way toward the being. Soaring through the sky, Vul placed his trajectory with the sun to his back, making his way toward the being. He could tell that the entity's focus was squarely upon Ustin, who was dodging in and out of trees and brush that lined the lake's shore. Once he felt he was close enough, Vul retracted his wings and dived vertically toward his prey. Catching a glimpse of something in the sky, the being quickly sank into the water. Thinking he could still catch the being, Vul continued his descent, slamming hard into the water's surface without penetrating it. He lay crumpled motionless as sprays of water thrown up from the impact landed around and on top of him. Ustin ran to his mentor, shocked to find that the water had become hard. Reaching Vul, he asked, "Vul—Vul, are you all right? Can you hear me, sir? Are you all right?"

Opening his eyes and looking up at the young man, Vul said in a low, pain-filled tone, "Ustin, we have a problem."

Patel and Norhi, who had been watching the action from outside the citadel, made their way to the shifters. Staying along the shore until they arrived where Vul lay atop the lake, the men were baffled at the characteristics of the water. They walked across it, taking cautionary steps, to their fallen comrade. After confirming that Vul was not mortally wounded, and with a breath of relief, all four shifters focused their attention on the lake.

Patel was the first to speak. "Norhi, have you ever seen such a thing?"

Norhi bent down and waved his hand through the water and noticed he could splash and even drink from it, but his hand was blocked by some kind of force that kept him from penetrating any farther. He stood, turned to Patel and said, "In the high mountains like the ones over there in the distance, pools and ponds freeze solid due to cold air, but this is not that. This is a barrier of energy. Can you feel the vibration from it? And a very low hum is even audible. It's not from nature—it's not natural. In my opinion, our enemies have placed it here. Did you notice how the entity was able to descend beneath the waves with ease, whereas our friend here was abruptly halted from following after?"

Vul slowly got to his feet after morphing into a lion-headed man, Vul angrily responded, "So these demons are able to generate force fields now? Well that's just great! How do we fight against a power like that, fearless leader? They can have at us while staying safe and free from any retaliatory attack we dare launch—let alone even thinking of protecting ourselves from them!"

Patel shot back, "Vul, shut up; you're not even a part of the group anymore, right? We need level-headed thinking about this. Now, I think it was a test! It's a test to see if the barrier worked—but why the lake? Why not try it on land?"

Annoyed with what he considered a waste of time, Vul replied, "Probably because it could escape under the water. Who in the blazes cares why? Norhi, please talk some sense into this guy; he's your friend. We are getting nowhere with this; let's send a legion of men against them now before they use this barrier on a larger scale."

Looking around the area, Norhi suddenly lit up. "Patel is correct. Why the lake? Look over there close to the shoreline and you will see a cave entrance which extends about six and a half stadia to the west. This being could have lured you there just as easily as here—so why the water?" He ran to the shore, grabbed a large stone, and returned to the group. "Now watch." He threw the stone farther into the interior of the lake, and everyone watched as it splashed and sank to the bottom.

Once again, Vul's temper manifested itself as he spoke. "Great. I thought you were the intelligent one out of the two of you, but I was wrong. Why am I surrounded by nitwits that want to show me how far they can throw stones? What next, Norhi? Let's play tag, or perhaps hide-and-seek, maybe—hmm?"

Norhi changed into a cheetah. "What a great idea! Tag—you're it!" He took off across the surface of the lake with a cheetah's grace and speed, turning this way and that, making contact with each side of the lake's shoreline before returning to the group. He then morphed back into his human form and said, "See, the whole lake is a barrier, and I'll bet you every body of water is the same way. Somehow limits were assigned to nature, keeping us from penetrating water completely."

Laughing it off, Vul said, "Ridiculous. You are definitely out of your mind on this notion, Norhi— getting as bad as your friend."

"Then how do you explain what I just did—running across the length and breath of this lake?"

Vul pointed to the lake. "Just because you did it here doesn't mean every body of water is off-limits to us, idiot. This area is affected; this one here, and that's all! Besides, if water were somehow off-limits, we wouldn't last too long, let alone people. Such foolishness!"

Patel cut in. "There's only one way to find out if Norhi's hypothesis holds water—no pun intended. We each find a body of water—ocean, river, pool—and try to enter it. Second, it would appear that we have access to the water for bathing and drinking, Vul. It splashes and coats us as we move across it; we just cannot enter it."

Relenting, Vul answered, "Fine I'll play your silly game; but know this, the both of you: Ustin and I will round up our followers and move off to an area where we can properly build our own empire. It's bad enough he must endure these foolish and fruitless escapades you two put together—every place holding a large body of water off-limits my left foot."

As they walked off toward the ocean, which was conveniently adjacent to the old village, Patel said, "You know, Vul, it's that sense of cooperation and understanding which makes everyone feel so at ease when in your presence—that's awe-inspiring."

"Blow it out your ear!" Vul bellowed.

***

Reaching his own citadel, Azel, still in dragon form, looked for Torel and found the entity gloating in the throne room. "I saw the whole thing, Torel, and may I say congratulations on a successful mission."

Laughing, Torel shrugged. "It was nothing, really. But I tell you this: never again will I underestimate the cunning and craftiness of our enemy. That vulture practically made me its carrion; they were very clever to keep my focus on the jackal that crept its way toward me."

Azel pointed out, "I wouldn't rule out overconfidence making you... shall we say... careless."

"Yes, well, you are entitled to your opinion. Regardless, the barrier does work—quite well. I say we take an army through the underwater tunnel and raid their stronghold by surprise. Then you can lead the dragons from the sky and assist in the attack."

A grim look of puzzlement crossed Azel's reptilian face. "Superior thinking—spot on, really, except for one slight detail: our remaining army is composed of halflings! They would not survive the long swim underwater. Good thought, though."

As if a veil had lifted from his mind, Torel said, "Hybrids—right, right. My apologies; the idea of ending the shifter's reign on this accursed rock clouded my thinking." Pacing back and forth within the confines of the throne room, Torel searched his mind for a better way to attack, with relative safety, his rivals.

Azel sat upon the throne, watching as his comrade moved about the floor wondering what possible plans he might conceive to bring about the demise of the shifters. Just as he was about to nod off from a lack of energy, Azel shot to attention upon hearing a shriek of excitement from Torel. "My dear dragon, I have it! We will travel to the southeast, where the giants Hamath and Karish reign. They have developed flying machines which they use to take halfling angelics and humans into space to study the stars, the universe, so forth and so on, but the vehicles should do just as well underwater."

"Think about this for just a moment. There is a vehicle which can transport non-celestials through space unharmed and you want to use it—in water? Why not fly straight to them, Torel, cutting out the water way altogether?"

Frustrated, Torel explained, "Azel, if we are to succeed, we must be able to attack quickly—take them by total surprise or face swift interception while still in the air, giving our enemy a perfect target to hone in on and destroy. The vehicles hold about thirteen personnel, including the pilot. Now think of losing them in just one attack by a single foe. Six of them could, in theory, eliminate seventy eight of our troops. No—surprise is our only chance. In all honesty, neither of us knows what their full capabilities are, and I don't want to be taken by surprise—do you?"

Azel let out a long, deep sigh. "I do not. Lucifer has done enough with 'surprises' to last me an eternity; I don't need the enemy providing more of the same."

Chapter 23

Large flakes of snow blew wildly at the most northern apex of the planet. Giant gusts of wind tore frozen tufts of ice from mountain peaks, only to release it back to them. An enormous entrance some seven hundred stadia in circumference was hidden from sight by the blizzards of the north, but Lucifer was very knowledgeable of its existence, for within the earth huge continents moved about on rivers of molten magma. Heat from the magma rose, melting snow and ice to form water all around the entrance. That water was then funneled through an extensive network of dormant lava tubes, providing fresh water for plant and animal life to thrive far away from the surface.

Varieties of reptiles ranging from small to large roamed the continents. All of them were fearful of Lucifer and stayed a good distance from him whenever he was present. There were only two animals he had hidden within the inner world that most interested the angelic, though, and that was the reason for his visit this day. He heard them before catching sight of the pair and rushed over to meet with the couple.

As usual, they were raging at one another, oblivious to his arrival. While sitting quietly atop a boulder, Lucifer listened and watched the volatile situation unfold.

Lilith shrieked. "Why I ever agreed to mate with a hideous beast I'll never know!"

"Hideous! Hideous? You're no beauty queen yourself, sister! Why is it you have to moan and groan about every little thing? 'The water is too cold… now it's too hot. Why can't you kill a mammal and bring it home for dinner for a change of pace?' Look around you, Lilith; not much variety in the way of meats, dear. Reptiles—reptiles for as far as the eye can see! I'd need to go to the surface for anything different, but you won't let me go by myself, and when I ask you to go with me—Oh, no! 'I don't feel like it; besides, too many women are up there, and they might seduce you away from me.' Geez, give it a break already! Another thing: why, if I'm so hideous, do you even care if I am seduced away from you by another woman or two?"

Laughing fully now, she sarcastically replied, "Or two? Someone sure thinks highly of himself! No woman anywhere dreams or desires a green scaly thing to lie with; we want power, fame, and wealth, as well as physical strength and virility!"

An annoyance and feeling of frustration infused Serpent's response. "Just be happy with what you have, because I'll tell you something: no one else would have you. You're the whole purpose I'm here in the first place—against my will, I might add. You materialistic, shallow, self-centered, egotistical she-demon."

It was then Lucifer made his presence known. "Please, please. I truly hate to see my number-one couple at odds with one another. We have work that needs to be done, and throwing barbs at each other is unproductive. Speaking of productivity, how is my army coming along?"

A great silence fell like a thick blanket with neither wanting to speak until finally Lilith said forcefully, "Come with me and I'll show you the beginnings of your wretched army. Perhaps my other half can leave and go hunting for a mammal or two for dinner while I take you around. Do you think you can handle a simple task like that, Serpent, dear?" His head low, he nodded and left Lucifer to incur the remainder of her wrath, all the while feeling as though he was free from Lilith, even if it was for only a short time.

As Lilith and Lucifer walked along the hard crust of the earth's inner core, Lilith led him to different caverns that held various entities that made up his army. "These are my darling shadow men, or mastemas. Each is capable of possessing the bodies of men while remaining invisible to their sight, so they can easily tempt mankind into doing evil toward one another. My sweet mastemas lack wisdom but latch on to any task given them with great ferocity."

Lucifer nodded and smiled. "Very good, Lilith—very good. Can they reproduce on their own—to make more if needed?"

She shook her head. "I'm afraid not, but with a little more time I could generate enough of them. I doubt you'll require more anyway. Now we move to another cave, where I've taken great steps to ensure the next soldiers are quite intelligent."

Walking some distance from the first cave, they arrived at the mouth of a second and entered. Stepping into a large auditorium, Lucifer marveled at what he beheld. Large numbers of entities moved to and fro, busily constructing various machines of different sizes and shapes. Some of the beings entered and flew a few of the machines around the room and even to the outside of the cavern, which had a vast opening at its apex. His awe turned to confusion, however, when he focused on the beings' appearances. Some were tall and others short, with large bulbous heads that held two large, dark almond-shaped eyes. The rest of their bodies were very thin, making their heads seem out of proportion. The skin was a grey, bluish-pink hue, which Lucifer found most unusual. "Lilith, I must say that you have given birth to quite a variety of beings, but why are these so … different from the others?"

She laughed. "Diversity, my dear angelic, just as in heaven and on earth. The samaels here are quite different because they possess different skills and abilities. Although mankind can perceive them better than the shadow men, their intellect will keep them safe from capture or harm. The machines you see will give them the advantage of attacking from the sky or large bodies of water, allowing them to slay more rather than a few. The ariyon spawn of fallen angelics have the same technologies, so they should all get along nicely, wouldn't you say?"

Pondering all she had showed him, Lucifer wasn't sure. "Who really knows? One can only hope. How soon before I can have them? I'm in a real time crunch here."

Teasingly, Lilith replied, "Time is such an illusory concept, isn't it? Besides, if you want the best, it takes a little time. Come with me and I will show you something magnificent!"

Lucifer bantered with her. "Lil, illusory or not, I need this army to be ready very soon. Second, the last time you said there was something magnificent to show and share with me, I barely escaped undefiled from your grasp."

Coyly glancing back at him as they walked on, Lilith brought Lucifer to a third cavern, which held three leathery, transparent, oval-shaped structures suspended from a low ceiling by a thick thread made of the same material as the structures. Something appeared to move and trilled from within a greenish-yellow fluid of some kind. Lilith hugged and caressed each one as she spoke to them as only a mother could to her children.

Scrunching his face, Lucifer asked, "What are they, Lil?"

Responding she said, "These, dear Lucifer, are my pride and joy—three of the most powerful demons ever to exist. Immortals of first caliber, and oh so rare—none shall surpass or come after them. They are a product of a liaison between Stul and me; and a wonderful affair it was indeed."

Lucifer was taken aback, "Stul? Lilith, I brought you a person to sire my army. There was a reason I didn't want any angelics mating with you. The army must be comprised of the seed of man and demon, not demon and angelic! When did this take place, and how was it kept from me?"

She answered defiantly, "You don't need to know everything that goes on, Lucifer. You're not God, and it happened before you brought me that reptile of a man you call perfect. Writhing, developing within these cocoons—here is perfection. They cannot be killed by man. Their appearance is in the form of mankind, but they will be exceedingly beautiful—one male and two females. My seductive abilities course through their veins; they can turn the most pious to a quivering mass of flesh. They will thrive upon energies contained within the corpuscles of their victims, draining them of blood and life force. Perfect killing machines, they will know no fear—more than a match for your enemies." Still caressing and kissing the eggs, Lilith continued, "They are my most precious of all my children."

Impressed, Lucifer asked, "When can I have them? With these three I doubt there will be any troubles with annihilating mankind."

Glancing over toward Lucifer, Lilith said, "Oh, you cannot have them, I'm afraid. They are far too precious for me to give over to you."

Surprised and upset Lucifer responded, "What are you talking about? Can't give them! The whole purpose of you being here is to give life to my army! My army! Not to play house or mother, but to generate spawn to do my bidding and nothing more!" Walking seductively toward him, Lilith attempted to entice the angelic; after all, he wouldn't be the first to fall. Her long, dark hair shimmered and draped over her shoulders, creating a frame that hugged a triangular face. Her strong almond-shaped eyes glistened, beckoning him to take her. Perky breasts slightly obscured from sight by her long, flowing hair gave way to sculpted abs that possessed the jewel that was her navel. Placing her arms over his shoulders, she looked deep into his eyes and, with a teasing smile, said, "Let's not fight with each other over such silly little things. We're on the same side, aren't we? I'm sure we can work something out which would be mutually beneficial for the both of us. Like maybe you and I could bring forth even more powerful demons by loving one another. What do you think, my bright morning star?"

Smiling, Lucifer reached up and took hold of her arms. He pushed her back with great force, causing her to fall hard to the ground. "I told you once; I'll not defile myself with any creatures, let alone one that has had more partners than there are stars in the sky."

"You venomous snake; how dare you judge me! Who do you think you are?"

Haughtily, Lucifer said, "I'm your superior in every way. Now, do I need to bring further pain upon you, or are you going to cooperate? When can I have these specimens?"

"I won't give them to you! They are mine!"
Lucifer moved toward Lilith as she begged. "Wait!
Please—I can't give you the three, but you can have all
their offspring! Just please let me keep my babies."

Glancing over at the eggs, Lucifer asked,
"When will they hatch and be ready to mate?"

She explained, "They are incapable of
reproducing sexually. However, when they bite, venom
is released from their fangs which turn the lifeless
corpse of their victim into one of them—a shadow of
my children. The more they feed, the more they create
copies of themselves. The only thing is, they can only
feed upon the truly lost of mankind."

Lucifer thought for a moment. "If what you say
is true, I'll leave the three in your care; but if not, and I
find that you're trying to deceive me, I'll kill them
myself in front of you before ending your life as well.
Understand?"

Bowing in silence, Lilith stood between him
and her developing offspring, keeping to herself the
limitations those people her children turned would
possess. After all, Lucifer never asked.

Chapter 24

After returning from checking bodies of water for entry, the shifters met in council to speak. Everyone present talked among themselves until Patel rose from the table and motioned for silence. "Thank you for your attention, and I will begin with my findings. In checking every kind of jar, vat, and small man-made pond no larger than two meters deep and just as wide, I was able to place my hand through the waters with no problem. That said, the wells and other larger natural ponds I could not enter."

Norhi nodded. "Yes, and we are blocked from the oceans as well. I couldn't breech the force field below its waves. Another thing: I took along with me two elders, and they had no problem swimming and diving under the surface, which tells me that the enemy will use these areas as bases or fortifications to elude and escape our grasp."

Slamming his fists on the table as he stood, Vul cut in, "Well thank you, Captain Obvious, for such an insightful report! Now, perhaps you can shed some light on how it's being done and what it will take to defeat it? Otherwise, we can be attacked from any body of water these snakes wish to use as a pathway!"

Nyeve spoke up in defense of Norhi, "Vul, stop being abusive and calm yourself. This is new to us, and no one expects Norhi to have all the answers all the time. What do you propose as an answer to this problem, huh? We're all ears; please feel free to share with the whole group."

If it were possible, wisps of smoke would have risen from Vul's ears, physically showing the rage within him. After a moment of silence, Vul turned his gaze from Nyeve to Patel. "Get your wench under control before I do it for you."

Patel lurched out of his chair, shaking, with a burning anger directed toward Vul. "Nyeve is her name—not wench! Nor will you lay one finger on her, or you'll answer to me, as God is my witness!"

Trying to relieve the tension in the room, Norhi said, "Gentlemen, I have an idea to the water barrier problem if anyone is interested. I can explain it—the plan—now!"

All eyes were on Norhi as they waited to hear what he had to say.

"Okay, thank you. Um, I was thinking we could use a vessel to enter the water—a submersible— allowing pursuit of the enemy."

Patel asked, "What type of vessel do you mean?"

Norhi continued, "Far to the south, past the jungles, near a large lake, two great citadels of the giants sit. Within the massive rock walls, an enormous bay holds various machined craft. We may be able to use them to our advantage."

Cutting him short Vul spoke up, "And you know this how? Have you been there and seen these machines, or would this be another wild goose chase?"

It was then that Ustin stood and replied. "Sir, Norhi speaks the truth. I know because I escaped from that evil place—just barely."

Patel asked, "Ustin, why didn't you say something earlier?"

Ustin explained, "Sir, I wanted to but was afraid. I didn't think anyone would assist me in freeing my people—my family unless I helped you first, making it harder for you to turn my request away."

A fatherly look of understanding washed over Patel and could be deciphered in his answer to Ustin. "I can understand your motivation. You show great character, my son, but now I need all the information you possess regarding the citadels and the machines within them."

Shaking his head in disagreement, "Respectfully, I must decline, due to the great dangers involved—many would die."

Placing a hand on the young man's shoulder, Vul prompted, "Ustin, you can tell us. Believe me, we will be fine."

Trembling in rememberance, "Master, it's not any of you I worry for, but my people. Demar and Utt were gentle giants compared to Hamath and his brother."

Slightly irritated with his potential second in command, Vul became stern and pressed for information. "We are running out of precious time, Ustin; the ariyons could attack us any time now, and we are the ones at a disadvantage. So a few people may lose their lives, but the majority will be safe, and that's what counts."

Shock washed across the young lad's face as he listened to the words of his mentor. Turning aside, Ustin addressed Patel. "Sir, I will tell everything and even take you to the fortresses if you promise to free the people before absconding with any ships. If you promise, I will believe you, because you always tell the truth. I could not live knowing my family and others died because of me."

With sincerity in his voice, Patel responded, "Not one craft shall leave its place until all your people are free and safe; you have my word."

A gasp left Vul as he voiced his protest to Patel's statement. "Have you lost what little is left of your mind, Patel? You have no idea of either citadel's strengths or weaknesses, nor the number of enemy soldiers stationed within them!"

Cutting in, Patel stood and adjourned the meeting with a request that Norhi, Vul, and Ustin remain behind for further discussions. As the other members filed out of the room, Patel turned to Vul and said, "People and their safety Vul, is our priority first and foremost. We cannot abandon this ethos or we risk becoming that which we stand against. No innocent life lost is worth any amount of gain that we might obtain, and you know that well. Ustin, your apprentice, is here to help us help them." He turned his attention to Ustin. "That having been said, young one, you should have come to us sooner. Perhaps your people would have been freed before this very day."

Ustin answered humbly. "Sir, freedom for my people has never left my mind, and it wasn't that I did not think you would attempt such a thing. Rather, I wasn't sure you could pull it off."

Ustin took out a large piece of dried animal hide and, using charcoal as a marking utensil, drew a map of the land between them and the land of Hamath. Patel, Norhi, and Vul watched intently as Ustin created symbols and images foreign to the men. Once the drawing was complete, Ustin explained to the group what the images meant and the perils awaiting them. "The journey took me six suns before making it to your border. The jungle is dense and thick with large reptilian life; some are harmful, others not so much. Then, as you come out of the jungle, a large mountain range looms forebodingly in your path. Waterfalls of solid ice cascade down its sides, producing huge knives of frozen water that may come loose and fall upon you at any time.

"There is—was—a pass in between two peaks I used to traverse the mountains, but it may be impassable now. I cannot be sure. On the other side of those mountains, a valley containing all kinds of fruit-bearing trees and vegetation that is good to eat covers the floor all the way up to a giant river which runs parallel, cutting off the bad land from the good. I looked to see if the river ended from atop a mountain peak and could not find its source or ending point— that is how long it is. It also runs quickly from east to west, never stopping or slowing as it goes. At its narrowest, the river is just under a stadia or so—this is where I passed using a thick rope extending from one side to the other. I pulled myself along in a small boat."

Stopping him, Vul cut in and asked, "Where did the boat and rope come from that you used to get across this river?"

Ustin told him, "The boat I made from one piece of wood and the rope was already in place." Everyone could see that Vul was working out something in his mind, which he kept to himself for the meantime. Ustin continued. "Once across the river, everything turns to waste. No vegetation grows, and stones—some jagged and reddish-black—litter and stick up out of the ground like the teeth of a giant snake. In the distance, if you know what to look for, you can just barely see the top of one of the citadels over the horizon. Karish, brother of Hamath, lives in it. He is not as bloodthirsty as Hamath, but he is just as deadly. He does not prefer to eat men raw but well roasted, whereas his brother enjoys drinking the life blood before roasting. As I recall, Karish was quite paranoid after hearing the news of chosen ones running loose in the world. In fact, he doubled the amount of ariyon soldiers protecting his citadel—about a thousand men for each of the four sides."

"Four sides of what?" said Vul.

Ustin described the citadel, "The outer walls. His citadel is configured into one large square with walls sixty-five cubits high and twenty cubits thick—a mountain unto itself."

Norhi questioned Ustin, "Are the machines inside his citadel or Hamath's?"

Ustin shook his head. "Neither. I will explain, but let me finish with the fortresses first, so I leave nothing out." Norhi nodded and gave a smile of apology, and he remained silent until Ustin had completed his report. "Farther south of Karish, about thirty three stadia away, lives his brother Hamath the Terrible—one born of men, sired by those of the heavens. He despises mankind and loathes his father for consorting with the dust and mud of the earth. Rage and vengeance are constant companions to him, turning an already black heart even darker."

Just then, Patel asked, "Vengeance against whom? Mankind? The celestials? Who?"

Ustin answered, "Not who, sir. Vengeance against being born—against the whole idea of it. He didn't ask to be born, and the person he holds ultimately responsible for the abomination that is his life is the Lord of Hosts."

"Then why doesn't he just kill himself and be done with it, making our job easier?"

Ustin explained further, "Hamath believes he must be killed in battle after fighting valiantly. Fighting poorly or killing himself will lead to exile in the abyss. A valiant combat leading to the loss of his life will bring him face-to-face with God, allowing him to strike out against the Lord and take his vengeance—his belief, not mine. So you can see how incredibly unstable Hamath is, thinking he can take on the Creator. We are an annoyance to him—nothing more than insects in need of extermination."

"His citadel," said Vul, "is it the same as his brother's? What is different? I'll be more than happy to make a house call to put him out of his misery."

Ustin laughed. "His citadel is different, my master; the walls are about the same height as Karish's, but they are double the number. Each of the eight sides is composed of very hard interlocking stones—one atop another. Both citadels were built using a method of heating rock to softness before pouring it into place to harden. Most of Hamath's stone was molten, poured into molds, and put into place after hardening. A tyrant unimaginable, and yet the artistry used to build his home is unsurpassed. No wood was used in either construction. Rather, beams of stone were made to support and hold in place the roof and upper chambers. All furnishings are of gold, silver, precious stones, and granite. Nothing exists within the walls that will burn."

Vul asked, "How, then, do these giants roast people if nothing burns inside the citadels?"

"Equal in distance between the two citadels stands a great pit," said Ustin. "This is where all the firing is done, because Hamath believes his father is commander of the center star, which resides close to two other stars in the sky. The roasting of animals and men act as sacrifices to this star in hopes they will entice his father to come down and visit."

Patel then asked, "I thought he hated his father; seems strange to want to venerate a person hated."

Ustin nodded. "He wishes for the visit so he can slay his father; Hamath's motivation for anything he does is vengeance and nothing else. If he could, he would set the world ablaze—if only to mock God and the luminaries."

Vul pressed. "Is that all you can tell us about the terrain surrounding the citadels, or is there more? Namely, are there any vantage points we can use to spy out the areas without being seen?"

Ustin frowned and shook his head. "I'm sorry, but most of the land is flat, barren. Except for a very large lake southwest of Hamath—its banks rise above the level of the citadels. It sits less than twelve stadia from them. The only issue I see, master Vul, is the water. We can't go in or come out of it."

Vul smiled as he began making alternate plans in his head. "Just leave the details to me, son; I will make do with the information you've shared this day."

"Sir," said Ustin, "if I may continue, during my stay inside the citadels, it was my responsibility to quarry underground tunnels and construct large bays for storage of the flying machines. The bays are located under the water—the lake. The machines can enter and leave through the water."

Vul, still thinking of a plan, asked, "Are there other ways for the machines to be taken out from the underground bays?"

Ustin replied, "None I am aware of, my master; I fled soon after their construction."

After thinking for a moment, Patel said, "Perhaps some of your people that escaped with you have knowledge of the bays."

Ustin shook his head as a sad look crossed his face. "I'm the only survivor of six. The others were caught and destroyed by Hamath or became prey for the thunder lizards which roam the jungle and forests between the two lands."

Patel was curious, "Ustin, if the giants possess these ships, why haven't they attacked us or other settlements? Demar was the only giant I knew of with the power of mechanical flight."

"Sir, as I said earlier, Hamath could care less about the inhabitants of this world; he neither wants to conquer nor possess any of it, but to take revenge against those who made and placed him upon this rock in space."

Nodding his head in understanding, Patel said, "Thank you, Ustin, for a very thorough report."

Ustin, appearing nervous and worried, said, "Patel, sir, does this mean you will still assist me in freeing my people?"

Patel smiled. "Of course we will. I stand by my word, Ustin; believe in it."

Vul, grasping Ustin by the shoulder, said, "If that's all, son, you may leave so Patel and I may discuss plans of attack."

Ustin nodded, turned, and started for the door. When he reached the threshold, he stopped and said, "Sirs, one last thing I just thought of: six suns from now the sky waters will fall, giving concealment since the brothers detest its coming. They will stay deep within their respective homes until the waters end."

Everyone in the room glanced around in confusion as to what Ustin was saying. Rain and clouds were unknown to them, since only the sun shone where they lived. They had never experienced rain. Ustin tried to relate the best he could. Finally, Norhi spoke up. "Ustin, what are 'sky waters,' and how will they help conceal us, exactly?"

"From time to time, bright white mists can be seen forming in the sky. They look cheerful, but as they begin to pass over the brothers' domain, the mists turn grey and black. Loud noise which shakes the earth echoes as flashes of light like tree branches go forth from within the mist. Then tiny sprinkles of water float toward the earth from the mist, sometimes lightly and other times with great anger and ferocity. Even the ariyons will not come out during this period. They are fearful of the great light mixed with water. Some of them have been struck by the great light while holding spears and were consumed. They have words for all of this, but I forget them. A great room exists within one of the chambers under Hamath's citadel that holds tablets of gold, silver, and something called quartz, which gives testimony to all angelic knowledge. They call it 'written in their language,' made up of symbols and markings unknown to me. We have nothing to compare it with, I'm afraid, but…"

The faces of the onlookers took on expressions of shock and confusion. Instead of continuing, Ustin bowed, left the counsel, and headed for his room. Several minutes passed in complete silence as the remaining members of the counsel tried to absorb and understand the information given by Ustin. After looking around, Norhi gave a nervous laugh and said, "Quite the imagination your apprentice possesses, Vul."

Vul dismissed the stories told by Ustin, "Yes, well, I think he was just nervous speaking with all of us, and the strain of being away from his own people probably didn't help things…"

Patel asked, "Why couldn't what he said be truth?"

Vul snorted. "Patel, please. If I were to have a son, I would want him to be just like Ustin, but even I cannot accept a story about sky water and angelic tablets. He's under a lot of stress and wanted to impress us—to please me—and that is all."

Norhi chimed in. "Patel, as much as it pains me to say this, I think Vul may be right. I've studied many things in nature, and never have I seen water fall from the sky, let alone strange powerful lights that seemingly attack warriors holding spears."

"What about the mist which comes in from the ocean and settles over our beaches and even stretches inland for some distance?" asked Patel.

Norhi agreed. "Well, sure, that does happen, but there are no lights or loud noises accompanying it, and though damp it hardly fits the description of water falling from high in the sky, Patel."

Patel further argued, "Before we experienced it, though, we didn't know of its existence, right?"

Vul's anger began to grow more intense as he sat listening to the banter going back and forth. "Patel, Norhi—enough! This is pointless. You might as well say that stones can fall from the sky as well; it makes just as much sense. We need to begin working on a plan to free Ustin's people since you opened your big mouth and gave your word to do so. Of course, before we do that, Norhi, I need some of your white bark powder; my head is throbbing."

Put off by Vul's temper, Patel suggested everyone get rest first and they would meet to develop a plan first thing in the morning.

Waving the idea off, Vul replied, "I need no rest, and I already have a plan worked out. We'll only require six thousand men and at least seven days of supplies to accomplish our goals."

Sitting back in his chair and with a look of total disbelief on his face, Patel replied, "Six thousand? We barely have four thousand shifters to choose from, and our mission is to release people from bondage and procure, if possible, some flying machines—not invade and conquer lands!"

Vul tried his best to show restraint despite his disdain for Patel. "We do not know the brother's strengths—not completely. Nor do we know how truly difficult assaulting their citadels will be, sir Patel. I have developed contingency operations for any and every scenario possible. These are not fortresses in our backyard like the others; this mission is taxing in a number of ways. Just leave strategy and tactics to me, Patel, while you take the glory for it all."

On his feet now, his fury growing, Patel said, "Is that what you think of me, Vul? An empty seat that squawks of achievements rather than praising those who truly are deserving of acknowledgement?"

Vul replied, "Control yourself, lord Patel! Rage is very unbecoming of you, especially since it's unwarranted."

Patel questioned him, "Define 'unwarranted.'"

Vul shook his head in disbelief. "There's no time for this. Once the mission is over, we can deal with this in private. Now, do you wish to hear my strategies or no?"

Gaining his composure, Patel glanced toward Norhi's direction to find his friend attempting to ignore the situation altogether. "My apologies, Vul… Norhi. Please, why do we need so many warriors?"

Continuing, Vul explained. "When we cross the great river, I intend on forming ranks in the shape of a spear tip made up of four columns. Two on each side comprised of five hundred men each form the tip and sides. Another thousand will take up the rear, while a thousand archers will make up the body within the spear. It will ensure a strong, formidable army against their ariyon soldiers. Once their army is crushed, we then assault the first citadel, capture and maintain control of it, and prepare to take on Hamath. We only need a small squad led by Ustin to find and commandeer as many machines as he sees fit. Then we prepare for home, leaving the land and fortresses to their own fates."

After thinking for a moment, Patel asked, "Correct me if I'm wrong, Vul, but I only see four thousand men comprising your spearhead, and you asked for six thousand. Where are the other two?"

Explaining, Vul said, "I call them a 'reserve' force; I will keep them back by the river in case they are needed to restrengthen our lines, should we lose too many warriors. Additionally, as stated before, we do not know everything about the land and defenses; having extra men would cover any unforeseen dangers... so?"

Waiting for either man to respond to his proposal, Vul put out his hand toward each of them as if asking for alms. Finally, Norhi spoke up. "Your plan seems quite plausible, Vul; yet, as Patel has pointed out, we do not have enough shifters to cover four thousand bodies, let alone six. What if our home is counterattacked by ariyons from Demar's citadel? It will be defenseless against any onslaught launched from there."

Vul nodded. "You're correct. I intend on leaving this citadel and village abandoned, since we have underground cities to protect the people. Upon our return from the land of Hamath, we'll have superior weapons to take back the entire area if warranted. As for the two thousand soldiers, it's my plan to use regular men to fill the positions; after all, they can be trained to fight as warriors, and it's time they stood up and worked for their freedom and that of their fellow man as we do. Don't think them weak; remember, we were all men before the chosen ones ever existed."

Patel perked up and said, "I was against the idea until you said what you did, Vul. Very well. Your plan is approved. Let's get some rest for now and begin tomorrow coordinating training and logistics. We march forty days from tomorrow. May the Lord's power and will be with us in all things."

***

After exiting the council chambers, Patel headed for home and Nyeve. They had been apart far too long, and he wanted to make it up to her, even though their time together would still be too short, since he desired to lead the assault on Ustin's giants. Every now and again he fantasized about leaving everyone behind except for Nyeve and finding a deserted island where the couple could live out the remainder of their years in each other's arms—living and loving, unconcerned with problems of the world.

Upon entering his quarters, Patel found the woman of his dreams lying in bed asleep. Standing silently next to her, he watched as she took in a breath and released it softly through her nostrils. Long, dark hair crowned her head like a halo, making her face seem even more angelic to him. Not wanting to wake her, he slowly slid into bed lying next to her. Nyeve instinctively rustled, placing her head on his chest. With a smile of contentment, she fell back into a deep, peaceful sleep. Smelling her hair as he softly stroked it, Patel slowly fell into a deep sleep as well, to dream of better days to come.

Chapter 25

Pacing back and forth across aged black lava flows, Lilith pondered how to keep Lucifer from taking her most precious children once they hatched. *Only their father can provide a proper place for them to develop and be safe. I must go to him and demand he watch over our brood, keeping them well away from Lucifer until they are able to take care of themselves.* Looking around the caverns, she ensured all the other demons were well. Then she found Serpent and charged him with protecting all her children until she returned.

"It is vital that you pay close attention, Serpent; my children mean more to me than your life."

Arguing, Serpent replied, "Just a minute, wench; these are my children as well, so don't think for a moment that—"

"Enough, Serpent! I don't have time for any of your masculine banter. Maybe they are your children, maybe not; but you will protect them as if they were your own, understand?"

Confusedly, Serpent said, "May… be… mine. Maybe mine! I'm the only person here to assist in propagating Lucifer's army—maybe mine indeed!"

Not wanting to insight his wrath against her children while away, Lilith tried to smooth things out with him before leaving. "Of course, my strong lover, you are the father of the big man's army. I'm just restless and a little moody. Can you forgive a moody demoness like me, sugar loaf?"

Relenting, Serpent said, "I guess so. Women can't help but be moody every now and again. Go. Take some 'me' time and I'll watch over our kids."

Lilith smiled. "Thank you, dear; I'll be back as soon as I can. You can believe that! Listen, do me a favor and place herbs and spices near my—that is, our—hanging eggs in the third cavern. Lucifer is repulsed by any aroma from nature, which is the reason we are underground rather than topside. I'll be back soon, my pet. Thanks again."

Energetically he replied, "You bet. I'll do all you requested; just go and relax. Enjoy, okay?"

After blowing an imaginary kiss to Serpent, Lilith took off, exiting through the north entrance of the underworld and heading toward the aura of Stul—the true father of her three special egg sacs. She had been attracted to him even before he fell and became one of Lucifer's demonic dragons—second in power now that Bael had been banished by a shifter to the abyss. They sneaked out of their respective groups to enjoy intimate encounters lasting many earth days, unable to satiate their desires for one another. She found it odd to see his aura within Demar's citadel, and seemingly dimmer than normal.

Appearing within the throne room, she found her lover sitting upon a throne not of his own making, with a veil of grief upon his face. "I expected to find you sitting upon a throne ruling this world, but with a far more majestic face of a conqueror, my love." Excited, Stul jumped up from his seat yelling. "Lilith—Lilith, is it really you? I thought I'd never see you again!"

Running to him, "It's me, my love; how I missed you so!" The lovers embraced and kissed, joyful to finally be in each other's arms after a long time away.

Stul pulled back. "I didn't want to be kept from you, my love, but Lucifer forbade me from seeing you. He wanted an army sired by someone called Serpent—"

Lilith placed a finger across his lips. "I know it wasn't your doing, and yes, he made me mate with his reptilian man. But not before I gave birth to our children."

Stul released her and took a few steps back, attempting to process the information given by his lover. "I'm... I'm a father? You've graced me with offspring?"

She smiled. "Well, I had a little help, but yes, you are a father, and they are so beautiful, Stul; so wonderful. And they are why I have come to you now. Lucifer means to take them from me to use as he sees fit. Stul, I need you to take our children and protect them from him—please."

Fury grew within him as each word was a blow to his insides. "I'll not allow Lucifer or any other entity to harm my—our—children; this I vow with my life! Where are the little ones?"

She told him, "Safe for now within the underworld, but Lucifer means to come and take them once hatched; that's why I need you to take and hide them. I'll tell him they died before hatching, so they'll be safe forever."

Stul nodded. "Yes, that sounds good to me. They have yet to hatch? Seems a long time, Lilith; are you sure they live?"

Lilith smiled. "Of course I know they live. I'm their mother, you know." Suddenly, her mood changed, and with eyes downcast, she continued. "I'm sterile, though—all my eggs are depleted. I'll never know childbearing again. I feel so empty—a shell. That's why our children mean so much to me, Stul. Once I give over the others, I'll come back to you so we can live as a family forever."

"I'd like that very much, but for now we need to get you back and retrieve our offspring." Stul transformed into a dragon and had Lilith climb onto his back, and the couple made their way to the underworld and their children.

***

Birdsong tickling her ears slowly brought Nyeve awake. Early morning light fell upon cool bricks on the floor, heating them. As Nyeve moved to stretch out her body, she realized Patel lay sleeping next to her. Her glowing smile was the first thing he saw as his eyes opened, ready to take on a new day. Saying not a word, they ran hands over each other with each caress expressing words. They remained in silence, wanting their lovemaking to tell each other what was held deep inside. Many hours later, the two lay spent in an exhaustive embrace, happy to have a mate so perfect— so incredible.

Moments passed, and finally it occurred to Patel he had a task to perform. "Ny, I'm sorry, but there's something I need to do, and I'm already late. I'm actually surprised Norhi hasn't showed up to drag me off like he usually does." He kissed her forehead and jumped up from bed to wash and put on clothes.

Watching from the bed, Nyeve asked with a coy tone, "What's so important, sweetie? I'm feeling a bit neglected. Come back to bed and keep me company— please? I'll guarantee it'll be worth it, lover."

Smiling back at her, he said, "Believe me, if I could stay here with you, I would, happily. But we are putting a strategic plan together to attack two new citadels, rescue villagers from their oppressors, and abscond with flying machines in the process, so …"

Nyeve sat up. "Well, then I'll go with you to the planning since I'm sure archers will be needed and my archers are the best in all—"

Interrupting, Patel replied, "I'd rather you stayed here, Ny; I don't want you to go on this mission. However, on the next one I will take you up on leading our archers in battle."

Feeling dejected and frustrated at her lover's response, Nyeve got up from the bed, keeping herself covered, and stood by Patel as she waited for a reason she had to stay home.

"Nyeve, please don't fight me on this, okay? We've never gone after tyrants simultaneously—and in a foreign land, no less. I can't take the chance of losing you."

A serious look fell across her face. "Am I not a warrior? Have I ever asked for protection? I am a part of you—your helper; don't turn me away or ask if I'll stay behind to cower. Please, if you love me…"

He could feel his heart melt as the answer left his lips, "Ny, what was I thinking? Forgive me. I didn't mean to state that you were a coward. On the contrary, I do worry about and want to protect you from everything harmful; that's all I meant by asking for you to stay behind."

Answering she said, "I worry the same way about you, and yet you'll go off to war regardless of those feelings because you want to help people whether they are of your kin or not—and so do I. It's better for me to stand by your side and perish than stand on my own in everlasting sorrow. I'm strong, Patel, and I will be strong for you always. Please don't shut me out."

Patel gazed deep into her eyes and, with great authority in his voice, "You're not dressed yet! We have a planning meeting to get to, master archer. Do not make me any more late than I already am. Scoot!"

Leaping with excitement, Nyeve complied with the order by washing and dressing as quickly as she was able. When her tasks were complete, she ran up to Patel, placed her arms around his neck, and passionately kissed him.

After many moments passed, Patel pulled away and said, "I never once thought of you as being weak. You are the best part of me, and don't ever forget it."

Nyeve smiled. "… and don't you forget how much you mean to me and always will—always."

Just then Norhi barged in, frantically saying, "Okay, that's it! I waited as long as I could, but we're on our very last nerve with Vul running the meeting. So stop pawing at each other, get dressed, and run—don't walk—to the council chambers now!" Finding the couple standing a few feet away, dressed and ready to go, Norhi fell into a state of confusion.

Patel's next words didn't help to clear his confusion either. "Norhi, really, high blood pressure will be your undoing. Learn to relax; maybe take up a hobby. Okay, let's go to meeting then, shall we? We don't want to keep people waiting, right?" Smiling, but still very confused, the couple left their room and walked to the meeting place with Norhi following close behind.

Upon entering the chambers, Patel surveyed the room to find those present looking as though they all sported painful toothaches—all but one of them.

Vul stood near a board fastened to a wall and pointed a stick at some symbols drawn on a piece of animal hide. Looking toward the couple, Vul said, "It's about time you showed up for your own meeting, Patel. Perhaps if you learned to control your baser instincts, we might have the privilege of knowing what professionalism means to a leader of men."

Taking immediate control of the meeting to show he was indeed leader, Patel said, "Sit down, Vul, and remain silent until spoken to. Gentlemen, I wish to extend my deepest apologies for my tardiness, especially to the elders. I'm aware of how important your time is and will not keep you away from the people much longer since your part in this operation is small." He acknowledged their nods of understanding. Patel continued, "I'm sure Vul explained our intentions to go to war with another pair of giants in the hope of freeing more villagers under their control. That said, we will require all humans to remain underground when we leave. No warriors will be left to protect your people. Additionally, we intend on conscripting two thousand men from your ranks to fill ours—mainly as a reserve force in case we run into any unforeseen challenges. If there are no questions, I would like to respectfully dismiss the elders, since the rest of the meeting does not concern them."

After speaking among themselves, the elders stood, bowed, and silently filed out of the room.

Once they had left and the door had been secured, Patel stood and continued, "Regardless of Vul's lack of character or personality, he is one of the best tacticians, and his plan for assaulting the citadels appears sound to me."

Vul gave Patel a stern look. "Thank you—I think."

Patel smiled. "Don't mention it. Continuing, I confer the title of general of the army to him. He is responsible for organizing our army into a well-defined fighting force, as well as naming commanders and lieutenants to lead our soldiers. Second, Nyeve is named general of archers and ballistics division and will coordinate with General Vul regarding the best way to deploy her men during battles and counterattacks."

Put off about upon hearing Patel's appointment of a woman as general, Vul protested, but he was quickly silenced by Patel once again. "Now, as I was saying before Vul's interruption, Norhi is appointed general of sciences, research, and development; he is responsible for capturing and replicating any and all foreign technologies to the benefit of mankind. Additionally, his second title is that of deputy supreme commander, which makes him an executive in overall command of forces. I know there are many questions, and I humbly ask that you hold them in check for now. Our primary mission is to ready the army to move in a short amount of time, and weapons training is essential, especially for the two thousand humans comprising our reserves. Generals Vul and Nyeve, I leave that training in your capable hands; do not disappoint—as if you could. If there are no questions, we'll close out the meeting."

Vul stood. "Yes, supreme commander, I have one. Who do you intend on putting in charge of logistics? Since we have humans going with us, they'll require food, water, shelter, and other amenities to support them, not to mention additional weapons caches. What, then, say you, supreme commander?"

Without missing a beat, Patel said, "I leave the appointment of an individual to that position to you. Thank you, everyone. Meeting adjourned."

Vul, showing dissatisfaction with Patel and his decisions, kept thinking of when he would break off and begin his own culture and people to rule over. *Have your fun now, Patel, but understand this: I'll tolerate it for only so long, then it's done. I'll have my kingdom.* Looking in Nyeve's direction he continued, *And my queen.* Storming out of the room, Vul summoned Ustin. He appointed him general of logistics and began his training in the position.

Nyeve frowned and approached Patel. "I see the way he looks at me, my love, and I don't believe he will cooperate and work with me and—"

Stopping her, he replied, "Ny don't even worry yourself. He will cooperate or deal with me. Besides, I'll be right there with you when the attack begins, so just pay attention to me. Everything will be fine, okay?"

Nyeve still frowned and nodded. "All right, you're all I need. What do you want to do now?"

Patel further instructed, "While you prepare the archers and assist villagers to take provisions underground, Vul, Ustin, and I will take a trip to the mountains and observe routes and maybe even peek at the citadels. And don't give me the concerned face. I want this to go off without too many snags, Nyeve, and to do so, I must see for myself what we are going up against."

A look of concern still on her face, she said, "I know what you need to do, and it's fine. Just watch out for Vul. I don't trust him, and sometimes I think you're a little too overconfident that you can handle him. He has something up his sleeve, and it gives me chills."

Patel laughed, "Too overconfident—really? You feel I'm too overconfident? Very well, I'll sleep with one eye open—promise."

Turning up a side of her mouth, Nyeve said, "Now you're just teasing me, supreme commander; be careful"—she balling up a fist and shook it at him—"or else, mister!" After kissing him, Nyeve walked off to call and gather her archers for training.

Norhi, seeing that Patel was finally alone, approached acting peculiar by standing back and stammering a bit to Patel. "Sir, may I make a request?"

"Sir? Norhi, it's me—Patel. Why so formal, old friend?"

Norhi apologized, "I don't really know how to act right now, since everything's been made… well… regimented, for lack of a better word."

Patel Explaining, "I only did that to make it easier for Nyeve. Vul is an arrogant twit to me; imagine how he'd be with a woman in charge of something, let alone counted as an equal. You did notice I made you deputy commander, right? I trust you, friend, to do what's right, as opposed to Vul. Though a great tactician, he makes for a lousy leader."

Feeling a bit more at ease, Norhi replied, "What you did seems much clearer now that it was explained to me. I just wish I could have been in the know before the meeting."

Apologetic, Patel explained, "Honestly, Norhi, I didn't even know what I was going to do until I entered the room, but as my second in command you should be in the know. I promise to involve you in all decision-making from this point on—deal?"

Enthusiastically, Norhi said, "Deal! Now about going on this scouting mission without including me. I have a problem."

Looking confused, Patel asked, "Who said you couldn't go?"

Norhi continued, "Well, you didn't say anything to me. I only overheard it when you spoke with Nyeve—not that I was being nosy. Rarely do I listen to what you're saying—not that what's said isn't important, because it is; I—"

Stopping him, Patel said, "Norhi, it's all right. In fact, I want you to be nosy, since I'm human and from time to time may forget or leave something out. That's one of the reasons you were chosen as my second. Not that I'm saying you can't come with us, but why do you want to go?"

Norhi explained excitedly, "I'd like to get a look at this river crossing. Perhaps a prefabricated bridge or even multiple prefabs could be made and hauled to its banks. I'm thinking the river crossing will be our most vulnerable time to be ambushed or attacked while attempting to move men and supplies over it."

Amazed, Patel said, "Is it any wonder why I made you science officer? Of course you'd need to view the river yourself. Take measurements of the depth and speed of the water, determine whether one or more bridges will be needed—not to mention the types of material to use for their construction. I…"

Patel glanced toward Norhi and could see by his expression that he was stating known axioms. "Captain Obvious—right, old friend?"

Smiling and laughing, Norhi said, "I think you would have made a great science officer yourself, Patel."

Gesturing to Norhi, the two then walked off to find Vul and Ustin.

Chapter 26

Stul and Lilith glided to a soft landing within the underworld. She climbed down from Stul and waited for his transformation before setting off to their eggs.

Serpent came running at them at a full sprint; he appeared anxious and excited to see his mate return. "Lilith! Lilith! I did what you said, and it worked, it really worked!"

Questioning, she replied, "What do you mean it worked? All I asked you to do was place pungent herbs near my special eggs to repulse Lucifer until I returned. So what worked?"

With an evil grin on his face, he said, "I placed the herbs as you said. Moments later, he showed up—Lucifer—saying something about seeing you down in a valley heading toward a citadel, and he wanted to know if everything was all right. Anyway, I showed him the eggs, and the way they appeared plus the smell made him believe they were lifeless—well, that and the fact I told him you left grieving for their loss. So it worked!"

Puzzled, she looked over at Stul and then headed for the cavern sheltering her eggs. Upon her arrival, she found crushed onions and scallions covering the floor and strands of garlic wrapped directly around her eggs. Shrieks of despair left her throat as she realized the green glow of health had left her spawn and been replaced with deep darkness. She ran up to the eggs, and tore the garlands off her brood. She then clutched the eggs as she sobbed uncontrollably, stroking and kissing them as a mother grieving. Great rage grew within as she shot daggers of hate and loathing at Serpent. "You—you killed my children!" Looking over at Stul, she said, "Our children!" Tears of rage streamed down her face and with a low, dark voice her words escaped through clenched jaws and grinding teeth. "Kill him, Stul! Kill the murderer of our children! Peel the skin from him first, then muscle and sinew, until he is nothing more than a pile of rotting flesh and bones." Stul glanced at Serpent and then back at Lilith. "I cannot! Authority must be given to me by the one who empowered him."

A look of agony and confusion fell upon her. "What? What do you mean? What are you saying? Are you not Stul the Powerful, leader of Bael's dragons, father of my now dead spawn?"

Explaining, he said, "Lilith, I still am under the authority of Lucifer. Remember, I am a fallen one. He is my superior, and Serpent—once a man—was transfigured and empowered by him. Unless Lucifer commands it, I cannot take his life."

The shock of hearing Lilith's response to Stul finally released Serpent's mind from its grasp, allowing him to speak in protest. "Why try to kill me when I did what you told me to do? I killed nothing, and what do you mean by calling our children his?"

She responded, "I told you to place herbs around—*around*—the eggs. Not on them! The reason they are suspended is to keep them free from anything because of their sensitivity to things as embryos, you nitwit!"

Serpent arguing said, "Well, I didn't know that! You never said anything about them being sensitive to things; otherwise—"

Cutting him short, Lilith shrieked, "Shut up! Shut up! Shut up! I don't want to hear your voice right now! Leave before I kill you myself!"

Serpent's eyes flashed with anger. "I will not tolerate you speaking like that to me when I have been completely devoted to you while you go whoring around with every—"

Just then, Stul leaped at Serpent, grabbed him by an arm, and punched his face with great force, spraying the eggs with blood. As the two of them fought, Lilith noticed small signs of life returning to her eggs.

Excited, she yelled to Stul to hit Serpent again closer to the eggs so his blood would fall on them. After repeated blows, Stul sprinkled his opponent's blood on the brood, sparking them back to life. Once satisfied the eggs were sustained, he threw Serpent to the side and smeared blood from his hands on the clutch as well. It appeared that the blood was being absorbed through the eggs' leathery skins. Happy that her children lived, Lilith pleaded with Stul to take them and hide them away from everyone and everything that could harm them. Stul transformed into a dragon, gently removed each egg from its fastening, and turned to leave.

Serpent, lying on the ground, reached out and took hold of Stul's foot and said, with an exhausted voice, "I thought you had to get permission to harm me."

Pulling out of his grasp, Stul said, "To kill you I need permission; but threaten my family or talk down to their mother, and I'll kick your tail worse than this beating." As he took to the air, he turned and said, "You'd be surprised what you can live through, frog boy!"

After watching her family fly out of the underworld, Lilith approached Serpent, who was now sitting upright, and said, "You're fortunate that my children live, because I could care less about male authority. I'm through with you! The army I produced is it; no eggs are left within me, so your services are no longer required. I don't care where you go or what you do, just as long as it isn't around here. Leave!"

Getting to his feet and wiping the remainder of blood from his face, Serpent said, "I'm not going anywhere, witch! This is my home, and those are my children, but please feel free to leave here and take up residence with your dragon. If you think about giving me any grief, remember this: I know those eggs live. I have no reservations in telling Lucifer of their existence; after all, they're not mine, are they?"

Feeling trapped, Lilith said, "If I leave, it might raise Lucifer's curiosity … so I guess we'll need to work with each other. Truce?"

After thinking for a moment, Serpent said, "Truce, but it will cost you for me to keep quiet and allow you to stay here."

Sarcastically she asked, "And exactly what will it cost me?"

Serpent smiled. "Only 'companionship' where and when I require it, or Lucifer gets your most precious brood."

Repulsed at the idea but having no choice, Lilith relented to his demands, hoping to find a way out of the agreement in the future.

***

Soaring through clear blue skies, an abnormally large eagle, vulture, ibis, and falcon made their way to a mountain range that divided two lands from each other. Green forests and large, lush valleys passed quickly below them, giving way to foothills and craggy mountain peaks with elongated, cascading waterfalls and, finally, snow-capped tops.

Landing on the highest peak, the four birds transformed into their human forms and scanned the area opposite their land. Below lay a great jungle where mountain ranges abruptly terminated and beyond thick jungles a forest stretched on until it reached the banks of a large river. It was difficult for any of them to make out what lay beyond the great body of water from their vantage point, but what could be seen allowed Norhi to make some astute observations. "We have a few challenges to overcome. For instance, how will we get an entire army, a third of which are human, over mountains and through dense jungles before tackling such a large water barrier?"

Ustin said, "Not to mention supplies, armaments, and other materials needed to cross into the Badlands."

Looking intently at the both of them, Vul replied, "Easily. Our shifters will fly needed materials to the water's edge and stand by while the humans make their way on the ground. What's so hard about that?"

Ustin explained, "Sir, the moment anything—animal or man—enters the jungle below, it is watched by flyers, which then bring reports of foreign entities to their masters, the giants. Karish is quite paranoid, as I stated beforehand. He knows of our shifters' existence, and he is nervous. Additionally, there are great lizards—huge and nasty—living in these lands. Some eat plants, but a lot of them—the worst—consume meat, whether it's dead or alive."

Patel spoke up. "So we destroy their communications and slaughter the lizards with power swords—I don't see the challenge, son."

Interrupting, Vul said, "Since you didn't participate in the beginnings of our last conflict, let me fill you in. Ustin, transform into a hybrid for us—whatever one you desire." Nodding in response, Ustin changed into a wolf-man. "Now, Patel, look closely at our warrior here. Does anything seem amiss to you?"

After looking Ustin up and down, Patel glanced over to Vul with confusion on his face. "What am I supposed to notice? I find nothing wrong with him."

Just then Norhi spoke up, "No sword, he's missing an armband and hilt."

"Very good, deputy commander," said Vul. "I did not notice it either until we engaged the ariyons in battle. Our copies, for lack of a better word, are incapable of manifesting a sword of the Lord; and so, only brute strength and manmade weapons will they bring to a battlefield. Additionally, commander, is it your intention to wipe out every living thing from here to there so we keep our warriors safe and attempt to maintain an element of surprise?"

Taking a seat on an exposed boulder, Patel tried to work through the information he had just received.

Ustin walked up to him and said, "Commander, there may still be a way to reach the water's edge without being detected, but after that I cannot ensure surprise." Patel listened intently as Ustin continued, "A couple of elders from the village, while consuming fermented fruit beverages, talked of a hunting expedition to the foothills of this mountain range during which they came across vast caverns that went on for a long way. Lit torches allowed them to explore the caverns, which eventually opened near a great body of water running through a strange land. At the time, it seemed like more of a story at the time for the benefit of entertaining other villagers, but maybe there is something to it."

Vul stepped forward. "And you decided to tell us about this now? I gotta tell you, I'm not impressed, Ustin, keeping important information like this from me—us."

"Sir, I couldn't confirm their story. Believe me, if I had found caverns when I made my escape, I'd have used them. As a man, fighting through steamy jungles and climbing over cold mountains is not without perils."

After a few moments, Patel addressed the group. "Gentlemen, we need to make a decision; make plans to go above or chase down a story that may allow us access from below. Or should we call it off altogether? I don't want to needlessly jeopardize innocent lives for some strange machines that may or may not assist us in battles with our enemies."

Answering Ustin said, "Sir, it may not be my place, but this isn't just about machines; people are being held against their will to work and die at the whim of others. I'll get you to the machines as vowed; first and foremost, we must fight for their freedom." Looking around at everyone, he said, "Nothing means more to a man, nothing means more to me! Please, do not give up—not now. I know it can be done if only we keep our hearts and minds open. We can find a way."

Feeling ashamed, yet proud of Ustin's convictions, Patel stood and said, "Forgive me if I came across negatively. Of course we'll fight for their freedom! Let's head back to camp and find the elders you spoke of. If there are caverns large enough to accomplish our needs, we will take them; and if not— we'll knock a hole through these mountains if need be!"

All nodded in agreement as they transformed and took to the sky, returning home to find elders who might hold precious information on subterranean caverns.

Chapter 27

Coming together within the throne room, Torel and all the other angelics sat to discuss newly received information—except Stul, whose whereabouts were unknown. "Once again, Karith and Hamath's answer to lending some of their flying machines to us was just delivered; it will cost us two thousand."

Quickly standing Tubel's reply to his brother's statement was loud and hot. "*Two* thousand—what happened to only a thousand? We cannot afford such a drain! We'll be left defenseless!"

Gesturing to his brother to relax and take a seat, Torel said, "That is their price, and we will meet it regardless of cost."

Deenal, agreeing with Tubel, said, "Two thousand ariyon soldiers will knock our military strength down to citadel guards, plus or minus four; not to mention our weapons depletion from the last battle with shifters. It'll take almost thirty days to replenish and arm that many of them. The only thing we do have a great supply of is armor; otherwise, we'd need another sixty plus days at least."

Torel said, "Nothing said is new to me, and I understand the limitations. The gains override the risks. Yes, the citadel will sit unprotected; however, I believe the enemy will not attack, since all humans held by us were released to them. In studying their motives, we have found that their raids were conducted to release slaves, and the only citadel ever inhabited by them is Utt's, for whatever reason. No, I think we are safe here until we attack them."

Once again Tubel injected, "With what, brother? We're giving up our army for some empty carriages! We'll have no soldiers. Azel, Ridep—are you hearing this? Say something that makes sense—please!"

Azel answered. "We could ask Lucifer for a portion of his army, although I doubt he'll be receptive. Or maybe we can get them to deliver the ships and we take them without giving up our army."

Ridep, who mostly kept to himself and remained silent over most things, said, "Azel—everyone—we must stop and think. Most of the giants and ariyons littering this reality are from us. We cannot turn on our own and hope to take over the earth. We need to work together; even Stul would agree with me. In fact, it was his idea to build and use a detention cell—a cell which extracts and collects luminary energies, leaving our special enemies docile." Each person present glanced at one another with a mixture of possibility and intrigue beaming from their faces.

Deenal spoke up. "Do you know what materials are needed to develop a proper holding cell?"

Before Ridep could answer, Tubel and Torel, in a fit of rage, slammed their fists on the table in protest. "Torel and I have heard enough! Talked enough! We will rearm and resupply the two thousand troops requested, and my brother and I will deliver it to Hamath, take possession of flying machines, and plead with the giants to allow us a return escort of five hundred soldiers, which we will use against our enemy! No more rethinking or wild ideas from anyone. We do this and wait for Lucifer to deliver on his promises to us! Good? Yes? Thank you, this meeting is done!"

Azel transformed into a full dragon, and he bellowed and roared at the brothers. "I am not some entity that can be ordered about by the likes of you!" He moved toward them. "I will rip flesh from bone!"

Suddenly, another large dragon flew into the room and landed between Azel and the brothers to intercept him,

"Stop! This is not going to happen, Azel. Back off—now!" With a grunt of contempt, Azel backed down, allowing Stul to turn and address the brothers. "This is the first and last time I will interfere with my equals to save you. Remember the hierarchy or perish! Sit! Everyone present needs to know what I know."

After transforming into a more humanoid appearance, Stul said, "I have seen Lucifer's dark army, and it is vast, concealed within the bowels of this planet. Second, my offspring also live and now reside with me inside this very citadel. He also persuaded a third of our brothers in heaven to his side; they await his signal to attack Michael and his soldiers and take the realm. All we need to do is be patient, and I'm here to ensure that happens."

Curious Azel asked, "Giants dwell here now, within the citadel—your children?"

Stul shook his head. "No, brother, they are not offspring of men but of another."

Azel didn't understand. "Another? What other?"

Stul waved him off. "I cannot tell you now, but you'll know soon enough. My children rest and are still developing—never have such entities existed as these, my friends, nor will there ever again."

"Where are they located?" asked Deenal. "May we see them?"

Stul set his jaw and answered. "No one is to ever go to them without my permission; at least not until they hatch!"

Ridep asked, "Brother, we need to know so as not to accidentally come upon and disturb them."

Moments passed, and then Stul said, "Very well. It does make sense. But know this: since I shall show you where they are, your life is forfeit if any of you disturb them, understand?" All nodded, and when he felt satisfied with their answer, he motioned for them to follow.

After descending cobblestone staircases and walking through dark, damp stone hallways, they finally entered a huge great room that held three large elongated boxes. Each container was made of a wood bottom and a solid silver cover, and embossed on each lid was a dragon signet. "My children lie safe and secure down here, away from anything that could harm them. They are very delicate right now; nothing must touch them! I fear it may kill them. The mother and I already know herbs affect their metamorphosis somehow; they stopped thriving when an idiot placed a plant called garlic over them. That's why they are with me instead of the mother—for protection."

Cocking his head to one side, Deenal asked, "Forgive me Stul but if they are affected by external things, should they be encased in materials? Just wondering."

A look of horror fell upon the fallen angel's face as he raced to open one of the boxes. Peering in, he saw the egg black and lifeless within the case. "What have I done… what have I done?"

Deenal raced to his side. He looked into the chest and, thinking quickly, said, "Stul, do you have any of the ground they were hanging in or around?"

The grief-stricken Stul did not answer but stared in anguish at his languishing unborn. Deenal shook him and continued to ask the question until Stul answered. "I… don't know… I don't understand. Why dirt?"

Turning from him, Deenal searched the area and found a burlap bag filled with pulverized volcanic rock and ash. He filled a large empty vat with the dirt and then called for Stul. "Come here and bleed into the dirt. I need your organics—quickly!"

Anxiety propelled Stul toward Deenal as he hoped to himself it would work. He placed an arm over the vat and sliced a deep gash into his arm with one of his claws; he then splattered the dirt with his bright green and fiery red blood. Deenal stirred the mixture with a large piece of metal, Deenal kept at it until he felt the consistency was right. He then placed a large clump of blood and dirt on the tip of the piece of metal and smeared it on a low portion of the ceiling. As he repeated the action over and again, it dawned on Stul what Deenal was doing.

Deenal grabbing one of his eggs, moved to the ceiling, and placed it under the overhang. He watched as tentacle-like protrusions erupted from its top to burrow into the volcanic mix. Immediately, sparks of life danced underneath the now healthy membrane that made up the outer casing of the egg. Stul enthusiastically ripped open the other two cases and placed the eggs into their new ceiling residence.

After he was content that each egg was thriving, Stul turned to Deenal and thanked him. "You saved the lives of my children. How did you know what to do? Li ... their mother told me nothing, and when she placed the bag around my neck, she gave no reason. How did you know?"

Deenal looked at him, shaking his head as if to clear it. "I'm not sure; it just came to me. Perhaps the mother gave directions telepathically, but that is impossible unless she possesses angelic powers. But of course, there are no female angelics. Strange."

Knowing Lilith must have influenced Deenal, Stul decided to keep it to himself for now. "Well, I thank you nonetheless. We need to leave here now to ensure a safe place for development. Let's see if we can hurry in the rearming of our soldiers and get the machines needed before the enemy decides to attack this place, huh?"

Agreement among everyone led the group to begin smelting operations and the gathering of raw materials without the help of slaves.

***

Ustin sought out two elders from among the villages who had knowledge of caverns leading under a mountain range that directly exited to the banks of a great river when he was informed of one's demise. Ustin approached a young man caring for livestock "Have you seen the two elders from the last raid?" The young man nodded, "Yes, I know of the men you speak. One died during the last great battle, and another is on a hunting expedition with young ones—their rite of passage into manhood."

Ustin asked, "Do you know when they will return or in what direction to find them?"

The man said, "They shall not return until every youth has made a kill. As for the direction they may be found, take the path north which parallels the shoreline until you come to a dark forest; here you will find them."

Nodding, Ustin thanked the villager and made his way back to Vul and the others. Finding Vul alone at a table, plotting his siege attacks against citadels, Ustin said, "My lord, I have information on the elders we are looking for." Vul grunted, indicating Ustin should continue.

Waiting for an acknowledgement from Vul to continue, and once received Ustin replied, "One has passed away, and the other is on a hunting trip. I'm unable to find Patel or anyone else except you, sir. Do we wait, or should we look for the elder ourselves?"

Seeing an opportunity to undermine Patel, Vul stood up and said, "If you're aware of where this man went, we'll track him down. No need to alert the others. When can we leave?"

Ustin responded enthusiastically, "Whenever you're ready, my lord."

Vul nodded. "Then let's move out, lieutenant."

The two shifters exited the room. Before transforming, they looked around to ensure no man was present. They then took to the skies. Vul had Ustin take point since he knew what direction to travel. Climbing higher, Ustin spotted where the path ended and a dense forest started. He pointed to the forest and told Vul that the elder would be inside it. Circling high above, neither shifter could spot any type of human activity below, though there were parts of wooded areas denser than others. After many hours had passed, the two large birds decided to land within a dense part of the forest.

When they changed back into men as they touched ground, they heard many gasps come from bushes and shrubs near them. Vul commanded, "Come out! Come out of there and stand before us now!"

Ustin could tell they were frightened and so spoke softly. "Do not be afraid; we will not harm you but have come to speak with the elder."

An older man quickly moved from the brush and fell before them, begging for mercy. "My lords, please forgive us; we did not know this was your land! I was unaware this land was the land of gods."

Looking at each other, Ustin was about to explain they were not gods when Vul stopped him. "Rise and stand before me as a man. What is your name?"

Trembling, the man said, "My name is Enteppi, my lords. What is your will?"

Continuing, Vul said, "I require your services, Enteppi of man. You know of caverns which lead under mountains to a great river, do you not?"

Nodding incessantly, he said, "Oh yes, my lord, I know the caverns you speak of quite well and can take you to them, oh great ones."

Vul was enjoying the veneration he was receiving, never wanting it to stop. "Very well. You shall take us, Enteppi; but first, do you possess knowledge of lands farther to the north of this place?"

Confused by the question, he said, "My lord, I know all of the upper lands, for my people had a settlement there until the giants came and took possession of it. Many times ago, the giants abandoned the whole area, moving to low lands and even to the Badlands."

"Is the upper land habitable for men?"

"Yes, my lords, I just came from there to make men out of boys." Enteppi called the boys to come forward and presented them to the shifters.

Vul commanded, "Enteppi, these men are now my men. I will be your god; and you, my people."

Enteppi fell upon his face, as did the young men, at hearing Vul's statement. "Rise and return to the upper lands and settle there. Upon my return, you shall have more people brought to you and I shall make you a great leader among the people. You shall prosper, Enteppi—you and your household. But first you shall take me to the caverns after seeing these men home. We shall hover above and protect you all as you go. Now therefore go, and we will be with you."

Enteppi immediately gathered all the young men to him and led them back to his old settlement in the northern part of the territory.

Soaring high above them, Ustin confronted Vul as to what he was doing with people. "Sir, I rarely question your motives and express concerns with actions even less, but I must protest openly this one time! We are not gods! For us to misrepresent ourselves to those less knowledgeable seems … wrong!"

Flying closer to his apprentice, Vul said, "Leave it to me. I spoke with you earlier about breaking away from Patel and his puppets, and you were present when I threatened Patel it would happen. We are breaking away, my son. After Kareth and Hamath are destroyed, no power on this planet will be left to stop us from ruling over an empire greater than any in existence. Whether by accident or divine right, we were seen transforming from animals to humans; it wasn't intentional, and if they return to the village and talk of what they've seen, it could start an uprising, throwing everything into confusion and chaos. How would that help anyone? So they count us among heavenly realms—even better for us to keep a tight rule over them. Think for a moment, Ustin; I am limited in transformations to three animal beings but possess a sword of great power, whereas you, though not armed with a power sword, possess the ability to transform into many creatures. Together, you and I can rule this world and all within it. I need you, my son; I need you!"

Pride quickly swelled within the young shifter, and he felt honored Vul wanted him as a second in command of a future empire. "Very well, sir. Your will is my will, and your word is now my word. I pledge my complete loyalty to you—to our future."

Grinning with power, Vul beamed with enthusiasm as they soared high above their newly recruited subjects.

Many days came and went before the group finally reached its destination. Surveying the area from the air, Vul motioned for Ustin to come closer to him. "Look at the topography, my son! This is a very easy place to defend, with mountains, valleys, and great rivers to use as natural barriers. Plenty of food and water for our humans to sustain themselves with surrounds where my capital, our city, will be erected. If this is not a sign for building our empire, I don't know what is Ustin, my boy."

In agreement Ustin replied, "Yes, my lord. From what you have taught me, we couldn't ask for a better place to begin. Shall we touch down and speak to our people?"

"Yes, we shall, and we shall see if Enteppi requires rest before showing us the caverns." Vul and

Ustin dove to where the men stood and transformed before them. As they did so, the men fell prostrate in reverence. "Stand, Enteppi! We are willing to give you a few days of rest before taking us to the caverns."

Cheerful and more confident, Enteppi said, "My lord, the journey is many suns from this place, and I am old but will depart immediately if it is your will."

Vul placed a hand upon his shoulder and said, "Take food and water. Refresh yourself. Then I will fly you to the foot of the mountains, and it shall only take a quarter of the day to get there."

Confused Enteppi asked, "My lord, what does 'day' mean? I am unfamiliar with this word."

Ustin smiled. "A day is equal to the time it takes the sun to rise, traverse, and fall from the sky; just as the time from when it falls to rising again is called night." From the moment Ustin passed on this revelation to them, he was called and known to his people as the 'Wise One'; knowing all things." After making a fire, the men roasted meat and grains collected from the hunt and ate various fruits from the trees.

When he was full and felt refreshed, Enteppi drew close to Vul and Ustin and said, "Masters, I am ready to go show the caves to you now."

The two men nodded and transformed into birds, and Vul motioned for Enteppi to climb upon his back. Taking to the skies, they headed to the mountains with Enteppi elated as he rode on the back of his god. As he neared the mountain ranges, Vul decided to take an alternate route bypassing territories under Patel's control. They landed where Enteppi directed, and Vul and Ustin looked around for an entrance to the caves but found nothing.

Turning to Enteppi, Vul asked, "I thought you said an entrance existed here, but I see nothing."

Humbly, Enteppi approached them and said, "My lord, the entry point was right over there, I swear an oath, but it seems as though huge stones have fallen upon it and covered it from sight." The two men glanced over at a large pile of rubble with plants and small bushes growing from in between cracks. Without saying a word to one another, they transformed into huge lion-men. Grabbing stones and boulders many sizes larger than themselves, they easily tossed the rubble to one side, slowly revealing a dark, gaping hole in the side of the mountain.

Vul turned to Enteppi. "Is this the cavern of which you spoke?" The man could not utter a word, as he was still in awe at the sight of his gods and the power they possessed. Vul did not understand

Enteppi's behavior, however, and grew impatient with the man. "Old man, answer me; is this the opening or not?"

Vul's booming inquiry caused Enteppi to faint from fear. Ustin transformed into a human, went up to the elderly man, and cautiously roused him to consciousness. "Do not be afraid, my dear man; all is well. Remember, you have found favor with us; be strong and tell us if this is the entrance we've been looking for, all right?"

Standing now, and with his wits about him, Enteppi said, "This is the entry point, my lords. I shall take you in, but I will need a light source. We made torches from wood, cloth, and pitch. Some of them should be near the entrance, but I don't see any. My lords, where have you gone?"

A large stack of ready-made torches was piled against a wall within the cave. Ustin picked up one and snapped his fingers near the pitch, creating a spark that brought the torch to life. He handed it to Enteppi, and they allowed the man to move through the cave ahead while Ustin fastened twelve extra torches to his back. Moving on, Enteppi showed them where he had found symbols on the wall to direct where to go. Large chambers gave way to smaller long cylindrical tunnels that seemingly went on forever. When Enteppi became tired, Vul changed into a half-man, half-horse and allowed the elder to ride on his back. When even riding upon Vul's back tired the man, the three men stopped and made camp. Ustin fed the man fruit and roasted grain from a bag he carried and brought him something to drink from a nearby pool of clear, sweet water. Once he had his fill and fell asleep, Vul and Ustin left the camp to look ahead, following the symbols Enteppi had shown on the walls. After many more hours, Ustin caught a glimpse of light that seemed teasingly close.

A few hours later, the two emerged to see a thick jungle canopy overhead. The roar of rushing water filled their ears as they approached a great shoreline of soft yellow-white sand that slowly merged with a fast-moving body of water. "We found it, lord Vul; we found a way through the mountains which will be much easier for the men making up our army reserves."

Glancing around the area, Vul said, "Yes, this will do quite nicely—plenty of room to work on building a bridge to traverse the waterway and station defenses until everything is readied for our crossing."

Ustin glanced around uneasily. "Sir, we might not want to stay on the beach too much longer. We may already have been detected by their alert systems.

I'm sure Enteppi will wake soon and feel abandoned when he finds us gone."

"After one last look around we'll go back, collect our elder, and leave, but I'm wondering where this river flows, and if a natural land bridge exists, maybe—" Suddenly, the jungle that had been quiet came alive with birdsong and animal howls. "On second thought, let's go; no need to give away our presence early." Sprinting back into the jungle, the two men headed for the cave, making their way back to Enteppi. Finding him awake and eating food near a fire, Vul and Ustin approached him saying that it was time to return to his people and that his services there were no longer required. Quickly complying, the three beings reversed course, eventually reemerging from the cave. Vul placed a great boulder over the entrance and instructed Enteppi never to speak of it to anyone again.

While flying the elderly man back to his northern village, Vul said, "Since you have shown us the way to go, I will keep to my promise and make you a great people among the men of the world. This time next month—or thirty sunrises, as you know time to be—men and women will come to you in peace. Accept them and build my empire; then shall I return and live among you."

Vul and Ustin took to the sky as their men paid homage. They flew back to Patel's village, keeping silent of what had been done.

***

Watching as Nyeve taught archers under her authority to practice hitting targets as far away as a stadia greatly impressed Patel. She was a firm but forgiving trainer, and every pupil respected her ways. She turned around and saw Patel watching, and she quickly stuck her tongue out at him, retracting it just as quickly so no one but he could see. Smiling back as he leaned against a large threshold to the training area, Patel motioned for her to join him. Once she felt her student had nocked his arrow properly on his bowstring, she ran to Patel and, after looking around to see if anyone was watching, gave him a long, deep, and passionate kiss.

"Wow, some kiss!" said Patel.

Coyly, she said, "You're some lover." As they embraced, she felt great comfort in his arms. It was then that she spotted Vul and Ustin walking in their direction. "Here comes trouble."

Reacting to her comment, Patel swung around to see their approach as well. Yelling out, Patel addressed them. "Greetings. You've been away for some time; almost thought something happened to the both of you until I realized who I was worrying over."

Vul motioned for silence and gestured for them to head for the council chambers. As they entered the room, Vul told Ustin to stay silent while he explained their whereabouts for the last few weeks. Patel and Nyeve took a seat and waited to hear from Vul. When Vul realized Norhi was not with them, he waited until Ustin was able to track down Norhi, who was busying himself in his lab.

Once everyone was together, an impatient Vul explained. "As you all well know, Ustin and I went on a journey to find the elders who spoke of caverns that went under the mountains. Unfortunately, we discovered both had perished—lost due to war. However, we took it upon ourselves to search areas around the foothills, where we stumbled upon a cave entrance obscured by a couple large boulders." Immediately, those present—with the exception of Ustin—perked up, excited over what they were hearing.

"So it is true, then; a pathway under the mountains does exist!" said Patel.

Annoyed at Patel's interruption Vul continued, "…as I was saying, we entered the caverns and found symbols directing us through the many catacombs to a large chamber used for camping which contained fresh water and enough room for at least ten thousand men. Additionally, charred wood filled a massive fire pit probably used for heating and cooking. As we continued through the tunnels, eventually they opened to the outside, concealed by a dense jungle canopy. We walked out of the jungle, and there before us was a vast shoreline terminating into a great river. Therefore, the pathway exists and is usable. All we need to do is leave as soon as possible. Any questions?"

Norhi spoke first. "Vul, you said symbols were used to navigate through the caverns; how did you know what the symbols meant?"

Thinking quickly he replied, "We made an assumption which turned out to be correct. Anything else?"

Patel tilted his head to the side in confusion. "Yes, you said the elders were killed in our last battle, but I don't remember regular humans accompanying us."

Vul exhaled in frustration. "We used a few humans as armor bearers, and unfortunately, they perished during the fight."

Jumping in, Nyeve said, "That is true; we chose several as armor bearers for resupply if needed."

"I know of what you speak," said Norhi, "but I thought they were young men, not el—"

Interrupting Vul replied, "They volunteered. Strong and brave they were, but are no more! Now, does anyone else have a question not pertaining to the elders?"

Vul's demeanor troubled Patel. It seemed to him as though his general was holding something back, deliberately hiding information. Keeping his suspicions to himself for now, Patel said, "No more questions, Vul. We thank you for such initiative; true actions of leadership which we all need to emulate."

Tossing Patel's words to the side, Vul continued. "Well, when do we depart for the caves?"

Patel said, "We are three days out from the tentative date set of forty days, but Ustin has been gone for a long time and I'm unaware of the logistics completion.

Suddenly, Norhi stood and said, "Nyeve and I saw to everything since they were gone. Also, taking into consideration our need to cross a river, I built a prefabricated bridge-way in twelve detachable parts for ease of travel. When we arrive on the shoreline, the pieces can be put together in a few hours. We should be able to move about a hundred plus men across at a time, but I wouldn't want to try for any more than that.

We've never attempted anything like this before; no sense in taking too many unnecessary risks, right?"

Just then Nyeve injected, "The bridge, of course, is only for our human reserves and supplies. The rest of us can fly across and set up a perimeter to protect our people in the rear. A small contingent will ensure bridge security, and I believe Ustin will take a squad of twelve men to infiltrate the flying machine hangars while the rest of us engage the brothers and their army; is that right, Ustin?"

Vul's arrogance was felt by all as he responded for his lieutenant, "My war plan will be studied and utilized, no one makes a move unless I allow it." He looked directly at Nyeve. "You are responsible for preparing archers and ballistics and nothing more; I'll be satisfied with that accomplishment by a woman. Stay out of more complicated areas so as not to feel overwhelmed."

Both Patel and Nyeve took in deep breaths while their blood boiled at his remarks. Glancing over at her lover, Nyeve waited for Patel to chastise Vul for his attitude and comments toward her, but he sat silent with his teeth clenched. She urged him to say something with her eyes, and Patel finally said, "We will leave in three days, everyone; please ensure all tasks are complete before then. Generals, we will meet exactly one day before departure to finalize plans. Thank you all."

Vul left the room with a smug look upon his face, knowing he had placed a wedge between the couple.

Nyeve walked over to where Patel was sitting, where she stood in defiance and said, "I'm waiting."

Patel looked up at her. "For what?"

"An explanation as to why you would allow him to speak of me in such a way! What do you think?"

Patel shook his head while simultaneously getting to his feet. "Ny, I cannot treat you any different when in council; you are a general just as he is, and—"

Shutting him down, she replied, "And you are my lover—we are partners! Nothing should override that fact, Patel—nothing! I am your everything and should be treated as such. So why are Vul's lungs still in his chest and not on this table?"

Softly cupping her shoulders, he tried to reason with her. "Please try to understand; as commander, I must treat everyone the same. If I show preferential treatment to one or another, then leadership will break down and all will suffer. As a general, you have the ability to stand on your own with him—go toe to toe;

tell him the way it is. You are his equal, and you'll accept nothing less."

She nodded as she backed away from him. "I see. I see now how cowardly you truly are; you fear him and always have. Oh, you speak of being tough, but when it comes right down to it, you're nothing but a little coward!" She stormed out of the room, leaving Patel slack jawed and confused. Once outside, she transformed into an eagle and flew off to nowhere specific just needing to get away.

Patel was leaning against a dark stone wall, trying to comprehend what had happened between him and Nyeve, when Norhi entered. "Commander, I compiled the data you requested earlier if you wish to go over it now."

Glancing more through Norhi then at him, Patel said, "I'm a coward—in the eyes of the woman I love. I'm a coward. Why?"

Shaking his head, Norhi asked, "Are you asking why you're a coward, or why Nyeve sees you as such? It doesn't matter, Patel; you're not a coward. Far from it, in fact; she's emotionally unstable right now and just needs time to work through her issues. Believe me, she doesn't think of you as being cowardly. We have so much to go over, though… is this problem really more important, or can it wait?"

Shaking his head as if to clear it, Patel conjured up a half smile and took a seat next to Norhi to go over mission plans.

***

Nyeve found an isolated spot far away from camp, landed, and changed back to her human form. As she sat weeping and looking up into the night sky, a voice called out from the darkness. "It's not safe to be this far from camp on your own."

Turning, she found Vul standing next to a palm tree, fiddling with a fallen leaf. "What do you want, Vul?"

"Nothing. I was just out and about looking for something to eat."

Sniffling, she said to him, "Liar, there's plenty of food in the citadel, and since when do you need to eat? Have your powers been taken from you? One could only hope."

Vul slyly walked over to her and before taking a seat next to her, he said, "My powers are stronger than ever, but it doesn't hurt to indulge in food every once in a while." He sat close to her. "Forbidden passion fruit, perhaps; after all, it is the sweetest."

Nyeve shook her head. "Passion fruit is not forbidden; we col—" It was then that she looked into

Vul's eyes and knew the real fruit he spoke of, which was her.

Getting to her feet she said, "Why are you bothering me Vul, really?"

Smiling, "As I said, I was out looking for fruit and found you sitting and weeping. Why were you crying anyway?"

Frowning she snapped at him, "It's none of your business, and you were the cause of it, so don't try to play coy with me!"

Craftily, he replied, "The cause—you mean because of earlier in the meeting? I had no idea my words touched you so; please accept my apologies. If I had known you took my words to heart and cared so deeply about our relationship, I would have chosen better—my words, that is, of course."

"I don't care about your words and never have. Still, you knew exactly what you were doing, running me down in front of everyone. And we don't have a relationship, so…"

As he drew symbols on the ground, Vul said, "If you don't take to your heart my every word, and since they do not bother you, then I must repeat my question—why are you here alone crying?"

Becoming exasperated, she answered him. "Fine, Vul, fine! I'll tell you. It has to do with Patel not ripping your throat out earlier. See, so it doesn't have anything to do with you."

Grinning with satisfaction, Vul said, "I see. My words that did not affect you in your heart should have riled another into viciously attacking me—is that right?" Confusion danced across her face and spilled forth from her response. "No… or yes, it… he did nothing, letting you get away with… not that it matters."

Moving in for the kill, Vul said, "It gets confusing, though it needn't be; a beauty such as yourself should always be first in a man's mind. It pains me to see you taken advantage of every day by a man that puts his work before a warm, loving woman such as you." He stepped behind her and caressed each of her shoulders as he continued speaking. "A queen you are, and as a queen you should be treated. Think about it, Nyeve; can he dive into your heart, swim through the waters of passion to bring desire as I can? Where is Patel's heart? Let me tell you—working for others and thinking only of a future for him that may, or may not, include you. Whereas I can give waves of excitement and perform somersaults, diving into the depths of your heart. Safety, security, and comfort with a man lead only to routine and blandness of life; whereas with me, danger, unpredictability, and forcefulness keep the embers of passion alive—never going out."

Vul's breath upon her neck, mixed with his words, melted away all rationale from within her. She leaned back and closed her eyes, allowing him to kiss deeply on her lips. He spun her around and grasped hard at her waist with one arm while holding the back of her head with his hand, kissing her with greater force.

Pulling away from him and pushing with a hand against his chest, Nyeve said, "Wait! Just wait... this is wrong on so many levels. I belong to Patel. You and I would never work out—not ever!"

Pushing against her hand with his chest, he asked, "Why couldn't we work, Nyeve? I felt the passion in you when we kissed. Is it because Patel gave a part of his soul to you? Give it back and I'll shower you with real love. Your feet will always have fresh rose petals to walk on as their sweet aroma fills every part of our palace. Boredom and routine will stand as bywords in a kingdom filled with nothing but spontaneous excitement." Her arm softened, releasing the pressure against his chest and allowing once more for an embrace and kiss.

Pausing long enough to speak, Nyeve said, "I don't want to hurt him. Give me a little time to think things over. I need time."

"All right, take some time to think it over, but don't hold yourself from me. It wouldn't be fair if you were to see him all the time but me for only a little; promise me."

As he continued to kiss her neck, she complied with his wishes. "I'll set aside time for you and him, and I'll make a decision as soon as I can."

"Make it quick, and make it me," He said. Laying her down on soft, plush grass, he began to know her, laughing in his heart an evil laugh, gratified that his plans to destroy Patel and take what was once his were going very well.

Chapter 28

Karish, riding in a chariot studded all around with gold and silver metals and precious stones that was being pulled by twenty-two large horses, made his way to Hamath's citadel. He was full of deep anguish from potentially bad information he had received and needed reassurance from his brother that everything would be fine. Cracking a whip over the heads of his horse team, Karish urged them to go faster, yelling as they went. Large plumes of dust and dirt flew wildly around the hooves and wheels until he came to his destination. Pulling back on the reigns, the giant jumped free of the chariot before coming to a complete stop and ran to Hamath's door. Banging fiercely, he couldn't believe how long it was taking his brother to answer the door.

Annoyed, Hamath ripped open the door and pushed his brother to the ground. "What in blazes do you think you're doing, shaking my citadel like that? Get to your feet and come in—crazy ogre!"

Picking himself up off the ground and brushing dust from his body before entering, Karish, upset countered. "I'm not a crazy ogre, and you shouldn't have pushed me down, brother. I have a report of strangers in our territory."

Paying little attention to him, Hamath poured two large steins full of a liquid, walked over to his brother, and handed him one. "I want you to try this new batch of wine and tell me what you think."

Frustrated, Karish said, "Are you listening to me at all? I said there are—" He paused for a moment to peer into the stein and take a short sniff. "What is this? It smells of grape but holds an amber-like hue?"

Hamath smiled and nodded. "Yes, I cultivated a green grape rather than the usual purple. Try it, and tell me what you think."

After a small sip, Karish smiled as he gulped the rest of the drink down, afterward wiping the residue that escaped his mouth from his beard. "Delicious, brother, truly, and it seemed less… acidic than your usual darker wines."

Hamath, sticking his chest out with great pride, said, "Thank you. My next attempt will be to ferment grains of various kinds and see what tasty treats they will make."

Karish liked that idea, "Oh, well now, that is interesting! Perhaps other fruits could be fermented as well. I—" He suddenly remembered why he was visiting his brother, Karish pleaded, "Hamath, please sit and listen to me for just a few minutes. This is important!"

After filling both steins again, Hamath walked over and gave in to his brother's wishes. "All right, but this better not be about your illusions again."

Dejected, Karish asked, "Delusions! When have I ever had delusions of anything?"

Hamath chuckled. "I said illusions, not... never mind."

Karish frowned and looked very worried. "Well, that's not any better. I'm trying to tell you of strangers in our territory, and you want to put me down!"

After gulping down his drink, Hamath said, "You do know you were dropped on your head as a child, right?"

Karish's frown deepened. "Yes, and I wish you would stop reminding me of it all the time!"

Hamath, calmly replied, "Calm down. Look, how many false alarms have there been? How many times have I gone out with you to search for these supposed invaders, only to find nothing at all or regular wildlife walking about, hmm?"

Nodding his head Karish said, "A few, but we know our enemies are shape-shifters; they could be any type of animal. So I think it's legitimate to check out animals acting suspicious."

Wiping wine from his beard, Hamath said, "Yeah, okay, brother! I'll agree, except the one time I followed your suspicion, it turned out to be one huge reptile eating another. What was that all about? Did ya think maybe they're trying to throw us off by having one eat the other?"

His teeth clenched, Karish replied, "Sarcasm is duly noted! Ya know, I'll just keep things to myself since you don't want to take me seriously anyway; after all, it's not like these shifters have stormed citadels and cleaved the heads of fellow giants or anything. Oh wait—yeah they have!"

Hamath let out a long sigh. "Very well, tell me of the strangers you encountered."

Correcting him, Karish said, "I didn't encounter them; my Terra birds spotted them walking along the shore."

Puzzled Hamath asked, "They were seen near the lake? Where at, exactly?"

Karish shook his head. "No, no, not near the lake but the river."

Trying to make sense of his brother, Hamath said, "Oh, they were spotted walking on a riverbank?"

Annoyed he answered, "Why must you correct me all the time? Does it really matter what it's called—shoreline, riverbank?"

Shaking his head Hamath responded, "In this case, yes, since our dwellings are near a lake and a river runs through the land. More wine? I do, because I know I need it."

Ignoring his last comment, Karish continued, "As I was saying, these were men and not animals. They may have been scouts sent to get the lay of the land in preparation for an invasion."

Shaking his head, Hamath returned to the table with three full steins and said, "Right away you jump to invasion because two men were spotted on a riverbank. Why can't they be hunters, explorers, or just plain lost? Do you honestly believe an army of *men* is preparing to attack us? It's ridiculous, Karish—come on!"

"Yes, brother, I do believe it to be a possibility! We have human slaves they would want to free and flying machines which could be used against us—if stolen."

Hamath's eyes were glassy and showed signs of intoxication, as did his speech. Leaning forward and slightly to one side he said, "There is no ... man on the fase a... a fase... I kill a... mee a... man—so yeah."

Disgusted with his brother's behavior, Karish chastised him. "Drunk again; why is it every time I come over here to speak with you about important matters, you get drunk?"

Clumsily wagging a finger while smiling, Hamath replied, "Ah, see—you… you ansurd your own queshun—he he he."

Karish shook his head. "I can't stand you like this. Look, never mind about the men. You're probably right. Who am I kidding; you're always right, and I'm always wrong. One day, though—one day I'll be right and you'll be wrong, and then we'll see who gets dropped on their head." Karish glanced toward the table and realized his words had fallen on deaf ears, as his brother was fast asleep. As he turned to leave, he said in parting, "Sleep it off, fat boy, and I hope your head feels like someone took a mallet to it when you awake!"

A grunt and the sound of gas being passed was the only reply Hamath gave before the snoring started. Karish slammed the door, boarded his chariot, and headed back home with anger and suspicion for companions.

✱✱✱

After rising from a troubled night of sleep, Patel found his bed and dwelling Nyeve-free. He worried for her safety, knowing she was upset with his lack of action from the night before. She was prone to taking off into the woods or jungles to get away and think. He located Norhi and Ustin, and the three men worked feverishly to ensure everything was in place and ready to go.

As usual, Norhi had a few concerns that he brought up to both men. "I'm sure the battle will go in our favor; however, my worry is with capturing the machines. We have no one who knows how to pilot them, let alone how to reengineer the captured craft—if, indeed, we are capable of capturing them. Yes, I know what you will say—I'm smart, highly intelligent, a true master of knowledge and wisdom; but this may show you my weaknesses."

Smiling, Patel said, "Someone here thinks very highly of himself—though it is true. I do hold your abilities in high regard, so I'm not worried at all."

Ustin then spoke up. "Sirs, if I may. I'm well versed in the flying machines' capabilities and have flown a few as well. Producing more will be a very daunting task due to materials and technologies used in their construct."

Both men looked at Ustin with surprise and awe upon their faces, prompting Patel to ask, "Ustin, giants allowed men to pilot these vessels? Why not use them for escape if that's really the case?"

Continuing, Ustin explained. "Those who showed an aptitude for flight were set apart from other villagers, and their families would be placed in protective custody whenever we piloted the craft. If we failed to return, the family members would have been tortured, killed, and consumed. As you may surmise, they never lost one craft. Second, ariyon soldiers accompany each flight to further ensure all craft return from scheduled flights. Hopefully we can take Karish's citadel by surprise since the villagers live within its walls. Hamath can't stand to have men or anyone else living with him. We must—*must*—liberate the people before taking on Hamath. The machines mean nothing to me, but I want my people freed."

After a moment of silence, Norhi asked, "Could we use flying machines to evacuate your people to safety in our village?"

Ustin nodded. "Yes, there are four craft that hold a thousand men and around another dozen or so with occupancy rates of thirteen personnel—maybe a few more, but not many."

Norhi questioned further, "Would Patel or I be able to fly one?"

Ustin seemed to hesitate in answering Norhi's question, and Patel picked up on it very quickly. "Ustin, tell us; it's all right."

The young lad nodded. "I doubt either one of you could. Not that you lack skills, by any means;

rather, it's the way these machines work. I'm not sure how to explain it, really, other than saying that they are living organisms. The engine and interfacing equipment live; a pilot uses a symbiotic relationship to control them—they become one."

Norhi, intrigued, said "Fascinating. And you think the symbiotic organisms wouldn't interface with either of us?"

Nodding, Ustin replied, "Exactly, sir. The ship may react to you as a foreign body and not allow for neural linkup. No worries, though; pilots are kept within the hangar at all times and watched over by ariyon guards. I'm not sure why, since Karish never launches them for fear of losing some to an enemy. Makes no sense, but that's what he does."

Patel asked, "Ustin, is there a way to get your people out in the ships without alerting Karish or other soldiers within the citadel?"

Nodding Ustin continued, "Sir, I wanted to evacuate the people from a room which is connected to a large tunnel leading to the ships. While you all engage in battle outside, Norhi and I, with eleven other shifters, will attack from within, free the people, and continue our assault inside, hopefully gaining access by unlatching main doors to the citadel and entering with our army fully intact."

Patel nodded as he thought over Ustin's plans. "Vul holds a great amount of respect for you, young one, and I can see why. Speaking of Vul, where is he—and Nyeve, for that matter?"

"You know, Vul," said Norhi, "We're a few days from moving out, and he's probably working her hard, teaching her new positions and explaining where he wants her. I wouldn't be surprised if he wasn't trying to dominate the poor woman."

All three men nodded, and Patel said, "Yep, that's Vul all right" under his breath. They then stood and left the room to look for the pair.

Chapter 29

A tiny pinprick of sunlight shot through a thick canopy of leafy branches, concealing the couple and striking Nyeve's eyelids, slowly rousing her to life. Suddenly, she realized where she was—and with whom. "Vul... Vul, get up! Get up! Get up! It's way past morning!"

Vul sat up and rubbed his eyes, trying to focus better. After raking his hair and letting out a large, roaring yawn, he got to his feet, slapped Nyeve on the butt, and said, "Don't tie a knot in your gut, babe; we're ready to set out today if need be—my plans are flawless." A glaring look told him she was upset, but about what he didn't know or care. "Hey, we'll get something to eat and check on our soldiers if that'll get you to take it easy."

Now even more at odds with his nonchalant attitude, she said, "I was supposed to meet with Patel this morning until—until this thing happened!"

Vul acted surprised. "You make it sound like it was a bad thing; and believe me, last night you didn't seem to be put off one bit."

She quickly moved to him and swung to strike his face, but he caught her arm, spun her around, and placed it behind her back. "If what happened last night bothers you, just remember this, sweetheart: you wanted it—more than I did!"

Turning her head to the side, he planted a hard kiss on her lips before throwing her to the ground and walking off. Tears streamed down her face as she sat pulling up clumps of dirt from the earth, clenching them hard, forcing streams of moist, dark soil to pass through her fingers. She despised herself for the attraction she felt for Vul, knowing his words held a great truth. She loved two men.

As the sun was about to set, coloring the sky a pinkish gold, Vul approached Patel, Norhi, and Ustin, who were readying troops to move out.

Patel asked, "Where have you been all this time? We're just about set to move out."

Waving his hand toward Patel as though swatting an insect from the sky, he said, "Working of course. We should take point with the humans behind us since they will need to camp and rest at the halfway mark."

Slowly nodding, Patel agreed. However, an itch of suspicion scratched at the back of his mind, and he didn't know why. "All right Vul, we'll take point. Ustin, have the men fall in behind us, and Norhi, everyone else. I'd like all generals up front so we can discuss actions as we get closer to our objective. Has anyone seen Nyeve? It isn't like her to be late."

Ustin said, "Sir, she may be with bowmen. I'll track her down once the men are in place, sir."

Patel nodded. "Thank you, Ustin. The rest of us will position ourselves forward and wait for you and Nyeve to join us."

After bowing, Ustin ran to the back of the line and began herding men to the front. Ensuring no one was paying attention; he moved quickly to the underground entrance of their village and spoke with a young man waiting for him. "Did you round up everyone on the list I gave you?"

The boy answered him, "Yes, my lord, they only await word and we will go."

Ustin handed him a scroll. "Here, this map will take you north to a new village—our home. On the other side of the map is a monument I want built in honor of Vul. Hew it out of rock in a single piece. Be careful not to break or deface it in any way. Our new god-king will reward you greatly for a job well done. Also, take this message with you for the people. Their king says 'be fruitful and multiply,' for he intends on making a great empire through them."

Bowing low, the young man complied with the instruction given him while Ustin returned to the column of soldiers. As he moved swiftly to the front, a voice caught his attention; it was Nyeve.

Calling to him she said, "Ustin," she said, "what's going on? Where's Patel and the others?"

"Waiting for us to meet them at the lead. And by the way, you were instructing bowmen, which is where I found you just now. Vul and I will cover for you when needed—fear not."

Shocked Nyeve asked, "You… you know of Vul and… how did…?"

Looking around to ensure they were alone, he said in a whispered voice, "Vul confided in me, so I know of his future plans. You are to be blessed and made a queen, my lady; but we must remain silent for now. After we take Hamath, everything will be made known to you as well. Now please hurry; they are waiting."

As she ran forward, Nyeve's mind swirled with increasingly difficult questions, mixed with fear and guilt. She knew Patel would be cut to the heart if he ever found out about her and Vul, yet she also knew she couldn't quit either of them.

✳✳✳

As they approached the entrance of the cavern, Vul halted the group and showed strange symbols on one of the walls to Patel and the generals. "These markings led Ustin and me through the inner caverns to an exit just within a jungle area close to the great river."

Examining the symbols closely, Norhi asked, "What do they mean, the symbols here?"

Vul said, "What do you mean what do they mean?"

Norhi said, "Well, you stated a translation of the symbols was made which assisted you in finding your way through the tunnels, right?"

Seeing a look of both confusion and anxiety on his face, Patel pressed him. "That's correct, Vul; what do the symbols tell you?"

Thinking quickly and speaking with pseudoconfidence, Vul replied, "It says 'entryway' here, and here, and 'caution' on this side of the symbol, of course."

In a suspicious-toned response, Patel said, "Of course. Well then, general Vul, please lead the way."

Vul nodded and moved to where the pitch torches were stored. He passed them out until the supply was exhausted. Once the torches were lit, the army entered the cave ten abreast, with Vul leading them all. As they walked on worn paths through deep, dark tunnel systems, Nyeve moved closer to Patel and said, "Hello, stranger!"

Puzzled, Patel replied, "Hello, stranger—really?"

Chipper, she said, "Well yeah, I haven't seen you in some time, you being busy with work and all. It was as if you had fallen off the face of the earth."

Patel smiled. "I believe you were the one that left, wanting time to yourself, Nyeve—not me."

After a short pause, and with a look of reflection on his face, he continued. "Ny, I love you. I really love you, and I know what I want in life, especially after we complete this mission; but recently I've been picking up strange signals from you that perhaps you're struggling with the idea of what you want in life. Because I love you, I'm willing to let you go so you can have time to think about what you really want. I hope it's me, but the only thing that matters is your happiness. Do you understand?"

Her face lit up as a smile covered it. "Patel, do you really mean it? You're letting me go?"

Looking a bit dejected, he said, "I didn't think you'd be so jovial about it, but yes, I'm willing to let you go because of the love I hold for you."

She said, "No, I'm not happy that you're letting me have time and space to think. Rather, I am happy because it shows how much you love me. Everything is fine, Patel, and I want to spend the rest of my life with you, but in saying that, there is something I need to work through, and it won't require us being apart. All I ask is time away every once in a while until I've figured it all out. Fair?"

Elated that Nyeve wanted to remain a couple, he focused only on that one thought, missing altogether the problem she had hinted at. "Great, sweetheart, and I promise this will be the last mission to come between us. I intend to devote my whole life to loving and taking care of you." After stopping long enough to hug and kiss each other, the couple ran to catch up with the leaders.

Upon reaching the midpoint of their journey, the group made camp, allowing the human soldiers to rest, eat, and sleep. Norhi sought out Patel and accidently walked in on him and Nyeve being intimate. Blushing, he quickly turned and left the area, saying to himself that what he wanted to say to Patel would keep for now. Some time later, Patel emerged from his shelter and found Norhi sitting alone. He approached his friend and took a seat across from him, and he watched as Norhi formed symbols with a sharp stick in the ground. "Hey, what are you doing pal?"

As if in a trance, Norhi did not answer but kept forming different images in the dirt. Finally, he broke his concentration and acknowledged Patel. "Oh, hello. How long have you been here?"

Troubled, Patel replied, "Quite some time; is everything all right, my friend?"

Norhi nodded. "Yes, yes. I'm sorry; the symbols written on the wall gave me an idea. What if we design our own symbols and assign different sounds to them, making a... written word?"

Interested Patel replied, "Sounds clever. We'll develop a writing of our speak—or is it speech ... speaking?"

Norhi smiled. "Absolutely. The potentials are infinite. Sending messages in written form, keeping track of all things, not requiring people to go here and there to count and recount things. Messages that may fall into the hands of foes would do more to confuse than help them ... So what do you think—honestly?"

Great respect flowed from Patel's response. "I don't believe these people understand how blessed they are to have you among them. Our own unique way of communicating with each other—I love it! However, it may not be easy to develop it, Norhi; you'll need to teach a large group and then have that group train others in it—a lot of work, my friend. If you can handle the extra workload, I'll ensure compliance."

Matter-of-factly, Norhi said, "Patel, come on, you know better than anyone else that projects like these are sweet honey to me. Once we conclude the mission, I'll begin a written phonetic symbolism for us. Between studying the flying machines and developing this, I'll be good to go."

Standing, Patel said, "Very good, commander. I'll leave you to your thoughts for now and go check on our soldiers. After a few more watches, we'll reassemble and march onward. I'm hoping to cross the river by tomorrow. We've never attacked with such large forces before—not to mention the fact that we'll be fighting as men, since our human soldiers have never seen us as animals. Vul assured me his soldiers know not to change under any circumstances; the shock may be too much for the humans. They might freeze up during battle, and we don't need any more aggravations. They are enough as it is, you know?"

Slowly nodding, he said, "Patel, I've stayed silent until now, and believe me, it took a great deal of self-control. I do not, nor have I ever, trusted that man. His sole motivation is self—self, Patel—and he will stop at nothing to get what he wants. I'm still trying to understand why he is here assisting us. What his angle is this time, I just don't know, but in no way do I trust him."

Staring forward and watching as shadows danced against irregular-shaped stone walls behind torchlight, Patel said, "My friend, I agree with you. Think of this for a moment: he may very well be using us for his own agenda, but aren't we doing the same? Good or bad, right or wrong, we are using each other for our own agendas. When the time comes, when he wants to move on—to leave us to pursue his own gains—I'll not stop him whatsoever. Well, provided his actions do not cause harm or endanger human life. Keep an eye out, if you will, Norhi, for a replacement as good as Vul—when it comes to battle tactics, that is—okay?"

Raising a hand to show his acknowledgement, Norhi said, "I will. I only wish Ustin wasn't under his thumb. He's a good organizer and leader, Patel; his only flaw is—for lack of a better word—venerating Vul. Well, anyway, I'll keep a lookout; trust me."

As he walked away, Patel said, "You're the only person I do trust. The only one."

***

Vul stepped into Patel's tent and moved to where Nyeve slumbered. He softly kissed her neck as he slowly ran a hand over her shoulder and arm. Smiling with her eyes still closed, Nyeve pressed against him until she realized a few moments later that it was not

Patel she was snuggling but another. "Vul, what are you doing in here? Patel could return at any moment!"

Placing a finger across her lips, he said, "He's out reviewing the men, and why should you care whether he returns to finds us together or not?" Pushing his hand aside, she stood up and departed the tent with him following close behind. A stern voice stopped her. "Listen, Patel will eventually find out about us one way or another, Nyeve. You are mine now, not his!"

She turned to face him. "This is not the way I want him to find out. And I am not yours, Vul!"

Folding his arms in contempt, he said, "I see. So you still belong to Patel, then; is that right?"

Nyeve twisting her mouth in confusion. "Yes... I mean no. I don't know; everything is upside down... confusing... and I need time to think free of your advances and his love, which I have betrayed and still betray."

In a firm, authoritative voice, Vul said, "Your confusion due to this situation you find yourself in and your love for Patel neither bothers nor concerns me. You are mine, plain and simple, so get used to it; and when we complete our mission, Nyeve, he will know one way or another that you're mine. The expectation I have of my future queen is that she should show strength and authority to rule the people during my absence." He took hold of her forcibly by the arms and pulled her close. "Now start showing it!"

He pressed his lips hard against hers, and she let out a small squeal as she attempted to break free of his grasp but couldn't. A part of her was repelled by Vul, and yet another part felt a strong and intense attraction to him. It was this feeling that won out as she gave in to his efforts. As they were locked in a passionate embrace, a person happened upon them. Shocked at the sight of them together as they were, he crept away, not wanting to be detected by the couple. A great pain grew within him, promising to rip asunder his very being. Silently, he sat and wept, wondering what possible future existed now that he had witnessed such a devastating betrayal that threatened to destroy the unity of his world and everyone's life as he knew it.

At third watch Patel decided to move the shifter soldiers to the cavern exit within the jungle. He rounded up his generals and explained his plans. "After thinking it over, I've decided how we will take the riverbank. Nyeve, pick out twenty-four of your best bowmen. They will go before us with orders to shoot down anything seen which has the power of flight, to ensure nothing can communicate with the giants of our arrival. Norhi, you said twelve shifters are all you require to haul, set up, and put in place the makeshift bridge for crossing; I want them directly behind the bowmen, emerging from the caverns once security is in place. Vul, keep all humans here until the bridge is in place and our shifters take on a human form; then we'll bring them forward as well. Please remember and pass it on to the shifters: no one transforms while humans are present. We cannot allow them to see us in such ways; they may not understand we are servants of God and may worship us as gods. We battle the giants and their armies as men unless I determine otherwise."

Speaking up Vul replied, "Exactly what determines whether we transform or not, commander?"

Patiently, Patel said, "Do so if extraordinary circumstances exist, such as greater numbers of soldiers or more than two giants attacking us, or if humans held by the enemy are in danger of being wiped out due to reprisal or we face a powerful weapon unknown to us which we cannot hope to counter as men. Will those suffice as legitimate reasons for you, general?"

Vul nodded and remained uncharacteristically silent, only glancing over at Nyeve with an esoteric grin upon his face.

Patel continued. "When you see me transform, consider it a signal for all shifters to do the same. Any questions?"

Norhi spoke up. "Yes, commander. Once we are over the bridge, how should we conduct operations?" He held his head downcast, seeming to be confused or lost as to what was going on around him. "I mean, do we destroy the enemy from within or without? I'm not sure how to proceed, or I do but ... could you explain it again? I'm sorry, my mind is ..."

Concerned with his friend's behavior but wanting to maintain an authoritative presence, Patel said, "No problem, general; we can go over the plan of attack. First, you, Ustin, and six others handpicked by him will move to the lake and enter a bay through concealed entryways and take control of the airships and their hangars. Vul and Nyeve have command of the army and will attack the first citadel and take it. Then they will reassemble and attack the second citadel while you and Ustin, using airships, free and evacuate the people. Once all objectives are met, we will level the citadels to the ground as a message to others that we will not tolerate enslavement of mankind. Additionally, those ariyons taken prisoner shall be fed, and their wounded cared for. They will eventually be released to give a message to others of their kind that we prefer peace to war and we are willing to live together in peace."

After hearing the last part of Patel's message, Vul broke his silence and protested. "Free prisoners after caring for them? Have you gone mad? Showing such weakness to our enemies will not ensure peace but bring their wrath down upon us! What prisoners of our people were ever returned to us? We must crush and wipe them from the face of the planet, not coddle them! Whose side are you on anyway?"

Rage mixed with an anxiety that cut to Norhi's very bones. "Enough! How dare you question the mind or motives of one such as Patel! He thinks only of others, and not himself! He gives love only to have it betrayed and thrown back in his face! I support his decisions and will not tolerate dissension among the ranks. If you want to discuss this more in private, general Vul, just let me know when and where you want to meet. Until then, shut up!"

Everyone in the room was in a state of shock as the area they were in fell silent. Patel couldn't believe his friend's uncharacteristic behavior. Lashing out against Vul was very unusual and unheard of for Norhi—so much so that Vul was caught completely off guard. After some time had passed, Patel spoke up and said, "Okay, if no one has anything else, let's get to work. Norhi, if I might have a moment alone with you, I'd appreciate it."

Silently nodding, Norhi waited for everyone to leave so they could speak in private. "Norhi, I'm the first person to state publicly Vul's flaws, especially his selfishness, but when it comes from you, a man of great patience and peace, I have to ask what's up, dear friend? Are you burned out, needing some time off or something?"

Norhi shook his head. "I'm sorry, Patel. I guess his antics had finally caught up with me and I see him as more of a liability then asset right now. I'll control myself better—perhaps by taking a holiday once the campaign is over with. But I'm good."

Patel grinned slightly. "Okay, pal, I won't push for now. We'll talk more after the battle. On another subject, how sure are you about the integrity of this bridge you've created?"

Perking up, Norhi said, "Very sure. In fact"—he ran to the room's entrance and summoned a young man to him—"this is actually the person who put the parts together, making a durable bridge for us to use. Commander, may I introduce to you Eningree—a person I could not do without."

Smiling, Patel approached and shook the lad's hand. "You are to Norhi what he is to me, and because of that alone, I promote you to subgeneral of engineering under Norhi. Congratulations."

Surprised, the young man said, "Thank you, sir… thank you… You're too kind and generous."

"Nonsense, son. Don't sell yourself short; you deserve it."

His eyes downcast, Eningree said, "Sir, may I always serve you well, and may God grant me the wisdom to know how to address issues which may impact our people for good or bad." Both men found his cryptic words strange but nodded.

"I'm sure you will," said Patel. "For now, I believe we are ready to move, correct?" The three left and headed toward the columns of men standing by to march forward into battle.

***

Nyeve took her twenty-four archers and emerged from the tunnel first. The sun was just beginning to peek over the horizon as they fixed their positions, watching for anything moving or flying in the air. Soon, many various birds were moving rhythmically overhead. Their behavior seemed quite normal to Nyeve, and therefore she kept her bowmen from firing. Suddenly, two great, flying grey-green reptilian creatures with elongated heads soared from their hiding place in the jungle, immediately making for the direction of the citadels. Nyeve shouted, ordering her soldiers to target and bring down the creatures before they made it over the water. Twelve pairs of arrows sliced through the air, penetrating their prey and instantly dropping them to the ground. Vul sent forth eight of his men to retrieve and bring the carcasses to him. As the soldiers placed them within the jungle, Vul, Patel, and Norhi examined the bodies, amazed that such creatures existed. Norhi was the first to point out markings on one side of each leathery wing. "They definitely belonged to the giants! See these markings—three lines in a delta or arrowhead shape. The ariyons call this their signet."

Suddenly, Nyeve showed up. "Well, are they what we are looking for, or did we kill innocent life?"

"You did very well!" said Patel. "They belong to the giants. Please congratulate your men."

Motioning to Eningree, Norhi ordered the bridge parts to be brought forward. Assembly took less time than first thought, which made Vul happy and Patel relieved. It took eight soldiers transformed as large eagles to pick up the bridge and place it over the river. Each side was fastened and secured to the ground. Once Eningree was satisfied, Patel ordered six large ballistic machines to be brought out and taken across the water.

Vul asked, "Why only six? We have eight in the inventory, and we may need them all for the siege."

Patel said, "I'm thinking we may not require all eight and would like to keep two on reserve just in case."

Vul snapped at Patel, "In case! In case of what? I'd rather have overkill then be underarmed!"

Attempting to keep calm, Patel said, "We err on the side of caution. Who knows what we may encounter, Vul? We've never taken on powers such as these before."

Keeping his voice down, Vul said, "There are two giants out there with ariyon armies, and in point of fact, you relieved two giants of their heads not too long ago. So what is there to worry about?"

Patel argued further, saying, "The giants did not possess airships, only a flying cloth, and they never deployed any weapons that we did not know of. But this time, my soul, in the last days of preparing for conflict, has felt strange about what we may face."

Annoyed the general relented, "Fine, fine, whatever makes you feel good. Just remember I am in charge of the army in the field. Do me a favor and leave that to me, okay?"

"Of course, Vul, you're the man in the field, not me. When we cross the bridge with our troops, I will not exercise power over them until the siege is complete. I honor my words, Vul, and this I vow to you."

Vul nodded and smiled. "Very good, then we do understand each other."

Checking to ensure all changelings were once again in human form, Vul directed his army across the bridge along with Nyeve and her archers. He then ordered his troops to form up as a giant spearhead with Nyeve's bowmen confined within its borders. Each side of the formation consisted of three columns comprising five hundred soldiers, each armed with a rectangular metallic shield that was two-thirds of a body length, a double-edge curved sword, and a spear twelve cubits long, including the one-cubit spearhead. Their armor consisted of various worked-metal plates sewn one over the other, like scales, to allow for freedom of movement. The helmets, made of polished metal, were pointed on top and covered the whole head except for eye and mouth openings.

Nyeve's bowmen were not as heavily armored, nor did they wear metal helmets; rather, a durable leather helmet served as protection for them. Each quiver held five hundred arrows with varying tips used for specialized situations. The bows were recurved made from flexible yet quite strong wood and strung with large, indestructible dried reptilian sinews. An expert marksman could hit a target the size of a melon at over three stadia.

Vul placed his artillery pieces in back of the formation, leaving the two thousand human reserves directly behind the artillery out of harm's way. When Norhi, Ustin, and their team were ready to move out, Vul gave the command and brought to life his war machine.

Chapter 30

Faint rhythmic rumbles flowed over the ground, resonating off large stone walls, stirring Karish awake. Attempting to focus, he sat up, rubbed his eyes, and cleared his head, concentrating on the rumbles, which seemed to be growing in intensity. It did not sound like thunder from the sky, nor did he perceive raindrops striking the ground. At that moment, an ariyon soldier burst into his room and told him a massive force was approaching from the river. "Do you see anything in the air or animals among their ranks?" he asked the soldier. He had heard what happened to his cousins Demar and Utt—shifters attacked their citadels and took the giant's heads for trophies. He hoped to avoid another such incident at all costs.

The ariyon soldier said, "No, my lord, nothing like that from what we are able to make out atop the tower. I believe they are humans, and they brought siege weapons with them."

After giving orders to deploy a bulk of his army outside the citadel, Karish busied himself putting on armor and retrieving weapons for battle. The giant made his way to the top of a fortress wall, where he looked out across the dry plain and watched as a huge army approached from a distance. Looking behind him, he could see large, dark clouds making their way from over the lake to where the battle would take place. "Thanks be to the fathers for this good fortune. The very sight of thunder clouds and lightning bolts should take the fight out of them, not to mention water falling upon them from above. Ha ha ha." He turned to one of his soldiers. Karish continued, "This will be a glorious victory; we shall crush mankind with the forces of nature as well as our own might!" He paused for a moment as he looked again at the approaching army. He then turned to the soldier and said, "Nonetheless, perhaps we should break out and prepare our aerial weaponry." The soldier bowed and ran to fulfill the giant's request.

***

Nyeve glancing every now and again toward aerial phenomena she had never before witnessed. After a while, she turned to Vul and pointed it out. "What do you make of that?"

Focusing on the growing dark mass of clouds that flashed from time to time, he said, "Ustin told us about it, remember? Water falls from them, and electrical discharges boom in the sky." Thinking of how it might affect his soldiers since none of them had ever experienced such a thing in their lives, let alone during battle, he told Nyeve to pass the word through the ranks to halt their advance. Vul climbed a boulder and, in a booming voice, informed his soldiers of what to expect from the thundering rainfall and ensured them that no harm would come to them.

Peering through an eyeglass, Karish watched as his attackers stopped in their tracks. He pondered what they could possibly be doing so far from his citadel. He turned around and barked orders to one of his soldiers to take all humans, with the exception of those working in the hangars, and lock them up in the great room until the battle was complete.

Returning his attention to the enemy, Karish watched as their columns resumed marching toward his position. His own soldiers were set up in line formations four deep outside the citadel walls. Ariyon metal, incredibly strong and perpetually sharp, comprised their armor. Only Ariyon metal can sharpen its own metal. Though technologically advanced, they considered sword and lance as honorable weaponry; they preferred to see the life drain away from their opponents rather than destroy them at a distance.

Karish, however, was willing to activate everything in his arsenal, including airships, to win—to survive. He wouldn't use them unless they were desperately needed, though, since it took Hamath's permission to deploy airships and he did not give it easily. As Karish glanced in the direction of his brother's fortress, he couldn't believe he was unable to communicate with him.

Karish hadn't seen hide nor hair of his flying reptiles, and he was not going to send a runner, as all soldiers were needed to repel the invaders. Two stadia from his stone walls, the attackers stopped, strengthened their columns, and set ballistic platforms in place just behind their formation. A person then stepped out from between the columns and addressed the people in and outside of the fortress.

"Giant, I am Vul, general of the freemen's army! We demand the release of all humans held by you and your brother. Second, we require all technology held by you and your brother. Third, you will make a peace contract with all men to never take up arms against them and to cooperate in every way to facilitate man's future in this world!"

Letting out a grunt, Karish said, "Or what, human?"

Vul confidently replied, "We will storm your citadel, slaughtering you and your soldiers. Then we will take what we want and put a flame to the rest! What is your answer?"

Thinking for a moment Karish grinned and directed his soldiers to target the ballistic platforms.

Once they were targeted, Karish said, "General of mankind, my answer is this. Fire!"

Puzzled at his answer, Vul tried to work it out in his mind. Suddenly, six objects moving quickly overhead separated and slammed into his artillery, erupting with great noise, flame, and pressurized heat. Vul's soldiers panicked, uncertain what to do.

Moving back into the formation, he gave orders to hold ranks and directed Nyeve to have her archers target the inside of the citadel using incendiary tips. Her bowmen listened to each command with great discipline. "Nock! Flame! Target interior! Loose!" Thousands of arrows passed over both soldiers and walls, striking various areas within the citadel, exploding on contact. Special gel developed by Norhi streamed out of the arrows shafts, setting fire to stone and wood.

Soon after, Karish ordered his soldiers to attack. Advancing against their foe, the ariyon soldiers marched with shields up and lances forward.

After another volley of arrows into the citadel, Vul directed Nyeve to target the rear soldiers with armor-piercing tips while he ordered the outer columns to execute a movement he had named 'clapping the hands.' Five hundred soldiers from each side pivoted at the tip of the spear formation, enclosing a great deal of the enemy in between their ranks. During the fight, dark clouds that had gathered over the battlefield burst forth, sending torrents of rain to the ground, surprising the shifters and creating chaos as they fought viciously against the ariyons.

***

Ustin and his group moved quickly up the jagged slopes, which led to a great lake. Landmarks served as reminders of which paths to take as they went. Coming to a large boulder, Ustin found and removed the top to a ventilation shaft. Silently, they climbed down a metallic rebar-type ladder encircling the inside of the shaft. After half a stadia, the vertical shaft traveled horizontally and then dropped again for another stadia. At the bottom, a small metal door opened to a great underground bay. Only a few soldiers guarded the area, and the group easily neutralized them before looking in amazement at the size of the flying machines kept in rows.

Norhi couldn't contain his excitement. "Ustin, they're... they're incredible! How was it possible for you to manufacture such magnificent machines?"

Before he could respond, a voice came from behind the group. "He only helped."

Turning in surprise, they looked to see who was speaking and found no one. Norhi asked, "Where are you? Who are you?"

The voice answered, "Down here, and my name is Gimet the Wise."

Glancing down and to the left, they beheld a diminutive man wearing a leather apron with a pair of goggles on his forehead. Ustin moved forward and said, "Gimet, old friend, you look the same and none the worse for wear."

Nodding, Gimet said, "And might I say I'm surprised to see you alive. We were told that everyone who escaped was caught and consumed. They lied." The two laughed and carried on while Norhi and the others stood back and watched in awe. Finally, Gimet asked, "So who are these with you, and why did you come back?"

Ustin said, "I'm sorry; these are new friends, and we're here to set my people free and abscond with your flying machines."

Shaking his head, Gimet said, "Of course, I should have known. I mean, why else come back here when you were safe and clear of the brothers? Not that I'm against the idea, Ustin; don't get me wrong. I'd help, but you're outnumbered, not to mention the brothers. How can you possibly get all the people and my machines past them—without dying, that is?"

Norhi stepped forward and said, "Don't you know? A battle is taking place topside as we speak."

Placing his hands on hips, Gimet said, "Well now, that makes sense. All your people were taken to the great room and secured inside. Tomorrow is Hamath's birthday, and I assumed they were being rounded up for choosing."

Curious, Norhi inquired, "Choosing?"

"Yeah, the brothers choose which humans to roast for the event." A disgusted look was all Gimet needed for an answer. "Ustin, these machines are very complicated, and I'm not sure if any of your people could maintain or manufacture them without me. What I'm saying is, I want to go with you."

Confused, Norhi asked, "Aren't you one of his people? Why would you think we'd leave you behind?"

His eyes downcast, Gimet did not answer; rather, Ustin answered for him. "Norhi, Gimet is an ariyon, having an angelic father and human mother."

Taken aback, Norhi said, "Ariyon? But he's… he's not—really?"

Looking up, Gimet said, "I know, my height is the issue, right? I could go into dominant and recessive genetics, but you wouldn't understand. I'm ariyon, but I want to live among men and take a wife for my own. Life is so futile among my kind, but when men see new machines and energy generators, they are amazed, not taking it for granted. I know how to develop and create these machines—great celestial chariots, if you will—plus so much more."

Norhi said, "Gimet, I cannot speak for our leader, Patel, but as second in command, I can tell you we will welcome anyone who wishes to live in peace with us."

Gimet happily said, "Very well then, my new friend Norhi. Behold, I give to you the chariots of the sky, along with their pilots." Placing two fingers on each side of his mouth, he whistled loudly within the bay, which brought much scuffling and moving about it. Twenty-three diminutive men ran up and stood in a straight line facing them. "These are the ariyon pilots and will take your people wherever they may wish to go."

Turning to his fellow ariyons, Gimet said, "Make ready all chariots for departure. Once we have released and loaded the spawn of men, we shall then take them to safety, where we may live among them in peace, treated as equals!" At this, a loud cheer went up from the pilots as they made their way to the craft within the bay. Looking up at Norhi and Ustin, Gimet said, "We need to move quickly. I cannot overpower the guards holding your people, but I can take you to them."

Ustin said, "You take us, and we will handle the rest."

Moving to a large staircase hewn from stone, the team with Gimet moved up to where the people were being kept.

***

Rain poured incessantly upon the battleground as the two armies fought with weapons of metal and wood. Water flowed along hard ground in curved, craggy veins, creating tripping hazards among the warriors. Visibility was obscured so badly that Vul's army broke ranks and began fighting in small groups, placing Nyeve's archers in jeopardy. Thinking the battle was favoring the ariyons, Patel sent his entire human force of two thousand men to assist Vul's army. He wanted to stay clear of the fighting to honor his word not to interfere, but thoughts of Nyeve needing him filled his mind. Suddenly, lightning from the sky slammed and whipped the ground where the army fought, stopping the humans in their tracks. They saw some of their fellow soldiers holding spears struck down by the great light. Patel saw it as well and wondered if it might be a weapon the giants possessed. He transformed into an eagle and took to the air, attempting to soar above the storm and find a way to disrupt it if possible. It was then that he noticed Karish's soldiers were being struck by the lightning bolts as well.

Patel turned to make another pass and watched as another ariyon army far off approached from a different part of the river. A dragon overshadowed them as they moved in the direction of the citadel. Patel soared back around and flew to inform Vul of the new danger approaching. As he moved closer, the rain slowed and suddenly stopped falling as the clouds begun to break up. Vul stopped fighting to look up at the sky, thankful that the rain had ceased. When he did so, he caught the image of Patel flying as an eagle. Thinking it was Patel's way of giving permission to change, Vul gave the order to what was left of his army to shift. Soon the entire battlefield was filled with half-man, half-animal fighters that overwhelmed the rest of their enemies, mauling, clawing, and slicing them to pieces.

His eyes wide, Karish watched as his army was laid to waste by hybrids, a few of which were armed with flaming swords of power. As if that weren't bad enough, every aerial machine he possessed came up and out of the water, flying over his head to parts unknown. Panicked, he left the wall and headed to the room where the humans were being kept, thinking he could use them as a means to bargain for his life. Upon reaching it, however, he found the place empty except for a note, pinned to the door with a dagger, that simply read, "I quit! Sincerely yours, Gimet." The blood drained from his face as he heard crushing blows, growing louder and more intense, landing on the large wooden entry doors of the citadel.

"Where are you brother?" he shouted to the open air. Then, as if by a miracle, the pounding to the doors ceased. He walked to the quad area and stood close to the doors, where he was able to make out the sounds of a quarrel of some kind just outside the fortification.

***

"Why did you change? I gave no orders to do so!"

Confused and irritated, Vul shot back at Patel, "Look, supreme commander, I saw you transformed and coming toward us and thought it was a signal; besides, we were getting our butts kicked."

Angrily, Patel replied, "That's why I sent in the reserves to assist you, but because you ordered everyone to shift—well—look at them!" Patel pointed in the direction of their reserves. Some of the men stood in awe, while others prostrated themselves to pay homage to what they perceived as gods. Patel roared, "This is exactly what I've tried to avoid all this time, Vul! They don't understand all this; how do you think—"

Nyeve approached and, getting in the middle of the two, said, "Patel, he did what was needed to be done. My archers were vulnerable to attack once the formation broke up. He saved many of us from destruction!"

Shooting back Patel replied, "What? You're taking his side? It doesn't matter what good came of it! Look at the evil it's wrought!"

Startled at first, Nyeve collected herself and said, "I'm not taking anyone's side. Please—"

"Look pal," said Vul, "I did what was needed. If you don't like it—too bad! What in blazes were you doing up there anyway? No one asked for you, so why did you enter the battlefield?"

Through clenched teeth, Patel said, "I was checking to see if it was possible to turn off or destroy the intense light source that was harming our troops— until I saw it was harming Karish's army as well. Then, when I spotted…" His demeanor softened. "The fight isn't over. I spotted an army coming this way from the river, and they have a dragon with them."

With an eyebrow raised, Vul inquired, "An army led by a dragon is on its way to us—from the river? Patel, no such army exists. We wiped out Utt and Demar's soldiers many times ago. You sent a dragon to the abyss; how many more do you think roam the earth?"

Nyeve pointed to the horizon and said in a low, soft voice, "At least one." As they glanced in the direction she was pointing toward, they saw a large dragon hovering over a growing dust cloud that was headed their way.

Vul was the first to react. "I'm really getting tired of being wrong and Patel right!" He turned to address the remaining soldiers. "All right, form up! This fight isn't over yet! Stay transformed; this battle we fight as gods!"

Patel, shocked, protested against Vul's statement, saying they fought as chosen ones, not gods, but no one heard him over the rumbling roars coming from Vul's soldiers. The humans, seeing and hearing the force before them, dropped their weapons and ran back to the bridge in great horror. Only two men stood their ground, and as they approached the group, they took spears in hand and launched them. Nyeve ordered her bowmen to target the men, thinking they meant to do harm to the army, but just then a scream of pain caught their attention. She turned to see two spears embedded in the arm of Karish, who had been preparing to attack from atop his citadel, as he fell back behind the wall with a large thud.

Nyeve approached the men and asked what their names were.

"I am Naki, and this is Anu; we are known as the fearless ones, and we are at your service."

Nyeve said, "Very well, Naki and Anu; walk with me and protect my archers." The men bowed, took up flanking positions, and readied themselves to closely protect the archers. Soaring high above his army, Patel watched as each army grew closer to one another.

Once the storm began to wane, Stul was able to make out a major siege erupting just outside Karish's citadel. Signaling to Deenal, he said, "You're correct; a fight is taking place, and it involves chosen ones! Your box will see the first of many victims this day!" Towed behind the army was a massive crystal like box made of pure quartz of virtual flawlessness. Waving in acknowledgement to Stul, he hoped beyond hope his theory that celestial powers could indeed be drained and held by crystalline rock proved true. He wanted to imprison the one who had banished Bael to the abyss, and as he watched his foe take to the air, he started to work out ways in which to snare him.

✳✳✳

Four lances apiece were given to Anu and his brother as the formation quickened its pace toward the ariyons. At three-quarters of a stadia from enemy lines, Vul halted his army and took up a defensive posture.

Nyeve directed her archers to target the dragon first. "Nock arrows! Target! Hold... Hold... Loose!" Hundreds of arrows sliced through the air, slamming into their prey with no effect. One of the arrows bounced off a belly scale, falling to the ground—but not before placing a small chip in one of the quartz walls of the cage. Drawing and firing more arrows, Nyeve targeted the center of the ariyon lines. A few arrows found their marks between shield and armor. Suddenly, ariyon soldiers broke ranks and ran directly toward Vul and his troops, yelling as they went.

Anu and Naki launched lances in quick succession, downing eight for eight. Each side drew swords and struck at the other in a ferocious melee. Both armies had met before and desired revenge upon the other, resulting in unmerciful carnage. Patel, hidden among the clouds, focused on the dragon below. When he felt the time was right to take it down, he dove quickly with talons brandished. Stul was prepared for the assault, however; he positioned himself over the quartz cell and moved aside just in time for the eagle to pass by him and slam deep within the box. The lid snapped shut, and Deenal secured it and turned the horses towing the cell toward home.

Clouds of dust on the battlefield concealed Patel's fate, and Stul added to the confusion by flapping his massive wings, kicking up even more debris among the fighters. When Stul thought the cell was far enough away, he recalled his troops. They broke from the battle and ran, making their way to a ridgeline overlooking the valley; only four hundred made it out alive.

Vul, seeing the enemy on the run, did not give orders to pursue, since he had lost many of his own warriors, including Anu and Naki, who had fought valiantly, keeping Nyeve from harm many times over. Exhausted, those surviving made their way toward Karish's citadel hoping to find water and healing plants for their wounds. The great doors to the fortress opened, revealing Norhi and Ustin waiting for them.

Walking through the threshold in silence, Vul spotted Karish bound and bleeding. Rage swelled within him; he pulled the hilt from his armband and brandishing a flaming blade as he approached the giant.

Knowing his end was near, Karish moved back against a stone wall, pleading for mercy. "Please spare me, my lord, and I will serve you. Yes, serve you, and provide energy to heal wounds and refresh you, my lord! I am beaten and swear allegiance to you, my lord. A slave for all time—me and my children. This I vow!"

Not paying attention at first, all Vul could see in his mind was a giant's head for a trophy on his lodge pole. As he raised his sword to strike, he suddenly stopped and thought about what Karish had said. "Your servitude you have vowed in return for your life. Very well, giant; I bestow mercy upon you and in doing so have become your god. You and your descendants shall serve me, but if deceit is found in your vow, I shall kill those you love in your sight before gouging out your eyes—swear it to your new god!"

Stammering, Karish replied, "I-I… swear to my new g-god. Lord, I do not know your name."

"Vul the Almighty is his name."

Continuing, Karish said, "I swear to Vul the Almighty; let it happen to me as he has said if any deceit is found in me."

Vul raised his sword once again and cut loose Karish's bonds. "Now, giant, where is this energy of healing you spoke about?"

Getting up from the ground, he said, "Yes, my lord, right away. I'll bring enough for all your soldiers, my lord."

Turning to Norhi and Ustin, Vul said, "You two go with him; if he tries to escape, kill him but leave his head for me to take."

Ustin bowed and immediately went with Karish, but Norhi stood in shock at what he was hearing. "Did you take a blow to the head during battle? Who do you think you are, setting yourself up as a god? This isn't what we're about, and who are you to take any person as a slave, Vul? Do you seriously think Patel will allow you to get away with this—any of this?"

Vul calmly said, "Norhi, I don't have time for insubordination. What I have done, I have done! As for Patel, he is no more."

Nyeve, who was attending to the wounded, stood up with a frightful look upon her face. "That's not true; he was fighting the dragon and—"

"Do you see a dragon?" said Vul. "Do you see Patel among us? I didn't want to say anything this soon, but I saw Patel fall before the dragon. It decapitated our Supreme commander and took his body with them, probably as a trophy." He scooped a cup of water from a large wooden barrel and poured it over his head. "Either way, he's dead and I'm alive."

Norhi and Nyeve glanced at each other in disbelief. Tears filled their eyes as Karish returned with spheres of energy—more than enough for everyone present. He warned them not to take in too much of this particular energy at one time or it would act as an intoxicant. Holding one of the balls of power, Vul took in small amounts of energy and watched in amazement as gashes and long, jagged slices in his skin closed with no signs of scarring. Soon, everyone assembled had taken in the healing energies—except Norhi and Nyeve, who still grieved for Patel. Vul walked over to the couple and put out his hand for Nyeve to grasp, but she was unwilling and inconsolable.

Norhi got to his feet and walked toward the entrance to the citadel, prompting a question from Vul. "Norhi, where are you going?"

Without looking back, he replied, "Out."

In an authoritative voice, Vul continued his inquiry. "As your king, I demand to know where my subjects go and when they intend on returning."

Anger laced Norhi's response as he turned to face Vul. "You are neither my king nor my god; nor shall you ever hold such a place in my heart. Play your games with those who care, but never think you hold power over me."

Norhi turned and kept walking, leaving the citadel never to return. Ustin tried to catch up with him, thinking he could change Norhi's mind, but Vul called him back, directing the young man to let him go. "We still have a giant to confront. I want all enemies crushed under my heel so peace reigns as I build an empire. Then shall I go out once again to conquer more lands and take other peoples as my own."

Ustin bowed and brought Karish to stand before Vul. "Tell me, giant, what are your brother's defenses, and are there any secret passageways to enter his citadel?"

Humbly addressing Vul, the giant said, "Master, Hamath is powerful—more so than I. He does not have an army but only uses six slaves to take care of him: three females to know and three males to clean them and his fortress. A servant's door may be found in the back wall that faces the great lake, though I'm unsure if it still exists since he had many slaves attempt escape in the past."

Vul dismissed Karish, "That's fine; I'll not need it anyway. From what you've stated, this man holds too much pride, thinking himself invincible. I shall call him out and defeat the giant in front of his own dwelling. Karish, you will stay here and see to my people. Bring out all metals and precious things here, as well as any armor and weapons. When I return, we shall leave for my city, understood?"

Karish bowed, turned, and began his work while Ustin watched over the giant. Vul grabbed a bow and quiver of arrows and readied to leave. Looking over at Nyeve, who was sobbing and long-faced, he said before departing, "You have until I return to mourn, and then you will mourn no more for Patel. As my queen you will be strong, standing at my side in confidence. I'll accept nothing less from you." Vul left the fortress, mounted a horse from Karish's stable, and made his way alone to Hamath's fortress.

Chapter 31

Walking to the bridge pondering what to do next, Norhi came across 1,998 humans that had fled the battlefield, sitting on the other side of the river. When they saw him, they immediately fell to the ground and worshipped him, because he hadn't transformed back into human form. Seeing a tall figure with an Ibis head and human body made them think of him as a god among men. When he spoke, they trembled. "Men, arise, and do not pay homage to me, for I am no god but a man like you."

One of the humans spoke up. "My lord, forgive me, but you are no ordinary man, for we cannot take on such an image."

Norhi sighed and reluctantly transformed into the figure of a man whom they knew quite well. "See, I am like you, and you know me from the village, for I am Norhi. Do not be afraid, and try to understand. I am a man no better than any of you. I've lost a great friend, the man you know as Patel, to a dragon of Bael. And now Vul, general of the army, has set himself up as king and god over men. This I cannot accept."

Speaking up once again, the man asked, "Lord, we fled the battlefield not for a lack of courage, but for a lack of understanding. We shall fuse our lives to yours and live under your word. Let us be your army, and we will follow whatever commands we are given, we so vow."

Seeing that the others all agreed with the man, Norhi shook his head. "What is your name?"

The soldier answered, "I am Tyndal, my lord."

"Very well, Tyndal. Let's go home. But no man shall serve me, for we are all free, as one great leader of men always wanted." His voice was broken with grief. "Patel desired for all men to be free, and so shall it be. To his memory—freedom!"

In one voice, the men cried out "Freedom!" So loud was their cry that birds took flight, echoes were heard from the mountains, and all those inside Karish's citadel looked every which way to find where the sound originated.

***

Vul arrived at Hamath's citadel and leaped from his steed before halting its stride. Shouting to the giant with ever increasing taunts, he waited for a response but received none. Puzzled that no sound or stirrings could be heard within the fortress, he picked up large boulders and hurled them against tall wooden doors. Soon after, he heard a great rumbling from behind the gates, then silence. Suddenly, a large shadow formed over Vul. Looking up, he perceived a huge mass falling toward him. He rolled to one side, barely escaping being crushed underfoot by Hamath. Vul leaped away and came to rest atop a boulder. Standing upon it, he viewed his enemy for the first time. Even though he had transformed into a lion-man standing twelve cubits in height, Hamath stood twenty-four cubits, and thick was his torso. Armor covered the giant from head to toe; the thick metallic scales gleamed under a shining sun. His lance, as thick as a tree trunk, brandished a large silver spearhead. His shield was as big as one of the doors to the citadel, and on a belt of leather he sported a double-edged curved sword.

Ominously Hamath stood, facing Vul with a look of disdain upon his face. Glancing about, the giant peered through his helmet at the area surrounding the two of them. Confusion gripped him. He once again looked about and saw nothing but one of his brother's horses and a lone shifter. "What's this, then? Where is your army? Did you not speak with arrogance, and yet you are here alone?"

Confidently Vul replied, "I require no army, Hamath of the giants. I have come to bring an ultimatum: surrender yourself and your house to me— Vul the Almighty!"

His brow drawn together, Hamath said, "Or what, little one?"

Vul answered haughtily, "Or your head will be added to my trophy collection." He gave a large bellowing laugh. "What, then, shall be your answer, giant—life or death?"

A stern-faced Hamath answered, "You dare come at me alone and speak as if a god? No man has ever defeated me, and before this day ends, I will gut and roast you like all the others!"

Hamath brought his lance up and threw it toward Vul. The lion-man ducked, moving to one side, barely escaping. But the breeze the lance caused in passing knocked him to the ground. Hamath leaped to where Vul fell and drove his shield into the earth, again missing his intended target. Vul drew his sword and leaped into the air and over the giant, slicing as he went. Vul landed on his feet and spun around in time to see his opponent's ear fall to the ground. Hamath stumbled to get to his feet, holding the side of his head as blood poured from the wound, prompting Vul to say, "That's what you get for removing your helmet."

When the giant bent forward, attempting to locate his ear, Vul mightily leaped into the air once more. He landed on Hamath's shoulder and, with both hands clutching his sword, sliced through the giant's neck, detaching head from body. "And that's what you get for underestimating me!"

Vul stood over the slain body of Hamath. Pride swelled his chest as adrenaline surged through his veins. Placing a foot on his foe's torso, Vul bellowed an intense roar of such strength that Norhi and the men with him could hear it. After grabbing up and affixing the giant's helmet on his severed head, Vul jumped upon his steed and rode swiftly toward Karish's citadel.

***

Upon reaching the fortress, Stul assisted Deenal and the brothers in moving their newly acquired prize to a room below the citadel. After they had set it across from Stul's spawn, everyone except the dragon returned to the great room to relax. Stul transformed into a more humanoid form and slowly moved about the exterior of the cage, tapping on its walls, staring down his enemy. Finally, the dragon spoke. "Greetings, shifter, and welcome to my abode; I do hope you are enjoying the accommodations."

Patel wearily replied, "How could I not? A room with a view. When's dinner? I'll need to wash up."

An evil grin across his face, Stul said, "I'll let you know. In the meantime, please feel free to roam about and take in the sights since you'll be here for a very long time."

Patel inquired, "Exactly why am I being shown such special hospitality?"

Stul rushed at one of the walls, seething with rage, but kept himself from crushing it to get at the changeling. "Because you banished one of the most powerful angelics ever created to the abyss, and for that I wish to hurt you; to torture the soul within that dustbowl you call a body for all eternity!"

An exhausted Patel replied, "You make what I did sound like a bad thing. I bet his domain is bigger than mine."

Stul sneered at the shifter. "Enjoy your joviality while you can, chosen one. You might be noticing an energy drain."

Laughing and nodding, Patel said, "Now that you mention it, I have been feeling a little off."

Stul flashed an evil grin. "Yes, well as I was saying, this box drains energy from you, storing it within these walls. Bael will be released in ten thousand earth years, but I'm afraid you won't be around to greet him. Since you're mortal, once all your energy is absorbed, you'll die. Oh, and when that happens I intend on preserving your shell for Bael to have as an everlasting trophy; how does that sound to you, shifter?"

Sitting with his back to a wall, Patel said, "It's always nice to be wanted … I guess."

Stul snarled. "You will fear, shifter! Make your jokes now, but I guarantee you will fear before death takes you."

Looking around, Patel noticed three sacs hanging from a lower part of the room's ceiling. "I hope I do a little better than those poor creatures in the corner." Glancing over his shoulder, Stul was shocked to see elongated, gleaming, dark cocoons where his spawn had once hung. He ran up to one of them and placed an ear against it and listened. He could hear and feel stirrings beneath the casing, which washed away the anxiety that was growing within him. "These are my children, shifter, and though you and your kind have made short work of our other spawn, these—my children—are quite special, for they shall be like me— immortal!"

Wearily, Patel said, "Well, when I escape I'll be sure to test your theory of immortality."

Stul rush the cage once again and ran his claws along it, unaware that he was gouging long marks along its wall. "I know what you're trying to do, shifter, but my rage is not without wisdom. You'll not taunt me into releasing you from this cage to rip your head from that body. My children are immortal, and unfortunately, you'll never get a chance to—"

Before he could finish, a crackling noise from behind caught the dragon's attention. He turned toward his children and watched as the cocoons split from top to bottom, releasing each child one at a time. The first to emerge was a young man with fire in his eyes, brandishing fangs. His body was muscular, with pale blue skin free of hair. However, upon his head, jet-black hair extended to just above his broad shoulders. The second child was female and most beautiful; long hair the color of corn silk draped over her shoulders, ending at her waist. Her skin was creamy blue-white, her lips red like rubies, and her body was toned, possessing an inviting navel and taunt abdomen. Patel was captivated by her; he found her so appealing that he could not look away. Finally, the third child emerged—a female as well. They were twins; the only physical difference between them was the color of their hair—that of the second of the pair was a fiery red. Both were endowed with fangs, like their brother, and possessed almond-shaped eyes with irises full of blue green flame. The symbol of a golden dragon was embossed on the left side of the male's chest and just under the females' navels. All three of them stepped forward, bowed, and went to one knee before Stul. "Greetings, father. We, your children, pay homage."

Joy filled Stul's heart as he moved to embrace them. Shaking his head, Patel said, "Gee, do I feel like a fifth wheel. Do you want to introduce me, or should I just go back to doing—well, nothing actually?"

Ignoring him, Stul pushed his offspring to the door but was stopped by them. "Father, we must have our first feeding to be fully charged." He thought for a moment and was about to bite his wrist to open it for them, but they gestured to him again, saying, "No, we need energy—spiritual energy." Hungrily, they stared at Patel, and rubbing their arms, they anxiously desired to feed on him.

Stul shook his head. "My children, I want to help you, but I cannot allow this creature to be freed. Take from my essence if you must, because this animal is off-limits."

At that moment, a voice came from the direction of the threshold. Spinning around Stul found Lilith standing near the door holding garments in her hand. "My children, approach the cage and place your hands upon it; slowly withdraw the energy stored within the wall. Slowly, now; too much all at once will make you dizzy."

As they drew energy into their bodies, a glow emanated from their skin. Once they had their fill, all three ran to Lilith and embraced her. When they were done greeting her, Lilith gave each one a form-fitting suit, black with gold trim, along with combat-style black boots for the male and knee-high stiletto boots for the females. A symbol of a golden dragon was embossed on the left side of his chest and just under the navel of the females.

When they finished dressing, Lilith said, "You may wear whatever clothing you choose, but I thought this would do for now. How beautiful you all are. No other mother could be as proud of her children or love them as much as I do you—the last of my motherhood."

Stepping forward, her son asked, "Mother, names we have not been given. What shall we be called?"

She walked up and took hold of his shoulders. "You shall be called Hakeldama, which means 'field of blood.'" Glancing over to her blonde daughter she said, "Barrab you shall be, which means 'most desirable,' and your sister's name is Eedn, which means 'flaming sensuality.'" Content with their assigned monikers, the family left the basement and made their way to the great room to meet the others.

Time slowly passed, leaving Patel alone and forgotten in a dank and dark dungeon with only memories of a life he had once shared with the woman of his dreams. It was not his pain that haunted his thoughts while he lay on a crystal floor that slowly drained energy from his already exhausted body, but the agony Nyeve faced. Patel knew she loved him more than anything in the world. He knew her heart ached at his leaving; she had clutched at him, sobbed, pleaded for him not to go. Images of them together seared his mind; if only he could go back, he'd never leave her again. "Let people take care of themselves. Why do I have to free them and chain myself to a life devoid of her—why?"

His entreaty fell upon deaf ears, resonating off cold, cruel walls that threatened to keep him buried alive for all time.

Karish sat against a back wall, speaking with Ustin as they waited for Vul to return from Hamath. A sudden silence fell over the land, and no wind blew upon the ground. The giant knew what was coming and explained it to Ustin and the others. "The great rains have come and passed; soon after they leave, a great wind comes bringing dust and sand with it. Visibility will become faint until it passes."

410

"How long will it last?" asked Ustin.

Karish answered, "Oh, about thirty or so minutes—not too long."

"Thirty minutes," said Ustin. "what are minutes?"

Nodding and smiling, Karish said, "You do not possess such knowledge. We, the sons of angels, divide time into small parts increasing from least to greatest." Seeing confusion on Ustin's face, Karish drew out on the ground what he meant. "Look. Sixty seconds—each tick here equals a minute, and sixty minutes equal an hour. Additionally, twenty-four hours are in a day, which is divided into twelve hours, dependent on what part of the globe you happen to be on at the time of the sun's passing."

Waving his hands toward Karish, Ustin said, "I'm fine, I'm fine. No need for storytelling right now. Let's wait for Vul's return, okay?"

Though confused, Karish agreed and sat back, folding his arms. "You know, I'm not trying to upset anyone, but I have reservations about his success against my brother. Hamath is a very strong and dark-tempered being holding great hate for mankind—greater than any other. You might want to take what you can and just leave here now. When he comes, not even I will escape his wrath. He entrusted me with technologies given by our fathers that are lost to you humans now."

Through open doors to the citadel, Ustin watched as winds mixed with earth raced sideways toward the great river, blotting out a ridge on the horizon as he spoke. "Do not underestimate Lord Vul, giant. He possesses a power and will unmatched among our kind. Even this dust storm he would subject to his will. He shall return—triumphant!"

Nyeve sat listening to every word. Sorrow filled her heart, and she didn't understand her feelings or know whether they were being caused by the loss of Patel or the possible loss of Vul. Her very soul seemed at war with her mind over what or how she was to feel: the memory of the one man who gave safety, security, and comfort to her very being, unceasingly sharing his very spirit with her; or the man that set fire to it with cruel passions and unpredictable primordial behavior. Either way, both were missing and one was lost to her for sure. As she gazed into the fierce storm, it appeared as if it were mocking her pain. Every now and again she could make out an image—a shadow, really—of a man-beast slowly walking, ever nearing the citadel's entrance.

Karish also made out a figure looming tall, slightly swaying in the powerful winds. As the storm slowly subsided, he perceived a glint of his brother's helmet. "See, I told you my brother would come he has defeated your champion!"

Soon an image of Vul also appeared out of the blowing dust and sand of the storm, his stride full of pride and arrogance. Before he crossed the threshold to enter the citadel, the winds died and the dust settled, giving a clear image of Hamath's head atop his own spear, which had been planted in the ground. Shock and disbelief fell upon the giant. He couldn't believe what was before him. Great fear clutched his heart as strength left his legs; prostrating before Vul, he prayed for mercy. Nyeve struggled with what to do—run to him or hold back; love him or not. When he looked in her direction, she obeyed his command without words, swiftly moving to him. "As my queen, you will reign, and my empire shall be great," he said.

He directed Ustin to his other side and said, "My son, you shall reign as a prince with the same authority; your words shall be law!" Turning his attention to Karish, he said, "You, giant, rise and pay heed; your fate will be that of your brother's if ever deceit is found in you. Serve me well and you'll live. Many women shall I give you and land as well, in exchange for the wisdom of angels. With it, I will construct an empire and a legacy rivaling those of the gods, and those who serve me will prosper." Not waiting for a reply, Vul ordered the remainder of his army to strip the citadel of everything holding value to take as wages for themselves. He then ordered the pillaging of Hamath's house, leaving the land desolate with the exception of the giant's lance, helmet, and head; these he left as a warning to anyone that found them. Vul declared his kingship and dominion over the lands, challenging the celestials as well as all of mankind who opposed him.

Chapter 32

Several decades had passed since the great war of the Badlands ended. Norhi had been elected leader of the people, taking Patel's seat at the council of elders. He was happy that the people embraced Gimet and other ariyons as their own. Soon thereafter, celestial knowledge among men was as common as water. They created calendars to mark the passage of time, and they developed a written form of their verbal language and started keeping records of their histories.

Norhi's people lived in peace, and though from time to time Vul's flying machines could be seen in the air engaged in battle with ariyons and other angelic hybrids, neither Vul nor the hybrids molested them. After all, Norhi's people were neutral, taking neither side and always giving refuge to those who asked.

Gimet taught a greater form of alchemy and metallurgy to Norhi apart from man, since he was fearful of its misuse. Chemicals extracted from certain plants, when combined in measured parts, created a liquid that dissolved the hardest rock; less of one component and the rock became as putty and could then be molded into various shapes that later hardened. He also gave man the ability to create electrical power by fabricating pyramidal generators. Only certain types of rock that possessed the best conductive properties were used in their construction. When proper amounts of specific chemicals were added to the pyramids in calculated measure, the pyramids produced energy that resonated in both sound and light waves. These waves were focused with large quartz-like crystals embedded in the center of the constructs. They also sent up a vertical shaft that terminated in an apex of pure silver that held a crimson-colored crystal with an aperture on all eight sides of the building. As energy passed through the apertures, it looked as if an eye were blinking, sending out energies to be collected and concentrated by large obelisks. The obelisks would then charge a circular in diameter area with pure energy to be used for operating different tools.

When asked about the weapons that had destroyed ballistic siege weapons many years earlier, Gimet would always protest. "Norhi, I have given to you and your kind great knowledge and provided machines of usefulness. Why do you still wish for knowledge whose only purpose is to take life?"

Leaning in as they reclined at a dinner table with the elders present, Norhi said, "Gimet, I am a man of peace, and you know this quite well, but Vul and his legions are growing rapidly. The giants and ariyons are also proliferating, each kingdom closing in on the other, and we are in the middle, my friend. I worry of what might happen when we are attacked and have no way to protect ourselves. How will we repel such sizeable armies?"

Gimet explained, "My friend, conquest was the motivation of Vul and his men; that is very true. But it was for the metal called gold which he treasured, not so much people and lands. Did you notice how quickly his plans of expansion trickled away once a pyramidal generator, the size of which even astounded me, was built for him? As you know, the sludge runoff of combining the chemicals within the generator is pure liquid gold. He coats everything with it. We never enter his mind; believe me. Now, my people, on the other hand"—he took a drink of fermented grapes—"they view us like we are humans—with disdain—even though from time to time we give them shelter and act as a refuge for those fleeing battle. You and I will always be hated."

Norhi said, "All the more reason to arm ourselves now that we have the means to do so. Something has me shaken to my very core, Gimet. I thought those of our people who come up missing every now and again had gone lost or fallen prey to some of the giant reptiles since most were hunters, but now I'm thinking ariyons might be picking us off one at a time."

Glassy-eyed from the effects of the wine, Gimet clumsily leaned closer in and said, "My people do not work that way, my friend; if they wanted this city and its inhabitants, they would take it." He sensed that Norhi was unconvinced and highly frustrated. Slightly slurring his words, he said, "Tell ya what I'm willing to do. Now, I'll build you weapons, I will, if—*if*—you join me in drinking this wonderful concoction, this nectar of the gods, and if you will accompany me on a scouting expedition to figure out if any danger exists… exists. Deal?"

Norhi happily agreed, and with many goblets of wine, they celebrated the rest of the night away. When morning came, each man consumed large quantities of water before setting out on a reconnaissance mission, seeking information on their neighbor's activities. Deciding flying machines were too overt, Norhi transformed into a large grey rhino and made Gimet his rider. After trotting through woods and thick forests, they came to the outskirts of Vul's kingdom. The two of them stood in awe at its radiance and beauty; in less than ten earth years, Vul had created a place of absolute splendor.

A massive pyramid covered in shiny, smooth white limestone and capped by a silver top with crimson apertures dominated the horizon. Gold obelisks peppered the entire area of the city, as did statues of lions, and carved human bodies with the heads of lions stood at the entry point of every building. There was one monument that caught their attention, however—an enormous gold-plated lion's head with a closed mouth; a great, flowing mane; and no body. This mammoth structure faced a large, winding river. Its detailed and sculpted magnificence left Norhi speechless, but Gimet was able to deduce that the statue faced the point where the constellation known as Leo rose in the night sky. A shimmering pool of gold filled a trench leading from the great pyramid to the lion. So incredible was the sight of the city that the two were unaware of soldiers coming up behind them.

Norhi felt a slight pain in his neck, became dizzy, lost consciousness, and fell to the ground. Hours later, his hearing was the first thing to return, then his sight. Once he could sit up, he looked around the room he was now in and found Gimet still lying on the floor. Norhi slowly got to his feet, checked on Gimet, and then studied the room. Beautiful carvings of animals and portraits of people filled each part of the walls and ceilings. The floor was made of brilliant smooth stones and lit all the way around. Gimet started to groan and move, prompting Norhi to come to his assistance. "Easy, my friend; you're safe."

Gimet groggily asked, "Where are we? What happened? All I remember is looking at the city."

"I believe we are in the city," said Norhi. "They used some type of elixir administered through a hollowed dart to render us immobile."

A voice from behind them caught their attention. "Very good… you would be correct, sir. Please come with me, sirs; her majesty awaits your arrival in the throne room."

The two men looked at each other, shrugged their shoulders, and turned and followed a man dressed in a white toga with a red sash across one shoulder. As they walked down a grand hallway, they could not believe the splendor unfurling before them.

They entered a large chamber dominated by three opulent thrones; the entire room would hold a thousand men easily and was covered completely in polished gold. Emeralds, dark rubies, and diamonds the size of pomegranates had been cut and polished to great perfection and embedded uniformly within the chamber walls. Two solid gold statues of lion-headed men twenty cubits in height stood on each side of the throne area; each one held a closed fist over his heart. As they admired the craftsmanship, a man wearing a blue sash announced Her Majesty's arrival. "All bow before Her Highness, Queen SedicEve, wife of His Highness, King Vul the Almighty!"

The two bowed in respect but did not notice her appearance until she spoke. "Norhi, Gimet, please rise. It is I, Nyeve."

Norhi couldn't believe it was really her. "Ny—I thought you… I mean, after Patel perished, you and Vul… really?"

She nodded. "Yes, I stayed with Vul and built all that you see."

Inquiring further, Norhi asked, "What's with the name change—SedicEve?"

Her eyes downcast, she said, "He did not want reminders of the past—of Patel—so he changed my name to serve his purposes."

"He named you—"

Cutting him off, she answered, "Yes, God's footstool am I! But I am a queen, even if it is his queen."

Feeling a bit awkward, Norhi said, "A beautiful queen at that. Why didn't you visit us so I could know you still existed among the living?"

"I'm forbidden to leave the city, since I must rule while Vul is away expanding his empire or fighting against ariyons and their kind." She looked at Norhi's diminutive partner. "No offense, master Gimet."

Bowing, he said, "None taken, my queen."

Now it was time for her to ask questions of them. "Why have you come to us as if spies? My soldiers informed me that you were found on a ridge overlooking the city, in concealment."

"We were not spying," said Norhi, "or rather, it wasn't our intent. My people suffer from an unknown force, in that they go missing. I wanted to find out why they go missing so frequently, and I thought maybe our neighbors were taking them as slave labor."

Speaking up, the queen said, "And so you thought we might be stealing away your people?"

He shook his head. "Not necessarily, Ny; I'm just checking every possibility is all. A lot has changed in the past decade, as you know quite well; and as you know, my people are a peaceful one. We hold no super weapons and therefore may be incapable of defending ourselves if ever attacked."

Nyeve took a seat upon her throne and called for chairs to be brought for her guests. A small table was also placed before them, and gold chalices full of wine were served. After taking a drink of wine, Nyeve asked, "It is as you say, dear Norhi; many things have changed. But not once did Vul or any of his soldiers ever molest your people. In fact, the king decreed that under no circumstances were your people or their city to be raided. So, you see, he has taken great steps to ensure your safety."

Puzzled, Norhi said, "I was unaware he had done such a thing, and yet knowing this information adds more questions than answers."

Cocking her head to one side, she curiously inquired, "How so?"

Explaining, Norhi said, "Well, as you pointed out, my queen, Vul went to great lengths to wipe out all things reminding him of the past, especially Patel; so why go to such extremes to keep a people led by him safe from enemy attack and free from the king's empire?"

A deep, authoritative voice from behind pillars near the throne area answered, "One would think gratitude, rather than suspicion, should be given to a power that is benevolent in its dealing with weaker neighbors."

Walking out and taking his place before the main throne, Vul waited for proper homage to be paid by his guests and queen. Norhi and Gimet followed

Nyeve's lead and fell prostrate. When he was content with their display of abject humiliation, everyone took seats and waited to hear Vul speak. After taking a drink of wine from a chalice brought to him by one of his stewards, he said, "As I stated earlier, why do you question my kindness toward you and your city's inhabitants?"

Clearing his throat, Norhi made an attempt at showing awe in the king's presence but failed miserably. "I was merely stating, O king, that it appeared strange—out of character."

"So I am unable to show kindness because it does not fall within the realm of my character?"

Norhi nodded. "Exactly. Or rather... no, no, that's what I meant."

A smile upon his face partially hid the anger within as he answered. "I see. Then I assume you'll understand why your city will be leveled tomorrow, as it is in my character to do so."

Bowing his head, Norhi quickly apologized. "Forgive me, King Vul, if I in any way disrespected you; it was not my intent."

Vul nodded. "Very well. I will spare your city on the condition that you explain to my satisfaction why this audience with my wife happened while I was away."

Gimet spoke up. "King Vul, we did not seek an audience; we were caught spying. Not that we spied on her, but rather your kingdom. Not that we were even spying, really—"

Cutting him off Norhi said, "Look, Vul we weren't spying. A number of our people have gone missing, and not in groups, but a few here and there. I was checking to see if they may have wandered into your city when Nyeve's soldiers found us and—"

Vul quickly stood and let out a great roar; he then pointed at Norhi and said, "I am King Vul, and this is Queen SedicEve. Never shall you utter the name Nyeve in my presence again—understood?"

Norhi and Gimet both got to their feet and bowed low before Norhi said, "Again my apologies, King Vul; perhaps it would be best if we took our leave of you."

Calm suddenly came over the king as he answered, "You are not subjects of my realm and therefore do not possess knowledge of the workings of my kingdom. Sit; I shall forget your blasphemies this one time. Just remember, dear Norhi, all which you have surveyed of my kingdom is indeed mine. All that live, work, and die within it are mine. The queen owns nothing, and everything she is or has was given by me, and she is mine. Your people are of no concern to me.

Yet for your sakes I leave you under my realm's protection as a courtesy and nothing more. Many years have passed, and so we evolve mostly by the knowledge given us by ariyons like Gimet. However, where you have squandered away such gifts, I have built upon them. Power, my dear Norhi, allowed for the expansion of my kingdom, not peace. 'Peace' is a word of the weak, and the weak always fall prey to those more dominant—would you not agree?"

Attempting to choose his words carefully, Norhi said, "I cannot refute your achievements, O king. Your empire is truly spectacular. Not even offspring of the fallen ones create incredible buildings of this great scale and magnitude; they create large rock structures, but not with such beauty and detail. Nothing on earth exceeds your excess, but at what cost? How many have died in battle for you to secure all of this?"

I did not force others to labor for me; they did so for themselves. My people live on their own successes in peace, sharing what they have with those in need and vice versa. Everyone works, my king, or they do not eat. Not by someone else's hand but by their own do they thrive or perish. We hold love and peace as our commodities and give of them when we can, freely to all who are found wanting. Recently, however, it has come to my attention that my people require defenses, and I have asked Gimet to produce weapons for our safety and security. Being intelligent as he is, though, he wanted to find out firsthand what might be happening to our people who go missing. If the reason is legitimate to him, he will begin the process of developing sophisticated armament to protect our city and its occupants. This is the reason we were found looking around the areas between our two cities."

Hearing all that Norhi had said and trying to keep a look of confusion since he was quite aware of what was happening to Norhi's clan, Vul said, "Sound reasoning, in that you wish to find the cause of some disappearances," said Vul, "but I should caution you both; developing weapons is a dangerous undertaking. Many enemies still exist outside our two realms, and so far they have not attacked you, but me. I think it best if you leave the making of weaponry and fighting to me with this pledge: I will focus my own resources on finding out what is happening to your people and will fight against any enemy which comes directly against you at any time. If you like, I can send a garrison to occupy your city to keep raiders and such from molesting the people. How'd that be for you?"

Norhi quickly said, "A garrison is unnecessary, and too generous, my king. However, with such vast resources at your command, we would gratefully accept any assistance in investigating the disappearance of our people. Thank you, King Vul."

Vul nodded to the men and called for one of his personal pilots. Upon reaching the throne room, his highness ordered the diminutive pilot to take Norhi and Gimet where they wished to go. "It was good seeing you again, Norhi—Gimet. And again, rest assured that sophisticated weaponry is not required; my people will get to the bottom of those disappearances."

The two men stood and bowed low to Vul; they then silently followed his pilot out of the throne room. While walking down a large hall once more, Norhi glanced into a room through a door that was slightly ajar and saw three beings with mantis-like heads working around a three-dimensional model sprawled out on a long, red table that appeared to be made of granite or a similar material. When he momentarily paused in his stride to take in the sight, a guard firmly pressed a spear shaft into the small of his back to get him going again.

When the group reached a large circular aircraft hangar, the pilot pressed his hand against a plate on one of the walls and the ceiling parted overhead, allowing daylight to shine in and upon their ride. A delta-winged craft, smooth in appearance and seamless, rested on three extended landing gear; it was unlike the aircraft they had absconded with from Karish's lair. Norhi and Gimet stared at each other in confusion. They entered the ship and took seats next to the pilot, noticing control panels made out of a smooth crystal that self-illuminated.

Gimet asked the pilot if the engine was still symbiotic in nature but received no response. He peered closer at the pilot's face, which was covered by a dark helmet visor. "Fluinceed, is that you? Fluinceed, it's me, Gimet! Don't you recognize me?"

The pilot still gave no response; he then asked, "To where shall I take you, my masters?"

Disbelief settled heavily upon Gimet staring at longtime friend. They had worked together on many construction projects until the Hamath brothers desired a fleet of flying vehicles and guided rockets filled with explosives to destroy ground troops. They even collaborated on a project to design a vehicle that would allow Hamath to enter space, since the giant wanted to take revenge against his angelic father for giving him life as a half-mortal. Now his friend did not recognize him and Fluinceed seemed more robotic than organic. Norhi gave instruction to take them home, and while airborne, he instructed the pilot to slowly fly over Demar's old citadel. Turning his attention from

Fluinceed, Gimet asked, "Why do you want to see those old ruins?"

Norhi explained, "I saw something back in Vul's city that—" Stopping himself, Norhi waved off Gimet's question, thinking their pilot may take information back to Vul. Peering down and into the citadel as they grew closer, Norhi saw more of the same type of beings that were in the room of Vul's city. Additionally, he saw three beings that looked human, along with dark, shadowlike entities darting to and fro within the castle walls.

Just then, the pilot put two fingers on the right side of his helmet and said, "Yes, sir." Placing a hand over one of the panels, he said, "I must drop you off and return immediately to my master."

The craft headed for Norhi's city, where it silently touched down in the town square. It swiftly took off again once its passengers were on the ground. Norhi turned to Gimet and directed him to assemble the elders in the conference chamber, stating that he would explain everything then. As Gimet moved to rally the elders, Norhi pondered all that had transpired that day. Nyeve was alive and reigned as Vul's queen, Vul's kingdom and its opulence had no bounds, beings never before seen resided within the gold city, and those same beings were present in Demar's old citadel. *What does it all mean?* Norhi wondered. He wrestled with the information over and again, trying to make sense of it and wondering if any of it involved his missing people.

✱✱✱

Rising from her throne, SedicEve directed all servants and guards to leave the throne room. Approaching Vul, she said, "My king, why so harsh with our friends? Norhi doesn't mean any harm against us. It was nice to see him again. Do you know he thought I was dead all these years?"

Vul poured another a glass of wine and took a drink. "You are dead; yet has your womb to produce even one offspring." He looked at her with glazed eyes. "What good are you to me? Without sons I cannot continue bloodlines or expand my empire further through marriages as the fallen ones' offspring do."

Sorrow and anguish filled her heart as she answered him. "I've given all that I am to you. When did I balk, or crow hop, that you'd say such things to me? Ask anyone in your precious kingdom, and they will tell you that every type of support you desired I performed as a perfect rip entry, never once rippling the water. I even gave up my own self-respect by knowing you while still with another."

Turning, Vul raised a finger in contempt and said, "Say his name out loud just once and it will be your last word!"

Screwing up her nerve and strength, she yelled, "I don't deserve to have his name spoken by these lips or uttered by this heart, but this once I will say it, in defiance of you and all you stand for; and I will say it with glee: Patel! Patel! Patel!"

Vul threw his goblet across the room, he raced to his queen, and picked her up by the throat, saying, "I am king, and your pathetic lost love is no more. Perhaps you wish to join him. Perhaps I should crush your neck and send you to him now!"

He pulled her close to his face and looked into her eyes as she struggled he said softly, "No, no, my pet, you will not join him just yet. I own you in this life and will own you again in the next. I give you one more year to sire me a son; after that, I shall take a new bride, and she will replace you as my queen." After kissing her hard upon the mouth, Vul released his grip, allowing her to fall upon the ground.

Looking up at him through tear-filled eyes as she rubbed her neck, SedicEve said, "Why not get a new queen now? Don't wait; take another and let me go free."

Laughing he replied, "My dear queen, whether I take another bride or not, you will remain in the city, eternally locked away; after all, you are my queen forever. If anyone else were to touch you, they would face death by my hand. Now go clean up and wait for me to arrive in our bedroom chambers; I'll be along shortly."

Picking herself up off the floor, SedicEve slowly walked with her head downcast across the room.

Just before she went through the door, she stopped to hear Vul say, as he poured another cup of wine, "And don't forget, SedicEve—I love you."

Nodding, she silently left the room to prepare herself for him, lost in feelings of both guilt and shame.

Chapter 33

Sitting at a table made of dark onyx, Hakeldama worked on painting a portrait of his sister Barrab, who enjoyed posing for him. Eedn could never sit still long enough to pose for her brother. Where he and Barrab were levelheaded, wanting to think through a challenge, Eedn acted on impulse and was driven by desire. She loved taking chances, to her father's dismay, but Lilith encouraged her daughter to go out and taste life. "Savor every feeling and flavor as if for the first time," she would say, knowing Eedn possessed her mother's need for sensuality and lustful desires. Killing men to absorb their life force and take in a physical part of them was Eedn's art, even though her siblings scolded her incessantly about playing with food.

They preferred a quick end for their victims, creating less of a mess and leaving them more free time for exploring the new world. But Eedn enjoyed the chase; striking fear in a victim added spice to their taste, and she liked that very much. What she loved most was seduction, and she was quite capable of luring men to their demise through sensuality and teasing coyness. Taking a dominant position as she made love, Eedn waited until bursting before swiftly dispatching the man with a bite to his carotid artery. She savored every drop of blood as it coursed through her, pulling in life energies mixed within red corpuscles and powerful endorphins until her thirst was slaked.

One night, forgetting what her mother had taught all of them never to do with the remains, she buried a victim close to the castle to hide it from her father. He never allowed corpses in the castle primarily because of decay, but also because if an enemy were to see it, it might bring trouble, and he was very protective of his family. That night, the man rose from where he had been buried and walked into the castle, surprising everyone except Lilith, who looked directly at Eedn. "Why did you bury this man? Now he will die twice!"

Eedn ran to him, shielding her victim from the others, yelling that a miracle had happened. Pointing out that he possessed fangs and pale skin as their own and eyes that glowed as well, she begged for his life to keep. "My child," said Lilith, "no one in the castle will harm him, but he is not immortal as you and I—as we are. Nothing can destroy us, with the exception of the Son's light. The venom in your fangs will turn ordinary man into shadows of yourselves, but they will have weaknesses: garlic, silver, wood, and sunlight, which you and your siblings were exposed to while still developing in egg cases. Because of that, any time a person is turned, they will inherit those ailments. Yes, they might live until the end of time if they avoid these things, but what kind of life is that for an immortal, my sweet?"

Eedn looked into the man's eyes and took pity on him; using one of her nails, she opened her wrist and gave it to him. The man suckled as if an infant at his mother's breast and grew strong. When he was finished, Eedn turned to her mother and said, "I wish to keep and take care of him; help me with what I must do."

Lilith reluctantly told her what must be done. "He can never be out during the day; take some of the earth he was buried in and scatter it at the bottom of a solid gold coffin. He must rest in it until sundown and return to it when the sun begins to rise. Ensure the coffin is made from pure gold; any silver or wood will make it unfit. Until you have fashioned a coffin suitable, take him to the dungeon and sprinkle dirt in a corner." She grabbed a black silk drapery with a red inner lining, Lilith continued, "Wrap him in this; it will have to do until the gold coffin is complete. Now hurry; the sun shall rise soon, and he will be vulnerable to it."

Eedn ran outside, filled a bag with dirt from where her victim was buried, and rushed back inside. She took the man by the hand, led him to the dungeon, and prepared a place for him to rest. Before wrapping the man in the black-and-red silk drapery, she asked his name.

"I am known as Eningree the Machinist; what has happened to me? Why am I here?"

Smiling, Eedn said, "I made you what you are; a god-man which will live forever. Since I made you, so shall I name my creation in this world: Nad, prince of Sasairy. Now rest, my pet, until your time to reign is begun." She wrapped him thoroughly and checked over her work one last time. Just before she left, a noise from behind caught her attention. A dim reflection glinted off a wall encrusted with dust and crud. She approached it and swiped away debris to reveal the image of a man staring back at her. Startled at first, she recoiled, and then she remembered who it was that looked back at her.

"You are my father's living trophy that was captured before my time." She looked into his eyes, captivated by the sheer beauty of his energy. Drawing closer, she placed a hand on his cell and drew in some of the energy collected from him and impregnated within his cell's walls. Orgasmic tremors racked her body; uncontrollable surges of euphoric delight sent shudders throughout her, making her stumble backward. She fell to the floor and writhed in bliss, never wanting that moment of pure lust to end. Slowly coming to her senses, she sat up glaring at Patel with glowing eyes, fangs bared, and a look of total, insatiable desire upon her face.

"I have not tasted such raw power since my birth into this world. Why my father keeps you here in the dark is a mystery."

Though exhausted, Patel mustered what strength he could and said, "I'm not sure. It's been so long, but I can only imagine it is to keep me from beautiful things such as yourself; he's quite jealous of me."

She got to her feet and walked toward him and replied, "Stul told me you were quite powerful. He feared you and only you in this world." She again placed a hand against the cell. "But how is something so desirable—needed—considered a pariah to everyone?"

Thinking quickly, he said, "Release me and I will show you how good I am. I will not harm you; free me from this cell."

Looking deep into his eyes, she wanted to believe him, knowing inside he spoke the truth.

Leaning her face against the wall, she said in a low whisper, "You are a shifter of the Most High, and I know you are bound by truth. Tell me—promise that if I let you free, you will not harm my family. Give me your word, and I will release you."

Sitting back, Patel wrestled with his own desires to take revenge upon those who imprisoned him and his word to not harm them if released. Coming to a decision, he moved to her and said, "I give my word. No physical harm will befall you or your family by my hand, this I vow."

Smiling, she savored his words, but she wanted from him even more. "I also want you, Patel. My very loins are afire with passion; please want and take me upon your release. I'll not ask for another thing from you; this I vow."

She was pleasing to the eye, and long had it been since Patel had held a female body, but the memory of Nyeve was what had kept him going for so long. *Other men would have given up their spirit by now, and yet I desired to stay in the hope of reuniting with her someday. But what good is reality if left to rot in a box? If being with Eedn means freedom, then it is a small price to pay.* Or so he thought. "Eedn, I am weak from energy drain, but release me from this prison that I may make passionate love to you, my beautiful one."

Her eyes sparkled like pale blue diamonds at his words. "Fear not, my grand warrior; I know where my father stores orbs of power and will bring you one. Consider it an aphrodisiac for the both of us."

Swiftly, she left the dungeon and entered the throne room, where her siblings were still posing and painting one another. "Eedn, we were just about to take a break and go hunting, do you wish to join us?"

Shaking her head, "No, my brother, I want to keep an eye on my new prince; protective, you know. Kind of my hobby to keep me out of trouble and all that. If you want, bring me back a victim."

Puzzled Hakeldama asked, "So you're not going out at all? Well, I must say this new hobby might be the very thing to rein you in. Of course, father always did say that your appetites would be your undoing; this should go a long way to quell his misgivings."

"Yes—yes, it should," Eedn replied impatiently. "Now if you don't mind, I want to get back to work. And please bring back an A positive if possible; I have a feeling I'll be quite famished later." Eedn rushed out of the room, leaving her brother and sister to look at each other in great confusion.

Nonetheless, her siblings went on their hunt, making it easy for Eedn to smuggle an orb to the dungeon.

After entering the room, she locked the door behind her and moved to the cell. She placed the orb of power on the floor and cleaned off a buildup of dust, dirt, and lime from around the outer cell door. She kicked at a latch lock that was frozen in place by years of sediment, and freed it from its place. Looking into Patel's eyes, she gave one more kick, releasing bolt from clasp and allowing the cell door to swing open freely. Cool air rushed, in pelting his face for the first time in decades. He slowly moved toward her and collapsed in her arms, passing out.

Eedn placed him gently on the floor, where she cradled his head in her arms as she softly caressed the side of his face. She found him quite appealing. He stirred emotions in her that transcended lust and desire, frightening her at first. Pushing them aside, she laid him on the floor and started a fire. She heated pots of water and filled a large tub to overflowing. She then lifted Patel up, moved to the tub, and placed him in it. After peeling off her clothing, she entered the water with a washcloth and bathed him. She then dried him off and effortlessly carried him to her room and placed him in bed. As she left to retrieve the energy orb, Patel started to slowly awaken. At first he thought it all a dream, thinking Nyeve would walk into the room at any moment and that, upon awakening, he would find himself locked in a cell in a dark, dank room.

In reality, however, an enchanting redhead entered with a bright white orb under her arm. She looked at him the way Nyeve did, and he felt good inside. Climbing onto the bed, Eedn placed the orb between them and said, "Draw slowly the energy as if taking sips of water or wine. Consuming too much at once will intoxicate to the point of unconsciousness, and we wouldn't want that, now would we?"

She placed a finger coyly to her mouth and then traced a line down Patel's chest with it. Silently, the two beings took in energy, and soon Patel was feeling more like himself. Once she felt each of them had had enough, Eedn took the sphere and dropped it to the floor as she moved closer to Patel.

In his arms, and for the first time, she wanted to be dominated during lovemaking. A symphony of pleasures enveloped her body as never before, and Patel reveled in it as well. Too long had he gone without human contact and companionship, and his thoughts always turned to Nyeve. Yet Eedn touched him in ways no one had before, awakening new feelings that had lain dormant. Hours passed like minutes, and soon the couple lay spent, exhausted from their lovemaking. Before falling asleep in each other's arms, Eedn thought about turning him so they could be together forever. Then she remembered Eningree and didn't want to imprison Patel again.

She wanted a world where only they lived, loving each other every second of every minute and every hour of the day. Yet she also knew deep inside it couldn't be, as long as her parents objected and Nyeve was in the world. She had heard him speak her name as he lay upon the stone floor of the dungeon. She admired and hated Nyeve, a woman who at one time had won his heart—a heart she wished to possess, though she knew she couldn't compete with a love as old and strong as theirs appeared to be. For now, she was content to lie on his chest and listen to the beating of his heart—so strong, so virile.

Upon awakening to screams and struggles, Patel saw four mantis-like beings pulling Eedn away from the bed and carrying her off as more mantises attacked him. Pushing a couple aside, he transformed into a giant ape-man and beat the entities down, which brought more pouring into the room along with shadow beings to back them up. Meanwhile, the demons that had hold of Eedn quickly took her to the dungeon and locked her in one of the old silver coffins. Muffled screams and bangs from the coffin did not travel out of the room, leaving her helpless.

Patel drew his sword and sliced at the entities, but their number was too great; it seemed as though they acted as one creature. He could hear them all chanting in a low, rolling hum, "Legion," over and over again. When he felt they might overpower him, he jumped from a window, morphing into an eagle and flying off. None of the creatures followed him as he went, but Eedn was still back there. He truly wanted to help her, but the confrontation with those creatures had drained him. Barely able to keep his form, Patel made for his old citadel, hoping to find Nyeve or Norhi. As he reached the front entrance, an arrow pierced one of his wings, taking him down. Unable to hold his form any longer, he returned to a human state and was met by two diminutive men and Norhi before losing consciousness.

Many days came and went as Patel slowly recovered enough to speak. Guards surrounded his room inside and out. Norhi sequestered everyone and anyone with knowledge of Patel's return to keep Vul from finding out.

When he received news that Patel was again able to speak, Norhi entered his room, smiling with elation. Patel had returned home, finally. He grabbed a chair, placed it next to Patel's bed, and sat and talked with his friend. "It's good to have you back with us, my dear friend; you have no idea."

Whispering, Patel replied, "It's good to be back."

Norhi inquired, "What happened, anyway? Vul informed us he watched you die on the battlefield, that the enemy dismembered you and carted your body away."

Surprised, Patel replied, "The enemy did cart me away, but in a crystal box of some kind; it drains your life force—making one quite helpless, let me tell you. Perhaps he meant something else."

Contempt for Vul dominated Norhi's response. "Like what? No, he didn't mean anything other than that you were dead; otherwise, we would have fought to the last man to get you back—you know that."

Patel humbly smiled. "I know you would have, as well as my warrior princess. Where is Nyeve? I didn't expect to see Vul, since he's usually tied up with himself, but Ny—I would think she would be here."

Suddenly, Norhi's demeanor changed, becoming less bright and more sorrowful. "Oh, Patel, if only someone else could give this information to you, I'd be eternally grateful."

Seeing the pain in his face, Patel stopped him and said, "No need, my friend. I can see in your appearance that she perished in that last battle. I was not there to save her, and so the blame for her death rests solely on my shoulders, Norhi; it's all right."

Tears of sorrow and rage filled Norhi's eyes as he rose from the chair in which he was sitting and flung it across the room. He ordered the guards out, approached Patel, and said, "Patel, Nyeve is not dead; she reins as queen in a city constructed by Vul—her king and husband."

Shocked, a slack-jawed Patel askedsaid, "That's impossible; they hate each other—could barely stand to be in the same room with the other. When did this happen, and why?"

Shaking his head, Norhi said, "The best I can tell is they had an affair stretching back before the attack on Karish. How far back, I don't know. Eningree caught the two of them together in the caverns while we were marching to the Badlands. Anyway, when we all thought you had fallen on the field of battle, I left Vul and Nyeve to return here with survivors. Gimet and other crews brought their ships here, but Vul claimed and absconded with them and the pilots and most of the engineers and architects as well. He built a city with the help of Karish and ariyon workers; he set himself up as a god-king and took Nyeve as his queen. Honestly, I didn't even know of Nyeve and Vul until recently. She gave an audience to us in her throne room, and that's when I found out she was still alive. Eningree tried to tell me of their liaison years ago, but I didn't listen. I'm sorry, Patel! I wish it weren't true—any of it—for your sake."

Trying to digest all the new information received, Patel felt sick in the pit of his stomach, experiencing a pain that would haunt him for many years thereafter. He did not speak. Waving his friend off, he turned away on his side and silently wept.

As night fell, Eningree awoke from his dirt nap ready to face the night. He heard sounds of muffled sobbing in one of the coffins, so he approached it. He knew the voice of his maker coming from within and reached out to release her. He grasped the silver lock handle with his hand; his flesh began to smolder, and he cried out in pain. He then moved back from the coffin and tried to think of a different way to open it. Taking his sleep cloth in hand, he moved to the coffin once more and carefully placed the cloth between the silver and himself. He pulled down, and the lock gave way, freeing her from inside. Eningree held her tightly in his arms until she was able to compose herself. Now grim determination filled her eyes, flaming a pale blue. With fangs bared, she headed for the door, and Eningree followed close behind. Entering the throne room, she spotted a few of the mantis beings. She swiftly tore out their throats and twisted off their heads.

A voice from the throne rang out, saying, "Stul, control your daughter immediately!" Suddenly, a pair of dragon's wings enveloped Eedn, keeping her from committing further damage.

"My daughter, please settle down; release your rage, I beg of you!" Becoming calm in her father's arms, she began to cry crimson-colored tears.

"They took my love away and threw me into a coffin, locking it! I want revenge against them— against all of them, father!"

The voice from the throne said, "You've done enough revenge-seeking, woman! It is now time for you to be silent; grownups are speaking."

Unfolding his wings, Eedn saw Lucifer for the first time. "Who are you, and why do you sit on my father's throne?"

Lucifer was both annoyed and impressed with the vision before him. She was a hybrid unlike any other: strong, fearless, beautiful, and deadly—a truly seductive warrior.

"I rarely talk with women unless giving them direction, and though you are quite unique in every way, my rule still stands. Now run along while the men talk."

Her eyes aglow once again, she took three steps and launched into the air with her hands extended in front of her to grab at his throat. Suddenly, she found herself suspended in midair by an unseen force. Raising a hand to her, Lucifer manipulated her head without touching it; turning it this way and that, he admired her fangs, which were razor sharp with two small holes at each point. "My, what big teeth you have."

She responded, "The better to kill you with, fiend!"

Impressed, he replied, "Truly without fear of any kind; Stul, you sired a child of superior genes."

From across the room, Eningree spoke. "Put her down now or face my wrath." Looking at Stul, Lucifer said, "You're her father; why aren't you fighting for Eedn?"

Just then, Lucifer pulled Eningree up from where he was and brought him to where Eedn was suspended. "Stul, why didn't you tell me you had a son as well?"

"He is not my brother," said Eedn. "I made him!"

Taken aback, Lucifer said, "You… made him? By what means?"

Matter-of-factly, she said, "Biting him. I am able to do it with all my victims if I so choose."

Lucifer was in awe. "By all the stars, Stul, you created a being that can manipulate a double helix to mutate a human genome—I honor you, sir."

Gently placing the couple on the floor, Lucifer turned to Stul and said, "This is precisely what I require for an army to send against the humans. The angelics are ready to stand by me in heaven, and I need Lilith's demons at the ready to take down mankind."

Stul replied, "It will be as you command, Lord Lucifer. We'll deal with the humans, but what is to happen to those hybrids that have allied themselves with them, and what of those men you have as allies?"

Lucifer grunted in contempt. "Vul and his kind have served their purpose; only one settlement stands outside our realm of influence, and soon it will fall as well. As for those hybrids having assisted our enemies, kill them and cast them into the abyss." At that Lucifer disappeared from the throne, leaving Eedn to question her father.

"He is unaware of my brother and sister? Where are they?"

Scolding her he said, "You spoiled child. How dare you set free and then engage in relations with my sworn enemy? When other demons brought here to battle man found you with a shifter, I had to send mother and your siblings away to hide from Lucifer's sight. In exposing yourself to him along with this extra abomination, you jeopardize their safety!"

Her head bowed low, she said, "I'm sorry, father; forgive me, but Patel was not a dalliance. I love him. He makes me feel different from any other creature I've known."

It was then Stul delivered a sharp backhand to her cheek, his eyes full of rage. "I will not hear such things from my daughter! You've been enchanted by him so that I might be harmed by my own blood. Get out of my sight, and do not return until summoned." He pointed a clawed finger toward Eningree. "And take that thing with you."

Her eyes full of sorrow and confusion, she quickly left the citadel along with Eningree, never to return. They took to living within the many caverns under the mountains, which a mighty army had once used during the siege of the Badlands. There they subsisted on lone men or animals that wandered too close to the cavern entrances.

Chapter 34

Colorful dreams intermixed with grayish nightmares tormented Patel as he lay in his bed. Thoughts and images of Nyeve gave way to sensual depictions of Eedn as his heart slowly ripped itself apart. Then a vision of Nyeve standing within a throne room he had never seen before filled his mind. A look of fright rested upon her face, unholy and ghastly. This bewildered him at first, until he saw the reason for it; a man standing across the room with many others shot an arrow, piercing her heart. Soon after, the men with him swarmed the throne area and, with swords drawn, cut her to pieces. Suddenly coming awake, and dripping with sweat, Patel yelled out in fear and anger at the vision still smoldering in his mind. Norhi rushed into the room to see what was the matter.

Upon seeing him, Patel asked, "Where is Eningree? I need to speak with him."

Puzzled, Norhi replied, "I don't know, he went missing some time ago; his disappearance was the reason I finally went looking for answers about all those who had gone missing. Why do you wish to speak with him?"

Wiping sweat from his brow, Patel replied, "Perhaps he was wrong about what he saw. Maybe Vul tricked her in some way or took her captive. She may be in need of rescue, Norhi. What if I didn't do enough for her, show her enough love, or give her enough things? Her being with Vul is my fault, not hers."

Norhi walked over and placed a hand on Patel's shoulder Norhi said, "Deep down, Patel, you know that's not true. It's not the things we do or possess, or even the things we give to others, that define us, but who we are inside. She chose to be where she is, and not because of some failing on your part. You were presumed dead to us all."

Patel stood and walked across the room. Patel interrupted, "Exactly. She didn't know I was still alive, and thinking there was no other choice open to her, she went with Vul."

Norhi replied, "Patel, she could have come with us, but she didn't. Vul is who she wanted to be with, and you know it's true."

Nodding, he silently agreed, knowing his friend was right. He turned to face him and said, "When can you take me to see her? I'm rested enough."

"My friend," said Norhi, "are you sure seeing her again is such a good thing? Let's not forget about Vul as well. After all, he stated he watched you die on the battlefield. I'm certain now he is mixed up in more than we know."

Unmoved, Patel replied, "I don't care, Norhi. I must hear from her own lips she no longer wants me."

Shaking his head in disbelief, Norhi agreed to take Patel, but he again warned him that nothing good could come of such a potentially volatile meeting. The two men transformed into an eagle and ibis and flew toward Vul's kingdom. Seeing the city for the first time, Patel was captivated by its beauty and magnificence. Viewing the palace from its front entrance, two bronze pillars flanked the main doors. Atop the pillars were a gold sun disc on the left and a silver moon disc on the other. An arch was suspended over the pillars, with strange tadpole-like symbols etched upon the keystone.

They landed near an obelisk situated at the center of a circular courtyard that faced the front of the palace. As they grew closer to the entrance, Patel noticed that directly behind it sat a huge gold pyramid with a bright eye-shaped form at its apex. The pyramid was seated perfectly upon a solid silver arc that was attached to the keystone over the palace doors. Upon entering, Norhi directed Patel to where the throne room was located but gestured for him to remain outside and quiet while he entered first. Moments passed, and then Nyeve emerged from behind a pillar to greet her guest. "It's good to see you again, dear Norhi, but why have you come? Vul is away, deciding the fate of your village as we speak."

Taken aback by her words at first, he forgot about Patel. He stood silent and confused, not knowing what to say. Finally, Patel stepped into the room. "He brought me to see you Nyeve. To let you know I live."

Stumbling backward and falling to her knees, she was in awe, wondering if a ghost of the past had come to torment her. Patel moved closer, extending a hand for her to grasp that she may know he was a living being and not an apparition. Hesitantly, she reached out and touched him; feeling solid, warm skin against her fingers, she cried out in joy and sorrow. Patel helped Nyeve get to her feet and took her in his arms. He thought back to times of great happiness, when the two of them lived as one mind, soul, and body. Snapping back into reality, though, he felt something was different, strange, and alien to him. He pulled back and gazed deep into her eyes, where he saw a blackness that hadn't been there previously. He released her. "Nyeve, you've changed. Your feelings about me have changed; I can tell."

She sat on her throne. "A lot of things have changed, Patel, but my feelings for you are not one of them. I very much desire you still, but there is another that I desire as well." Patel nodded and turned to leave.

Nyeve said, "Wait, where are you going? Didn't you hear me? I said I still want you."

Patel turned to face her. "Nyeve, you just told me you desire another—"

Cutting him short she said, "Yes, but I still want you as well! Don't you see, we could be together—all of us!" She watched as a surprised and hurt look developed on his face. "Patel, you possess aspects of life I love dearly—the safe, secure, and comfortable side—while Vul gives me a sense of unpredictability, danger, a rush to life. If I could roll the two of you into one person, I would. But this is the only way: having the both of you and enjoying it too."

Patel replied, "I gave my heart and soul to you, Nyeve, sacrificing them to no one but you, and it was not enough. I bestowed a piece of my soul upon a woman I intended to spend the rest of my life with exclusively. By trusting in your love, this is what has accrued, to my great disappointment: an internal and external grief!"

Disdain and contempt grew within her as she took in her former lover's words. A callous heart spoke out: "That's life; the heart wants what it wants when it wants it. If you can't accept that, then take it back! I never asked for it in the first place; take back what is yours, and never return to me again!"

Approaching once more and taking her in his arms, he placed his mouth close to hers and slowly took in a breath. A light whisp of smokelike energy left her body and entered his. Immediately, Nyeve's head and face took on the form of a lioness's. Releasing her and turning to leave, Patel said, "Farewell, SedicEve, queen of all she surveys."

Norhi stood silent, turned, and left the throne room with Patel.

A pair of feminine eyes peered out from white columns located across the room. The owner of them had seen everything that had unfolded earlier and now watched as SedicEve sat on a throne, staring into space.

Chapter 35

Ecegre suddenly appeared in the council chambers, surprising the eleven. "What have you done? Do you even see the evil unleashed on this planet?"

Gypet replied, "Of course we have, Ecegre this wasn't our intention when attempting to correct it, but how else were we to try to counter the negative effects of rogue angels?"

Furious, Ecegre said, "Well, not by giving man hidden knowledge and abilities they couldn't possibly understand how to use properly!

Aafric replied, "You weren't here, Ecegre, at least we tried to fix the situation; it just kept rolling out of control."

Ecegre, calmer now, said, "Your efforts have not gone unnoticed; the Lord of Hosts is coming to fix our errors."

A look of surprise and fear fell upon all within the room, creating an uncomfortable silence that was broken only by Ecegre's next statement. "You have three days in which to prepare for His arrival. Gather those of your people that you believe to be godly— those meek among the inhabitants that are not of angelic mixing—and take them out far beyond this galaxy and wait. Above all, do not confide in any angelics outside this room, or they might keep their hybrid children from destruction."

Moving quickly, the watchers did as Ecegre directed and drew out those people not affected by inner influences of rogue angelics, taking the people far out from the galaxy. All the moves, however, did not go unnoticed. Lucifer, being the highest of angels, went before the Lord and asked what was happening. The Lord said, "I am making a new thing, and have I not already? Behold, I have made man in My image, and he will be My creation after My likeness, and My entire heavenly host shall serve him. Come with Me that you may pay homage to My creation."

It was then that Lucifer decided in his heart to strike and rebel against God. He mustered a third of the angels by promising positions of worship, and a great war broke out in the heavens.

Lucifer and his army raged against the army of, God but to no avail. Michael himself flung Lucifer out of heaven with all those who followed him. The Lord remade the earth, splitting one continent into several and turning some areas into lush jungles while others were void of plants. He placed His new creation, a man and woman, in a garden, giving but one command—never to eat of one particular fruit tree that grew in the center of the garden.

Lucifer, however, placed his servant Serpent in the garden, where he and Serpent convinced the woman to eat the fruit and to give it to her husband, who ate it as well. When the Lord heard of their deeds, He cursed Serpent, causing him to take on the form of a snake, and He cast the man and woman out of the garden to live in the lands and toil for their food. God then made Lucifer prince of the world and the first and second heavens until the day of judgment. All who followed Lucifer were made demons, along with every child of Lilith. Their charter is to roam the lands and deceive and tempt man until that day of judgment. The watchers returned to earth and placed the remaining humans from before in many lands. Because of their inescapable charms and lustful desires, some took wives and sired men of great renown, beginning a cycle that continues to this day.

***

As the final images within the orb faded away, J. D. said, "Wait a minute; that's it? There are so many questions left unanswered!"

Patel stood up, and taking hold of the sphere removed it from the table, and placed it in a smaller room. He then returned and said, "What else do you need to know, and what purpose would it serve?"

J. D. said, "Well, for one thing, why are you the way you are? How did you survive? What happened to Vul, Nyeve, and Norhi—lots of stuff!"

Sitting once again, Patel said, "Very well. As far as SedicEve and Vul, a massive uprising of the people subjected under their rein led to their untimely deaths. It seemed Vul had made a deal with Lucifer: for success, fame, and wealth, he had to give people over to be sacrificed. When the people found out, they revolted, killing any shifters within the kingdom and then cutting to pieces their bodies, which they burned, poured bitumen over, and placed in a large granite chest to ensure they never returned from the dead.

Those shifters loyal to God were given immortality to serve mankind, but when man tried to venerate us, we went into hiding. We are God's creation and not meant for worship, and so I have stayed in exile ever since. Norhi keeps to Europe, moving from place to place, trying to help man as best he can; strong is his will, and great his character."

Mary replied, "Your will is just as strong, Patel. You want to help; I know it."

Patel grunted. "You know nothing, and even less than that, woman."

Starting to get upset, J.D. said, "Do we really have to go through this again?"

Mary cut in, "J.D., stop! He's had a bad way with women; it's understandable."

J.D. perked up as he wondered about something. "Speaking of females, Patel, I was wondering—a few decades or so ago, some hunters took pictures of what they believed was a bigfoot."

Patel rolled his eyes. "Great! Here it comes."

Continuing, JD said, "Yes, well anyway, when the footage was studied, researchers came to the conclusion that what had been captured on film was a female bigfoot. It seems the animal was sporting a pair of hairy breasts. Is there something you want to tell us but are too shy to, sweetie?"

Pride mixed with anger fueled his response. "It wasn't a film of me in drag. If you must know, it's a female shifter named Rephel."

Suddenly, J.D. leaped up from the table, pointing a finger at Patel. J.D. exclaimed,"Bzzzz! Wrong answer, pal; you said the only female shifter was Nyeve, which we all know by your own story is dead. So how could there be another female shifter then—hmm? What say you to that, my large, hairy friend?"

Entreating JD to cease from being cruel in his questioning towards Patel, though curious herself that another woman shifter might exist, Mary said, "J.D.

please sit down and be nice to Patel; let him explain this other woman in peace. Go ahead, Patel; who is this mystery woman?"

He replied, "First, I do not need you to fight battles for me, thank you. Second, her creation was another mistake I made after SedicEve. Perhaps I did stop the images too soon." Patel got to his feet and began pacing around the room as he told the couple about Rephel. "After my encounter with SedicEve, Norhi and I left the palace. My heart and soul were in tatters, my zest for life diminished to a point where I no longer wanted to be a chosen one. People would do what they willed; this was made evident to me by the city I found us walking through. Heading back to my citadel, Norhi and I gathered those shifters loyal to God, and after placing elders in charge of the city, we went into exile. We retreated to the mountains, vowing never to live with humans and only to assist them when called upon by the Lord.

"One night, as I lay on my bed after drinking much wine, I ached in sorrow, longing for my woman. A female I'd never met before appeared and began stroking my head. I thought at first it was a dream, and so I asked if she was real. Placing a finger over my mouth, she whispered, 'All is well.' Her eyes were almond-shaped and strong, her body shapely and firm yet soft to the touch. I believed it all was a dream even as we made love; I should have known better, though, because it was perfect in every way.

"The next morning, I awoke alone and was disappointed, still thinking it all imagined. It was after the fall of man that I saw her again, the woman in my dream, and found her to be real. She told me her name was Rephel. She was betrothed to Vul as a second wife, but they had never wed. She had witnessed the confrontation between SedicEve and me in the throne room. She watched SedicEve's transformation as I took back a piece of me knowing the secret—understanding the mystery of marriage. As time passed, we became a couple and I took her as my wife. We were happy together and argued very little, but during one argument she let slip that she had come to me the night of my so-called dream and coupled with me to obtain for herself the power of the chosen.

"Angry more with me than her because I had allowed myself to fall in love again only to be betrayed, I left everything and everyone behind. I crossed two continents and an ocean to rid myself of mankind and those that could hurt me, only to be followed and eventually found by her. She lurks about out in the open more than I care to do. No one is aware of this place—except, it seems, the both of you. Does that answer your question, young one? If it doesn't, I don't really give a rat's behind." Patel moved to another room, leaving the couple in awkward silence.

Mary rose from her chair and slowly walked over to the room where Patel sat drinking from a bottle of wine with a worn label that read "Rothschild 1812." Putting a hand on his shoulder, Mary said softly, "I'm truly sorry for your loss and everything you've had to face alone for so long. If I may, with respect, speak with you about an observation?"

Patel waved to a seat with the bottle and then took another drink from it. Mary gestured to ask if she might take a drink as well, and Patel handed her the bottle.

Mary drew in a swig. It tasted a bit tart and spicy for wine. She handed him back the bottle and said, "Thank you. Now then, my observation is this: I don't believe Rephel betrayed you, and from a woman's perspective, it appears to me she loves you Patel. Not many women would follow a man around the world to be jilted for millennia. What harm could come from talking with her? I'm not saying right now, but think about it first."

Just then J.D. said from the other room, "Not too long, Patel; we need you to fight against the dragons."

Shaking his head, Patel got to his feet and moved back into the main room and said, "That's right, you came here to enlist me in a fight against the dragons. My answer is no! Thank you both for a wonderful visit; there's the door! Don't be strangers now that you know where I live."

J.D. said, "Okay, now that's just the wine talking."

Snapping back Patel said, "It's not wine, "I do not drink that which is fermented; this is spring water with cinnamon bark for flavor. I try to reuse what I can scavenge, like this bottle. Now please leave!"

JD said, "Fine, it's not wine but that doesn't change the fact that we need your help, man! Think of the people!"

Roaring his answer, Patel replied, "I was thinking of the people long before you were ever a thought, boy! So don't think you can come to me and preach about the people! Every step they've made throughout history has been to the rhythm of the prince of this world, ignorant to the things around them and not caring until it involved them personally in some way. Their jubilations are orchestrated by and for the powers and principalities running this planet, and I fought against it with all my might but to no avail.

"They murder for money, use sex for control and manipulation, cry out love for the environment with self-hate. They loathe everything that is God and embrace the things of this world without shame, and you want me to fight against what they desire in their hearts?"

Standing his ground, J.D. replied, "No, I'm not asking you to battle man, Patel, but those who hide in the shadows tempting him and coercing him to stumble. It is written that we are to hate the sin but love the sinner. My fight is not with men—neither is yours—but those behind the men. Help me, Patel; help yourself out of hiding in caves and come with me into the light and fight."

Bowing his head, exhausted from the banter, Patel said, "I know where to find you; I need time to think things over. I'll let you know my answer later."

Dissatisfied, J.D. wanted to confront him again, but Mary raised a hand and silently shook her head. Turning to Patel, she said, "Take all the time you need; we understand it's a lot to take in. However, we don't really know our way out; could you guide us to the exit?"

After looking at both of them, he nodded and walked with them to the surface. As they went, J.D. asked, "Hey, just one more thing—it's been driving me nuts since seeing your visions of the past, for lack of a better term. Why don't you wear an armband and hilt? You're in a manimal form, so shouldn't it be on your arm?"

Patel replied, "It stopped forming once I gave up fighting demons full-time. Where is yours, since you are a strapping new shifter? I'm looking but don't see one on either of you."

J.D. smirked. "Yeah, well, don't think I won't ask Larz the next time I see him. He keeps giving me things piecemeal instead of all at once."

Patel nodded. "Sound judgment! Keeps you from getting too cocky... or it should, anyway."

J.D.'s sarcastic laugh was all Patel needed to know J.D. understood him. When they reached the top, where the boulder sealed the entrance, Patel moved it from its place and the three emerged into daylight. They shook hands, and before the couple transformed into owls to fly away, they ensured Patel that he knew where to find them. As she took to the air, Mary looked back one last time to see the bigfoot waving at them, which made her feel more confident that Patel would eventually join their group.

As he turned to head back through the tunnel, Patel picked up a sound that did not fit the woodlands. It was the sound of an animal in pain. He searched for the source, and as he got closer to the cries, he found a small female child of six or seven pressed up against a broken tree trunk, trying to keep out of reach of three wolves snarling and growling at her. Instinctively, he ran and jumped, landing between the wolves and their prey. He let out a roar of his own, and the wolves turned tail and ran as fast as was possible.

Watching as they ran, Patel suddenly felt a tug on his calf hair. He looked down to find the little girl smiling with outstretched arms, pleading to be picked up. He gently embraced her and cradled her with one arm. As he wondered how she had managed to make it all the way out in the woods by herself, he heard in the distance voices calling out "Hope." "So your name is Hope, I presume?" he said as she played with his chest hair and hugged him as if he were her very own massive teddy bear. Looking up at the sky, Patel said, "Okay, Lord—I get it." He hoisted the girl upon his shoulder and, keeping one hand securely around her, headed for the voices desperately crying out for Hope to return to them.

About the Author

J.E. Runnion is originally from South Bend, Indiana. He is a retired USAF MSgt who holds four academic degrees. He is married 25 years to his wife, Mary. She and their three children John, Faith, and Hope assist with the artwork of his books.

Contact Author

J.E. Runnion
P.O. 545
Plattsmouth, NE
68048

Website address:
http://thechosen.wall.fm
https://www.facebook.com/JERunnion

www.ingramcontent.com/pod-product-compliance
Lightning Source LLC
Chambersburg PA
CBHW071340020726
47502CB00001B/183